THE MAGICAL ENCHANTMENT
OF TALES WELL-TOLD

"The Arrow's Flight"—Without even knowing
it, Lord Revan was about to face a challenge
that each new leader must meet, a challenge
that would see him ruler or dead. . . .

"Stealing Souls"—Could a swordswoman-thief
and her minstrel companion steal the very
source of an evil wizard's power?

"Kayli's Quest"—Seeking to rescue a woman
stolen from her village, Kayli must journey
to the magic lands. But can she stand alone
against the enchantment of a dragon's spell?

"The Seven Year's Night"—When the harper
stumbled on a passage to the Otherworld, she
was caught in a strange land where all the rules
of magic and of time were altered in ways
beyond imagining. . . .

Join wizards, sword masters, mercenaries, thieves,
healers, bards, and other denizens of the fantastic
realms in adventures to the never-was and the
might-have-been. . . .

SPELLS OF WONDER

SPELLS OF WONDER

EDITED BY

Marion Zimmer Bradley

DAW BOOKS, INC.

DONALD A. WOLLHEIM, PUBLISHER

Introduction © 1989 by Marion Zimmer Bradley.
The Amethyst Carekeeper © 1989 by Barbara Denz.
The Arrow's Flight © 1989 by Stephen L. Burns.
Istar-Zu © 1989 by D. A. Bach.
The Siege of Kintomar © 1989 by Millea Kenin.
Stealing Souls © 1989 by Laurell K. Hamilton.
Ladyknight © 1989 by Susan Hanniford Crowley.
Festival Night © 1989 by Harry Turtledove.
Kayli's Quest © 1989 by Paula Helm Murray.
The Seven Year's Night © 1989 by M. H. Lewis.
The Dance of Kali © 1989 by Richard Corwin.
Ancient Heartbreak © 1989 by Diann Partridge.
Hero Worship © 1989 by L. D. Woeltjen.
A Matter of Life © 1989 by Cathy J. Deaubl.
The Moon Who Loved the Man © 1989 by Robin W. Bailey.
Last Quarrel © 1989 by Dorothy J. Heydt.
Crooked Corn © 1989 by Deborah Wheeler.

DAW Book Collectors No. 793.

First Printing, September 1989

2 3 4 5 6 7 8 9

PRINTED IN CANADA

COVER PRINTED IN THE U.S.A.

CONTENTS

INTRODUCTION

Editing an anthology may be tiring, tedious and eyestraining, but (for me, anyhow) it's never boring. I thought I'd start off this new anthology by trying to give you a sense of what goes on around here when I'm working on an anthology.

Why a new anthology anyhow? Well, every year I receive about twice as many perfectly good stories as I need for the SWORD AND SORCERESS volume, and I really hate to send them all back; so I decided on a new anthology, to use up a few more of them, or to find a place to publish some of the stories which I really liked, but did not quite fit the S&S format. So I talked to my editor and my publisher, and to my agent, and they agreed to let me have a go at it.

The first thing I do for the anthology is to read manuscripts, and either send them back (hopefully as soon as I receive them) or hold them. The stories which are amateurish beyond redemption, too short, too long, or perfectly good but hopelessly out of market requirements go back immediately; anything I think I might be able to use gets held for a second reading. When it gets its second reading, one of my criteria is this; when I pick up the manuscript, which has had a first reading, usually a once-over to see if it has a beginning, a middle and an end which I can identify, can I remember it without reading it all the way through again? If I cannot, I am apt to think my readers would find it forgettable, too, and unless it turns out to be *very* good, I reject it.

If it passes both readings, I put it in a file of "hold for final decision." On the day of the deadline, I get out the whole file, and start thinking hard about the introduction, what tack I should take to introduce the stories. At that time I read everything over again and make some final assignments of categories. At this point, I forget about the printed slips; anything I've held this long gets a personal letter of explanation. Usually I use printed slips only if: (1) the story is so far out of category that it might as well have been sent to *The Ladies Home Journal* or *Playboy*; (2) I've had a bad day with too many manuscripts and just can't make myself write even one more polite note, or; (3) sometimes, I feel a little guilty about so many rejections and want to hide behind the impersonality of a printed slip. I want to emphasize that the use of the printed slip is not in any way a comment on the quality of your manuscript, if you've received one; it means only that your manuscript arrived in a whole bunch of others and I was too busy (or too bummed out and overwhelmed) to start writing letters.

Well then, by that time I've sorted out all the manuscripts into three piles on the kitchen table (hopefully not on top of the butter dish or the place I'd spilled marmalade at breakfast); stuff that was crowded out, stuff for SWORD AND SORCERESS, and stuff for the new anthology. At that time there are some hard decisions to be made; what form should the new anthology take? The last thing I wanted was for it to be just an "overflow" anthology, containing all the stuff that wasn't good enough for S&S. So the selection was not to be done by creaming off all the best stuff for S&S. On the other hand, some of the stories—by Diana Paxson, Jennifer Roberson, Misty Lackey, and Dorothy Heydt—had to be in S&S because they were about a continuing character who had appeared there before; and I felt I owed it to them and the readers, to leave them in a familiar place. Then I make a lineup of good strong stories for the new anthology; some stories by known writers—like Stephen Burns and Millea Kenin, whose work I had published before and know the quality, and a few by really promising newcomers. Finally, I have enough for both books, lying in two piles on my table. To keep a good balance of short stories and long, strong stories paired up with stories slightly weaker, known and unknown writers—well, you get the picture. Especially good stories for the beginning and the end; stuff which especially appeals to me spotted at strategic points, balanced out with stories which don't really grab me but which might appeal to a special segment of the audience, and so forth. (For instance, horror stories don't especially appeal to me; but I know this genre has a special appeal for many people and they always want more.) A few stories I weeded out as being a little too shuddersome or gruesome for my taste; that's where personal taste comes in. I can't like all stories equally, of course; but sometimes it comes down to a gut feeling for what people will like, or not like; some stories very appealing to me, I wind up rejecting because I've learned the hard way that these stories will not reach my audience.

Having completed the lineup this way, I say to my assistant, "Well, here it is." And then, being hopeless at arithmetic, I turn it over to her to figure out the wordages. Every editor has her own way of figuring out how much space a story will take up in the book. I usually figure, on a pica-type, computer printout, eleven words per line, twenty-seven lines. Then I round it off to the nearest hundred or so—I never pay for "3,419 words; I'd call that 3400. She figures it out with her calculator, and gives me the bad news: "I hate to tell you this, but you're about ten thousand words over."

Something has to go. So I start pacing and tearing my hair. Can I let go of Jane Jones' story? No, that's really strong, and anyhow, I've published four of her stories and they all went well. Susie Smith's then? Well, maybe; it's a first story, but it will really be good. Well, she could probably sell it, maybe even to a better market. Hepsibah's? Well, maybe. And so it goes. Finally, by taking out one seven-thousand worder, and two really short pieces, I wind up with the number of words specified in the contract.

I breathe a sigh of relief. Then I sit down and write this introduction. The only thing left to do now is to write the individual introductions . . . and that won't be done till the contracts come back with biographical information. Does D. H. (for instance) in an author's name stand for Deborah or Doris, or for Donald or Douglas? Is J. a Joan or a Jeffrey? Is Lee a man or a woman? Who's graduated from college, who's moved or had a new novel published or a new baby? And then it's really all over—until the next time.

—Marion Zimmer Bradley

THE AMETHYST CAREKEEPER
by Barbara Denz

Barbara Denz submitted this story by saying "I finally decided I'd bite the bullet and start doing what I really wanted to do all along; start writing." She's not the only one; sometimes it seems to me that every other fan I meet wants to be a writer. However, a lot separates the fans who "want to be a writer" and the ones who really want to write; and there's another great gulf fixed between people who want to write someday—usually when they have time, as if *anyone* ever really had time to write—and the ones who sit right down, not when they have time, but *now*—who *make* time. As far as I can see, that's what makes all the difference. Maybe you, too, can sell what you write—or maybe you don't care about selling it, in which case you'll have a whole different set of problems—but in either case, you have to get it written first.

This is Barbara Denz's first fiction sale, but she's wanted to write since she took creative writing lessons at age six. (The mind boggles, if only at the wonderment at what kind of person would give creative writing lessons to a girl at age six. On the other hand, better that than some other things she could have been learning; but most kids wouldn't need such lessons; every kid I ever knew was creative to start with—until the wrong kind of school got hold of her. And better, I guess, to study creative writing than playing with Barbie dolls, or watching too much bad TV.)

She is 40 years old, and "considers herself a Northwesterner," but lives, at present, in Baltimore.

Elissa stood on the porch of her cottage, fingering the amethyst crystal dagger on her belt, and surveyed the havoc which had moved toward her from two sides for the past three days. Far below her on the sea, the red tide could be seen in the distance. From higher up the mountain behind her, a tracery sea of rusty red death ran through the ripe grasses. She had spent these three days trying to identify the source of the plagues. She did not like what she had discovered and had just come outside to let the beauty of the surrounding landscape work its magic and relax her. Her solitude was now in imminent danger, as from both directions loomed townsfolk who counted on her for protection from the elements, which was her primary function in this back corner Realm. She shook her silver streaked curls slowly, regretting the events ahead, took off her indoor slippers and began to pull on her boots. She knew that she had become a hermit during the past years, since the obligation of being this Realm's guardian fell on her rarely, and it had been a long time since anyone had needed her help.

Elissa looked lovingly over those who approached her. She had deliberately chosen this remote corner of this remote Realm and was fortunate that its Prince did not mind. She had never done the things which other Carekeepers did, but her dedication to her Realm was never questioned by anyone. This sleepy seacoast village suited her need to get away, and so long as the Elders were willing to accept a Carekeeper here, then here she would stay.

It had been Senior Elder Alvarson who had convinced the others that her presence would be a boon to their daily lives while the rest of the Realm would only get her services in times of crisis. Per Alvarson was close to Elissa's age, and had been young to be the Senior Elder when she arrived. They had been lovers occasionally over the years and maintained a warm, teasing relationship.

Elissa rubbed her hands over faded-mauve linen-covered thighs in a nervous gesture Per would know as impatience as the Elders finished their climb from the valley below and stood before her, breathless. As was customary among Carekeepers, she waited for them to give voice to the words which called her to duty. She was impatient, for she knew the questions they would ask, but the etiquette was important.

"There is . . . a severe . . . danger," puffed her least favorite among the Elders. "It is . . . your duty . . . to help." He could not continue. Per remained silent, a twinkle in his eyes. Another took up the message a bit more tactfully.

"Dear Carekeeper," this slightly less winded Elder began. "We are in dire need of your help. Can you cure these new ills?"

"As Carekeeper for this Realm, I am here to serve you. Perhaps you could explain the need fully?" She showed no sign of welcome and no inclination to invite them to relax. Per always saw the sparkle in her eye and knew the enjoyment she had in teasing this group, but the others took her quite seriously.

"Could we . . . sit down . . . catch breath?" puffed the first.

"Certainly," she smiled equably, and sat on the edge of the porch, dangling her not-so-lean legs, kicking forward at air and swinging her booted heels back against the cottage foundation. "Perhaps you would like to wait on the grass a moment before you present the task?"

Winded, flushed faces nodded assent. She was not going to make this process easier. She loved her privacy and hated to travel. She always forgot how much she hated life on the road until a task required it of her. Elissa sighed. On the other hand, she had become far too rooted to this place. At times she resented being tied to one place because the road always offered so much adventure. She didn't have the heart to tell the uplifted faces that these new threats probably had nothing to do with them or those they worshiped, but were more than likely a challenge to her own power. Signs warned her of Alven but could not explain why.

Elissa sighed again and quit drumming her feet against the foundations of the porch. She pushed off onto her feet, etiquette forgotten, and began to pace and talk.

"Now, I can disperse the tide and stop the plague killing the grass, but only for a time." As she spoke,

Elissa realized that there had been a subtle change in the challenge, and that now she could, indeed, disperse these ills. The realization puzzled her as much as had her inability to disperse them these past few days.

"To prevent their reoccurrence, I will need to find the cause and stop it at its source. You would do best to bring the livestock from higher pastures down around my cottage where they will be safe if I am not immediately successful. I can protect the area around the cottage, though I fear I cannot protect the fish as easily. With luck, the problems at sea will not begin again before I can stop them at their source." An audible sigh emerged from the throats of the Elders and the collected townsfolk. It was nice to know that their Carekeeper was indeed aware and able to take charge. No one but the Elders knew how much power and expertise she brought to their peaceful fjord.

Elissa smiled inwardly at the sigh and collected her energy through the crystal at her belt. With the efficiency of movement for which she was known, she turned, drew three runes in the air, and pointed out to sea. The sea's red coating immediately began to turn purple as the plankton began to sink back to their normal depths and disperse, having quickly completed their mating tasks. A murmur much like the tide began at her feet and swept down the steep hill toward the docks. The sun, which had been hidden behind the tall mountains at her back, broke over the hilltop and glowed up to the invisible line which the plankton had marked and began its ascent toward her, ending when the silver strands in her hair almost blinded those around her. This was not her doing, but the effect was the same as if it were.

Elissa turned toward the Elders. "And now, if you will leave, I can finish gathering my things together and prepare to travel." She gave Per a wink, turned from the group, and entered her crystal-studded cottage, leaving the door ajar, knowing Per would follow when everyone else had gone. She knew it would not be long.

As Elissa began preparing tea, she was encased in rainbows which soared around her as the sun illuminated the crystal spears in her windows. All shades of blue and purple seemed to gather around the single dagger in her belt and be soaked into its depths. A peace crept over her and her dark green eyes lost some of the strain of the past few days and danced in time to the rainbows. She heard Per's soft-soled tread on her wooden floors and felt his tension also diminish as the rainbows welcomed him. As she stirred honey into two steaming mugs, his arms went around her waist and a gentle kiss grazed her ear.

"So, now, amethyst lady," his soft accent burred. "What's really going on, eh?"

As they took their tea and a tin of cookies into her living area and settled onto the piles of pillows that served as chairs, Elissa thought about how much she should tell this peaceful man.

"Truthfully, I'm not sure what it's about," she began. "I sense rivalry, but I'm not sure why. I'm not sure I can explain, because something feels wrong, even to me. How does one explain the feelings and knowings of a sorceress?"

Elissa shook her head and the rainbow smile in her eyes faded as she stared unfocused into the cup in her hands. Per sipped his tea and waited. He had known her long and well enough to know that the full story would be his if he were patient. They rarely kept things from one another, and he was always a good ear and kept what they said to himself unless she let him know it was all right to say something.

Elissa's voice seemed distant even to her as she recounted the view she had seen in her crystal before the townspeople had arrived. No splash of simple sorcery would keep the plagues from reoccurring. She had been allowed to alleviate the symptoms. To effect a cure, she would need to go to the source of the problem. Elissa let her eyes focus on Per and took a gulp of tea.

"I believe that the source of these problems is Alven, but I can't explain why. She now rules the Carekeeper Guild and seems to be using new-found powers to attack me. That never happens among Carekeepers. This may have something to do with events in the

Guild which I no longer understand." She paused and looked at Per. "I've not told you much about the Guild, have I?"

Per stopped in mid gulp to shake his head slightly.

"I guess there was never any reason before," she said, surprised that he did not know everything about her.

"The Guild School will take you very young if you show any penchant toward sorcery. Although many may enter as apprentices, most are unable to master the skills needed to join the Guild as practicing members. There are two other guilds for "everyday" sorcerers, one for healers and one for war masters, but the Carekeepers receive special training and fill a unique role in the order of life in the Realms. We Carekeepers are few and we are taught that ancient laws made us the keepers of peace among the Realms, not within them, although we have become that, too. The ancient law which chartered the Carekeeper Guild also says that we are to make sure that other sorcerers do not abuse the rights of the people in the battles for power and land among the Realms. To keep these laws, we are trained in the use of tools and weapons far beyond those allowed other sorcerers. Those with aberrant behavior are . . ." she paused, searching for the right words. She focused her gaze on Per, unsure how much he should know. "The word the Guildkeeper uses is 'cleansed,' which is a polite term for erased. Our final oath as Carekeeper includes the training to destroy other sorcerers. It even includes the training to destroy one another. But in the long history of Carekeepers, that has never been done. I have heard of the Training being used when the Realm Wars raged, but that was many generations ago." Elissa paused again and took a gulp of cold tea. "Gods, I sound like my teachers and I frighten even me. More tea?"

Per stood up and took her cup to the kitchen to refill it from the kettle on the stove.

"I was six when my mother sent me to Old Gillam," she began again when she had the diffusion of strong, honeyed herbs in her hand.

"She told him I had a gift with crystal. I didn't know what she meant. 'I've heard her play them and make them sing to her in beautiful harmonies,' she said. I still remember her face when she said it. She was so proud."

"She had every right to be," murmured Per. "You must have been a wonderful daughter to her."

"For her, you mean. Whoever first sponsors a child who graduates from the Guild apprenticeship into active duty gets a home and expenses paid for life. I'm not saying she didn't love me, but she never knew the pain she put me through." Elissa leaned back on her oversized pillow and closed back tears, bewildered that those memories could still cause so much pain. When she opened her eyes again, through blurred vision she expected to see pity in Per, but she was surprised to see a smile.

"What's the smirk for?" she demanded.

"You wouldn't trade a day of it and you know it."

She laughed, setting the crystals to mimicking the sound.

"You know me too well," she chuckled, leaning back against the pillows. "Anyway, five years of training with crystals proved Mother right, and just before my twelfth birthday, I made my first crystal dagger from a rare and delicately shaded amethyst I'd found. It was rather rough, and I've made much better since, but it earned me the title of Amethyst Carekeeper. I didn't know that my gift was rare until I was somewhat older and noticed a deference shown when the title was voiced. It seems that one does not usually cut amethyst first and certainly not so young. I was just lucky." Elissa stretched and kicked off her boots.

"I still prefer the amethyst daggers for their ability to hunt or heal cleanly, but I have many other crystals among my arsenal. You've seen most of them hanging around here. Those which are used for the more sinister tasks are safely hidden so their influence cannot be felt on me or anyone else. It's the sound of the 'good' daggers and their rainbows that I love most. I wish I understood why Alven was using the Training so I would know what to take with me to face her."

Per shifted on his pillows and tucked his legs under him, settling back for more of this bizarre story from a woman he thought he knew. He wasn't sure he liked the undertones of what he was hearing, but he would be patient a bit longer. Elissa obviously needed to talk this out.

"I have never been on the best of terms with any of the Carekeepers, but I found the jealousy and vindictiveness of the women in the Guild especially odious. I wanted only peace away from the Guild's bickering, and I managed to maintain that peace for all of this Realm so long as Old Gillam lived."

Elissa was on her feet pacing, again fighting back tears.

"He had wanted me to succeed him, you see, and he placed a persuasive hex on several crystals he sent to me such that if breezes played them, they would gently try to convince me to assume my rightful place as leader. Over the years, I got so tired of their harping that I buried them far from playful breezes and sunlight. I got them out yesterday, and they play a more urgent tune now. They demand that I succeed him and they demand that I come back to the Guildhouse." She whirled mid pace.

"I don't want to be leader, Per. I just don't. Alven has succeeded as Guildkeeper and is welcome to it. I would not think of challenging her. But my wishes seem to be of little consequence here. She challenges me here in the Realm with deadly vindictiveness and I just don't know why. Although Alven was several years behind me in the training, we became unusually close before I found the amethyst crystal. Then something changed and we grew distant. I've monitored the situation for the past weeks since Alven came to power and it seems that she holds the confidence of the other Carekeepers, which leaves me two choices. I can either assume that the Guild knows what is going on and has approved of plagues on this Realm, or I can assume that the Guild does not know and that Alven is now operating above the Guild. In either case, my prospects for staying here in peace seem gone."

Silent a moment with his mouth on his cup, Per was

the picture of someone who was not listening. In frustration, she plopped back down on her pillows and stared miserably at the floor.

"You must go, Eli. That is clear," he began softly, looking into his cup. "Alven is powerful now, but if she is acting above the law in abusing this Realm. . . . Well, that cannot be allowed, no matter what your desires are in the matter. It is clear that there is danger here, and that you are better trained to face it than are we. Others must know what she is doing, and if they do not, you must make sure that they do. You know all this." He paused and looked into her troubled eyes. "What you seem to fear is that you will be required to stay. Perhaps for a time, your guidance of the Guild will be required, but if you truly do not wish to serve the Guildhouse as head Keeper, surely you will not be required to do so. There must be others who are capable of serving. It is only a matter of time until they can be trained in the necessary details and voted on by the whole. Is this not so?"

"I hate it when you're so coldly logical about matters, but, yes, you're right." She reached across the space which separated them and touched his cheek with the love of long friendship. He blushed.

"I guess that's why I've been Senior Elder since I was twenty," he shrugged.

Elissa punched him as hard as he could and laughed at his wounded look. He was just what she needed now. She had let her fear of losing this place, or perhaps her fear of gaining the other, color her duty to the Guild. Despite all else, she was the Amethyst Carekeeper and she always took that role very seriously. She was, after all, trained to face this task, even if she was a bit out of practice.

She sighed in resignation. "Best get these old bones moving," she said as she pushed herself out of the pillows, and turned from him to her packing, thinking about which daggers she would need. Per cleared their cups, cleaned up in the kitchen, and turned to leave. As he reached the door, he turned and looked back at the familiar room.

"Take care, Eli," he whispered into the empty room. "Come back to us soon." So saying, he turned and left quietly.

Elissa had spent nearly ten days riding through mountains, high desert, and heavily wooded terrain. She had reached the canyonlands and was within three days of the Guildhouse when something began to tug at her mind and cause severe pain behind her eyes. For the last two days, a voice had kept telling her of her duty to her Realm and that she was in severe violation of her vows for leaving the Realm unattended. This didn't feel like the Alven she had come to know through the attacks—this voice had well focused power, but who else could it be? At first she thought it might be a new message from Old Gillam's crystals, so forceful was it, but the message did not entice her on as the crystals continued to do. Elissa was too tired to block the message and so its influence ate at her mind.

And then it stopped as abruptly as it had begun. Although she had not slept in two nights, and was saddle sore, dirty, and now extremely out of sorts with this throbbing ache in her head, Elissa slumped forward in her saddle and massaged her temples while the horse worked his way along the trail. The gentle rocking and the massage on her temples lulled her into another of the fitful sleeps which were all the rest she could seem to get.

"Go back," a whisper woke her in a sound the color of smoky topaz. "You are not wanted here." This was the Alven she knew.

"What the. . . ?" She started awake to discover her horse plodding toward the edge of a precipice. It had wandered off the trail while she dozed and seemed to be in a trance as well. Elissa yanked on the reins, holding them as tight as the constriction which now held her throat. The wild eyes of her mount told her that he, too, had been unaware of the impending disaster. She turned him and moved toward the trail and safety. Once they reached a small overhang just to the cliffside of the trail, she dismounted and soothed him with her mind and her touch.

Elissa left him to graze while she walked pensively back to the spot where her life had nearly ended. Again, in her mind was that subtle nudge toward the edge. She had to resist with all her might, which increased the pain behind her eyes.

"Stop," she screamed, and heard her voice echo off the cliffs in tones of topaz. The voice in her mind stopped as the echoes reached her and penetrated. Instinctively, she was afraid. She had allowed herself to became dangerously run down, and had forgotten that messages traveled in crystal. Confused, she analyzed her fear to seek its causes. In the sudden silence, Elissa could hear nothing except the wind whistling through the rocks and the whisper of dying grasses around her.

"Just stop," she muttered again wearily, and slumped into a squat, her head between her hands, her eyes unfocused on the valley far below. "Is this really necessary, Alven?"

As if in answer, the ledge above her horse again rang of topaz, Alven's stone, and shuddered. Instantly alert, Elissa touched his mind and urged him forward, but not in panic. He lifted his head from his grazing, laid his ears back, looked at her and moved forward. She began running on an angle across the bare space which would intercept his movement somewhere down the trail. He had gone only a short distance when the shelf under which he had stood disintegrated and covered the trail. A chasm suddenly appeared just in front of Elissa where seconds ago there had been solid ground. She jumped the growing distance, and ran until she could scarcely breathe and the pain in her side matched that in her head. She watched as the sound of topaz singing around her increased to a screech and the road she had just traveled disappeared down the cliffside, leaving rubble and dust behind. Then, again, there was silence.

Elissa fought for internal calm, knowing herself too angry and too out of practice to get even without getting hurt. She felt a nudge on her shoulder and turned to see her beautiful stallion full of fear, yet trusting her to keep him safe. She patted his nose.

"It's okay," she said. "We'll be okay now. We'll just have to keep careful watch and make sure we arrive better rested than we are now."

Elissa's riding clothes and hair were full of dust. She shook her head and slapped at her clothes, causing her crystal daggers to chime. She took one of the amethyst daggers which Old Gillam had given her. It was silent now, neither encouraging nor discouraging. Disgust and anger flecked her eyes as the crystal reflected back from the hazy sunlight.

"Old man, why couldn't you just leave well enough alone? I don't want to go to the Guildhouse and she certainly doesn't want me there. And the irony now is that I can't go home even if I want to." She eyed the precipice and the clean, shiny cut along what had been her fastest route home.

"I don't understand this at all."

With one last flick at her dusty clothes, Elissa remounted and began the final leg of a trip no one seemed to want her to finish.

The end of the journey passed uneventfully. Elissa's anger at what had almost happened on the trail seethed inside her and festered in the pain behind her eyes. She warded herself and her mount at night, but was plagued with whispers just beyond her hearing. When she reached the edge of Mellerby, the central city, she was beyond exhaustion and knew that she must sleep before she met Alven. The Guildkeeper's power would be strong here, and strong brew and strong wards were her only hope for the sleep she needed.

Having chosen the lesser of several evils, Elissa took her horse to the stables next to what seemed to be one of the better taverns on the edge of town. She paid the stable boy well to be sure that the horse got a good currying, good feed, and whatever apples or carrots the kitchen might spare as a treat. She took her own pack and headed for the tavern. She had gotten no farther than the desk when the entire room went black and cold, and she seemed to be sucked into a tunnel. She grabbed for the crystals.

Instead of an attack, she was met with silence.

"Just what do you think you're doing," Elissa called into the dead blackness that had the smell, feel, and strength of Old Gillam's rooms.

"How dare you enter this city without being summoned," boomed a husky female voice, as though from a cavern. "You were given a Realm to defend, and instead you leave it in peril. You will leave at once."

"I think not, Alven. I've had my fill of the games you're playing, and it is you who imperil my Realm. That is above the laws of the Guild. I have come to see that you are either forced to obey the laws or replaced."

A throaty laugh mocked her, and the black emptiness was replaced by blinding light.

"You dare to challenge me?" the voice mocked.

"No," said Elissa carefully. "I dare to seek justice from my Guild, and if you will not be just then you will be replaced. It is that simple."

"Simple," screamed a voice in her mind. "That challenge will not be simple," it mocked. "I, Alven, will see you out of the Guild."

"On what grounds," demanded Elissa, her patience worn very thin.

"Dereliction of duty," Alven yelled back.

Elissa flicked her hand at the absurdity of the charge. As she did so, Old Gillam's voice sang across the space, "The Amethyst Carekeeper is Guildkeeper."

"NO," screamed Alven. "How dare you blaspheme?"

"It is not I, but your predecessor," Elissa said, confused at the outburst. "And although I do not want the job, I will take it if I must. You will lose, Alven. Despite the petty games and the sharpness of your wit these days, you must lose. Neither I nor any other Realm Carekeeper will tolerate a Guildkeeper who infringes on our Realms. Do you forget what it is we are supposed to do?"

Something in the room was suddenly very wrong. The feeling of strength and power she had first felt from the Guildkeeper was now replaced with a cacophony of shattering crystals and mind-splitting cries. Alven was suddenly and clearly out of control. Confusion changed to fear, and Elissa shrank from the noise that pummeled her eyes and mind and tried with all her might to set crystal daggers in protective wards around herself. She was losing all sense of direction. Above the cacophony came Alven's voice.

"I am more powerful than anyone now," the hysterical voice forced into her mind, again setting harmonics toward cacophony. "You cannot take this from me as you have taken everything else in my life."

Inside Elissa's head, tension built to unbearable pressure. The crystals in the room were beginning to feed one another, and the pitch was increasing. With her last bit of strength, Elissa took one of the amethyst crystals ensorcelled by Old Gillam and threw it as hard as she could at the central source of hum. She heard a high-pitched scream, the splinter of glass, a crash, and then she fell into darkness.

Her next awareness was of a place of total darkness with no entrance or exit that her senses could find. She sighed as she realized that the pain in her head was gone. Wherever she was, her pack and crystals had come with her. Either she had injured Alven and the reaction had sent her here, or she had missed Alven and been sent here. She wished she knew where "here" was. She was cold and tired and desperately wanted a warm bath and a soft bed. Beyond exhaustion, Elissa realized that she could do no more without sleep. Now that the pain in her head was gone, she might even be able to accomplish that—even in this empty place.

"Elissa," she counseled herself wisely, "go to sleep. Thank you," she answered. "I think I will."

So saying, Elissa took five of her crystal daggers and with as much concentration as she could muster, she stabbed them into whatever it was she sat on. One went into the ground at the point where she planned to put her head. This was her first amethyst blade. She could tell by the feel and sound of it. It was not her most powerful dagger, but the first blade one made held a special power which she hoped would work here. At her feet she stabbed two more and one on either side of her body, forming a five-pointed star. Thus protected, Elissa sat on the cold ground and fumbled in her pack for a blanket and for her water skin, bread, cheese, and meats she had left from the journey. There was not much left, but she could survive two or three meals if Alven insisted. Perhaps. It certainly didn't sound like this hysterical woman would or could negotiate rationally, but perhaps. Elissa decided that a bit of Per's optimism and logic would help here. In her mind, she went over the recent events to see if there was anything that made sense. After two times through the same recounting, nothing new came to her. She pulled the blanket over her and shoved the pack under her head, carefully avoiding disturbing the daggers which protected her here.

"I won't sleep," she told herself. "I'll just rest and try to get rid of all these aches."

She took two of Old Gillam's amethyst daggers from her belt, carefully keeping their cutting points away from her body. They seemed to hold some weird power over Alven. Even if she could do nothing else, she could be ready for an attack. Suddenly, her right calf cramped. She cried out at the pain and flung the daggers down as she grabbed to massage the leg. One of the daggers sang to her in Old Gillam's voice, "Fair Amethyst Carekeeper, the Guildhouse is yours for the asking."

Elissa began to laugh. At first it was the bitter laugh of irony, but it changed to the frustrated laugh of confinement and finally to a self-deprecating laugh as she reflected on how she, this glamorous Amethyst Carekeeper, would look to anyone if they could see her now. Shedding tears as her legs and sides cramped in new places, she whooped and pounded the floor, finally rolling in uncontrollable spasms. It was not until she rolled against the edge of one of her dagger wards that she was reminded of the seriousness of her situation. Still giggling, she situated herself in the center of her wards, pulled the blanket over her, and took the loose daggers in her hands. One again began

"Fair Amethyst Carekeeper . . ." but she buried it in the folds of the blanket and giggled herself to sleep.

Elissa awoke feeling stiff all over. She looked around to find herself in the stables in the wan gray light of dawn, her wards still safely planted around her. She shared the stall with her horse, who had been curried and fed.

"Wish they'd thought to clean and feed me," she mumbled, groaning into an upright position. The stable boy she had entrusted her horse to the night before was gone. His replacement came at the sound of her voice and looked most bemused.

"Amethyst Carekeeper, how came you here?" he asked in the accent of one from the Realm next to her own.

"I believe I was Guildkeeper Alven's guest," she sniped. "I think it must be time for a good bath and a change of clothes and some decent food, don't you?"

"You do not wish the Guildhouse?" he asked, startled.

"No, I think I'll save that pleasure till I'm clean and fed," she laughed.

She got up, offended by her odor, and headed toward the tavern she had entered the night before. This time, she had Old Gillam's daggers at the ready, just in case. As she stepped into the dawn, two of the daggers caught the first light and threw rainbows around the nearby ground while two others extolled her magnificence and immeasurable worth to the Guild. These latter she pulled off her belt and stuffed in her pack. No sense giving people ideas.

Without incident, Elissa acquired room and board with hot bath to be delivered immediately, and made her way upstairs. The room was clean and the bed well made with cotton sheets, down pillows, and comforter. The bath water was steaming when it arrived. It soothed the aches in her bones and muscles. As she luxuriated in its soothing effects, she reflected on Alven's words of the night before. A sudden thought jolted her and she sloshed water all over the floor.

"She thinks I've caused this . . . this whatever it is

that is bothering her. She thinks I've wronged her in some way in the past and I've taken something that was hers. I heard her say it, but it didn't sink in. But what have I taken that she could possibly want? I guess there's only one way to find out, and I'd better do it soon."

Elissa dried off quickly, dressed in her best purple linen breeches and tunic. She suspended all the daggers she had brought from her belt, with sheaths over Old Gillam's to keep them quiet. The amethyst dagger which had guarded her head the night before was in its favored position for a quick grab. Then she raced down to the tavern and wolfed down a plentiful meal, followed by a hastily gulped tankard of ale. It was clear that the barkeep considered her quite crude, but she smiled in her most self-assured way, pushed back from the table, and mumbled something about being late for an important appointment as she dashed from the room.

She sped to the Guildhouse, slowing only as her precipitous pace began to draw stares. She hastily followed proper ritual as she entered the old stone abbey which served as Guildhouse. She signed the arrival book and stated her intentions as "conference with Guildkeeper on matters of Realm." That should still wagging tongues.

She walked briskly down the long, sunny corridor which led to Old Gillam's rooms, the unsheathed daggers splashing sun ripples on the walls. At least the daggers seemed happy to be here. She passed other Guild officials along her way and was surprised at how few she knew. She approached Old Gillam's door with some trepidation. She could still feel Old Gillam's presence, but it had mostly faded now. She quickly unsheathed Old Gillam's daggers. Inside was Alven, and Elissa could tell that her presence was also already known. She reached to knock, but was greeted with a quiet "Come in" before she could.

She pushed into Old Gillam's rooms. They were not at all as she remembered them. The room was softer now, although she could not tell how. The furniture was placed in different arrangements, but it was the same furniture, the same wall hangings, the same books. Yet the aura was of a gentler power and a soft topaz glow suffused the room. Alven sat in a chair with a book in her lap and her eyes glued to Elissa, her demure demeanor disguising unplumbed intensity. Before she could rise, Elissa planted a circle of Gillam's daggers around herself. Alven settled back against the overstuffed chair.

"That was unnecessary," she began, but she could see that Elissa was unmoved.

Elissa watched her a moment, trying to assess how much threat the young woman would be if Elissa removed the wards. Although the elfin face seemed large under short-cropped hair, it was obvious that Elissa outweighed her by a good third. It was also clear that Alven was in excellent shape, and that she was braced to do battle at the slightest movement.

"What wrong have I done you?" Elissa asked, figuring the direct approach was the best under the circumstances. Alven suddenly looked confused.

"You truly do not know?" she asked, still wary and angry, but now more vulnerable. "You dare ward against me with daggers made by my own father, and you are not aware? They sing your praises in my head as he used to do and you do not know what you have done to me?" Tears stood on lower lids and then flowed over a tormented face.

"Your father!" Elissa stared dumbfounded at the younger woman. "Of course," she said to herself, looking into Alven's eyes with sudden understanding.

The story then poured from Alven. It was the story of a father who favored one of his students while professing total lack of favoritism, and of a daughter burning to please her father but not allowed by tradition to even tell the world of their kinship.

"I have always lived in your shadow," she said harshly, and pushed from the chair. She began to pace away from the startled Elissa. Alven's blonde hair nearly matched the flaxen-colored tunic and breeches that declared her the Topaz Carekeeper, now Guildkeeper.

"You even stole my stone and my name. Daddy

always called me the shining amethyst of his life when I was a baby. I learned the history of the amethyst at his knee." She stopped suddenly and turned to Elissa.

"Did you know that amethyst is a focus for a woman's power? I was seven when you presented the amethyst dagger and took your Keeper name. I had joined the Guild School just a year before, and Father had seemed to forget I existed. When they called you the Amethyst Carekeeper, I knew that you had finally stolen all that was mine, and I have hated you since. In the end, Father asked me to succeed him, and asked the Guild to accept me. He favored me in the end, but he never quite knew how to deal with the prophecy."

"What prophecy?" asked Elissa, the deepening bewilderment at the events she was hearing clearly audible in her voice.

Alven looked at her again with disbelief. The fury and wariness in her lavender eyes were unmistakable. But somehow, Elissa knew that something in Alven had broken—that she was no longer a threat.

"Surely you know. He must have at least told you?" Elissa felt a probe in her mind which no ward could prevent. Alven had indeed become very strong. Satisfied, Alven's touch disappeared. "You truly do not know," she said bemusedly to herself. "No one knew but me. I have tested them all, and no one knew but me." She paused. "The prophecy was told to Father when he was very young and the last Amethyst Carekeeper died. The Amethyst Carekeepers were all men before you. The prophecy told that the first female Amethyst Carekeeper would be the strongest Guildmaster ever known." Alven sank back into her chair.

"If only you knew about the prophecy, how do you know it existed?"

"You think I would make something like this up?" demanded Alven. "That prophecy was the first thing my father forced my mind to accept, almost before I could breathe. He forced it down my throat for seven years."

"Have you ever thought he might have been wrong?" Elissa asked.

"Father was never wrong," Alven blazed, and crystals began to sing in the room.

"Never? Wasn't he wrong about you and your needs?" Alven's eyes dropped and the crystals quieted. "He was most certainly wrong about me and mine. I had to fight him to get away from here and away from the bickering that nearly drove me crazy. I am not suited to the task of Guildkeeper, Alven. If you force me to challenge you for the right to be Guildkeeper, I would wound you with another of your father's blades or cleanse you and leave you again with nothing. And then I, too, would leave the Guild in other hands. You have nothing to fear from me, Alven. You never did."

Alven's eyes glistened. "I never knew that. Until a moment ago. When I read your mind, I saw that what you say is true. I also saw the attacks on you and know that I caused them, although I do not remember doing so. On the trail, I warned you fairly as a Guildkeeper to a Carekeeper who leaves her post unattended. But these other attacks, I . . ." Her voice drifted off and her eyes glazed for a moment. She sighed deeply and returned her focus to Elissa.

"I barely remember last night. I apologize for forcing into your brain, but I had to see the attacks as you did."

She shook her head slowly.

"You are right, you know. I have achieved what was most important to me, and I have risked it for revenge. I have been so stupid keeping all this to myself all these years. But I couldn't tell Father, and you left before I could talk to you. I have blamed you for so much that is not yours. And I have used my powers improperly for revenge. I will tell the Guild what I have done and let them decide my fate. For Carekeeper to attack Carekeeper is unthinkable." She shuddered at the thought of being cleansed, then straightened her back. "But what is important now is that you forgive me. Can you?"

Elissa stepped over her wards and grabbed the younger woman in her arms, hugging as hard as she could.

"Of course, friend. Just straighten out my Realm and let me go home." She pushed Alven back and stared into her eyes. "No one else need learn of this. I know now that the attacks were not a matter of Realm but a deeper hurt which neither of us could know or control. If you let me go home and you correct the wrongs, then I think that we are even. You have the strengths that a Guildkeeper must have, and it will be good to have you here. Do not judge yourself harshly—your father did enough of that for a lifetime."

Elissa stooped over and tried to pull the daggers she had used as wards from the floor. As she did so, the morning sun shone through the room and caught their light. Through the rainbows, Elissa examined Old Gillam's daggers. Somehow, during the night or today, they had changed. Two had cracked, and the others no longer spoke. She gave them to Alven.

"He meant these for you," she smiled through the rainbows which bathed both their faces in peaceful and calming light. "He just didn't know it."

THE ARROW'S FLIGHT
by Stephen Burns

The title of this story, "Arrow's Flight," is the title of another writer's first novel; Mercedes Lackey, whose first story appeared in *SWORD AND SORCERESS*.

Stephen Burns said, in sending this in, that I had "the honor of receiving his second word-processed manuscript. I am running way behind because my first system . . . melted down while printing out a story for *Analog*; three weeks' work went down the tubes on that, as the stories are safely on disk where I can't get them out without using another SCM. The one I had was shipped back with various suggestions as to its disposal." I know exactly how you feel, Steve; I had a book die on me that way, and getting another word processor is a mighty act of faith. The reason I did it was because I had heard of a lot of writers who had refused to try a word processor; but I have yet to hear of one who had a good word processor and still went back to a typewriter . . . or to longhand.

Still, let's remember that the *real* word processor is the brain; everything else, whether a #2 pencil, or a #2000 Osborne, is just the *tool*. In one very real sense, every writer uses that word processor. And to hell with the Industrial Revolution.

Of course, reading some people's fiction, you'd never know . . .

Stephen Burns lives in upstate New York, on an island, and made his first bow in the pages of the very first *SWORD AND SORCERESS*. Since then, he's written for many more prestigious markets, but we're glad to kick off this new anthology with his work. Write on, Steve, and may your word processor never go down—the real word processor, that is.

I must tell you that I do not much love the water.

Oh, to bathe in it is a pleasure, as is drinking it when one's throat is parched and no wine is at hand. But to travel across it is to needlessly risk consuming enough of the stuff for the whole rest of a very short, very wet life.

I knew that the craft which was bearing me to Grimstone Island leaked. There were three widely separated holes cut in the big flat boat's cargo and passenger laden deck. Those holes were occupied by crewmen assiduously bailing out that part of the Saloran River trying to remake the areas above and below decks a place hospitable for its fishes.

The ferrymaster, a shaggy, stubble-chinned, spark-eyed little wretch who addressed crew and passenger alike as "my darling," noted my discomfort and sought to reassure me. I was little surprised that he noticed me. I was a stranger, an unaccompanied, unusually tall female dressed in travel-stained leathers, and perhaps most noticeable of all, my complexion was of a most striking greenish cast.

"She takes on, my darling," he told me, "only 'cos she's lade heavy and low in the water. That puts her dry seams below the waddy-line, y'see. Empty, she's tighter'n a gnat's ass."

All my fears flew like birds at this proof that we were sinking because we were overburdened enough to sink. He then launched into a long-winded explanation about how the leaks in a wooden boat are what keep it from leaking. But before he could finish elaborating on this paradoxical jewel of boatman's philosophy, he had to break off to go berate the rowers. They had apparently taken their master's inattention as permission to slacken their efforts. He hobbled up and down the crowded deck, threatening them with an immense whip and calling them "my darlings" all the while.

One cannot reach an island without crossing the water. I would not have tempted the Saloran's cold and clever currents but that on Grimstone Island was the stronghold of the man known in those wild parts as Lord Revan.

The very same Revan who had so generously taken under protection all the lands and islands for over a day's ride in every direction. The Revan who was on the way to becoming a king. The closer to this place I had come, the more tales of the man and his exploits I had heard.

The news of his empire building had spread far and wide. All such news eventually reaches the Order. They had sent me forth, and if all went well, I would soon be meeting the fabled Revan face-to-face.

He would be a changed man after that meeting.

After all, I was going to poison him.

Grimstone was much more beautiful than its name had led me to expect. I do not believe my perceptions were overmuch colored by my overwhelming relief to back on unmoving, unsinkable land once more. Autumn had wielded its madman's brush, painting the leaves gold and fire. The whole island seemed a living tapestry stitched in riotous color.

But I had not come to watch the waves lap and the leaves turn and fall. *Be an arrow*, as we say in the Order. Fly swift and sure to your target.

A detachment of bored-looking guards waited at the quay for those passengers who had not drowned or died of seasick. The one chief among them chose to stir from his wine and ask my business personally.

My delightful trip over a watery grave must not have left too much a mark on me. He lumbered toward me doing those things which no man would call primping—as if spit in the hair made that much increase in a man's attractiveness.

I am not uncomely, though many men are uneased by my height. This bearishly built man was tall enough to look me in the eye, though he did not. He spent most of his time looking everywhere but my face, and every so often cast a longing glance back at his abandoned flask as if wishing he had taken time for just one more nerve-steeling swig.

"You have business here?" he asked with what was doubtless supposed to be stern courtesy. But he looked more bashful than brutal. All around us the other guards joked with my fellow passengers while half-heartedly attempting to extract bribes of the bread crust or chicken leg variety.

"My business is pleasure," I replied, my tone and smile hinting much but promising nothing. I gave that a moment to sink in and take effect before pulling my slung *thoma* around in front of me.

My instrument must have been of less interest to him than my breasts. His gaze circled my face like a fly, finally lighting at my shoulder. "So . . . you are a minstrel, then?"

"What thought you me to be?" I asked sweetly.

His blunt, good-natured face reddened. He gave his wine a longing glance, then stared at my chin. "Nay, I did not think you a—" He swallowed hard. "It is just that I have never heard of a female minstrel," he finished lamely.

"Then you'll not have had the joy of hearing one, I'll warrant. Should I give you a lay?"

That turn of words took him two wine glances and a head scratch to untangle. He solved his confusion by retreating to form. "Then you seek to play here on the Isle, ah—"

"Sardhana," I replied, bowing as I supplied my name. "I would play for your Lord, if he would hear me." I pushed my long black hair back, and could not resist adding, "Many a king has heard me and remembered me ever after."

Of course a goodly number of them did not *live* long after. But that was a fine point, and there was no need to bring it up and further confuse the man.

He frowned, scratching his chin. "Well, anyone seeking audience with Lord Revan—"

"I would have him be *my* audience," I pointed out.

A long, longing glance wineward. "Anyone seeking Lord Revan's presence must first pass muster with his chief advisor, Al-Lord Bromelas."

I let my *thoma* hang from its strap behind me once more. "How would I go about meeting this Al-Lord Bromelas?" I asked, making it sound as if I thought such a feat nearly impossible. The guard's gaze dropped from my chin to the front of my shirt. I heaved a deep sigh as a coinless bribe. "Could you please advise me on this, kind Captain?"

My ranking him so highly brought him back to less physical matters. His face colored like the fall-fired maples growing along that stretch of shore.

"Cadre-leader, not Captain. Cadre-leader Sand. I, ah, could perhaps . . ." He shook himself, drew himself up straight, and came very near to looking me in the eye. "I will escort you to him."

I looked properly awed. "Could you truly do that?"

He puffed out his chest. "It would be my pleasure."

We set out right after he put one of his subordinates in charge and procured a full skin of wine for the journey. Thinking me a frail flower, he insisted on carrying my pack.

Poisoning a king—or in the case of Revan, a would-be king—is simple enough. All one needs to do is bring the poison and the royal victim together. This uncomplicated set of requirements applies to the dosing of queens, princes, princesses, and other sundry nobility.

Any reputable poisoner will tell you that the difficult part of this process lies in getting close enough to your noble victim to administer the potion. Second hardest, but of signal importance, is leaving your workplace alive. A surprising number of people who would not think twice about hanging someone who has stolen a single crust of bread raise strenuous objections to the poisoning of their king. When one considers the fact that the thief never passed a single law over them, and never lightened their pockets of a single coin of tax, one is moved to wonder what this world is coming to.

An afternoon's walk along a leaf-scattered path that led into the island's heart, past farms and garden-quilted fields busy with harvest, brought us to the narrow-necked inland bay upon the shore of which Revan's stone and timber keep was being built. Cadre-leader Sand's presence carried me easily past the guardpost at the end of the winding road leading to the keep, and through the gate in the high timber palisade around it. We were greeted often. It seemed that he had been drinking with every guard—and at least half of the island's numerous inhabitants—we met along the way.

He had escorted me all the way to a small anteroom inside the keep, little better than a cell. One splintery wood bench had been provided for our comfort, along with a barred window facing east. The sweet breeze passing through it hinted that we were somewhere close downwind of the privies.

Al-Lord Bromelas was making us wait. Sand fussed and fidgeted. He seemed to have had second thoughts about bringing me to meet the man who, judging by the tales he had told as his traveling wine had loosened his tongue and his present nervousness, he plainly feared. Most distressing of all, he dared not drink so close to the seat of power as it might have endangered his own seat.

The wait was not unexpected. No man of power grants instant audience. This holds especially true when that man has not yet had enough time to insulate himself behind several layers of underlings. Lord Revan's realm and rule were still too new to have collected the requisite number of obstreperous, pinch-faced drones necessary to proper governance.

There was no way for me to judge how long I would be made to wait. Sand could fret and second-guess himself to fill the time, but one does not become a minstrel—or a master poisoner—by wasting idle time. Instead one practices her craft. Since I had no desire to hone my art by poisoning Sand, I retrieved my *thoma* from the end of the bench.

Thoma are still rare things. Only Vlas of the Order makes them, although most of them are played by people who have never heard of us. In truth, no more than two dozen people outside the Order know of it, much to their regret.

Mine was one of her finest, made especially for me. Its long, graceful fretted neck is of the darkest rosewood, its amber-wood bell as sweetly curved as a pregnant woman's belly. Its flat top is a smooth, long-grained wood the color of sunlight, and it is stringed with drawn silver. At the top of its neck, just above the carved bone tuning pegs, are the fourteen *thoara,* the reeded pipes that enable a *thoma* player to wynd a melody at counterpoint to the deep, ringing music of the plucked and strummed strings. If one can sing, the interplay between singing and piping stretched like a bridge over the flowing string-play makes a music few can resist.

I chose not to sing this time. Using only strings and pipes, I played a song from my own land known as "Sueryn's Romance," the story of a beautiful witch who fell in love with a troll. It is a sly, sprightly tune, and few notes had sounded before Sand was grinning and tapping his feet.

One sure way to cut short the time spent in waiting is to appear to be enjoying yourself. That makes the author of your wait believe that you are being done a favor, and that is hardly the sort of attitude befitting a supplicant.

I had not even reached the end of the song when two men arrived to cut short our tuneful sojurn. One was tall and black-robed, with the long-jawed, indignant face of a landed fish. The shorter, muscular one was garbed in the same brown guard's leathers as Sand. His moon face was blandly impassive, but his striking green eyes were restless and watchful.

"You will come with us," said the taller of the two in a grating, nasal whine, his bulging eyes fixing on me like lampreys. "Al-Lord Bromelas will receive you now."

Sand scrambled to his feet and gave a belated salute. "Cadre-leader Sand," he said, "Ah—escorting the minstrel." He swallowed hard. "Sir."

Blackrobe's baleful stare never wavered. "That has been well noted, Cadre-leader Sand." This was spoken in such a way as to be more likely taken as threat than anything else. "You are dismissed." Only then did he look away, and for just long enough to watch poor Sand beat a hasty retreat.

Then my respite was over, and I was again treated to his cold, silent scrutiny. This was supposed to reduce me to cringing submission. I smiled, leaning in so my face was close to his. "Say there, soldier," I said "you look like you could use a good time."

His lipless mouth twisted like that of a hooked fish. "You will be silent and give me any weapons you carry."

I have been more intimidated by reproachful trout watching me raise my fork. I judged the silent one to be the more dangerous of the two of them. I had been watching him out of the edge of my eye. He appeared cat-quick and powerful, and I doubted that those sharp, ever-roving green eyes missed anything. He did not seem the sort to be taken in by feint or ruse. I threw him a wink, and was rewarded with the merest hint of a smile before I again faced his vinegarish cohort.

I stood up, forcing him back a step. "Have you no pricker of your own?" I asked while handing over the long knife at my belt. "Poor man, that you need a woman to equip you!"

"Silence, bitch!" Now he had to look up at me. He was tall, but I was taller. I let my smile widen.

"With your tongue so honeyed as your disposition, you must bid fair with the ladies," I said, sliding my hand along his bony forearm. He shuddered and jerked away, his piscine face twisting in distaste. "—Or is it the boys?"

"I pray your tongue wags so sharply at Al-Lord Bromelas," he hissed, one bony hand curling into a fist.

"How so?" I asked all coy and wide-eyed.

That fist opened into a claw. "Because then he will give you to *me*." For the first time he smiled. It was no pretty sight. "I have the tools to blunt it once and for all. Now *move!*"

He gave me a helpful shove to speed me on my way.

Al-Lord Bromelas was a huge mushroom of a man, pasty-pale and puffy, all hairless bulges and dimples. With mushrooms, one is well advised to know which ones are poisonous. As some of the loveliest poisons come from mushrooms, such lore is of more than passing interest to me.

He had been all beaming welcome when I was

brought in, and that smile had never left his face. Nor had it touched his pale eyes. He played the jolly fat man with the same zeal that apparently went into his meals. But was only a part, a mask.

This was a poisonous mushroom, of that I was certain. One whose appetite for riches matched his physical hunger, judging by the opulence of his chamber.

My pike-faced friend had been sent away to spread his sunshine in some other quarter of the keep. The short, silent guard had taken up vigil outside the door. It appeared Bromelas felt he had little to fear from a female minstrel. After all, had I not already been disarmed and thoroughly cowed by his winsome lackey?

My host's chair was a throne in everything but name. He settled his ponderous bulk more comfortably in it, the wood and leather creaking in protest. His smile broadened, his all but colorless eyes nearly disappearing in the folds of flesh around them. They had all the loving warmth of a steel knife in the back.

"So, you are a minstrel, come to play for Lord Revan?" His voice was soft and smooth, his accent highborn.

I returned an equally sincere smile. "That, and other things, Al-Lord."

A faint spark of interest flickered in those empty eyes. He pursed his liverish lips. "Other things?" He looked me up and down. "You are passing fair. Think you to become a queen?"

"Lord Raven is a king, then?"

There was a darksome mirth in Bromelas's dry chuckle. "He will be, in his day." I got the distinct impression that perhaps that day might not be a long one.

"I heard many tales of brave Lord Revan as I journeyed here," I said carefully. "He is much loved."

Bromelas inclined his massive, hairless head in agreement, but remained silent.

"But then, so are whores." As I spoke those words that faint spark of interest brightened. The frown he showed me was no less real than his earlier smile.

"You dare much, to speak so." His voice soft, silken. Like a Tuvangare garrotte.

"Do I?" I sat back and crossed my legs. "Recall Buggerfish."

His puzzlement at least was genuine. He rubbed his fleshy triple chin. "Who?"

"The fish-faced charmer who brought me here."

Another arid chuckle. "Ah, Pickernel. To what end?"

"Instruction, Al-Lord. Instruction and understanding."

He paused a moment, weighing me and the enigma I represented. Then he stamped his foot. The silent guard reappeared instantly, looking at Bromelas questioningly.

Bromelas said, "Pickernel. Here. Now." The guard nodded curtly, then departed.

"A deaf-mute?" I said. "That might be useful to a man who values secrecy."

Bromelas frowned. "Have a care, minstrel. You have piqued my interest. Pray that I am not angered—or disappointed."

There ensued a long period of silence. Bromelas simply sat there with a toadlike stillness, soft jeweled hands laced across his ample belly, watching me through slitted eyes.

This was supposed to fray my nerves. I began to softly whistle the old song about the fat man who fell asleep in the kitchen and was mistakenly taken for a pig by a nearsighted cook, thus becoming his own dinner, while giving his chamber a closer look.

No mean wealth was on display there. The wood and stone walls were hung with tapestries, and there was a thick rug on the floor. The tables and shelves were all carved hardwood or stone, and they bore books, mirrors, and articles of gold, silver, and brass. I counted far more wealth than could likely be gathered by the second of an upstart kingling in a place so poor and wild as this. But this was no barbarian's hoard of pretties. There was an order in their display, evidence of a refined taste and an understanding of their relative values. Seeing what was displayed made me wonder what remained hidden.

During my journey there I had never heard the

name of Bromelas mentioned but that it was carefully
pointed out that he was an outlander. It appeared he
had enjoyed some wealth, power, and position before
becoming the mover behind Lord Revan's ascent. Perhaps he had been a highborn exile, or a cast-out vizier
before becoming a kingmaker in this land.

A kingmaker who planned to usurp his creation.

He stirred in his chair. "You have not yet told me
your name, minstrel," he said, breaking the silence.

I turned back and gave him a smile. "Sardhana,
Al-Lord."

"A pretty name. Has it a meaning?"

"Yes, Al-Lord." I waited, wearing a half-smile.

"Pray tell me that meaning." A pettish tone burred
the smooth silk of his voice.

I let my smile widen. "Why, it means 'Laughing
Death,' my Lord."

The silence returned.

Not long after there was a sharp knock at the door.
The deaf-mute guard pushed through hard after. He
had friend Pickernel slung over his brawny shoulder
like a sack of wheat. A fox-faced graybeard in a stained
white robe trailed after, wringing his hands and muttering to himself.

"Put him down, Chaff," Bromelas ordered once the
mute guard had turned to see his face. Pickernel must
not have been too dear a friend of Chaff's; he dumped
his burden with the same tenderness he had shown in
carrying him. Pickernel's teeth snapped together as he
hit the floor. He lay there in a sprawl of bony limbs,
moaning piteously.

"Pickernel appears unwell, leech," Bromelas remarked mildly, leaning forward for a closer look.

The graybeard ducked his head. "He came to me
scarce-time ago, complaining that his gut burned and
his head was filled with ringing. No sooner was he in
my chamber than he collapsed, howling at the pain.
He bit and snapped like a wild dog when I tried to
examine him."

"Perchance he was afraid your fee would be too
high."

Graybeard started to take offence, then thought better of it. He licked his lips. "Perhaps, Lord. He now shows all the signs of Wound Fever, yet I found no mark upon him."

"He seemed his normal, miserable self when last I saw him," Bromelas began, hard thought moving behind his soft white face. I knew myself to be much in those thoughts.

Before he could say more, Pickernel suddenly let out a bloodcurdling shriek, his bony body arching like a bent bow. His face had been a livid red. Now it turned a most spectacular purple, and blood began to gush from his nose and ears. He shrieked again, his heels beating a furious tattoo on the floor. Then all at once he slumped, going limp as death.

That was no great surprise, as his gentle spirit had indeed departed. I knew. After all, it's a poor crafter who does not recognize her own handiwork.

Bromelas' faint eyebrows rose. He heaved his bloated body up from his chair, waddled over to Pickernel's corpse and nudged it with his booted toe. "Dead," he said as if informing the corpse of the behavior now expected from it.

"Dead!" wailed the leech, wringing his hands at the tragedy of his unpaid bill.

I moved to Bromelas' side, laying my hand on his shoulder. He jerked away, turning on me with a murderous glare which gave me a true look at his unguarded self. He opened his mouth to speak, then thought better of it. His smiling mask dropped back into place, and he spoke offhandedly.

"I can scarcely believe that Pickernel could be so ill-mannered as to die on my floor." His dry laugh rustled like a viper slithering under fall leaves. "But I can hardly chastise him for it, can I? At least I can be certain that he will not do it again. You, leech. If you wish your fee to be paid, then haul this unsightly carcass away."

"But—!" Graybeard began. A single glance from Bromelas silenced his protest. He sighed, and stooping down, grasped Pickernel's bony ankles and began dragging him away. He showed himself an expert at the removal of the unwanted body. Most leeches are; they get much practice, for the corpses of past customers do little to encourage further practice.

Chaff let him out the door and took up his station once more. Bromelas dropped back into his chair. I sat down as well, folding my arms and waiting for him to speak first.

The jolly smile was discarded now. "Pickernel brings you in to see me. Not long after he is dead. Is this chance?"

I shrugged. "Life is chance. But Death is in every roll of the bones."

"He died before my eyes, brought at your behest. You said I would find calling him instructive. Now that I have been . . . instructed, I am reminded of a question which you never answered. I shall ask it again: What else have you come to this island to do?"

I gave him a smile that has melted many a man's heart.

"I have come to poison Lord Revan, of course. I have a question of my own: Should it be done in concert with you for some mutually agreeable fee, and to further your aims, or simply because it is what I have planned to do all along?"

The closer I had come to Revan's lands, the more often people had smiled when his name was spoken. Once in his lands, the tales of his kindness and courage had come thick as flies in summer. I had stopped at many homes, taverns, and campfires along the way. At each one I had heard stories from those who had fought with him against the river mauraders or the Keebooka, worked behind him at storm-harvest or in building the keep's walls. They all loved him, men and women alike.

Oh, there were grumblings about the splendid new wonder of taxes, and about the number of men who had left fishing or farming to join the guards or help in raising the keep. But it was good-natured, and most ills were laid at the feet of Bromelas. Most spat after speaking the Al-Lord's name, but they trusted Revan to control him.

Revan was well loved, but not like a whore.

It was no painted harlot who pleasures his people only for the gold he can pick from their pockets that I found seated on a low stool by the cherry fire burning in his austere chamber's hearth. Nets and good, simple weapons hung on the walls, not tapestries. The floor was bare plank.

The near-king Lord Revan leaped to his feet when I entered, a most unkingly gesture. I bowed, keeping my face downcast. No few moments passed before he spoke.

"Oh!" he said, "please be at ease." I lifted my eyes. His sunburned face wore a sheepish grin. His teeth gleamed very white against his short black beard and ruddy skin.

He ducked his head shyly. "I forget myself sometimes," he confessed in a low voice. "This Lord business is like a too-large cloak. It slides off me more often than it stays on."

"It suits you well enough, Lord," I said, taking a long look at my intended victim. He was dressed in a rough jerkin and trousers, but his boots were fine leather. His hair was black and tousled, long at the back and bound in the local fashion. He was handsome enough to open nearly any woman's legs with no more than a wink, and the thin diagonal scar that crossed his left eye and cheek did nothing to make him any less so. His eyes were the color of the river, a clear admixing of green, blue, and gray. His gaze was honest and direct, yet sparkled with humor.

"Well, everyone tells me that I should wear a crown," he said, gesturing that I should sit on the other stool before the fire. "But I fear that it would fit less than this Lord's-cloak, and end up slipping down over my ears and hanging slantwise over my face." He chuckled at the picture that conjured.

I sat down, my *thoma* still riding at my back. "A king is made by more than the wearing of a diadem," I told him.

"Let us hope so." He regained his own stool and sat facing me. "May the office invest knowing, for I fear my poor head is empty of any kinging."

He held up the coil of fine thread and the other of heavier twine he held in his big rough hands. "I know fishing better, though little do I get a chance to angle. This plaiting of line is the closest I can manage these days."

"You make fishline, my Lord?" I could not help but be curious about this unkingly pursuit. It seemed I stalked a most unusual prey.

"At idle moments. My hands itch if not busy, and these lines I plait have become sought after as lucky. I bestow them as gifts, and believe it if you will, they are seemingly more treasured than jewels." He shook his head in disbelief, yet I could see that it pleased him.

I believed it, and now I knew more of why this man was so beloved. His appeal was such that I could only wonder that he was not king already. His warmth and honesty shone just as brightly as the fire crackling in the grate, and warmed me just as surely. Already I liked my victim very much. I knew it would be all too easy to tarry a while and enjoy the pleasure of his company.

Be an arrow, I told myself. You have work to do.

"I would play for you, Lord," I said.

His smile was boyish and devastating. He pushed his crow-wing hair back from his eyes. "Old Bromelas was adamant that I should see and hear you." That smile grew wider. It was a weapon, that smile, though I doubted he thought of it as such.

"If the playing is as lovely as the player," he went on, "Then I will surely at least lose my heart to the music."

I brought my *thoma* around before me. "You are too kind, Lord. Al-Lord Bromelas liked my playing so well, did he?"

His eyes glowed with mischief. "More like the look of you, though even that was some surprise to me. It often seems the only things in that hairless head of his are riches, making me king, his dinner, and riches again for dessert."

"Seeing you enthroned is so important to him, then?"

Revan laughed aloud. "It is the only thing dearer to

him than his wealth and a full board." He shook his head, his expression becoming serious. "Oh, I can well see where he leads when he speaks of strength in unity, of peace being more easily kept when we are gathered together and led by one. He argues convincingly—else I would not be here tending to the affairs of others instead of my own boat and nets."

"You led in war, Lord," I prompted.

"I did. Understand me, it did not ill-suit me to take the lead in defense against the wild Keebooka when they swept down from the North, or to organize a resistance against the river raiders who have too often stolen the fruits of our labors. Those things had to be done, and I found I could do them." He sighed. "But to tax my neighbors to put me in a fine house, to sit as judge over others? To make laws by which people will live and die? Such labors would better suit Bromelas, and often have I told him so."

I struck a chord, purposefully flatting one note. I made as to retune, and spoke offhandedly. "You would have Bromelas be king in your stead, Lord?"

He shifted uneasily, frowning down at the work in his hands. "Nay," he said at last. "Nor would the people have him. He is too much a starveling wolf under all that laughing lard. A wolf with a nose whetted for wealth and power, for opportunity. In these parts we train wolves to protect our sheep from other wolves, and he has done much to protect this flock— although sometimes it has been in spite of himself. I think good and ill are balanced within him, both in supply equal to his girth, and I believe I know how far to trust him. He has done much to turn these shores into something like a united kingdom. I may be the arrow, but he is the bow."

Be an arrow.

What delicious irony to have him remind me that I tarry, that my task is yet undone. I wrenched the peg around, forcing the string back into tune.

"I would play the song of King Narm, who ruled for five hundred years, to bring you luck," I said, wearing a mask stolen from the face of Bromelas. "If it please you, Lord."

His smile was as true as mine was false. He settled himself comfortably, his fingers going back to their plaiting. "You please me entire," he said. "How could any of your works please me any less?"

I came near to saying: *You have no way of knowing* out loud, but played him the song of a deathless king instead.

Of the act itself there is little to tell. I played one song, then another. Revan told me that he almost wished it were someone else providing the tune, for then I would be free for the dancing it deserved. He said he dearly loved dancing.

It was during the third air that the arrow the Order had shaped me into struck Lord Revan. He had his head bowed in an attitude of reverent listening, the work of his hands forgotten. There were no words to this haunting song. It was all strings and pipes, and the music held him enmazed.

I pushed a breath through the highest pipe, a pipe as yet unsounded.

Revan started, his eyes flying open as he slapped at his neck. *"Damn!"* he cried in pain and surprise.

"My Lord?" I asked, stilling the strings with my fingers.

He grinned sheepishly. "Your pardon, Sardhana. I was stung—a hornet, mostlike. They creep in this time of year, seeking warmth." He rubbed at the small red welt on his neck. "Play on, I beg you. It is only a sting. I will live."

I laughed. "Perhaps to rule for five hundred years."

I finished that song, and played only one more before leaving, pleading fatigue but promising to play for him again. That song was one of which I had long been fond.

To some it was a lullabye.

To others, a dirge.

It was in the very dead of that same night when I was torn from my warm bed, bound hand and foot by several silent, grim-faced guards, and delicately wafted away in a sack. I was then unbagged and shown the hospitality of a deep, muddy pit inside a walled-off area attached to the keep. The faces of my captors became clear in the flickering torchlight only after a half-dozen of them dragged a heavy wooden grate over the top of the pit and peered in at their catch.

Cadre-leader Sand was among them, his blunt-featured face red and swollen with a mixture of anger and tears.

"Why am I treated so?" I cried up at the circle of forbidding faces frowning down at me through the grate.

One with a pale, hard face spat down at me. "So gently, you mean?" he jeered. "Al-Lord Bromelas wills it. But do not become accustomed to such fine quarters and loving treatment! Soon you will be handled in a manner more befitting the foul, soulless bitch who has poisoned our Lord Revan!"

He looked around at his fellows. "Who will stand the first watch over this treacherous viper?"

"I will," Cadre-leader Sand said in a low, miserable voice.

It was dark in the pit, the floor carpeted in mud. At least I was not to be lonely. I could hear the chitter of rats discussing where best to kiss their guest in welcome, and from above me came the muted grumbling of Sand talking to himself.

I spoke softly. "He said Revan has been poisoned."

"Silence!" Sand's reply was more a sob than a command.

"I only ask what has happened that I might be able to defend myself against these vicious accusations."

That fetched Sand to the grate. The torchlight let me see the anger and anguish warring across his face. His voice came out in a tormented hiss.

"I accuse you, foul temptress! As I must accuse myself, for who was the credulous fool who brought you here?" He beat his breast. "It was I! You betrayed the witless trust I placed in you, and out of my own weakness I have betrayed the finest man to ever live on these shores! Now my Lord lays dying, and it might as well be by my own hand."

"Lord Revan dies, then?" I asked gently.

His upper lip curled in disgust. "Do not play at innocence with me! Who would better know than the one who so cruelly poisoned his cup?"

Dear Bromelas had not let me down! I had told him that there would be no evidence. He had, of course, provided some, and made certain it pointed at me. I spoke haltingly. "A . . . poisoned cup, you say?"

"Aye, as if you did not well know it! Al-Lord Bromelas himself pointed out the flagon of wine and the two cups, one with sweet wine in it, the other still holding dregs just as poisonous as you yourself."

Much hung on the next few moments. I spoke as if confused. "But . . . I shared no wine with Lord Revan! He asked if some should be brought, but I declined."

"You lie." A slight hint of uncertainty tinged his voice.

"I do not! But if you do not trust me, then ask your fellow guard. The deaf one—what was his name?"

"Chaff."

"Yes, Chaff. He brought me into Lord Revan's room, stood guard outside while I was within, then escorted me back to my own room. Ask him if he saw any wine in your Lord's room, or if any was brought while I was there. I know he cannot speak, but it seemed his eyes were sharper than an eagle's."

"They are. I know him, and in truth his wits are no duller than his eyes."

"Seek him out," I said urgently. "*Ask* him! If what he tells you leads you to see that I am telling the truth, then return with all possible haste. I have traveled much, and possess a wit or two myself. It may be that I know the remedy for the potion which has been given Lord Revan."

I could see new hope struggling to surpass Sand's fear and self-recrimination. "I—you say Lord Revan might yet live?" His voice throbbed with entreaty.

"He might—if you are quick, and the potion given him is one of which I have heard."

He rubbed his mouth, at last coming to a decision. "I will do this." He leaned forward, his hands gripping the bars and his expression turning grim. "But I swear, if this is more trickery, I will come down into that pit and kill you with my bare hands!''

He lifted his head and shouted, *"Hoy, Wrackler!* Come guard the bitch! I have an errand that will not wait!''

I heard a distant reply. Sand's face filled the grate once more. "One way or the other, I shall soon return," he vowed. "Pray that Chaff does not call you a liar. I do not like spilling blood, but yours will wash my hands if he does." That said, he hurried away to find and question Chaff.

I smiled to myself as I dropped the ropes which had bound my wrists onto the ground. There is more to a poisoner's art than mere potions, and I had reason to be proud of my work.

Sand was not long in returning. I heard him exchange words with the guard at the outer gate, and soon after he sent the guard away who watched over me.

His face appeared at the grate. He wore the look of a man enwebbed in a situation beyond his understanding, and I knew he wondered if I were the spider, or just another trapped fly. Chaff was with him, his bland moon-face impassive as ever.

"Well?" I demanded, looking up at them.

"Chaff confirms what you told me," Sand replied slowly. "He said you took no wine with Lord Revan."

"Then let me up from here so—" I began.

Sand held up his hand. "He has also told me that old Pickernel died this day from what may well have been *poison.* He had no love for Pickernel, but suspects that his death may have been your handiwork."

I wondered if Chaff could read my words from my lips. After all, I was in the bottom of a lightless pit. But did that matter to those green cat-eyes? The way he stared straight down at me like an owl at a mouse made me feel as if he could see not only my face, but everything else behind it as well. I dared not lie.

"I gave Lord Revan no poisoned wine," I said, speaking with slow care. "Is that not all that matters?"

Chaff stared down at me a moment longer, and I

well knew that I was being judged. Then he gave his answer by bending down and heaving at the grate as if he meant to lift it off by himself. He was even stronger than my first guess, for he started to move something put in place by six. Sand added his own strong back to the task, and soon there was starry, open sky above me once more.

"Step back," Sand hissed, and moments later a wooden ladder slid down into the muck beside me. I wasted no time climbing back out. Too much of the night had been spent there in idle luxury.

There was work to be done. Work which I had begun, but had not yet finished. The arrow was in flight once more.

We were nearing Revan's chamber. So far the combination of Sand's and Chaff's grim-faced authority, plus an occasional bit of politic slinking, had taken us past all challenge. But I doubted that such fortune would hold much longer. Unless Bromelas was more a fool than I thought him, the area immediately around Revan's room would be cordoned with men whose loyalty was to him alone.

I glanced at Sand as we scuttled along one silent, torchlit hallway, three mice out to dare the cat. He and Chaff held my arms pinioned so that anyone we encountered would think me their prisoner, and indeed I was part prisoner, part accomplice. How could they know that I wanted no escape?

Pitching my voice low, I asked Sand, "Have you given any thought as to who *did* poison your Lord if I am not the guilty party?"

The grim set of his face deepened. "Aye," he murmured, "I have." There was nothing of the good-natured sot I had met only the afternoon before about him now. He looked me in the eye. There was fear in him, but he was determined to risk all to save his Lord.

"It could only be Bromelas," he whispered hoarsely, as if fearing the walls had ears. "Only he has the cleverness and the ambition. Only he could gain by all this. He remains an outsider for all his years here, and he is too feared and mistrusted to be accepted other than while under Revan's control. Yet were Revan to—" His voice broke. He turned away for a moment, sighed deeply, then he faced me again. His eyes were damp, but his voice was steady.

"Were Revan to die, then perhaps he could usurp his better's place while we were all lost to grief and confusion. I do know that were he to take control, there would be no breaking his grip as he squeezed us dry."

The corridor turned just ahead, and not far beyond was Revan's chamber. I looked into Chaff's face, saying, "Let me go now." He released me, Sand following suit soon after.

I stretched my arms to limber them, then produced the knife I had been carrying the whole time. Sand's eyes widened in surprise. Chaff smirked and gave me an approving nod.

"Bromelas' men are not going to let us simply walk in," I said. "We have a fight ahead of us."

Sand pulled out the long hardwood cudgel scabbarded across his back with a quick, sure motion. "Never liked spilling blood," he said. Then something of the Sand I had met the day before returned as he grinned crookedly. "But cracking heads? Ah, that's another thing entire!"

Chaff simply pushed up his sleeves. His green eyes gleamed with a light all their own, and he looked like he could not wait until the mayhem began.

By then we were rounding the corner. There was a shout, and indeed it did begin.

"The intruders have been met, Al-Lord," the leader of Bromelas' personal guard rasped. "Their assault is over!"

There was a grating sound as the door's bar was pulled. The heavy oak door swung open to reveal Bromelas.

"We won," I said. The Al-Lord's pasty face drained of all color. He moved to slam the door in my face. But before he could, I flung the guard I had been holding by the throat behind me and blocked its swing with my body. I caught a fleeting glimpse of Sand's efficient dispatching of the man with one artful blow of his cudgel as he tumbled past.

Then the three of us were inside, Chaff rebarring the stout door behind us. The corpulent Al-Lord retreated before me, his eyes on the bloody knife I carried, at last halted by the footboard of Revan's bed. Revan himself lay on it, his handsome face ashy and lax, the rise and fall of his chest short and rapid. Dark, blood-bloated leeches clung to his face and neck. The graybearded leech who had applied them cringed by his bedside.

Three elders, two men and a woman, had drawn back fearfully when we entered. No doubt Bromelas had brought them there to witness Revan's death, and to testify that he had not eased it along with a comforting pillow over the face. Sand placed himself before them, saying, "Peace. You know me, my friends and elders. We are come to try to save Revan, not to hasten his demise."

"They lie! They have—" Bromelas began. I silenced him by pricking his vast belly with my knife, though I doubted the blade was long enough to reach through the layers of lard and find any vital organ. He swallowed the rest of his words.

Chaff came to my side, his eyes on my face. "Find the Al-Lord a chair," I said. "Break whatever pleases you if he dares stir." He nodded, then showed Bromelas a smile that told of a hope his charge made a break, and so purchased one.

I went to Revan's bedside, snatching up the leech by the front of his robe. "Have you *syratamin* in your stores?" I demanded. "It is sometimes called foxfote or foxdock."

"Y-yes," he stammered, "But my leeches—"

I shook him until his teeth rattled. "I am going to remove your lovely pets from your Lord's face. If you have not returned with a pitcher of boiling water and the herb I require by the time I am done, then I will send them up your nose one by one until you choke on your own livelihood!" I dropped him. "Now *go!*"

He scuttled away with the dignity usual to his kind. Sand let him out. I bent over Revan. "Soon," I whispered, "soon your ordeal will be over." I used a burning straw to prod the leeches loose, and finding salt on his bedside table, used it and water to cleanse the wounds they made. He lay unresponsive to my ministrations, but that was not unexpected.

The leech soon returned, and I slipped a powder I carried into the tea I made from the herbs he brought. The hot liquid had to be forced past Revan's slack lips. In less than a hundred heartbeats his color came flooding back, and in a hundred more his eyes opened and slowly focused upon me.

He smiled weakly. "I . . . wish I . . . felt better," he rasped. "Having you this . . . close to my bed tempts me . . . to ask you go join me in it."

Oh, yes, he was recovering nicely.

The candles were guttering low, and the sweet taste of wine was in my mouth, wetting my throat after my long tale was fully told. I lowered my cup and smiled at my host. "Well, Lord Revan?"

He rubbed his bearded chin. "It is too strange a tale to be anything less than true. You were sent to poison me, and you got Bromelas to pay you to do so."

I nodded. "Ten gold talents."

His black eyebrows rose. "So much? That I would be worth such gelt is enough of a wonder to occupy my mind for a day all by itself. I had no idea that Bromelas had such a long-made plan, or that he had gathered so much wealth and power about him. You must think me the veriest fool."

"Would I save a fool's life that he could be king?"

"After the tale you have told, I could make no guess as to what you would do or would not do, dear Sardhana. I suppose the most important thing is that you saved me in the end."

Now came the point to all I had done. I spoke gravely. "You are not quite entirely saved, my Lord."

He crossed his arms and smiled. "No?" If he was discomfited by this revelation he hid it well.

"I fear not. The first poison would not have killed you. You are strong, and would have fought off its effects in three days or less. The rub lies with the antidote I gave you."

He shook his head in unconcealed wonder. "I cannot wait to hear about this rub, Sardhana."

"The antidote was in itself a poison. A very special, slow-acting poison whose nature and cure is known only to the wisest, grayest heads of the Order. It will kill you in just over a year."

Revan's smile never faltered. "Judging by what I know of you, there must be a *but*."

"But there is a draught which will postpone its effect for yet another year. If you rule justly, then you shall be spared, but I am afraid as of now you live one year at a time, and only at the Order's sufferance."

He shrugged. "Do I not already? But what of this Order of yours? Who are you? What?"

I took a sip of my wine. "Our rules are strict, and there is little I am free to reveal. You are aware that there are several great, peaceful kingdoms to the south?"

"So I have heard."

"We of the Order overwatch them all." I thought hard for a moment, at last deciding to bend the rules just a little. Revan had proved himself no ordinary victim. I felt I could trust him, and was more than a little curious as to how he would react.

"Who runs the world, women or men?" I asked.

"Men," he answered promptly. "For better or for worse."

"Most often worse. The Order is made of women who see men's need for some governance. We are content to let men be, as you said, the arrow and the bow. You might say that we are the soft feathers which guide the arrow's flight."

Revan laughed out loud, slapping his knee. "The men rule the kingdoms, but the women secretly rule the men!" He shook his head with delight. "Well, why should the wide world be any different from the affairs inside most men's houses? So you are saying that where the Order rules, order reigns."

"That is the rough shape of it. There is more, much more, but the rules of the Order forbid my telling of it."

He held up his hand. "Oh, I am *sure* of it, my

tempting poisoner. For the moment, there is but one thing I would ask."

I took another sip of wine before replying. "Ask, and I will answer if I can."

He leaned toward me, his face intent. "This Order of yours, does it demand celibacy of its tricksters?"

It seemed I was the target of Revan's arrow now.

I laid my cup aside. "We are extremely dedicated," I said, "but we are not *fanatics*. . . ."

ISTAR-ZU
by D. A. Bach

Deborah Bach said in her biography (I didn't remember, because I all too often throw away cover letters, whether D. Bach was Deborah or Dorothy or David or Donald; so I had to ask her gender) that she's 28, single, and "I'm so excited about my first professional sale. This will give me something to brag about at my high school reunion." She says she's been trying to write for twelve years but only succeeded in the last two when she switched focus to what she knew: science fiction and fantasy.

I wish someone had told me that; people were always telling me to write what I knew, without adding science fiction; they kept telling me not to "waste my mind" on science fiction (back then fantasy appeared only in hard covers), and what I "knew" was boring: school, farm work and cows. But I, too, succeeded when I "switched my focus" to fantasy and science fiction. I'm glad someone else did.

———————

"Into this night, the name of your childhood is lost," rumbled the chief's voice above the crackle of the blue flame. *"You are no longer called Lorell, you are only She, Daughter of the Tribe."*

The girl Lorell kneeled in the sand, muscles taut and still. Her eyes flickered along the ground. Bronze-red clumps of hair lay in limp coils next to her; a soft breeze tickled her newly bare skull.

Lorell lifted her eyes, catching the absent motion of her younger half sister who stroked the precious jeweled bracelet that had belonged to their mother. Lorell had been forced to give the bracelet up before the ceremony. Noticing Lorell's gaze, the sister swept her waist-long hair forward, brushing her fingers through it, a taunt-ing smile on her full lips.

Lorell dropped her eyes to the ground.

The chief finished the last invocation of their gods.

"Seek the relics, daughter, earn your name, and re-turn to us," he finished in a low voice.

"I will, father," she answered, rising.

A chorus of voices filled the air as She stood, straight and tall, facing the tribe as they chanted:

> *"Claim the stone of Istar-Zu,*
> *Its power will protect and guide.*
> *Free the soul whose life it keeps,*
> *Trapped and helpless deep inside."*

Dagger clenched firmly in her teeth, the voices of the tribespeople echoed in her mind, reaching across the cold landscape to the mountain she now scaled. The power that had filled her at the midsummer festival seemed limp and useless, like the hair that had been sheared from her head that night.

Above her, patches of ice hid in shadows cast by the weakened winter sun. The tips of her fingers were numb with pain and cold while sweat matted her short, thick hair, plastering it to her forehead. One drop traced a path down the bridge of her narrow nose, clinging to the pointed tip. Leaning into the cliff, she clutched the dagger with her right hand, rubbing her face against the shoulder of her rough fur vest.

She reached over her head, digging at a narrow crevice with the blade of the dagger, freeing the loose shale. It sifted past her with a hiss as she replaced the dagger and grasped the new handhold, hoisting her body another two feet higher. She bent her head back, surveying the distance above her.

"Only three more body lengths, maybe four," she mumbled around the dagger, forcing herself to sound cheerful. "I wish I had wings," she sighed.

At the top of the cliff, she took her bearings, noticing the contrast of the flat green valley she had crossed to the sharp brown mountains she stood among. To the North, the crags grew narrower, taller, and steeper; rising from the ground like rotting serpent's teeth. A pinnacle, slightly higher than its brothers, pushed its tip into the mist. Shining dully like an angry beacon, its smooth sides reflected the setting sun. As she stared at it, she noticed a web strung from the man-formed tower to the natural peak at its side.

"Lovely place," she commented, shaking her head as she sheathed her dagger. She shifted her pack and continued, following the trace of a path left by marauding mountain goats.

Three more days of hiking and scaling brought her to the eastern face of the tower's nearest neighbor. Below her hung the narrow bridge that connected the two in umbilical fashion. She studied the structure of the tower and noted soldiers crossing the bridge at uncertain intervals.

The sides of the tower were not as smooth as they had appeared to her in the distance, yet there were no outcropping niches large enough to aid a climber. It was not made of rock, but of something she had never seen before. The only way in was to cross the bridge.

She sat back to think as night settled on the mountains. The full moon was obscured by high clouds, its light diffusing across the layer of mist that clung to the tower. Only one guard walked a narrow causeway that jutted out from the tower, leaning over the bridge. The last movement across had been at dusk.

A low bleat ricocheted across the rocks. She pivoted onto one knee, dagger to hand in a single fluid motion. A herd of goats drifted closer and she smiled, an idea forming as she reached into her pack and drew out a ball of twine.

Trapping the goats was not as easy as she expected. They twisted from her grasp, tangling together. As the moon swung overhead, throwing the tower's shadow across the bridge, she managed to loop the twine around the necks of the two largest goats.

Crouching between the animals, she lured the bleating herd forward. As they gained the bridge, its swaying motion caused panic among the animals. They swarmed each other, knocking her to her knees. She tightened the grip on her two captives and crawled forward. The leaders moved at her urging with the rest of the herd following close behind.

"It's just goats. Be happy to chase 'em off," the guard on the causeway called down in answer to an unheard question.

As his head bobbed out of her view, she abandoned her animal covering and loped toward the thick shadows gathered at the tower's entrance. The broad doors swung slowly inward, groaning with effort. As the guard stepped onto the bridge, brandishing a dull pike in the direction of the goats, she slipped softly behind him, raising no notice of her intrusion.

She flattened herself against the wall of a small guardroom as her eyes adjusted to the bright flicker from witch light and torch. She was alone. To her right, a metal ladder led up to the causeway. To her left, the gentle sound of snoring wafted out through a slightly open door. The plain hide shields of mercenaries hung on the far wall and a large trunk lay open in the corner, a pile of blankets and discarded clothing billowing from it.

Opposite her was a rusted double door. She crossed to it, raising the latch with careful precision. She nudged the door open slowly, wincing as it scraped the ground. Stepping through to a high open chamber, her eyes darted about her, on the alert.

Rumors from awed valley dwellers served as a guide once she had entered the tower. Its occupant, the wizard Lothar, was said to be cruel and clever. As his power grew, he gathered more soldiers to him; for protection, and for control.

Raids on mountain villages would have filled the dungeons below, she thought, but she was not here to free those unjustly held. What she sought would be above, as close to the pinnacle of the tower as space would allow.

Lothar had stolen the stone of Istar-Zu, and it was up to her to get it back.

Once she had located the stairway, she took no time to notice anything else. She ran swiftly up the stairs, stretching her long legs to cover three steps at a time. She paused to listen for signs of life before plunging through a large archway that opened onto the next level.

The design of the tower was too simple; there would be no place to hide if anyone crossed her path. She continued to ascend, unchallenged.

The seventh stairway ended in a door that had a moon and stars etched into its face in bronze. She could see no handle or hinges. Mounting the top step, she placed her palms against the door and pushed with all her strength. She breathed in through clenched teeth as the door held firm, not even noticing her presence.

"All this way for a door that won't open," she sighed, kicking at it with the toe of her boot.

She pressed her ear against its smooth wooden surface, listening to the silence within.

"I seek the stone of Istar-Zu," she whispered to the door.

The bronze star at its center brightened, bathing the steps in an orange glow. She felt the wood warm beneath her cheek. She pulled back and watched the door dissolve into a misty shadow of itself. She stepped through, her hand on the hilt of her dagger. The door became solid at her back.

The chamber she stood in was small and round with reddish walls that slanted into the darkness above. A triangular frame of bronze, a full head taller than she, stood erect in the center of the room. Suspended by a thick gold chain from the peak—the amber stone of Istar-Zu.

A faint green-blue light clouded the air above a low pedestal that was centered beneath the stone. She drew closer, her fingers trembling as she reached forward to touch the stone.

A shock tingled the ends of her fingers and she stumbled backward. The green-blue mist thickened, swirling round like a miniature storm. A streak of light shot out from its center as the cloud coalesced into the figure of a small woman.

Her hair was as yellow as the sun and her arms were raised over her head, palms pressed together, her fingertips brushing the bottom edge of the stone.

The small woman's form was still more mist than flesh when her eyelids fluttered open. Her green crystalline eyes pierced the haze, resting on the face of the other.

"Oh, you're new," the woman of mist said, her voice soft and light.

"I seek the stone of Istar-Zu," whispered the other, her eyes unblinking.

"This?" the woman of mist asked, lifting her eyes to the stone dangling above her head.

"You must be the goddess Istar," the other stated timidly, her right hand still gripping her dagger.

"Me? Oh, no. I'm Shayna. I'm a sorceress, although not a very good one," she said, glancing at the triangle. "I'm still learning," she added.

When she got no answer, the sorceress continued.

"Lothar used the stone to trap me here. He's not a very good wizard either, you see, except that now he's using my power as well as his. He can do that as long as he keeps me like this," explained Shayna. "And who are you?" she asked pleasantly.

"I am She, Daughter of the Tribe, seeker of the relics," She proclaimed in a strong voice.

Shayna bobbed her head from side to side, jutting her chin out like a dove.

"I get so stiff standing here," muttered the sorceress. "Do you know how long I've been here, She?" Shayna asked.

"Since the Great Raid," She answered.

"And, how long ago was that?" Shayna prompted.

"Many ages."

"Yes, but how many years was that?" Shayna asked slowly.

Lifting one eyebrow, She stared at the sorceress, releasing her grip on her dagger.

Shayna sighed.

"Why don't you tell me about the stone and this Great Raid, from the beginning," encouraged the sorceress.

Taking a deep breath, She straightened her back until she was standing at her fullest height. Focusing on a spot near the sorceress' head, She began to recite.

"Our tribe has protected the relics for age upon age, since before the fall of the Dark Time. Then, a group of mercenary soldiers from another land raided our village and stole the relics, not knowing of their power. Each relic fell into different hands and was lost to us.

"To remedy our shame, we sought the relics. As the firstborn child of each chief came of age, he or she was called to forsake her name and possessions, leaving the village to search for the relics and return them to the tribe, earning her name," She finished solidly, then dropped her eyes to the ground. "There have been four seekers before me, and none has ever returned," she added with pain in her voice.

"So, that's four seekers . . ." Shayna mumbled, figuring out loud. "And how old are you?" the sorceress asked.

"I have seen the winter come again ten and ten times," She answered.

"And how many years after one seeker left was another born?"

"Ten, ten and five seasons; ten, ten and ten? I do not know," She answered, shrugging her shoulders.

"Twenty-five, thirty seasons between, twenty-one years to come of age, call it fifty; four seekers plus you . . . Oh, piff!" Shayna shouted. "That's over two hundred years!"

As an echo to her anger, the walls of the room shuddered, sending a spasm downward toward the base of the tower.

"You have to get out of here," Shayna said, directing her eyes from She to the door.

With a loud crack, another spasm rumbled through the structure, setting the suspended stone swaying. As it swung out of touch with her fingertips, the sorceress' form began to fade.

"Remember I told you that Lothar wasn't a very good wizard," Shayna called out from what sounded like far away. "Well, sometimes, when he sleeps, his power fades; and since this tower is only made up of one pretty weak spell, it winks out."

The walls groaned as large dark splotches stained them, seeping through and opening holes that peered out onto the night. The noise rose in a crescendo of grinding and groaning.

"Head for solid ground, but come back when the moon is overhead—to get me out of here!" Shayna shouted above the din as her image collapsed into a cylinder of swirling mist.

Darkness dripped down the walls and pooled onto the floor, gnawing away the edges of the chamber. A void opened next to the door and She jumped through it, landed on her knees on the fifth step down, clinging to it as its edge was lapped at by the darkness.

She fled downward, zigzagging her way past dissolving pieces of stair, barely staying ahead of the flowing destruction.

Dodging through the archway at the top of the first stairway, She halted, gulping back her breath. This chamber was real, carved from the mountain that the false tower stood upon. Seeking the only hiding place she had seen earlier, she snuck inside the empty guardroom. Stepping inside the open trunk, She pinched off her nose with her fingers and burrowed under the pile of dirty clothes and blankets, resting beneath them at the bottom. Before long, she was fast asleep.

The groan of the tower doors opening awakened She at first light. Breathing silent deep breaths, she prepared to leave her hiding place. The scrape of swords brushing the ground mixed with voices, high pitched and low, passing through the guardroom and into the chamber beyond the double doors.

The smell of frying meats reached past the stench of her enclosure and woke her empty stomach. Moving one limb at a time, she worked her way up through the mound of clothing until she was squatting near the top of the trunk, a large blanket covering her head. She lifted one corner and peered out.

The gurgling of her stomach became more urgent. Her mouth was wet with saliva as the smells from breakfast grew stronger. A moment passed where no troops entered the guardroom. Taking a deep breath, she leaped from her hiding place and sauntered into the meeting chamber.

Seating herself at the nearest table, She grabbed at each plate of food that passed by her. When there was no more room on her plate, she lifted her eyes to the rest of the chamber, turning her attention to her surroundings while she ate.

Fourteen long tables were crowded into the room in an irregular pattern. The table nearest the kitchen was occupied by two neat organized troops of twenty men each. Bunches of mismatched men and women sat at the rest of the tables, gaps forming between them. At her table were seven men and one woman, all of different coloring and height, style of dress and table manners; no one spoke a word.

After the meal, she rose and followed close behind the woman from her table. At the door, they were assigned to take the leftovers from breakfast down to the dungeons to serve to the prisoners.

"Kitchen duty. No matter where you go, when you're a woman, you always get stuck with kitchen duty," was the only thing the woman said all morning.

Listening to the whisperings of the prisoners, She learned that Lothar had planned an attack on the valley that was to begin the next morning.

The rest of the day was spent performing duties that took her to the troop exit below the dungeons, and through the barracks that housed the mercenaries. Her eyes and ears were open to secrets and gossip, and by nightfall, she had gathered all she could.

As she lay in the darkness waiting for the moon to peak, she shifted through everything she had heard. There was no hint that anyone knew of the stone, or of the strange-speaking sorceress.

Quiet gripped the barracks; all were asleep and dreaming of dawn's battle. She rolled off her cot and stole through the shadows, quickly making her way to the central room under the tower. Once she was clear of the first stairway, she bounded openly up the others, knowing that no one would enter the tower at night for fear of being trapped by the inky voids.

Opening the ornate door as before, she recalled the form of the sorceress by lightly touching the stone.

"Oh, good to see you, She," Shayna said as she solidified.

Nodding her head, She smiled at the tiny woman.

"Did you see Lothar today?" Shayna asked.

"No. but I learned many things. Lothar has gathered close to four hundred soldiers to him to lead in an attack on the valley. He pays them every day in gold he makes from stone," She replied solemnly.

Shayna's lilting laughter rode the air like a running stream; first bubbling up into a pool, then flowing down fast and hard. A tear fell from her eye and dissolved into mist.

Taking in a sharp breath, She frowned at the sorceress.

"Don't you see, when I get away from here, all that gold will turn back into stone. They'll probably tear Lothar into teeny tiny bits," Shayna explained, her laughter turning harsh. "Which he deserves," she added.

"Why would he attack the valley?" She asked.

"Because that's what wizards do," Shayna answered. "Evil serves no purpose but its own." The amusement had dropped completely from the sorceress' voice.

"I must have the stone," said She softly.

"And you will. But you must free me to get the stone," the sorceress stated. "You must memorize the words I give to you and say them when Lothar's power, and these walls, begin to fade.

"We do not have much time."

After the first spasm of dissolution rocked the tower, She began to circle the bronze triangle, reciting the words of reversal, using the exact tone and inflection as Shayna had instructed. The void oozed along the walls of the tiny chamber, spilling tendrils of darkness toward her feet. Fissures opened beneath her, shaking the floor.

She finished the spell. The sorceress hopped down from the pedestal and spun around, arms flung out to the side.

"I can move my arms!" Shayna cried, a smile claiming her face.

Reaching the stone down from its place, She poked her head through the circlet of chain and tucked the stone beneath her tunic.

"We should go before this tower . . ." She started to say as she turned her attention to the dancing sorceress.

Silence, dark and menacing, cut off her last words. The tower became still as death.

"Oh, did I neglect to tell you that breaking the spell would wake Lothar and make him aware of our presence?" Shayna asked in a timid voice.

Rolling her eyes at the sorceress, She snorted.

"I see that I did. Well, let's get down to the dungeons and free the prisoners. In the confusion, we can just slip on out," Shayna stated lightly.

"Why take time to free the prisoners? Won't the mercenaries help us once the gold turns to stone?" asked She, moving after the sorceress toward the door.

"Yes. But the gold won't turn until I'm no longer in physical contact with the source of the stone—which means, not until we're out of these mountains," Shayna answered, gesturing with her hand to dissolve the door.

Putting her hand on the sorceress' shoulder, She stopped at the top of the stair.

"It took over three days to climb here from the valley," she commented, concern riding the edge of her voice.

"There's a short cut through a ravine that takes less than one day," replied Shayna lightly. "That was the way they brought me in."

"And you remember it?" snorted She.

The sorceress put her hands on her hips, thrusting her chest forward.

"I was suspended in *nothing*. No time passed, except when I was called to appear. So what is two hundred years ago to you is last week to me. And don't forget that!" Shayna's eyes glowed with anger.

Snorting back a chuckle, She gripped Shayna by the elbow and led her down the steps.

*   *   *

Halfway along the stone stairway to the first level, She paused with Shayna close behind her. A figure cloaked in darkness floated into the high chamber. Fifteen soldiers with swords drawn filtered slowly in behind.

"Lothar," Shayna said in an expulsion of breath.

"And I don't even have a sword," commented She.

"Will it help?" Shayna asked.

"It won't hurt," She answered.

Shayna untied the rope belt from around her waist and handed one end to She.

"Here, hold this tight," whispered Shayna.

Gripping her end, She glanced briefly back at the sorceress, keeping her attention on those gathering below.

Shayna ran her hand over the rope, pulling it tight and straight.

"Change rope to sword!" Shayna commanded in a hard voice.

With a shimmer of haze, the rope hardened into sharp, gleaming steel.

Her eyes widened as the end She was holding bit into her hand. The sorceress exchanged one end with the other.

"Now that your lackey is armed, perhaps you will come down and face me," a voice hissed up to them.

Lothar lifted the hood of his cloak. His eyes were dark pits rimmed in red. His hair hung below his shoulders in a cascade of jet black. Two wide streaks of silver framed his face, lending his sharp features a sallow color.

"Lothar, let us pass and you will not pay for what you did to me," Shayna called down to him in a strong voice. "If you try to stop us now, I will bring a punishment on you that your limited mind could never imagine."

A squeaky giggle, like a rusted door hinge, escaped from Lothar's throat.

"You haven't the skill," he answered.

"And you have no power! My power has made you strong enough to hold the interest of these troops," Shayna countered.

"The sorceress lies," Lothar stated flatly, glancing around at his guards with a shrug of his shoulders.

"You others, Lothar has tricked you. When the sorceress is free of these mountains, the gold he has given you will turn to stone," She called to the mercenaries.

"No, no!" Lothar shouted. "The sorceress will change the gold to stone, to turn you against me," the wizard claimed in a rush of words.

Shayna put her hand on her companion's arm.

"This could go on forever," whispered Shayna.

"Can't you send a spell at him?" She asked.

"No, we're opposites and anything I do to him backlashes against me. He can't do anything to me, either, just to you," the sorceress answered. She looked up into the eyes of her companion. Seeing the strength in the young woman's face, Shayna smiled. "If I create an illusion around you, will you be able to continue fighting and take down as many of his guards as you can?"

"I can try. I must get the stone free of this place in order to claim its name as my own. I will try anything to accomplish that," answered She, fingering the stone through the fabric of her tunic.

"When we get to the valley, I'll ask you what that means," the sorceress replied. "Let's go!"

As they descended, the guards flanked the stair, forming an open wedge along either side.

"Your lackey will die, Shayna," Lothar hissed as he backed slowly toward the edge of the room.

"I'm no one's lackey!" shouted She. With the screech of a hawk, she leaped from the stair.

Her sword plunged through the first guard before her feet made contact with the ground. Two others rushed her at once and she feinted toward each of them with short strokes, drawing them closer together. Dodging between them, they swung at each other, locking their blades.

Shayna glanced at the remaining guards as they shifted their positions, spacing themselves out before the open doorway. A stiff look of boredom claimed their faces.

"We need to even this up," Shayna mumbled as she

scurried down the last few steps. Ducking below the arc of the sword, Shayna placed her hand on the small of her companion's back, shifting her balance to maintain contact as She lunged toward a new opponent.

"Make one appear as twenty!" Shayna commanded.

Like heat rising, the floor of the chamber wavered. The strong figure She cast was multiplied. As She lifted her sword in a slow arc aimed at the neck of the man facing her, ten images on either side did the same. Four guards nearest the doorway turned and ran, while her true opponent lowered his sword and lost his head.

"Child's play, child's play," Lothar moaned from his position beside the doorway. "Do not run," he whined to his guards.

"Circle round, circle round," Shayna whispered, lifting her eyes to Lothar as her hands danced in command of the images. In answer to her prompting, the images formed a tight line surrounding the remaining eight guards.

"Help us, you damned fool," one of the guards yelled to Lothar as he sliced through an image, his sword striking the stone floor instead of bone.

The wizard slid his back along the wall, muttering phrases over and over under his breath as he snaked out of the chamber.

"Forgot the words again, eh, Lothar?" Shayna called after him, laughing. "Let's go for the dungeons," she turned back to the fighting to say.

One image broke from the circle and followed the sorceress through the doorway. The guards hesitated, confronted by twenty images wiping their brow with the back of their sword arms.

Slipping into the shadows, She hurried the sorceress past the barracks and into the passageway that led to the dungeons below. Lothar's voice shouted an alarm.

"Rise! Rise! Follow the intruders!" his voice squeaked.

The clanking of quickly grasped swords and the voices of sleepy confusion echoed as She and Shayna sped down the ramp.

They gained the first lower level. The corridor before them was clear. Gruff shouts reached their ears as they loped along the second ramp.

"How could Lothar control those mercenaries when he can't even fight against us?" She asked, easing her pace to let the sorceress catch up.

"Greed did most of it," Shayna panted in explanation. "Without me, Lothar's memory is lousy," she added.

Steps echoed in the passage behind them, accompanied by the scrape of weapons against the narrow walls.

"One more level," She commented.

They rounded a corner, stopping at the top of a steep stairway dampened with moss. They descended, step by step, carefully avoiding the slippery patches. At the bottom, the passageway split into two directions.

"That way is out," said She, pointing to the left. "The other leads to the prisoners."

Shayna nodded.

"Prisoners first, escape later. We won't have to run so fast if someone's covering our backs," Shayna replied quickly in reaction to her companion's frown.

They shot off down the right branch as the first mercenary came bounding down the stair, sliding on the moss and landing on his back. More poured out behind him, tumbling over one another as they skidded down the steps.

"We'd better find some keys, fast," She cried as they reached the heavy wooded door that closed off the dungeons. A thick metal lock hung from the crosspiece.

"We don't need keys," Shayna stated, indignation edging her voice. She placed her palms against the door. "Change wood to water!"

A gentle waterfall flowed from the frame; the lock clanked to the ground. The two stepped through, the water feeling cool and light. Shayna snapped her fingers and the door returned to solid form.

"Hold it shut and I'll get you some help," Shayna exclaimed as she ran along the corridor, changing the doors of the cells to water or mist.

A cry of confusion went up among the prisoners as the diminutive sorceress freed them. Some milled into the corridor while others were afraid to pass through the altered barriers.

"Some of you help me hold this door before that whole troop of mercenaries breaks it down," She yelled to the nearest group.

The heavy door groaned as a human wave battered it from the other side.

A tall man with a thick dark beard nodded and ten of the prisoners moved in to steady the door.

"I thank you for freeing us," the man said.

"It wasn't my idea," She snorted, inclining her head toward Shayna. "If I can get the sorceress free of these mountains, all of Lothar's spells will dissolve. Can you hold them here?" She asked, glancing at the door.

"We can hold them, but without weapons, we can't clear the passage for you to get through to the exit," the man replied.

Shayna sidled up to her companion, her hands clasped behind her.

"There's another way out," she said with a wink. "When the tower has completely vanished, have the mercenaries check their pockets," Shayna directed the man.

They dodged past prickling bushes and leaped over boulders, the faint sound of pursuit ringing in their ears and urging them to run faster. In the form of caterpillars, the sorceress and her companion had inched their way along the walls, clearing the fighting forces and slipping past Lothar and his guard. Changing back to their own forms, Shayna's cry of delight on locating the shortcut to the valley alerted the wizard to their presence.

Panting, She and Shayna paused as they cleared the last ridge, their feet coming to rest on the verdant grass of the valley. Lothar and his guards burst out from the path behind them.

"Wait," Shayna gulped, holding her hand up to the nearest guard. "If you have any of that good Lotharian gold, pull it out and take a look at it," she instructed.

Beside the sorceress, She inhaled deeply.

The nearest guard lifted his tunic and drew out a small tattered pouch. He untied its drawstring and peered inside. Lothar's eyes shifted nervously left, then right. The guard turned the pouch over, spilling the contents into his free hand.

A pile of tiny red stones sat dully in his palm.

The other guards grabbed for their pouches, pulling them out from deep inside the fronts of their leggings. One by one, piles of rock filled the hands of the mercenaries.

"I'll get you, Shayna, you will not rest!" Lothar cried as he turned and ran.

Shayna and She laughed at the sight of the wizard—feet flying, his hair streaming behind him.

"So, what was that about claiming the name of the stone now that we're free of the mountains?" Shayna asked as they watched the mercenaries fling their pouches to the ground and take off after the fleeing wizard.

"Now that I have the stone and have freed the one trapped by it, I can claim the name of the stone for my own," She stated, her voice going flat with recitation. "I am no longer only She, I am now Shezu."

"I like that better. It will make it much easier if we're going to travel together," Shayna replied. "And we are going to travel together."

Shayna looked up at Shezu and smiled.

"I have my own traditional obligations to uphold. I must aid you the best that I can for the rest of your quest. That is my payment to you for freeing me from Lothar," Shayna explained.

Shezu nodded. The two started walking on the soft grass, heading into the valley.

"My father said it would be a good thing to have an older, wiser traveling companion," stated Shezu.

"Oh, piff!" Shayna swore. "I told you that the two hundred years I spent in limbo *do not count!*"

Shezu snorted back a chuckle as the sorceress mumbled under her breath. The smell of food reached out to them, providing their first destination together.

THE SIEGE OF KINTOMAR
by Millea Kenin

It would be a cliché to say Millea Kenin needs no introduction to our audience; she has appeared in most, if not all of these anthologies (my assistant keeps the list), and was doing desktop publishing before the phrase was invented. I remember Randall Garrett saying that about me once . . . that I "needed no introduction" and added, "That being so, I'm not going to introduce her," and sat down.

With this precedent I can only say "Neither am I," and add that if you really want to know about Millea, you can look her up in any of these anthologies. But read the story first.

Aiduri shivered and drew her cloak close about her. She was standing with the king and queen of Kintomar at a lookout post on the city walls. The night was overcast, its heavy darkness hardly relieved by occasional fitful gleams of moonlight that came through gaps in the clouds—now white, now blue, now amber. What there was to see, the three of them saw by the light of hundreds of campfires scattered along the riverbanks and on the plains beyond. Countless dark shapes huddled there or moved to make silhouettes against the flames: narrow, upright shadow shapes of humans or humanlike creatures; larger forms of antelopelike tricorns; still larger, covered wagons.

From those fires thick columns of yellowish-gray smoke rose at first toward the pall overhead, then bent and converged from all directions toward the city, as if winds from all quarters drove them. The smoke stung the eyes of the three watchers, and there was a faint acrid smell.

"That is the smell of the wraith-wind," said King Niethos, putting an arm around his young wife, Niara, but turning his head to speak to the young warrior-woman who stood at her other side. "The Lenash must have won the aid of the half-men of Distor." In the dimness, Aiduri could not see the king's expression, but she saw a shiver pass through his spare frame.

"How do you know?" she asked.

"Whenever the wind blows from the northwest, from Distor, it has that same stench. People in Kintomar fall sick of it—coughing, choking, fever—and if it blows long enough, they start to die. It is the work of the wraiths who live in the ruined cities of Distor. You can see how it comes from our enemies' campfires, from all directions. You were the captive of the Lenash, Aiduri. Did you see anything to make you think they had such sorcery?"

"No, my lord king. But I saw nothing either to make me think they dealt with wraiths. I learned very little from them, and told it all to you when I first reached your city."

"The more fools they, to seek such allies," went on Niethos, dryly, "but little good it will do us if Kintomar falls and the wraiths destroy the Lenash, too, afterwards."

"My father must have sent aid by now," Niara said. "It is four weeks since Iraud rode to Imvainor. They should be here soon."

For a moment the clouds parted, and one of the three moons cast an amber light on her face, turning her pallor to gold. The long dark lashes lay against the broad cheekbones, and the shadow beneath it outlined the delicate hollow of her cheek. Her black hair fell fine and thick and lustrous down her back. At the sudden sight Aiduri stifled a gasp, as if a blow had struck a half-healed wound.

They were the same age, nineteen. Niara was the daughter of one king and married to another. Though Niethos was twice her age, no one could doubt the love between them who had seen them together or with their infant son, as Aiduri had, almost constantly, these past four weeks.

She had been traveling west from the mountains to the coast, seeking work as a hired sword, and had come to the barren moors of the Lenash, known for their fighting women sworn to the raven goddess Vayel. She felt a chill now to think she'd offered her services to them; she might have been one of the folk out there, attacking Kintomar. At the time, though, she'd been offended when the moorfolk took her captive, along with anyone else traveling westward through their country, lest word come to the fertile peninsula of Riedona that they were planning an attack.

How Aiduri had escaped was, so far, still her secret. She had brought warning, barely in time, to Kintomar, farthest northeast of the Riedoen city-states.

A Kintomartan soldier came toward them. "My lord king, Iraud has returned." Niethos turned toward him. Like Niara, like almost all Riedoen, the king and the soldier both had small, rather flat noses, narrow dark eyes and broad cheekbones, faintly yellowed ivory-colored skin and straight black hair. They looked as like as kinfolk to Aiduri's eyes. She herself was light-skinned and dark-haired, but her features were bold and aquiline, her hair curly, her eyes gray-green.

"Iraud came through the sluiceway alone," the soldier was saying. "He's wounded, but able to report at once."

They followed the soldier to a room in the gatehouse, where a young man lay on a cot, naked but for a sheet thrown across his torso. A pile of wet, bloodstained clothes lay on the floor nearby. An elderly woman was tending gashes on the man's right arm and leg. Iraud struggled up onto his left elbow, and the healer settled him back into place. "Lie still, lad."

"I've got to report!" He went into a fit of coughing. When he could speak, he said, "If I die without telling the king, it's all been wasted."

"These are flesh wounds, they won't kill you." The woman's tart competence reminded Aiduri of her grandmother.

"Not that. Came through the worst wraith-wind I ever—" Again a spasm of coughing wracked Iraud. "They followed me to the water-sluice," he gasped.

"Chased me. Wraiths, not moormen. Have to guard or block it. Wraiths in the city. If not yet, any minute now."

Niethos spoke to the soldier in a low voice, giving him orders Aiduri could not hear, no doubt regarding the sluice. "Aye, my lord king." The man bowed and went out.

Niethos pulled up a stool and sat down by the messenger's head, out of the healer's way. "The sooner you tell me all you can, cousin, the sooner you can rest."

"No help coming from Imvainor." Iraud stifled a cough. "Your father's dead, my lady queen. Your cousin Erior has seized the throne. Far's he's concerned, he hopes the Lenash get you, so he'd be the rightful king. He as much as told me so. That's all. That's all." He coughed again till tears poured from his eyes. The healing woman supported his head and held an earthenware mug to his lips. He managed a few sips, then lay back, spent.

Niara put her hands over her face. Niethos rose and gathered her into his arms, and she leaned on him and wept. He stepped back, still gripping her upper arms lightly. "Niara, go back to the palace and try to get some sleep. You, too, Aiduri. I'll see to the sluiceway before I come." His face looked haggard.

Aiduri had never felt less like sleeping. She went to the room where she was staying and bolted the door behind her. Then she looked through her gear till she found a packet of gray powder. She hesitated a moment. She had so little of the Sight, what she was about to do was unreliable and could even be dangerously misleading. Still, it was the only thing left that she could think of to try.

There was a basket of logs next to the fireplace. Aiduri built up the fire, then sat down cross-legged before it on the stone hearth, as close as was safe. She sprinkled the powder on the fire, and it flared up peacock-blue and green. A picture gradually took form amid the flames, until it became a moving scene whose vivid colors eclipsed those of the fire.

In that scene, a young man armed for war escorted

a young woman great with child aboard a ship with gaily-patterned sails. The man mounted a chariot drawn by a pair of white tricorns and drove swiftly back to join an army defending a city. The city was Kintomar. Now Aiduri could see that the man was a much younger Niethos. What appeared now in the flames would have occurred—if this was a true Seeing—about twenty years ago.

The flames blazed up; the scene changed. The ship was driven before a storm and wrecked on a rocky coast. The young woman was cast ashore, apparently the sole survivor, and the people who found her helped her, but it was clear from their gestures that they could not understand her language, nor she theirs. She give birth to a baby, and died. Next Aiduri saw the child being taken secretly, by night, into a palace, and later proclaimed as the royal heir. Further swiftly changing scenes showed this princess, always treated by the king and queen as a beloved daughter, growing from infant to child to young maiden of surpassing beauty—

Aiduri groaned aloud. It was Niara. Aiduri could feel tears streaming down her face, but they did not affect the vision. Not until this moment had she let herself recognize her feeling for Niara.

Niethos came to that seacoast city—which must be Imvainor—looking much as he had when Aiduri saw him that evening, except that his expression was relaxed and happy. He won the heart and hand of Niara. Aiduri saw them sitting in the palace garden of Kintomar while Niara nursed their newborn son, and she saw herself, all dusty and disheveled, entering that garden to warn them of the impending attack. Then she saw them with the wounded messenger.

The next scene showed Niara at the bedside of her baby, weeping while he coughed and thrashed about. The Seeing dissolved into chaotic scraps that faded swiftly, leaving no memory beyond the vague sense that these were alternative futures, some or none of which might come to pass. Aiduri's Sight had never worked for the future yet—which meant that the last clear scene must be happening right now. She rose to her feet—but before she could look away from the fire one last image took form: a woman's face, barely clear enough to see, and yet Aiduri was sure that it was the most beautiful face she had ever seen. And though all the rest of the vision had been silent, now Aiduri heard a voice, so faint she did not know whether it came from the flames or from inside her mind. The voice said, "Pray."

Then there were only the red flames, dying down, and the crackling sound of the fire.

Pray. Yes, that made sense. Such legends as Aiduri had heard about the wraiths hinted at their origin in some other world—and such matters were the concern of the Guardian. She could not think of any means other than prayer to attract the attention of that goddess. But prayer was chancy at best, and before she did anything else she must tell Niara and Niethos what she had Seen. It would be harder to do that than to fight half a dozen battles, so best to be done with it.

The baby, Yelendon, had the wraith-wind sickness, as the flame-vision had shown. Neither Niara nor Niethos looked as if they had slept at all; neither had Aiduri, but she was fighting exhaustion with an inner-chant, syllables repeated over and over in the silence of her mind, as her grandfather had taught her. She taught it to the others, for those particular syllables were not secret. Some chants were too dangerous to teach to the untrained—such as one Aiduri knew, that called forth the body's last reserves. But this was a simple, healing chant that produced relaxed alertness.

When all three had benefitted by it, they sat together at the far end of the nursery. In a low voice, Aiduri told the two what she had seen.

Niara turned to Niethos. "Is this true—from what you know?"

Niethos nodded gravely. "When I was barely of age I married a lady of the western islands, whose name was Verial; my tutor had been an islander and had taught me their speech. Before she had time to learn Riedoen, the Lenash attacked Kintomar for the first time, and I had her sent back to her kin for safety. The ship was wrecked, and till this day I had believed she had died, and our unborn child with her. I had no desire to marry again till I met you, thinking you were the—the daughter of—" His voice broke, and he fell silent.

Niara took his hand, then snatched hers away, then took his again and held it fast.

He smiled at her wearily. "Well, dearest love, I cared for you from the first, though I was old enough to be your—" He swallowed.

"Hush," said Niara, listening. A choking sound came from the cradle, then a scream. She went and picked Yelendon up, took him back to her chair, unfastened her shoulder-clasp and gave him the breast. The baby kept trying to suck; stopping, gasping and choking for breath; trying again. Niara brushed her tears away with her free hand lest they fall on his head.

Niethos stood up. He had mastered himself, and his voice was clear and firm. "It is I that must pray." He walked to the center of the room and looked up as if he were trying to see through the ceiling to the sky. His broad-browed face looked drawn, hollow-cheeked, like a skull; his eyes were sunk deep in their narrow sockets.

Aiduri glanced from him to Niara. Her eyes were just as sunken, her cheeks' hollows of just the same shape and depth. She had always thought they looked as like as kin—but she had thought it was no more than the racial likeness among Riedoen.

"Ethreya, Guardian, Goddess!" Niethos cried in a loud, hoarse voice. "Hear me, help me." He sank to his knees, hands clasped, still looking upward. "Save my city and my children."

At that word Niara gulped. She looked at Aiduri, her eyes wide and shocked, then at the baby, then back at Niethos, biting her lip as if to prevent herself from interrupting him.

"They are guiltless," Niethos prayed. "If there was a sin, it was mine, only mine. Let me pay. Let my life pay." He said no more, but stayed where he was, licking his lips as if he were trying vainly to think of more to say. Finally he shook his head, rose to his feet and came over to Niara, resting a hand on her shoulder. "It's no use. I don't know how to pray."

Aiduri tried to think of anything she might do. Would her prayers help? But what had she to offer, in comparison with Niethos' life? Was there anything else? She had used all her open and hidden skills so far except one: she had a limited ability to teleport—only to a place she had been before, and only at the cost of totally exhausting herself. Last time she'd done it—to escape from the Lenash—she'd set it up to look like an ordinary escape. If she had to face them again, with luck she'd have that secret in reserve. But what could she use it for now except to flee, leaving her friends to be killed? Was there anyone she could go to to ask for help? She could not think of anyone.

She realized that the room was filling with light, as a cup is filled with water. It was a clear, fresh, early-morning light. In the midst of it the face she had seen in the fire took shape. Even when it was hardly more than a thickening of the light, its beauty seemed the center and focus of all things. The lips moved, and a voice spoke—the same voice Aiduri had heard faintly before, but now warm and kind and full of power: "It shall be as you have asked, Niethos." Meanwhile the being's whole body was taking form, as a tall woman robed in flowing golden beams. She kissed Niethos' brow. "Your life shall pay for all. None shall destroy Kintomar or harm Niara or Yelendon, for fear of my curse, and they shall live and prosper, though neither shall ever rule in Kintomar."

"No!" cried Niara. "I will not buy my life with his."

The Guardian Ethreya kissed her in turn. "That is how you must pay. Your child's life depends on yours. I do not offer mercy. I restore balance." For a moment it seemed there were tears in Ethreya's sunbright eyes. Then she bent and kissed Yelendon. The flush faded from the baby's cheeks, and he sighed and nestled against his mother's breast, nuzzling her sleepily.

Last, Ethreya turned her gaze on Aiduri. "Aiduri," she said, saying the name as if she knew the person who bore it more thoroughly than that person could ever know herself. "We shall meet again." The light brightened, and her image melted into it. Then it faded, and she was gone. Only then did it occur to Aiduri how strange it was that none of them had been the least surprised by the whole occurrence.

Niara laid the sleeping baby in the cradle.

"Come with me," Niethos said to both the others. "There are things each of you will have to do." Stopping only for Niara to rouse the baby's nurse, they walked out together.

The next couple of hours passed swiftly; Niethos summoned his council and told them what had happened, and explained the plan whereby he would fulfill the Guardian's promise. "Iraud is my only other living kinsman," he said. "You must choose one of you to lead until he is well enough to take command, or to be king if he dies." Aiduri and Niara were present throughout, though neither spoke. Niara because she would not be parted from Niethos for the time that remained to them, and Aiduri because she would have work to do for the king.

Finally the three of them walked out toward the walls, and on the way Niethos gave the two young women final instructions. Now the king's voice and face were calm, but Aiduri could see Niara using all her strength to keep her self-control.

She leaned toward Niara and whispered in her ear, "Here's the inner-chant you need just now," and gave her another brief set of syllables.

Niara looked at Aiduri, surprise lightening her features as if she were really seeing the other woman for the first time, and seeing, too, what Aiduri would never tell her. "You are so kind to me," she murmured, then fell silent and turned away, her lips moving as she practiced the chant.

They reached the gatehouse, and Niethos gave orders to the gatekeepers. Then he took Niara in his arms. "I love you," he said quietly, but for all in earshot to hear. "You are the love of my soul. I would not do this if there were any other way."

"If there is any mercy in the world, one day we'll be reborn and live together as lovers for a hundred years." They clung together and kissed.

Then Niethos climbed the steps to the lookout post, and from there to the top of the walls. A moment he stood there, dark against the blue sky, his black hair and cloak streaming behind him in the wind. Then he leaped down onto the thicket of bronze spear points. There was no sound from outside the gates; he must have died instantly. At Aiduri's side, Niara gave a choked-off cry. When she turned to look at her, her face was hard and still. She clasped her hands a moment—hers were cold and dry—then nodded to the gatekeepers.

They opened the gates just far enough for Aiduri to go out, unarmed and holding a truce flag high. She was a witness to the Guardian's promise, and was known to the Lenash, so she must be the herald for the Kintomartans.

She could not prevent herself from taking a quick glance about, to try to see what had become of Niethos' body. Before she could see anything, she was seized by two Lenash: a burly, sallow man and woman dressed alike in battle leathers, with their long reddish-brown hair tied back with thongs; the man had a long, stringy mustache. They searched her hastily for weapons, then, apparently satisfied, led her through the cap, among many similar folk who were busy at various tasks.

Sometimes, in the shadows, Aiduri saw other people who looked grayish and misshapen, whose forms seemed tenuous and fluid, almost like shadows or shapes made of smoke. But they kept to the darkest places, and she could not see them clearly. She supposed they were wraiths. If so, they could handle material weapons. She remembered Iraud's wounds.

A heavy-set, gray-haired man sat on a folding chair of wood and leather. He wore a cloak sewn of many pieces of richly dyed leather, over well-worn armor. Behind him stood a tall, thin being, grayish yellow like a heavy fog. It made no sound and had no discernible features except for a pair of glowing golden eyes, larger and higher-set in its head than human eyes.

"Lord Ekarnem," said the woman, in the Lenash language, which Aiduri understood, "this vowed-one has just come out of the city carrying a flag of truce."

Ekarnem looked at Aiduri narrowly through slanting blue eyes. The wraith behind him leaned over his shoulder like smoke bent by a slight, persistent wind, and stared at Aiduri likewise. Ekarnem pressed hairy knuckles to his lips a moment as if stifling a cough. The Lenash must have something, Aiduri thought, to protect themselves against the wraith-wind, or they'd all be coughing their heads off; but this close to a wraith, it wasn't working perfectly. She wondered how soon she'd start to cough, herself. A brief moment of inner-chanting nipped her fear of the wraiths in the bud.

"You're the vowed-one that got away from us and warned the Kintomartans," said Ekarnem hoarsely in fluent Riedoen. Aiduri nodded. "No hard feelings," said the lord of the Lenash. "Didn't do them much good after all. Well, what have you got to say to me?"

"I am empowered to discuss terms of surrender."

"Terms?" Ekarnem snorted. "We've got you like this, and you know it." He held up one hand, flat palm up, and closed it into a fist. The wraith hung gloatingly over his shoulder.

Aiduri told him of the Guardian's answer to Niethos' prayer. "I swear by my true and secret name," she finished, "that this is true. Queen Niara and the Council are waiting to let you into the city, if you will vow not to sack it, but to rule peacefully and to let her and her son depart under my protection."

The wraith reared back, and its yellow eyes narrowed as if it were amused; then it leaned its distorted head close to Ekarnem's ear as if it were whispering to him. Ekarnem's eyes lost focus as if he were concentrating on listening to a sound that was hard to hear; but Aiduri heard no sound at all, not even the faint hiss of a whisper. A mind link?

Abruptly, Ekarnem rose and began barking orders to his guards.

A delegation of moorfolk entered the city. None of the wraiths came with them; Aiduri did not know why this was. Although the absence of the wraiths certainly made it easier for the Kintomartans to deal calmly with the invaders, she doubted that was why the wraiths had stayed away. Perhaps they simply found a human city an uncomfortable place to be, and preferred to stay outside. They might well still be in mental contact with Ekarnem, and have no need to enter Kintomar to know what was happening there.

Hours passed while formal oaths were exchanged in the main hall of the palace. Iraud, limping and with his arm in a sling, sat down on the throne and swore peace in the name of the Kintomartans. His people could not prevent Ekarnem sending his moorfolk on errands about the building as if it were already his own. Presently an armed moorwoman came into the hall, shepherding before her the nurse who was carrying Yelendon, now wide awake and staring wide-eyed at everything around him.

"Let me take him," said Niara.

The moorlord shook his head. "Not yet. I have sworn to rule Kintomar in peace, Niara, but I have not yet sworn to let you depart. And I will not so swear. I will keep you here at my pleasure, till you marry me."

Niara had kept going all day on sheer nerves. Now, she snapped, "I'd rather die!"

Ekarnem snapped his fingers. Several of his followers uncoiled the ropes they wore at their waists and flung their looped ends skillfully. Aiduri's arms were pinned to her sides, Niara's likewise, and the nurse and baby were tangled together in a third loop. None of the Kintomartan warriors or courtiers had been touched, but there was nothing they could do now.

"*You'd* rather die." Ekarnem chewed his mustache and stared at Niara. "And your baby, too?"

Niara was breathing heavily, her fists clenched. Aiduri thought the other woman was close to an outburst of hysterical rage, but she could not try to catch her eye. Hoping Niara could hold on just another minute, Aiduri began silently to repeat the inner-chant that would summon up the last reserves of her strength. Still chanting silently, she teleported out of her bonds, snatched a sword from the scabbard of a startled Lenash, and confronted Ekarnem.

"I challenge you, Ekarnem, sword to sword, here

and now, Niara to go with the winner." If wraiths could teleport, she thought briefly, she might have done nothing but seal her own doom. But no smoky figure appeared. "Abide my challenge," she went on, "or abide the Guardian's curse." The inner-chant sustained itself in her mind, and its power filled her voice. Her words rang and echoed in the dome overhead.

Ekarnem sat very still a moment, as if he were listening to something he alone could hear. Aiduri felt a chill up her spine at this confirmation of her suspicion. Then the Lenash lord looked at the ring of faces turned toward him and nodded brusquely. "Fight a vowed-one? I'll choose one of my own to fight you."

Aiduri shook her head. "You yourself, Ekarnem."

He laughed shortly, "It's your funeral, girl. Tanik, you're about her size, lend her your armor. Take it off, right now, and help her put it on."

Aiduri inner-chanted ceaselessly during the hasty preparations and was still at it when their blades engaged. The unfamiliar bronze sword was heavy and clumsy in her hand. She thought longingly of her fine Azien steel that lay sheathed in her room; if only she could have spared the energy to teleport twice!

Ekarnem's technique was as clumsy as the Lenash swords, but he was bigger than Aiduri, outweighed and outreached her, and showed no signs of weariness. So far Aiduri had been able to parry all his attacks without having to think about it, but she had not been able to get past Ekarnem's guard either, and it would not take the moorlord long to wear her down. No inner-chant is strong enough, in the midst of violent physical action, to draw strength from an outside source. That needs quiet concentration. Aiduri had been tired before she began, and had not eaten for many hours; now, her body was using itself up like a log burning in a fire.

Already she felt her strength beginning to surge and ebb in waves, as her body's real weakness fought the power of the chant. She continued to block Ekarnem's strokes mechanically. She would be dead in five minutes at this rate, even if the moorlord never touched her. It was foolish to keep guarding herself. She staked everything on one reckless thrust, leaving herself wide open, and felt Ekarnem's blade rake her side even as she drove her own up into the Lenash lord's throat.

The next few days passed in a blur, from pain, loss of blood, fever, perhaps even the effects of the healing drugs. Aiduri remembered later only that her side hurt, though she was lying on something soft; that her throat was dry, though she tried to drink whatever anyone put to her lips. There was always someone sitting by her bed, and she had a sense that it was not always the same person, but she never knew who it was.

Full consciousness returned gradually. She lay, sorting out her thoughts and her pains, realizing that the person who sat beside the bed in weary stillness was Niara. Their eyes met; Aiduri tried to speak and managed a faint, hoarse sound. Niara held a cup of water to her lips, and she swallowed gratefully.

"The Lenash—the wraiths—?" she asked.

"They're gone.' Niara's voice was subdued. She was so obviously shielding herself against her own pain that Aiduri found it hard to listen to her words. She forced herself, for the other woman was telling her what she needed to know. "Once Ekarnem was dead, the Lenash decided that to stay was to risk the curse. They demanded tribute, and took the first year's payment with them. As for the wraiths, no one has seen them since that day."

Aiduri frowned, and chewed on her lower lip. "I wonder what they'll be up to next. But you and I are not the ones to deal with them. If you can wait till I'm ready to travel, I'm still ready to be your bodyguard when you go."

Now that she was clearly mending, Aiduri was left to herself. She spent much of that time thinking, to no immediate profit, about herself and what she planned to do with her life. It seemed to her that when she had set out a year earlier she had begun a quest from which her adventures so far had been little more than distractions—a quest which she could only name in terms that put herself to the blush. A quest for herself, and she did not know where to look next. Probably if she were to meet herself at the crossroads, she would not recognize the woman.

She was aroused from these thoughts by the sound of the door opening. Iraud came in and closed it behind him. His arm and leg were still bandaged, but he was walking steadily now and looked much better than when she had last seen him. He sat down on the stool at her bedside.

"Aiduri," he said, and then sat, swallowing several times, looking at his hands. She wondered what business he was finding so hard to discuss. He must be a few years older than she, but at the moment he looked like a half-grown boy.

"Yes, my lord king," she said gently. She could not help feeling kindly toward him, he looked so much like Niara. After all, it was he, not the odious Erior, who was Niara's cousin.

"That's right," he said, "now I am king of Kintomar, and—and I am in need of a queen. I would like to—wraiths take it, I've never done anything like this before, and I'm making a mess of it. Aiduri, will you marry me?" He looked her in the eyes, and a blush gradually spread over his face.

Her first impulse was to laugh; she bit her lip and checked that. Her next was to hug him, and it was as well that she was in no shape to do so, for it would certainly have given him the wrong impression. After all, it was a reasonable offer. He could use her help; they would make a good ruling team. And he did look a lot like Niara. She could probably stand sharing his bed, though breeding his or any man's heirs was not something she really wanted to do.

Yet this was not what was making her hesitate. She was just not interested in staying—even if she could do so as full co-ruler—in a small tributary kingdom, when the only person in it that she really cared for was going to have to leave soon. Besides, the Guardian had promised her that they would meet again, and somehow she knew that this meeting would take place far from here.

That must be her answer. "Iraud," she said, still

more gently, "I am vowed to the Guardian, some way; for what, I myself don't understand. I must take Niara wherever she wants to go, and after that I don't think I will be able to return to Kintomar, or that it would bring good luck either to you or me or the city, if I did. I'm sorry."

"So am I." Iraud took Aiduri's hands between his own for a moment, then without another word stood up and walked out.

"Have you decided yet where you're going?"

Niara shrugged. "I don't care what I do now. I could even go back to Imvainor. The ironic thing is that Erior could have helped us without hurting himself, after all. I've no real claim on his throne. But if you ever meet Erior, you'll know why I don't want to be his pensioner."

"I know now," Aiduri answered. "Even a halfway decent usurper ought to have had the grace to offer you his troops in returning for waiving your claim to his throne. I thought of that myself—it's what I'd have done in his shoes."

For the first time since Niethos' death, Aiduri saw Niara laugh. She wracked her brain for some other silly thing to say, but could not think of any.

"Maybe I'll go to the islands, to my—mother's people. Who knows." Once more Niara had sunk back into that numbness, out of which she was forcing herself to go through the motions of living. Once one has survived a doom out of the ancient tales, it is hard to put much faith or energy into everyday life; Aiduri felt that a little, herself.

Perhaps one day, Aiduri thought, Niara's heart would heal; but then, most likely, she would turn to someone who had not seen it break—a man, almost certainly. Aiduri did not know how she would bear it if Niara chose some other woman as her life companion. But Aiduri might never know. They would go on the next leg of the journey together, and after that—Aiduri's fate might take her where it would, until the day she met the Guardian again.

STEALING SOULS
by Laurell K. Hamilton

Sometimes I get a story which for one reason or another just doesn't make it, but the person doesn't take the rejection personally—which is grand because I never mean it personally—but I should always add that "if you can't handle rejection you're in the wrong business"—and simply goes away and writes something better for my present purposes. Laurell Hamilton was one of these; her first story was about elves—which are even more of a cliché in fantasy than dragons, and probably should be left to Tolkien. Her second story, to our good luck, was the delightful and original one we present here. It is her first sale, I think . . . she didn't sent me biographical information in time.

———————

Stealing souls was hard; stealing them back was harder. Sebastiane had spent fifteen years learning just how hard.

The Red Goat tavern was full of people. They swirled, laughing, round Sebastiane's table but did not touch her. For she was the mercenary Sidra Ironfist. And she had passed through many lands as Sidra until she had more stories told about her under that name than her own. She towered over most of the people in the room. The two swords at her waist, one long and one short, looked well cared for and much used. Scars decorated her arms and hands like spider tracings. Her cool gray eyes had a way of staring through a person, as if nothing was hidden.

She had been Sidra so long that sometimes she wondered where Sebastiane had gone. But fighting was not her true occupation. It was more an avocation that allowed her entrance to places her occupation would have closed to her. Most people did not welcome a thief. Especially a thief that had no intention of sharing her prize with the local thieves guild.

Sidra had traveled half a continent and bartered a piece of her soul to be here. She would share with no one.

But then the local thieves guild did not traffic in souls. And that was the goal this time. There would be jewels and magic items to bring out, but like every good thief, she did not allow baubles to distract her from the main goal.

The herb-witch had said that the bones she sought would be in two earthenware pots. They would be bound with black and green braided cord and suspended from a thin-branch made up of some white wood. They would be hung high up in the room where the wizard performed his magic.

The souls in question belonged to Sebastiane's older sisters. They had vanished when she was ten. No one knew what had happened to them, but there were rumors. Rumors of a wizard that had needed twin girls for a forbidden spell done only twice before in all history. A spell to bring great power to a mere herb-witch. Enough power to allow the wizard to taste other magics.

The spell was forbidden because not only did the girls have to die but their souls were imprisoned. Imprisoning souls was a very serious offense if you never intended to let them go.

Sebastiane, the child, had been an apprentice thief and had little hope of confronting such a powerful wizard. But Sidra Ironfist, mercenary and master thief, had a chance.

The little girl of long ago had vowed to Magnus of the Red Hand, god of assassins and god of vengeance. The vow had held firm for fifteen years until she sat only an hour's ride from the wizard who had murdered her sisters.

The hatred of him was gone, killed in the years of surviving. Her sisters' faces were distant things that she couldn't always see clearly. But the vow remained. Sebastiane had come for the bones of her sisters.

The wizard's death would be an added sweetness, but she was no true warrior to go seeking blood vengeance. She was a thief at heart which is a more patient and practical creature. Her goal was to rescue her sisters' souls from the spell. The wizard's death was secondary.

She had left Sidra's friends behind—all save one, Milon Songsmith. The minstrel leaned back in his chair, a grin on his face. He drained his fourth tankard of ale and grinned wider. He was her bard and had been so for eight years. He had made Sidra Ironfist a legend and his own talents in great demand.

He would follow her until she died and then perhaps he would find another hero to follow.

Sidra had not denied him the right to come on this adventure. If she died here, then Milon would sing of it. There were worse things to leave behind than songs.

But somehow she was not the perfect vengeance seeker she had wanted to be. Her life seemed more precious now than it had fifteen years ago. She wanted to live to see her mercenary band again. Black Abe was all right for a temporary command, but he let his emotions carry him away at awkward times. Sidra had welded them into a fighting force that any king in the civilized lands would welcome. Gannon the Sorcerer, Brant the Ax, Emil Swordmaster, Jayme the Quick, and Thetis the Archer. She would have Black Abe's heart if he let one of them die without just cause.

Sidra waved the barmaid away when Milon called her over for the fifth time. "You've had enough, Songsmith."

He flashed a crooked smile, "You can never have enough ale or enough adventure." His rich tenor voice was precise, no slurring. His voice never betrayed him no matter how much he drank.

"Any more ale and there won't be any adventuring tomorrow, at least not for you. I am not going to wait all morning while you sleep it off."

He looked pained. "I would not do that to you."

"You've done it before," Sidra pointed out.

He laughed, "Well, maybe once. To bed, then, my fair Sidra, before I embarrass you any further."

Morning found them the first ones up. They were served cold meat and cheese by a hollow-eyed barmaid. She clasped a shawl around her nightdress, obviously intending to go back to sleep after they had gone. But she brought out some fresh, though cold, bread and dried fruit. And she did not grumble while she did it.

They walked out into a world locked in the fragile darkness just before dawn. The air seemed to shimmer as the dark purple sky faded to blue and the stars were snuffed out like candles in a wind.

Milon drew his cloak about him and said, "It is a chilly morning."

She did not answer but went for the horses. The stable boy stood patiently holding the reins. Sidra had paid extra for such treatment, but it was worth it to be off before curious eyes could see.

Sidra led the way and Milon clucked to his horse. He and the horse were accustomed to following Sidra without knowing where they were going, or why.

The forest trail they followed turned stubbornly away from their destination. Not even a deer path led to where they wanted to go. Then, abruptly, the trees ended.

It was a clearing at least fifty feet across. The ground was gray as if covered in ash. Nothing grew in it. Grass and wildflowers chased round the edges but did not enter. In the middle of the ash circle was a tower.

It rose arrow straight toward the brightening sky. The first rays of sun glimmered along it as if it were made of black mirrors.

The tower was all of one shining ebony piece. There were no marks of stone or mortar; it seemed to have been drawn from the earth whole and complete. Nothing broke its black perfection. There was no door or window.

But Sebastiane the thief knew that there was always a way in. It was only a matter of finding it.

She led the way onto the ash ground and Milon followed. The horses were left loosely tied to the trees some distance away. If neither one of them came back, the horses could eventually break loose and find new homes.

The ground crunched underfoot as if it were formed of ground rock. And yet it couldn't be stone; stone did not crumble to ash. Milon whispered to her, "Demon work." She nodded for she felt it, too. Evil clung to the black tower like a smothering shroud.

Sidra stood beside the tower. She laid her shield on the ground and knelt beside it. She ran hands down the scars of her arms. The scars were far too minor to be battle wounds.

She unlocked the sword guard which held the short sword in place. Rising of its own accord, it sprang to her hand. And the sword laughed, a tinny sound without lungs to hold it.

Milon shifted and moved far away from the naked blade.

Sidra noticed it and politely moved so he would not see the entire ritual. This was one thing that her bard did not like to sing about.

The sword crooned, "Free, bare steel, feel the wind, ahh."

Sidra said, "Our greatest task is before us, blood blade."

The sword hissed, "Name me."

"You who were Blood-Letter when the world was new. You who were Wound-Maker in the hands of a king. You who were Soul-Piercer and took the life of a hero. You who were Blood-Hunger and ate your way through an army. I name thee blade mine, I name thee Leech."

He chortled, "Leech, Leech, I am Leech, I live on blood, I crave its crimson flow, I am Leech. So named, power given."

Sidra had risked her soul five years ago to name the sword. But it had seemed inordinately pleased from the very first at such a name as Leech.

Milon had complained that it wasn't poetic enough. But she left the poetry to the minstrel. Her job was to survive.

The blade whispered, "Feed me."

Sidra held the blade out before her, naked steel at face level. She pressed the flat of the blade between the palms of her hands. She spoke the words of invocation, "Feed gently, Leech, for we have much work to do."

There was always that moment of waiting when Sidra wondered if this time the sword would take too much and kill her. But it bobbed gently between her hands. The razor sharp blade brought blood in a sharp, painful wash down her hands. But the cut was narrow, slicing just below the skin. The blade said, "Sacrifice made, contract assured."

Sidra ignored the wound. It would heal in a moment or two to become another scar. She did not bother to clean the blade as all blood was absorbed cleanly. For it truly did feed.

She resheathed the blade and it hummed tunelessly to itself, echoing up through the leather sheath.

Sidra set to searching the black stone with her fingers. But she found nothing. It was like touching well-made glass without even a bubble to spoil its smoothness.

There was nothing there, but if illusion hid the door, then Leech could find it. She bared the humming sword and said, "Find me a door, Leech."

The humming picked up a note to a more cheerful tune. She recognized the tune as the new ballad of Cullen Tunemaster. Leech seemed very fond of Cullen's tunes.

They paced the tower three times before the sword could make the door visible to her. It looked ordinary enough—just a brown wooden door with metal studding. It was man height.

"Can you see the door now, Milon?"

"I see nothing but blackness."

Sidra reached her hand out toward him and he moved to take it. Leech fought her left hand grip and slashed at the man. Sidra jerked the sword sharply, "Behave, Leech."

"I hunger. You did not feed me."

"You did not ask."

It pouted, "I'm asking now." By the rules she could have refused it, for it had done its task. But keeping the sword happy assured that she could wield it and live; doing both was not always easy. An unhappy blood blade was an untrustworthy blood blade. She held the blade against her left forearm and let it slice its own way into the skin. It was a mere nick of crimson.

She offered her hand once more to Milon.

A drop of sweat beaded at Milon's hairline and he took her hand tentatively, as far from the sword as possible. "I can see the door." He released her hand and backed away from the sword once more.

Sidra knelt before the door, but before she could touch the lock, she noticed the door moved. It wasn't much of a movement, just a twitch like a horse hide when a fly settles on it. She asked the sword, "What is it?"

"It is an ancient enchantment not much used now."

"What is the quickest and quietest way to win past it?"

"Well . . . fire."

"The wizard will notice us setting his door on fire."

"True, but would you rather chop through that much meat? Even I cannot kill it, only damage it. Oh, it would be a glorious outpouring of blood. But it would not be quick." It sounded disappointed.

Sidra hated to use the day's only fireball so early on. She hoped she would not need it later. She faced the door and pointed the sword's tip toward it. A fireball the size of her fist shot from it. It expanded in a whirling dance of heat. The wildfire exploded against the door. A high keening wail sounded. When the fire died away, the door was a blackened hull encircling the doorway. The ruined door was screaming.

The sword said, "Such work deserves a hearty meal."

Sidra did not argue but let the blade slice over her left wrist. The vein was slashed and blood welled dark and eager over the hungry blade. It stayed near, lapping at the wound until it closed.

"Follow close, Milon, but be wary. Not everything in a demon made tower will be civilized enough to know you for a bard."

He nodded, "I have followed you into many adventures. I would not miss this one out of fear."

She said, "Then, come, my brave bard, but watch your back."

She stepped over the blackened rim of the door creature. It whimpered as she and the sword passed through it. They stood in a circular chamber made of the same black rock. But a staircase made of good gray stone curved downward in the center of the room.

"Light the lantern here, Milon, and carry it high." The lantern's flickering yellow light soon danced in the small room.

Sidra led the way and tripped the first trap. Three darts clanged against her shield and fell to the steps. She knelt carefully, shield up and alert. The dart's tips were blackened with a thick tarry substance. She did not touch it.

She spoke for Milon's benefit, "Poisoned. Don't touch anything unless you have to. Watch where you step."

Sidra found the next trap and tripped it with the sword. A spear shot out and buried into the stone of the far wall. It would have taken her through the chest.

And still the stone stairs wound deeper into the earth. There was nothing for a long time save the lantern's golden shadows and their footsteps echoing on the stairs. Then the stairs ended at a small landing in front of a door. But there was one last trap. And Sidra was not at all sure she could trip it without being harmed.

She studied it for a time, directing Milon to point the lantern here and there. There were six separate pressure points on the stairs; that she had found. They were set at a pattern that would make it difficult if not impossible to walk the last five steps. They could jump, but Sidra didn't trust the landing either. And they were too far away for her to find traps on it yet.

She could not pass the stairs, but the sword could. If it would do it. Moving without human aid was something Leech did not prefer to do. Only twice before had she asked it to and each time the blood price had been high.

"Leech I want you to set off the traps on the stairs and then come gently back to my hand."

"Payment." He whispered.

"Blood, as always."

"Fresh blood." He asked.

She offered the blade her naked arm, but it remained unmoving against her skin. "What do you want, Leech?"

"Fresh blood."

"I'm offering it to you."

"Fresher blood, new blood."

Milon said, "Oh, no, no."

Sidra said, "I agree. You are my weapon. You taste my blood, no one else's."

"When we kill, I taste blood."

"I will not sacrifice Milon to feed you."

She could almost feel it thinking, weighing its options. "A taste, a fresh taste, just a nick, just a bite."

Milon said, "No, absolutely not. That steel monster is not going to taste my blood."

Sidra sighed and said, "Then I will attempt to remove the traps."

He gripped her arm, "You said you couldn't do it."

"I said, that I didn't see how I could do it without getting killed."

"It's the same thing."

"No, it isn't."

"I can't let you be killed."

She just looked at him, waiting for him to make up his mind.

He shuddered and held out his arm. She unlaced the sleeve and pushed it back to bare the pale skin. The sword chuckled, "Just a taste, just a bite, just a nibble." She held the sword firmly two-handed, for she didn't trust it, and placed it against Milon's arm. The sword bit deep and quick like a serpent's strike. Milon cried out, and opened his eyes to stare in horror as the blade lapped up his blood. The wound quickly closed and the sword sighed, "New blood, fresh, good, yumm." Sidra felt that the last was added for Milon's benefit.

Milon took it very seriously. He yanked down his sleeve and said, "Yum or not, that is the last of my blood you ever get, you bloodsucking toothpick."

The sword laughed.

Sidra pulled Milon back up the stairs and then released the blade. It settled onto the first pressure point. A rain of poisoned darts filled the hall like black snow.

Leech floated back to her, obediently. "I have cleared the way, O master." Sidra ignored the sarcasm and led Milon to the landing. It was not trapped.

But the door was.

The poisoned darts were soon removed. And the well oiled lock clicked under her pick. The door opened into a short straight hallway. Doors dotted the walls in geometric lines to right and left. Torches were set at regular intervals along the walls. In the still air there was the sound of chanting.

Milon started to blow out the lantern, but Sidra stopped him. She spoke close to his ear so the sound wouldn't carry. "We may need light if we have to leave quickly."

The sword started to hum in time to the chanting and she hushed it.

Sidra stared at the floor and said, "Place your feet exactly where I place mine."

He nodded to show he had understood and then concentrated on following her over a five-foot-wide area of floor. She let out a breath of air as if she had been holding it. He relaxed as well, stepping back just a half step. The floor fell out from under him and he was tumbling backward helplessly. Sidra caught his arm, but his weight pulled them both downward. He was left dangling over a pit and she on her stomach holding him by one arm. The torches glimmered off of silvered spikes set into the floor of the pit.

She hissed, "I told you to walk where I walked."

"Let us argue this later. Pull me up." She did, rubbing her shoulder, "You're lucky you didn't dislocate my arm."

He shrugged an apology and picked up the fallen lantern.

The chanting seemed to be coming from the last door on the right-hand side. They were only three doors away from it when Sidra stopped the bard with a hand movement and knelt to study the floor. She shook her head, sending light bursts from her helmet to the walls. She said, "When I say jump, leap forward as fast as you can."

"Why?"

She stared at him a moment and then looked upward.

He would have missed it, but with her gaze to direct him he saw the portcullis spikes ready to come crashing down. He swallowed and said, "When do we jump?"

She stood beside him and said, "Now." They stepped forward and flung themselves across the stones. Sidra rolled easily, coming to her feet before the spikes had bitten into the floor. They were trapped.

There was a swimming in the air near the torches in one corner. Sidra pointed Leech at it and concentrated. Illusions bled near fire. A demon stood at the end of the hallway.

He was perhaps eight feet tall, fairly short for an ice demon. His scales were the color of new frost and winked in the light like diamond glints on snow. His teeth were ivory daggers. His four arms were crossed over his chest and his tail rustled over the floor. He grinned and said, "Welcome."

His bat-ribbed ears rolled into tubes and then unrolled. "I would speak with you before we fight."

Sidra found herself staring into its smooth blue eyes, no pupil, just empty blue like a frozen lake. Peaceful. Milon gripped her arm and pulled her back. "Sidra."

She shook her head roughly and faced the demon in a fighting crouch, shield close, sword ready.

He said, "Perhaps you are right. Enough talk, let us fight." He strode forward and said, "And you, bard, I know the rules; by touching her you gave up your safe conduct."

"I do not regret what I did, ice demon. You cannot harm me if you are dead."

It chuckled, then, low in its chest.

Sidra whispered to the sword, "I want you to burn for me and aid me in slaying this ice demon."

It said, "Price will be high."

She had expected nothing less. "When is the last time you tasted demon blood."

The sword paused and said, "Demon blood."

"If we kill it, then all its blood is yours to consume."

He gave a nervous expectant giggle. "All that demon blood, all of it. You won't remove until I have drunk my fill."

"I won't remove you."

It chuckled, "Payment is more than generous. I will do as you ask."

The ice demon strode forward, still laughing to itself. Its claws clicked together with a sound like breaking ice.

Sidra kept Leech half hidden behind her shield as if she meant to only cower before the demon. Leech burst into flame with its blade like a wick in the center of the good orange fire.

The first threads of cold oozed round her shield and she knew, magic weapon or not, the first blow must be a good one. Milon simply stared up at the creature with his back pressed against the fallen portcullis.

The demon stood almost directly in front of Sidra and she kept her head down as if she could not bear the sight of him. He spoke to the bard, "Your protector is not doing much protecting, but be patient. When I have finished with her, you will have my undivided attention."

Sidra forced Leech up while the demon was looking at Milon. The sword took him through the chest, burning brightly as the demon blood gushed over it. The blade bit through a clawed hand and sent fingers spinning. The demon screamed.

A casual swipe of the tail knocked her to the ground and a claw raked along the shield. The nails left grooves in the metal. A hand caught her helmet and sent her head ringing back against the floor. Leech moved of its own accord, bringing her hand with it. The blade shot through the demon's throat and blood poured out acrid and stinking. Sidra struggled to her knees gagging from the stench. She fought upward with the blade and shield. A claw slipped past the edge of the shield and she felt claws sink into her thigh. Leech bit into the demon's arm, half severing it. And it began to fade. It was running as a proper demon does when it is hurt badly enough and has the choice of leaving.

Leech screamed after the fading creature, "No, no!"

It flamed in her hand a while longer and then faded back to normal. "Cheated."

Sidra leaned against the wall, favoring her wounded leg. "It was not my doing that the demon left. I kept my part of the bargain."

The sword was dangerously silent. Sidra was almost

relieved that all its magic was spent for the day. It was never reliable when it was pouting.

The last door was not locked. It opened easily to reveal the wizard in the middle of a spell. A protective circle chased the edges of a pentagram and the wizard stood in the center of it all. He was short, balding, and did not look a demon master or an evil man. But standing outside his magic circle was no mere demon but a devil.

It was why the wizard had not aided his ice demon. It was death to abort the spell. He was trapped as if in a cage until he released the devil to its home plane.

Now their only danger was the devil.

It was still only half formed with the bottom half of its body consumed in a strange black smoke. Its upper half was vaguely manlike with shoulders and arms. It resembled the demon they had banished with its bat-ribbed ears and teeth, but it was covered in black skin, the color of nothing above ground.

High above it all, suspended from the ceiling, were the two earthenware jars on the end of a white pole.

A rope held the pole in place and the rope was tied off near the door around a peg. Sidra smiled. She raised the sword and chopped the rope. The wizard seemed to notice what she did. But he could not stop to plead with her. If he stopped, then the devil would be freed and it would kill him. Devils were very reliable that way, or unreliable, depending on the point of view.

The pole came crashing to the ground, but the jars did not break. They were spelled against such mundane accidents. Sidra stepped toward them carefully, one eye on the devil. She sheathed Leech, for fighting devils was not a matter of swords.

She untied the two jars from the pole and passed one out to Milon. The other she balanced under her sword arm. Just before she passed out of the room with his precious power, the wizard broke and shrieked, "No!"

The devil laughed, "Take your pots and go, warrior-thief. Your business is finished here."

The floor quivered. Sidra turned to Milon and said, "Run."

They ran only as far as the fallen gate. It blocked their way completely and the floor shivered once more. "There must be a hidden lever that will raise this. Search." They felt along the walls to either side and Milon found something that he pressed. Slowly the gate raised upward. The walls lurched as if someone had caught the tower and twisted it.

They ran full out. There would no more fighting, no more trap finding. It was a race to the surface.

Milon said, "The pit, what about the pit?"

"Jump it."

"Jump it?"

"Jump it or die."

He ran harder to keep up with her longer legs and he tried not to picture the spikes on the floor of the pit. It was there suddenly and they were leaping over it. Sidra went down, betrayed by her wounded leg, but was up and running with the blood pumping down her leg. The floor twisted under their feet and cracks began to form on the walls.

The stairs were treacherous. The lantern was a bouncing glow that showed widening cracks and falling rock. They came up into the tower room.

The door had healed itself shut. The tower gave a shudder as its foundations began to crumble.

Sidra drew Leech from his sheath and pointed it at the door. She decided to bluff. "Open, door, or I'll burn you again." The door whimpered uncertainly and then it swung outward. They raced through the door and kept running across the ash circle and into the trees. With a final groan the tower thundered to its death. The world was full of rock and dust.

They lay gasping on the ground and grinning at each other. Milon said, "Let me look at your leg."

She lay back in the grass, allowing him to probe the stab wound. "Deep but not bad. It will heal. Now will you tell your minstrel what was so important about two earthenware jars."

Sidra smiled and said, "I have a story for you, Milon. A story of a little girl and a vow she made to a god."

LADYKNIGHT
by Susan Hanniford Crowley

Although Susan Crowley is the editor of a religious news-letter—and has been published in her local newspaper, small presses, and religious publications—this is her first sale of fiction. So much for those people who picket science fiction and fantasy conventions, openings of *Star Wars* and so forth by saying that fantasy is incompatible with religion, as some people do. Personally, I think that if humanity is a special Creation at all, as distinct from the beast-kind, we have only one thing going for us—and that's our imagination. I know my dog sometimes dreams—and I once owned a dog who had nightmares—so the beast-kind must be capable of *some* imagination—but there are, so far as I know, no canine or feline Tolkiens. More's the pity. Crowley has a Bachelor of Fine Arts from the University of Connecticut; she has studied theater, poetry, and short story writing. She also is married and has two children (sexes and ages unknown—maybe she didn't think we, or you, would be interested) and "like every other writer" is working on a novel. In other words, she is a typical housewife-writer. There's a lot to be said for combining housewifery and writing; unfortunately, words characterizing it would be unsuitable in a family publication such as this one.

Awaking, I stretched my arms along the grass. A sword fell into the ground near my face. I leaped to my feet. Towering over me was a knight in white and silver on a fine white steed.

"Pick it up, woman. Just don't stand there."

I tried to reason it out. If I picked it up, he'd have every right to cut me down.

"No, I won't do it," I said:

"Pick it up. I'm giving it to you."

"Why would a knight give his sword to a beggar?" I asked.

"I'm dying," he said. Then he fell off his horse. I poked the heap of motionless metal and flesh on the ground. When I was satisfied he could do me no harm, I rolled him over. I took off his helmet and cascades of brown curls shot through with lightning tumbled out. Agonized eyes of deep blue reached out to me, as I gazed in wonder at the ladyknight.

A dark gash spoiled the silver of her breastplate. She labored to breathe as I struggled to free her from her broken armor. A strong tug released a gush of blood. Exposed, her wet body shivered. I could see the wound clearly. A battle-ax had cut through very near her heart.

"He found my weak spot. Beware my enemy, Jackonan the Gray."

"I don't understand," I said.

"You are Sorrel?"

"Yes, I am. How did you know. . . ?"

"I was given your name in a dream. The sword will serve you now," she said.

Tearing strips of cloth from my rags, I bound her wound and propped her up near my firestones. While I set to work building a fire, she chewed on the bit of rabbit I'd given her.

"Thank you for your hospitality, Sorrel. But no matter how you try to heal me, I will still die. I am Cassandra de Martaine. I was on my way to you, when I was waylaid by a rogue. Well, actually laid, I should say. Well laid at that." She laughed, but the pain prevented her from fully enjoying her joke.

I laughed cautiously and put more wood on the fire.

"So he is after you?" I asked.

"No. He is after the great sword, Rhet. In ancient times, Queen Nor used this sword not only for protection but as a key to her treasure chamber."

"Where is this treasure chamber?"

"Somewhere deep in a cavern. The legend says that someday the sword will choose to lead its lady to the hidden treasure. It didn't choose me."

"So you were taken by this man—Jackonan?" I asked.

"It was my own fault. I sought to use him for my pleasure. I did not see the black heart beneath his beauty."

She spit up blood, and I wiped her up the best I could. Her shining eyes watched as I concocted a gruel in my cooking pot.

"Why do you live in the forest, Sorrel?"

"I have no home. No family. My parents died when I was just beginning to walk. They are shadows in my memory. A family took me in for a while. I became their dog—fit to do their work but not sit at their table. I waited, learned. Ran away when I knew I could do better. I keep moving so as not to become a slave. There's men that rape and beat you, and there's men that wive you. But for me, I'd rather be free."

"Very wise, Sorrel, very wise." Again she laughed, her hand pressed against her heart. "So you must be a pure maid, then?"

"How's that?" I asked.

"A virgin?"

"Oh, no." I laughed. "I remember it clearly. It was midsummer's night festival. He was very comely in the moonlight."

"Did you love him, Sorrel?"

"For that night at least." I chuckled slyly, and she joined me. Then suddenly she grew very pale.

"Please, Lady Cassandra, rest yourself."

"No, I'll be just fine. Dying is a tiresome thing. I wish at least to be good company in my last hours," she said. "I want to tell you how the sword came into my hands. My husband, Barius, had died, killed in a Holy Crusade."

"Did you love him?" I asked.

"Yes, very much. Barius was my friend and my cousin, too. As children we played together. As he learned the bow and sword, he took great pleasure in teaching me. I remember one day he said, "Cassandra, my love, master these skills of war, someday you may need them to defend everything you hold sacred." He kissed me that day for the first time. No one saw and I told no one. One year later, he demanded me from my father. We were married and two months later he marched off to die. The family waited to see if I was bearing Barius' child. There was no child. Barius had been the oldest, his father's heir. Now his brothers wanted their rights, but I was a burden to the family. They told me that I would be sent to a convent to live out my life there."

"God," I said.

"Exactly. I am not really very religious. By myself, I never pray. It was a dark night, blacker than any I'd ever known. I cried for Barius, and I demanded God to give me a task, something that was mine. I was so utterly wretched. Then a servant came to my chamber door. There was a strange woman below who asked to see me."

I took the gruel and went over to her. With my fingers, I fed her. She protested.

"Do not waste your food on the dead," she said.

"It's my business what I do with my food. Now eat it."

She ate very little, coughing up more blood. I stopped and put the gruel aside. After a short rest, she continued her story.

"The woman's name was Half Moon. She was from China. She told me how she got the sword and was now led to passing it on to me. After she left, I sneaked out of the castle and went to see the village smith. He had been a loyal friend of my husband's, and I trusted him and his wife with my new secret. I hired him to make me a suit of armor. When the armor was finished, I put all my jewels into a pouch and with my horse, Lightsong, rode away in the night. At my first opportunity, I sold all my jewels, even my wedding ring. I did not want to provide a trail of jewels in the event the family sent someone after me."

"Did they?" I asked.

"Yes. On the twelfth night out, I broke the promise I made to myself—not to kill. He came at me. When I raised my sword, he laughed at me. The fool laughed at me, underestimating my strength and my anger."

She sighed and pressed her hand to her heart. Blood seeped out between her fingers.

"Sorrel, what is your full name?"

"I can't remember any other but Sorrel."

"Then I will give you mine, Sorrel de Martaine, and you are my heir. I give you my purse, my armor and my horse. The sword is already yours. I regret I will not be able to teach you how to fight. Beware of Jackonan the Gray and other men who want the sword. Trust no one. Let the sword lead you, Ladyknight."

She drew three painful breaths, and then there was a rattling sound. The lady was dead.

"Lady Cassandra?" I shook her, but her spirit had fled the body. Looking at the corpse of the beautiful lady, I ate gruel and wondered what to do.

Her horse, Lightsong, stood over her neighing softly. I stood up and patted his muzzle. A tear came out of one eye and fell down the long nose. Before that moment, I didn't know animals cried. Lightsong rubbed his face against mine. I was crying, too. I had never wept for anyone in my life before. Never. I had watched death. Once I had been in a village with plague and watched children following the death wagon carrying their parents. Not a single tear from me. Now I cried like a baby over Cassandra. No one had ever given me anything. In death, Cassandra gave me everything, even a reason for living.

Suddenly I became aware of something different in the forest. I knew every creature sound, the wind through the trees. There were hoofbeats coming fast. My heart took on their rhythm, pounding so hard I ached. Dragging the ladyknight's body into some bushes, I covered the trail as I went. Almost as if he knew my mind, the horse lay down near the body behind the bushes in perfect silence. I returned to my firestones. Why I didn't hide, I don't know.

He appeared in the clearing. With the sun behind him, he was all shadow. Nearer he came. His horse was black and his armor gray.

I heard her voice echo in my head. "Beware my enemy, Jackonan the Gray!"

"Come here, beggar." His voice was deep and rich with promise.

I stood and cautiously approached the gray knight. Only a few feet away my eyes fell on the battle-ax, red with blood, which hung at his side.

"Tell me. Have you seen a white knight pass this way? A beautiful knight all in white and silver?"

Silence pressed my lips together. *What if I gave him the sword,* I thought. I wanted no trouble. Could I betray the ladyknight's trust in me? She had given me everything. Is this how I repaid her? I raised my arm to the distant east, indicating Lochlin.

He sat there and then slowly rode around me. His black steed snorted and restlessly pawed the ground with each step. My ears ached with the internal drumming of fear. Then, quite abruptly, he threw a gold coin at my feet and galloped away.

Gazing at the gold in the dirt, I considered whether to take it or not. I picked it up. Gold, like death, is cold to the touch. I walked over to Lightsong who was regaining his feet.

"Look," I said, "Jackonan the Gray pays handsomely for lies."

I carried the body deeper into the wood and with the sword dug a crude grave. After stripping the armor off, I laid her in the hole. She looked so small and delicate, almost childlike. I wept as I covered her, making a mound over her. The sword, shield and armor, I stacked in a pile. Next to it was her purse. I was slow to open it, but when I did I was surprised by the amount of gold she carried. I would never be hungry again.

Scrubbing each piece of armor in the river, I set it on the bank to dry. Cassandra's blood was now part of the river. A part of me didn't want to wear her armor, but I knew better.

From that first moment that I dressed as the ladyknight, I knew I would never again be satisfied with the crumbs the world threw my way. Rhet felt good in my hand, not as heavy as I expected. Soon I was riding south to Bresthaven, leaving my ragged life behind.

We had just cleared the trees when I saw him. Apparently Jackonan the Gray had not believed me.

Pulling the reins hard, I tried to turn Lightsong to flee. The fool horse wouldn't do it and instead charged full speed at the enemy. I had no choice. Dropping the reins, I held the shield against the open place in my armor. Rhet was long and rigid in the wind. The hand that held it was frozen with fear. Everything was dream-like. I didn't know how to fight, but somehow I did.

He screamed as Rhet pierced his shoulder. I with-drew the blade with such force that he fell with a crash to the ground. The shoulder joint in his armor spouted blood. I paused over him, considering whether or not to help him.

"I'll kill you, Cassandra de Martaine."

My decision made for me, I rode hard, changing directions many times and taking time to obscure my path. Finally I chose the hunter's route west to Greendale.

Riding into town was a revelation to me. The towns-folk watched me with reverent silence. The innkeeper hurried into the street and bowed before me, offering the hospitality of his inn.

I thought it best to wear my disguise of knighthood as I entered the great dining hall. I chose a table in the corner near the hearth. With my back to the wall, I could sip hot brew and eat gruel with relative safety. From my place, I could see everything that happened.

The cold autumn night blew open the door. A tall figure of deep purple entered and approached the bar, and the room filled with hushed whispers. It took a seat at the now empty bar. Long, delicate fingers pushed back the hood, revealing a beautiful lady with flowing night hair. Beneath the folds of purple, I saw a bright blue gown. The innkeeper bowed many times and put his best stew and bread before her. She ate, quietly surveying the room. Our eyes met and some-thing inside me stopped forever.

Putting a silver coin in the innkeeper's hand, she took her leave. I retired to my private room immedi-ately, and from my window, I watched her walk down the road and disappear over a hill.

The next morning I gave the innkeeper two gold pieces. He bowed over and over, calling me "lordship." I rode away annoyed when the man prostrated himself in the street.

The path the woman had taken led into a large forest. I journeyed for days without coming across a human or hovel. The path soon disappeared, and I had to create my own.

On the fourteenth day, I found a strange cottage made from the hollow of a living tree. There was a well in front, so I stopped to get water for Lightsong and myself. Dipping my helmet, I held it while Lightsong drank.

"Welcome, Ladyknight."

The surprise was so complete, I spilled water all over myself. The woman laughed and in one fluid motion had retrieved my helmet, filled it, and was holding it for Lightsong. Her long black hair nearly touched the ground behind her. Her gown was the color of a spring day. Her eyes. Her eyes. I looked deeply into them and was so stunned by what I found there, that I didn't even notice their color.

"You are looking for a teacher, Sorrel de Martaine?"

"How did you. . . ?"

"Your heart told me."

"How can my heart tell you anything?" I asked.

"Yours is a pure heart. It has no deception in it. I knew you when I saw you at the inn. I knew you again when I saw you give your horse water before drinking yourself," she said.

"The well could have been poisoned," I said.

"You did not think of that until just now."

I was speechless. She continued the talk while watering Lightsong and rubbing his muzzle lovingly. Her name was Torn Gown. Above her small white feet, the ragged edge of her gown's torn hem fluttered in the breeze. She, too, was on a quest. Until she could accomplish it, she would walk on earth. She had already lived for 2,000 years in this one form and her greatest desire was to return home to the Supreme One. Her only way home was through the giving of a gift. She did not know what the gift was or who would receive it.

I nodded as she spoke, pretending to understand. She looked at me sternly for a moment then laughed.

"In town, they say you are a sorceress. Are you?" I asked.

"I am not," she said.

"Then what are you?"

"For what I am, the word has not yet been created. For you, I will become many things. Do you want me to teach you, Sorrel?"

"Yes, but how will I pay you?"

"Be a good student and someday teach someone else."

I agreed and on that day I struck the best bargain in my life. She took me into her strange living home. Carefully removing my armor, she examined the damaged breastplate and then tossed it with the rest of the pieces. When she saw my rags, she laughed.

"Sorrel, you are disguised again? How many disguises have you?" It was not so much a question as a joke.

Disposing of my rags, she had me sit in a large tub while she poured warm water over me from a cooking pot. Then she poured a frothy liquid over my head and began to scrub so hard I was raw. My protests were useless. She said this was a bath—my first lesson. After a while I began to enjoy the experience.

Torn Gown gave me a pale yellow gown to wear and slippers of soft leather.

"Come here, Sorrel, and gaze into the looking glass. Have you ever seen such loveliness?"

I saw my reflection and looked down.

"Is that me?" I asked because I had never seen the image that stood beside Torn Gown's in the glass. It was not the dirty, distorted face I had seen in the rippled surfaces of ponds.

"Did you know I would look like this when you saw me, Torn Gown?"

"Even now, Sorrel, you wear a disguise. For when I look at you, I see the shining being of light that inhabits the flesh. That's your true beauty."

I followed Torn Gown everywhere. On our long walks through the forest, I learned to measure time by her shadow. She taught me the broad stroke of the pen and the broad stroke of the sword. When the first snowfall came, it crowned her dear head with snowflakes. That did not stop her vigorous hikes in the wood. I slid and stumbled trying to keep up with her. My complaining did not even slow her down.

At night, safe in the tender warmth of her tree cottage, she taught me to read. I watched the candlelight flicker across her eternally young face as she mouthed the words in the book.

It was a bad winter. Food was scarce. Often we would see herds moving through the high drifts to chew on saplings and strip bark. One such day, I was trudging behind Torn Gown when I fell headfirst into a drift. When I got up, I was horrified that Torn Gown was gone. I stared at the overhead sun that signaled midday. It was the wrong thing to do. Torn Gown had taught me other ways to tell time for just this reason. I was blinded and fell, half slid in my attempts to find her. Then I heard a low growl. That quickened my pace and I was more the fool. Too late I discovered that I was encircled by a wolf pack. I saw their dark images moving closer.

"My brothers, forgive the cub trespassing in your territory. It is only a cub, my brothers." It was Torn Gown speaking. I closed my eyes and could see the mind images she used to communicate with the wolves. The blurred deep purple form of Torn Gown approached, took my hand and led me past the now silent sentinels of the woods.

Safe in the treetrunk home, Torn Gown placed moist bandages on my eyes.

"You looked into the winter sun, didn't you? The injury will heal by tomorrow. Tell me, have you learned anything from your experience?"

"Why did you call the wolves brothers?" I asked.

"Because every form of creation is our brother," she said.

"I saw a kind of picture language in my mind."

"You saw a part of my inner communication with the wolves."

"Only part?" I asked.

She smiled.

I could feel her smile in the silence.

"There is a deeper language still that you have yet to hear. But you've done well, Sorrel, considering you panicked. When you make a mistake, don't stumble on and compound it. Stop and find your balance. Give yourself that time. I am pleased that you are relying on your inner senses."

Torn Gown's storytelling lulled me to sleep. In my dream, I pictured her in the forest with our brothers, the wolves.

Spring brought new lessons. I walked slowly, listening to the sweet music inside my heart. My eyes darted to and fro with rabbit swiftness. When I turned to look, I saw no bent blades of grass or broken flowers. The meadow was as fresh as if I'd never passed through it.

Torn Gown laughed. "Very good, my young friend. There is always a great benefit to traveling unnoticed by the world."

She skipped and leaped through the forest, and I followed this time more surefooted and stronger. We came upon a crossroad. In the distance was a farmer on his wagon. Torn Gown bent over and feebly laughed. I followed her motions. When he came near, he called out.

"Old woman, which way to Fairclover?"

Torn Gown cackled and pointed to the west. For a moment, I thought I saw a long bony finger.

After he had disappeared around the bend, I questioned my teacher.

"The mind sees what it wants to see. Remember, Sorrel, always look beneath the surface."

I couldn't sleep that night and crawled through the knothole in my bedroom wall out onto a bough. I sat there dangling my feet far above the ground. Spring called to me in the twinkling stars and fragrant breeze.

"Can't sleep?" Torn Gown was beside me, playfully kicking me. Somehow I was not surprised by my teacher. I had got used to the idea that she might be everywhere.

"I dream about us all the time. In one dream, we are walking on stars, I in my leather slippers and you in your bare feet. Then there's the dream where I can't find you. I gaze in every face looking for you. In some I see your wisdom or your smile. Some laugh with your sense of fun. But all just bits and pieces of you, not you," I said.

She smiled to herself and looked up at the stars.

"Come on, little one. Let's go inside," she said. We crawled through the hole to my hollowed bedroom. I climbed into bed and just like a mother she tucked the blanket in all around me and kissed me on the forehead.

That night I dreamed against of following her on endless adventures through the invisible worlds.

Summer's heat beaded on my brow, as I pushed scrub brushes across the floor. Stopping a moment, I sat up straight and let loose with profanity and a list of complaints. I wasn't here to be a scrub maid. I wanted to learn to fight, to be the ladyknight. Torn Gown made me do every dirty job in the house.

"Stop making that ugly noise, Sorrel."

"Does it bother you, Teacher?" I was sarcastic.

"No. You harm only yourself by complaining," she said.

"I'm sick of this, Torn Gown. Sick of this job and sick of your philosophy."

A sudden painful kick sent me sprawling into the bucket of soapy water.

"Why did you do that?" Drenched from head to toe and dripping with anger, I wrung out my gown.

"To stop you from creating ugliness in your life." She laughed as she spoke, pointing and chuckling each time I wrung out my gown. I began to laugh, too, imagining how foolish I looked.

During sword practice, I used Cassandra's shield which bore the image of an eagle descending from a mountain. Torn Gown had instructed me to keep a written record of my dreams. I tried my best though my script was still crude. During one particularly hot evening, I dreamed that a being of light gave me a gift. In my hand, I held a gold star.

On hearing this the following morning, Torn Gown took the shield down from its place on the wall. We worked all day building a small, hot fire in the clearing. By evening, Torn Gown had decided it was ready. She brought the shield into the blue-white flame. I watched the eagle fade and melt. While the metal was still pliable, she carved a picture with a thin iron poker of an open hand holding a star. From her pocket she took a pebble of gold, put it into an iron cup which she set in the flames. Later, she poured the liquid gold carefully onto the star. Then, when it was precisely right, she drenched the shield in a tub of cold mountain water. During this time, she also repaired the breastplate.

"You will be strongest at the heart," she said.

There was change in the crisp autumn zephyr that ranged throughout the forest. Already a year had passed. I had hardly noticed. In that time, Torn Gown had become many things to me. Sometimes my friend. Sometimes my sister. Always my teacher. Sometimes when I managed some profound wisdom, she would gaze all wide-eyed at me like a student. When I was deeply sad, she would comfort me like my far-off memories of my dead mother. Sometimes she angered me so that I trembled. Sometimes she made me laugh so hard, I tumbled in the leaves like a child. But the golden times were when she moved me so that instead of my heart breaking, it danced in the rain of joy. We both knew it was almost time for me to go.

Finished with our swordplay, Torn Gown returned hers to its place on the cottage wall and embarked on her daily forest trek. I knew there was no real place for weaponry in her life. Carrying Rhet, I dallied behind her, feeling its balance and examining its deadly beauty. The amber leaves at my feet scolded me with hush, hush, hush. Torn Gown didn't seem to notice my noisy trudging. She hummed happily to herself, totally absorbed in whatever world she was seeing.

At the crossroad, she became abruptly aware.

"Hide your sword in the folds of your gown. Do as I do," she said.

I obeyed. I quieted even the noise in my mind, when I realized we were to become invisible.

Soldiers on horseback were approaching fast. They were upon us and still did not see us. Then I saw the banner they carried—an upraised fist on a field of gray. I remembered a battle-ax red with blood. In my head the echo came, "Beware my enemy, Jackonan the Gray!" Anger broke my focus, making me visible.

Startled, one soldier's horse reared before me. He shouted to the others.

"Look. A woman all alone."

Like a hidden serpent Rhet struck. The four remaining soldiers came at me. I knew they meant to take me alive. I glanced around for my teacher. She was still invisible. She was safe. I fought fiercely, until finally I faced only one. Like a bellowing monster, he charged. I cut him down.

Then the air behind my head whipped and bled. Turning I saw Torn Gown's dear head fall to the ground. A soldier I thought slain had risen again. When he rose up behind me, Torn Gown had gotten in the way. My anger died a cold death. I gazed at her murderer and felt a strange compassion. He had killed beauty without knowing it. I was to blame. I had started the battle and he was just doing the only thing he knew. He stood tall and silent, his body a river of blood. Suddenly he shuddered and died.

I stood helpless among the slaughtered. My beloved teacher had given her life for mine. My memory was fragmented and hazy. I saw a dagger of carved bone in the shape of a fleeing stag and picked it up from among the bones and blood. I was numb. I don't remember how I managed to carry Torn Gown's body home.

My searing pain roared high, flamed by the funeral pyre. My tears fell hot and left their bitterness in my mouth. Cassandra de Martaine had given me a reason for living. Torn Gown had taught me how to live. I had failed her by my uncontrolled anger, and I had failed myself. Lying in the dirt, I watched the flames consume her body.

"Failing one test is not failing everything. Next time you will not let anger control you."

Rising slowly, I turned. A shimmering golden form stood near me. I knew that voice and loved it.

"Torn Gown?"

"I wore the torn gown, just as you came disguised as a knight and as a beggar," she said.

"What about your quest?" I asked.

"I gave my gift to you. Your life is now a treasure to give to others. It's all up to you."

I smiled and with it came the release of my sorrow. In the coming days, I set Torn Gown's house in order. Putting on my armor, I mounted Lightsong and rode away from the forest that had been my home.

Many times I was sidetracked from my quest by helping others. After a while a mystical legend grew about the ladyknight, some of it fact but mostly fiction.

I was tired of the dust and endless traveling, when I chanced on a clear woodland pool. Since no one was around, I carefully hid my clothes and went in. The cool water relieved my weariness.

Lightsong snorted. I turned. A man stood on the shore staring at me. To say he was beautiful was like saying the sun isn't radiant. Sunlight literally danced in his blond hair and beard. His eyes were blue like wildflowers. If I had to fight him, his towering strength was certain to be a challenge.

"I did not know there was a mermaid in this pool," he said.

"I am not a mermaid. I am a lady. Please, sir, turn your back so I may fetch my clothes."

I did not know what kind of man he was. When he turned, I was surprised. I hopped into the woods and quickly put on my yellow gown and slippers. Within the folds of my gown, the stag dagger rested in a hidden scabbard. I bundled my armor into Torn Gown's old purple cloak.

He introduced himself as Lord Jacob, the landowner upon whose estate I had trespassed. I called myself

Lady Sorrel de Martaine. Did I see him flinch or had I imagined it?

"Where is your chaperone, Lady Sorrel?"

"My chaperone died. But I am able to take care of myself," I said.

"Where are you headed?" he asked.

"Home to my father's land beyond Lochlin."

Again he flinched.

As he escorted me around the grounds, a servant came to him. Lord Jacob whispered to the man, who then bowed and led Lightsong to the stable.

"I will not be staying," I said.

"But you must. It will be nightfall soon, and you cannot travel at night. All manner of evil hides in the dark. Please, accept my hospitality."

His home was so much grander than I could ever imagine, handsomely carved oaken tables and chairs, embroidered fabrics and thick velvet draperies. Though unaccustomed to the great castles of the nobility, I sensed something was missing. My host was open enough with the matters of his wealth and estate, but I felt he was hiding something from me. He showed me my room where the servants had already put my bundle. The next room was his. He said he wanted to be near in case I had need of him. I kept myself from laughing, as I knew full well what he needed.

His feast table was spread with such delights that I lingered and savored each dish. Wine flowed into my goblet. In the year I spent with Torn Gown, I had forgotten the warm pleasure of wine. I tingled and laughed. After a few goblets, I felt befuddled but happy.

Taking a goblet from the table, my host showed me his garden by moonlight. He sipped a little and offered me some. Then we danced, swinging each other until we fell tumbling into the grass. His body pressed against mine. I quickly got up, as I did not want him to feel my hidden dagger. He mistook my actions for maidenly modesty.

I headed for the door. Just as I touched it, his hand held it closed. He leaned toward me, kissed me. His arms closed around me. Every inch of me wanted him.

Pushing past him into the room, I wanted to see how long I could make the game last.

More wine collapsed me into giggles, as he tried to impress me with tales of daring. Apparently, he was a knight, too. His tales were filled with grief and loneliness and a quest ended badly.

Then he fell to my feet and kissed my slippers. I jumped away from his lunacy.

"My dear lady Sorrel, I am a slave to your beauty. Command me."

I didn't know how to take him. Then I laughed, and he laughed. I touched his beard. He kissed me. His hands caressed me before carrying me to his bed.

He was such a sweet lover, so completely satisfying. Watching him as he slept, I wondered what luck brought him to me. Then I saw the strange scar on his shoulder. A cold fog crept around my heart.

Wobbling, I got out of bed. Across the cold stone floor, I tiptoed so as not to wake Jacob. I was still very drunk and wanted to vanish the nightmarish thought that crept nearer each second. With all the draping and tapestries, I couldn't find the door. I pushed aside a curtain and walked into a small dressing room. The bright moonlight reflected on something in the corner. Metal? I pulled off the cloth that almost covered it. The weaponry, the banners and other flags displaying his coat of arms were piled near his gray armor. The ax was dark with dried blood.

I closed my eyes and remembered Cassandra's words: "I did not see the black heart beneath his beauty." Rage swelled in me, heart-ripping, face-tearing rage. But as my hand closed on my dagger, I remembered Torn Gown. My anger defeated me that day. My heartbeat slowed and my fever cooled. Anger would not defeat me again. His deception would not be complete.

I found my room and my belongings untouched. Dressing quickly, I readied to depart. I slipped back into his room and placed a note on the pillow near his head. My dagger rolled across my palm. I looked at him, thinking the killing would be easy. Torn Gown had tried to teach me compassion. Asleep, naked but for a coverlet, Jacob was like a defenseless child. I thrust the dagger into the note and into the pillow beneath. He smiled in his sleep. The note read:

On this night, I spared your life, Jackonan the Gray. I will not do it again.
                                Sorrel de Martaine, Ladyknight

I sneaked Lightsong out of the stable. Within minutes we were galloping north. I wanted to be far away by dawn. Maybe then we could hide and rest. I had a long time to think. I could easily understand how Cassandra's passion had led to her death. I swallowed hard, as I thought how close I'd come to mine. Yet death really wasn't that frightening, if you could die like Torn Gown. I wondered if I was really a golden being of light, too, that would live after death. My dear teacher had continued to teach me after all. I had finally learned compassion.

I traveled west. In the beginning, I obscured my trail but after a while I didn't bother. We rode hard on dusty roads where our path mingled with many others.

After weeks of avoiding anyone, I came to a small village in the highlands. When I stopped to water Lightsong, a woman named Kerry offered me lodging.

The village folk of Aor were very respectful of me. Even the men bowed whenever meeting me. The children followed me everywhere. Sometimes they would steal up and touch me, then run off. Kerry explained that they had never seen a knight before and it was an old belief that magic and courage could be shared with a touch. All in all, they were very comfortable with my presence and I was very happy in theirs. So I broke my rule and stayed several days in Aor.

Kerry was kind to share her meager fare with me. She managed a household of six children. Her husband was very sick and slept most of the time. In the one-room hut, my bed was a pile of straw in the corner nearest the hearth. I shared it with her youngest daughter, Neara, who wasn't hers at all but an orphan she'd taken in. Without her telling me, I wouldn't have known it for she loved them all the same.

The longer I stayed in Aor, the more I wanted to make my home there. One night, I dreamed I saw the village slaughtered and in the flames was the banner of Jackonan the Gray. I knew the sword was telling me not to stay.

By dawn, I was away. A shadow behind me crossed my vision. It was little Neara. Lifting her high onto Lightsong, I rode back and left her at the first hut. I felt her eyes still follow me. I remembered myself as a child, and I wept as Lightsong made his way over ever steeper rock.

The sword began pulling me in one direction, drawing me into the mountains. Soon I had to dismount and lead Lightsong along. Higher I climbed until there was nothing but a sheer face of stone.

Rhet fell from its scabbard to the ground. Picking it up, my hands tingled. The sword vibrated so loudly, it sang. Looking at the rock more closely, I found five little holes that corresponded with the five gemstones in the hilt. I matched them up, and Rhet the Key slipped into place. Moving with the sweet music that now played gently inside my head, I twisted the sword until it was upright.

The stone slid aside, revealing a carved staircase going down. Leaving Lightsong outside, I made a torch from a bit of cloth and some nearby weeds and plunged into the darkness with Rhet in one hand and the torch in the other. At last I came to an open area with old torches on the wall.

When I lit them, the room glistened with gold and precious jewels. So blinded was I by the splendor reflecting in my visor that I took off my helmet and dropped it at my feet. Falling to my knees, I thrust my arms into the mounds and tossed them into the air. It rained pearls, sapphires, diamonds. Rubies like red flowers blossomed everywhere. The treasure of Queen Nor was mine.

The throne in the center was a giant gold lion, its mouth stretched wide was the chair, its pink tongue a velvet cushion. On the cushion was Queen Nor's crown, a small gold band with crests of gold and on each crest rode a diamond teardrop. Though tempted to place the crown on my own head, I didn't.

I was sitting in the mouth of the lion laughing, when I noticed a grayness dim the room.

"I will share with you, Jacob, if you will leave me in peace," I said.

Jackonan the Gray stood tall with the darkness he carried in him.

"I will take what I want, beggar. Though you call yourself a lady and a knight, Sorrel, you are only a beggar. You will forever huddle over firestones in some dark forest."

He won first blood, grazing me just above the left eye. Lightning quick, I sprang at him. Blade struck ax blade. Each time Rhet struck, a tone rang out. My full strength pushed Rhet on. Then I fell. A heavy blow of his ax crashed my breasts, and I collapsed backward. Dazed but unhurt, the armor held. Torn Gown had indeed made me strongest at the heart.

Laughing, he stood above me, ready to deliver the final blow. Rhet waited secure in my hand. I was not trembling. I was not afraid. If anything, I saw quite clearly for the first time.

His ax plummeted downward. I rolled, then thrust upward. Rhet found the opening at the neck and cut through.

Jackonan the Gray quivered for a moment, then fell dead. Blood splattered the pearls, dimmed the sapphires. I became aware of hushed voices, studying eyes. The entire village of Aor must have been there. Neara came to me and hugged me around the knee. I put Rhet down and picked her up.

The villagers knelt. Some shouted, "Hail, Queen Sorrel." I shook my head, carrying Neara to the lion throne. I placed the crown on the small curly head and shouted, "Long life, Queen Neara."

"For your kind hospitality, I give all of this and a new queen," I said. Picking up my helmet and sword, I made my way through them.

Hours later I rested alone on a hill above the village. Twilight was my friend and hid me while I watched their celebration unobserved.

Rustling dead leaves disrupted my surrender to silence, and Rhet slid out of its scabbard, ready.

"Hail, Sorrel de Martaine, Ladyknight," said a figure stepping into the moonlight. It was a knight in gold-colored armor bearing a shield, its only decoration a half moon.

"Who are you?" I asked.

Removing her helmet, straight jet hair fell out. Her skin shone yellow in the dim light. I had never seen anyone like her.

"My name is Half Moon. Torn Gown came to me in a dream and told me where to find you. She said you could use a friend."

I lowered my sword and took her hand in friendship. Together we watched the festivities below.

"Why did you give it all away?" she asked.

"I didn't want it. Funny, after all that work getting it, I didn't want it," I said.

"You didn't keep a few gems for yourself?"

"What about the crown?" she asked.

"Not a single stone," I said.

"I didn't want it."

"There is a legend that Queen Nor had another treasure even greater than gold and jewels."

"Really?" I smiled to myself.

"That's how the legend goes," she said.

The village below had quieted down and the morning star was rising.

"Shall we look for that treasure together?" I asked.

Half Moon nodded, and we rode off into the new morning on the best quest of all.

FESTIVAL NIGHT
by Harry Turtledove

I don't usually buy horror for these anthologies—but as I've said before and will say again, I will break all my own rules if the story grabs me. And I had a special reason—quite apart from the excellence of the story—for wanting to take this. To start with, it was a story with this title, "Festival Night," by somebody who, as far as I know, never wrote anything else in the field of fantasy, which made me realize that, in addition to having always wanted to write, I wanted to write *science fiction*; that the spaceship need not always be the hero, but there was room for human values; that story had, in the immortal words of Rick Sneary, "atmosphere in drab slabs."

Harry Turtledove seems to be quite a new writer, and a young one—compared to me, that is. But then everyone's young compared to me, except Lester Del Rey—but in two years, I am told, he has had no less than *seven* novels published. These include hard science fiction and fantasy. He's also had stories in magazines too numerous to mention; in every magazine I've ever heard of, and some I haven't. And now, from him, a horror story—but one of the old type of "strange and dreadful," not one of the "new horror" which says frankly "if you can't scare 'em, gross 'em out." That kind of horror leaves me speechless—only because I am too much of a lady to say what I really think—but for this kind, I have a great deal of admiration.

Festival time at Cathaly, the high point of the year. Merchants with gray beards and thick middles promenaded through the marketplace, calling to one another and doing their best to ignore the swaggering young bucks with whom they shared the square.

The young bucks, of course, ignored them quite without effort. They were watching each other, to see whose sleeves were puffed the fullest, whose doublet most elaborately ruffed and whose of the most eye-searing shade, whose mustaches came to the sharpest point, and whose rapier, whose hose were tightest, and whose codpiece bulged farthest.

In those spaces of time when they were not scrutinizing their competition, they devoted their attention to the reasons for the contest. For the maidens of Cathaly were in the square, too, having more freedom at festival than all through the rest of the year. In satins and velvets and bright silks, in silver and gold and precious stones, their eyes flashing or coyly lowered, they made a lovely spectacle. No wonder the young men watched them.

(So did the graybearded merchants, though their sons and grandsons might not have believed it. But then, they had been young once, and none of the young bucks had yet grown older. But this is not the tale of a merchant, and their sighs will go unheard forever.)

Only Ricold seemed above the game of seeing and being seen. Not only was he scion of house Botron, the grandest trading house of Cathaly, he was also judged the handsomest young man in the city, not least by himself. The combination was ominous, but Ricold could have been much worse than he was. The friends with whom he was drinking wine *were* his friends, mostly, not hangers-on sniffing round the scent of gold.

They were enjoying themselves, as anyone should at festival. They laughed and joked, flung ribald insults at passing members of rival houses, and had the courtesy to wince when, as sometimes happened, those jibes were fielded and hurled back. And whenever a pretty girl passed, they cast such sheep's eyes at her that after a while Taurizo, the real clown among them, slipped away and came back with a crook and a bell of the sort a wether might wear.

The crook he kept himself, using it to try to snare such lasses as pleased him. Had someone else acted so, it might have meant swords, but no one could take Taurizo seriously enough for anger. One or two maids let themselves be caught, and paid a kiss for their freedom.

"Bait your hook with a bonbon, or a ruby, and you'll have even better sport," Ricold said, grinning, which led to a round of suggestions, progressively randier ones, as to the best sort of lure to use.

"Here, I can top the lot," cried a sallow young man named Ermony.

"Ah, that'd be a change," Taurizo chuckled: Ermony was the shortest of them all, the top of his head barely coming to Ricold's chin. He was an appendage of the group rather than a member, clinging more from sheer persistence than for anything he brought with him. He was certainly not known for his wit.

Now, though, he stepped forward, took the wether's bell from Taurizo, and put it round Ricold's neck. "There!" he said. "Now he need only say 'Baa!' and the wenches will come trooping after him as he walks down the street."

Half the company, or a bit more, roared laughter with Ermony. The rest looked this way and that, waiting in some embarrassment to see what Ricold would do. The festival, after all, was one of increase.

Under the circumstances, his reaction was mild enough. He simply took off the bell, saying, "I am no wether, Ermony. I have a perfectly good pair of stones, the gods be praised."

But Dayne, who of the group was closest to Ricold, spat angrily on the ground to turn aside the omen. He grabbed the bell from his friend and threw it over the roof behind them all. Even before it came down with a clatter, he had seized Ermony by the front of his doublet and lifted him off the ground, hissing, "Do you aim to curse the whole city, lackwit, taking away a man's virility on this of all days?"

Ermony kicked and wriggled, to no avail. His face went purple-red, from effort, shame, and strangulation together. He stammered, "Please, Dayne, no! I meant no-nothing of the sort!"

"Let him go, Dayne!" several of the young men said. "He meant no harm."

With a contemptuous shake of his head, Dayne dropped Ermony like a sack of meal. "What a fool means and what he works too often are different things," he said darkly.

"Oh, away with such cobwebberies; today is too fine for them," Taurizo said. "Let's to more important matters—who'll pay me for my bell, as an instance." He stuck out his palm, like a banker dunning some luckless tradesman whose loan is overdue.

Despite his japes, though, some of the luster had gone out of the festival. Before long, Ricold made an excuse and left the group. Dayne followed, still grumbling at Ermony's bungling and muttering about the disasters it might bring.

At last Ricold had heard all of that he cared to. He said, "If I wanted to listen to carrion crows, I'd find a knacker's yard."

"Have your own way, then. You generally do," Dayne said. He could not resist a parting shot, "You would have done better with me, I fancy, than with anyone else you might find today." Still shaking his head, he spun on his heel and turned back toward the marketplace.

Ricold laughed and shook his own head; he was not looking for anyone. He ambled through the streets of Cathaly, buying a bowl of marinated chickpeas here, an iced sherbet there. Several young ladies, and one or two not so young, sent smiles toward him. He returned their smiles, having been trained by his father to politeness, but pursued none of them.

When dusk came, it took him by surprise. Away from the central square, Cathaly's streets grew narrow and wandered as drunkenly as the revelers who lurched along them. Although no more than mildly illuminated, Ricold, too, had let his feet take him where they would. He found himself in a part of the town he did not know well.

He shrugged. If he had to, he could eventually find his way back to the marketplace by walking in the direction of the loudest noise. He did not fear foot-pads, not with his rapier at his side.

Like any city ancient and famous, Cathaly had grown more by builders' whims than according to plan. No one thought a thing of finding a merchant's mansion and broad gardens in the middle of a row of little shops. Such was the dwelling Ricold came upon in his peregrinations.

Although he had not visited the place before, he recognized the crest over the gate: this was the center of house Caffilos. They were not great friends of house Botron, nor enemies either. The two scarcely impinged on each other. House Caffilos took its small, safe profit from trade in wine and woolen rugs, and left to Botron the risks—and the gains!—to be won from jewels and spices and silks.

The mansion gate was unlocked, as was fitting at festival time. Ricold caught himself in a yawn. The idea of making the long trip back to his own bedcham-ber made him sigh. "I'd sooner beg a pallet from Caffilos," he said aloud, and stepped through the gate.

The trees and shrubberies of the garden were hung with lanterns of every size and shape. As Ricold walked the winding path that led to the house, he thought he might have been transported to fairyland, so magically did their soft glow illuminate the scene.

Rude reality returned, however, when he saw the mansion without its screen of plants. The gray stone building was almost entirely dark; either the folk of Caffilos had already drunk themselves insensible or they were out celebrating elsewhere. When Ricold rapped on the front door, he heard a dog bark some-where deep in the bowls of the building, but no one came to see who was there.

He knocked again, louder, with no better luck. "A plague take the damned rug-peddlers," he muttered. He was decided to go first to the one ground-floor window he had seen with a light in it, to tell whomever he found there what he thought of house Caffilos' treatment of would-be guests.

His angry shout died in his throat when he looked in at the open window. It belonged to a bedroom; lying on the bed inside, fast asleep, was the most beautiful girl Ricold had ever seen. His body reacted before his mind could say him nay. He put his hands on the sill and vaulted up into the chamber.

Setting his feet as carefully as if he walked on soapbubbles, he moved to the side of the bed. There he stood in wondering silence, staring down at the sleeper on it. It was madness, it was folly. If the men of house Caffilos found him here, they could kill him on the spot, with no one to say they did not have the right. He did not care.

The girl was about sixteen, three years younger than Ricold. Relaxed in sleep, her face seemed younger still, but her body had ripened sweetly. She wore only a thin white shift against the mild air of summer. She lay on her back, very still, her breasts scarcely rising and falling as she breathed.

Afterward, Ricold was never sure how long the spell of her loveliness held him unmoving. It might have been only moments; surely it was not long enough for the little lamp on the table next to the bed to burn all its oil. Yet the blink of an eye would have sufficed to brand the vision of her forever on his memory.

One thing he did know: it was no sound or motion from him that caused her to open her eyes, for he made none. Perhaps, he thought later, she somehow sensed his longing even through sleep; it might have been thick as smoke in the small chamber.

When she did wake, her smile was like the coming of sunrise after blackest night. She stretched out a hand toward him, murmuring, "What a sweet dream you are."

Then her fingers brushed his sleeve, and she perceived the dream was real. Sudden fear filled her face; she opened her mouth to cry out. "I mean you no harm, my lady," Ricold said quickly, and to prove it stepped away from her bed, belike the hardest thing he had ever done.

"Who are you? How did you come here?" she demanded, at the same time tugging at her shift to save such modesty as she could.

He named himself, then said, "I came to curse

anyone of your house I could find for your lack of hospitality, but I discover I was mistaken." He watched, enchanted as a slow flush mounted from under her shift to her throat, her cheeks, her forehead. He asked, "Where are your kinsfolk, to leave you alone here, untended?"

"Oh, them." She made a face, waved a hand, much more at her ease now that she saw him possessed of manners. "Every other year we and house Aversa host each other at festival time. House Aversa," she said with the devastating certainty peculiar to maids of sixteen, "has the dullest people in the world in it, so I stayed behind with a book." It was on the bed beside her; until that instant Ricold had not noticed it.

"Ah," he said. He realized something more was needed, found it: "What's your name?"

"Ellene," she answered, and politely dipped her head; despite irregular circumstances, she managed a dignity of her own.

In reply, he swept off his splendid hat of maroon velvet with its pheasant-feather plume and bowed himself all but double. Then he strode forward so quickly Ellene gasped in fresh alarm. "What are you doing?" she cried, shrinking from him.

"Two things. One is this." He took her fright-cold hand, brushed it with his lips. He let it go at once, bowed again, even more deeply than before, and withdrew to the window.

"What is the other?" she asked faintly.

An elegant eyebrow lifted. "Why, marry you, of course." Ricold stepped down into the garden and was gone.

Festival in Cathaly made light of darkness. Ricold walked by diversions, passed up delights. After Ellene, for him they would have been as broken crockery after plate of gold.

He recalled the jibe Dayne had sent after him, and laughed until he had to lean against a fluted column for support. As an oracle, he thought, his gloomy friend would never make anyone forget the haruspices.

*   *   *

The next morning, he spoke with his father. Feature for feature, Rigobert, master of house Botron, closely resembled his eldest son; the weight of decision and responsibility, though, had given his face a heaviness, a watchfulness that made an observer discount his good looks, which no one ever did with Ricold.

Moreover, Rigobert had drunk a good deal too much wine at festival, and was feeling it. "Can it not wait?" he growled when Ricold plucked at his sleeve.

"No," his son said.

Rigobert grunted; he had cultivated that tone of voice to ward off the importunate, and prided himself on how well it served him. Against Ricold, till now, it had proven sovereign. Something new, then; the boy was turning into a man. "Well?" Rigobert said, not altogether displeased.

Ricold was still youth enough to plunge straight in without preamble: "I've found the woman I want to take to wife."

Rigobert opened his mouth, slowly closed it again. The boy was turning into a man, indeed. "Not so much as a by-your-leave, eh?" he said. "Come to the study, lad; you'll need to have more to say than that."

Having closed the shutters to ease his headache, Rigobert sank into a deep-cushioned leather chair, steepled his fingers, and directed his steady gaze at his son. "First things first. Is she with child?"

"No."

Rigobert did not show the relief he felt. No forced ceremony, then, or gold to pay, or, worst, feud begun. The matter was still under his control. "Who is she?" he asked, expecting Ricold to name some serving-wench or sausage-seller's daughter for whom he had conceived an infatuation, if nothing more.

But the boy, it seemed, was full of surprises. "Her name is Ellene, of house Caffilos."

"Beneath us," Rigobert said at once. But Ricold recognized it for automatic protest; house Botron acknowledged no equals in Cathaly. His father's next questions had more substance to them: "Is the lass willing? What of her parents? The head of the house?

'Of house Caffilos,' you say? How is she connected to the head?''

To all of those, Ricold had to reply that he did not know. "What, what do you know?" Rigobert exploded.

And so, awkwardly, Ricold explained how he had come to meet Ellene. The tale was flat in the telling; his tongue limped when he tried to describe what the sight of her had done to him. When Rigobert said only, "Lucky you weren't spitted there," he was certain he had made a botch of it.

His father, however, was still rubbing his chin in consideration. Ricold could make out some of his mumblings: "Not the worst house . . . a connection to give us influence where we had none . . . whole new area of trade . . ."

After a while, Rigobert emerged from his maze of calculations. "Well, I suppose it can do us no harm to sound out house Caffilos on the match."

"Father!" Ricold cried, and rushed over to hug him, something he had rarely done since his whiskers began to grow.

"Here, what's all this? I've made no promises," Rigobert said gruffly, but his hands, gentle on his son's back, told better than words how pleased he was.

"You didn't say no, either," Ricold said, and Rigobert had to laugh.

Being who he was, he soon turned practical once more. "First things first," he declared; it was a favorite saying of his. "Let's to the haruspices. If the omens are bad, Caffilos will dismiss any suit out of hand, as well they should."

However often it was sluiced down, the temple courtyard stank of old blood. At the arrival of such distinguished clients as the head of house Botron and his son, several haruspices in their scarlet robes came forward with greetings. Rigobert was brusque. "Take me to your chief." They scurried to do his bidding.

Hilarion, High Haruspex of Cathaly, acted to no man's bidding save his own. To his credit, Rigobert was wise enough to know it. He spoke with the prelate as he might have to a merchant prince from another city, setting forth what he required and asking what more Hilarion needed to learn.

"I know enough, I think," the High Haruspex replied, nodding once. His face was like those sometimes carved on old gems: all planes and angles, with no loose flesh anywhere, and a jutting nose like a galley's ram. "You will sacrifice a goose for this question, or perhaps a cat?"

Ricold gasped. "He's trying to offend us, son," Rigobert said calmly. "It's his manner, to save time in dealing with fools." He turned to Hilarion: "It will be an ox, as you very well know."

The High Haruspex summoned an assistant, ordered the sacrificial beast fetched to the altar. He led the men of house Botron thither. They waited in silence, for Hilarion had no small talk. Before long, the ox made its appearance, lowing and tossing its head so that its gilded horns gleamed in the sunlight.

A brighter flash came from the blade Hilarion unsheathed; it was honed to perfect sharpness. When he drew it across the ox's throat, the animal made no more than a puzzled gurgle before its legs failed and it toppled into the spreading pool of its own blood.

Hilarion stooped beside it. The knife, now smeared with red, cut again, opening the belly of the beast. The High Haruspex plunged both arms into the steaming body cavity. Blood dripped from his elbows as he drew out the liver. He rose and placed it on the altar for examination, while lesser haruspices began butchering the ox and clearing the courtyard of the traces of its death.

For long and long Hilarion stared at the soft, red-brown mass before him. He prodded it gently with his fingers, turned it to study its anterior surface. His hard face revealed nothing of what he thought.

"Sir?" Ricold said at last, unable to bear uncertainty any longer.

The High Haruspex's eyes were gray as flint. "Your marriage to Ellene of house Caffilos would serve both houses well. Nay more, your failure to marry her will bring ruin with it."

"Do you hear, father; do you hear?" Ricold burst out, fairly squeaking with excitement.

"He is not yet done," Rigobert said.

"I am not," Hilarion agreed. "There is one thing more: the marriage shall not take place."

Ricold gaped in dismay. His father's jaw set. "Its failure will do harm?" he asked. At Hilarion's nod, he declared, "Then it will not fail." His voice was harsh and firm as the High Haruspex's. He had been of two minds, but saying he could not bring the marriage to pass only raised the fighting spirit in him.

He bowed to Hilarion, stiffly, as a man might to an enemy before a duel. "Your fee will be paid, of course," he said. "Come, Ricold." Determination stiffened Rigobert's back as he stalked away. Ricold followed, doing his best to imitate his father's assurance, but he could not help glancing back over his shoulder at the High Haruspex.

Hilarion paid him no attention. Long after the two men of house Botron had gone, the High Haruspex stood behind the altar, still studying the liver there even after the blood oozing from it had begun to turn black. His underlings wondered at the expression on his stony face. They could put no name to it, but had they seen it on anyone else they would unhesitatingly have called it fear.

After Hilarion's grim augury, Ricold was certain the negotiations with house Caffilos would prove fruitless. Instead, they advanced with a speed and ease that left him breathless. Ironic amusement glinting in his eyes, Rigobert said, "Fat old Famagost is all but panting to meet you."

"To meet me?" Ricold echoed, astonished. "Already? Why?" In Cathaly, the meeting of the groom with the head of his prospective bride's house normally signaled approval of the match.

"Why not?" his father replied. "We've settled the dowry and the other arrangements, so it's time he had a look at you. No doubt he wants to see what his favorite granddaughter's getting."

"Er, yes." Ellene's place in house Caffilos still sent thrills of wonder through Ricold.

This time there were guards at the gate of the Caffilos mansion, but they swung up their swords in salute and stood aside to let Ricold pass. One ran ahead to announce his coming to Famagost. He took the winding garden path slowly; he had, after all, never walked it in daylight before.

When he came in sight of the mansion itself, he was amazed to see women's faces in half the windows. Many of the women ducked out of sight the moment he appeared. He heard their giggles as he approached, and felt his ears grow hot. He did not see Ellene. He would have picked her in an instant from a crowd of thousands, of that he was sure.

No need now to rap on the door; it was open, waiting for him. The chamber to which a steward led him was comfortably furnished, if not so lavishly as it would have been at house Botron. The sweetmeats he was offered conformed to the same pattern: good, but not of the very best. The wine, however, was excellent.

No sooner had the steward carried away his empty goblet and the plate of sweetmeats than Famagost came in. As Rigobert had said, he was fat and old, with a bald crown and a bushy beard going white. He wheezed when he walked and came up panting from his bow to Ricold.

"Well, well, young sir," he said, settling with relief into an overstuffed chair, "you know you've sent all the womenfolk of my house into a tizzy."

"I saw them peering out at me when I arrived, your honor," Ricold agreed in some puzzlement, "but why?"

Famagost laughed till he coughed, turning alarmingly red in the process. "Why, you ask? Lad, the poor dears have been raised on romances since the day they began to crawl, but how much of such things is any one of 'em likely to see? Precious little, more's the pity. And then in you sweep like a lover from a troubadour's song. Is it any wonder the lot of 'em are grass-green jealous of Ellene?"

"I never thought of that," Ricold whispered.

"I know you didn't, young sir, indeed I do—were

there thought in it, it wouldn't be romance, am I right? Don't worry your head. They're happy for her, too; that she's of the house casts a reflected glow on them, don't you see? . . . So. Your father and I have dickered until we're sick of each other. I thought it was time to count your teeth instead. Come here to me, boy; let me look you over."

Famagost poked and prodded as if Ricold truly were a horse up for sale, watching his face all the while. The old man's eyes were tracked with veins, but gleamed disconcertingly keen from under tangled brows. By what standard he was judging, Ricold had no idea, but at length he said, "You'll do, lad; you'll do."

"Do you mean yes, then?" Ricold breathed.

"I just said so. Didn't you hear me?" Famagost chuckled at the expression on Ricold's face. "Here, save your great foolish grin a moment." He rose, puffing, and went to the door. This he opened, bawling, "Ellene! Where have you gotten to, confound it? Come tell this lovesick lackwit whether you intend to make his life miserable the next forty years!"

"Oh, hush, grandfather," she said fondly as she stepped into the chamber; she had, of course, been waiting in the hall all this while.

She was as lovely as Ricold remembered, although when he thought of her he would always see her first in his mind's eye as she had been there in her bedroom on festival night. She dipped in a curtsy, her long skirts rustling. Ricold surprised himself by how steadily the formal words came out: "Is it your will, my lady Ellene, to join with me in marriage?"

"It is," she answered, her eyes cast down. Then she raised her head, and he saw the spark of mischief in them: "For, sir my husband to be, is it not already proven nothing will keep you from my chamber?"

As Ricold blushed furiously, a beaming Famagost said, "Now, the wedding date." He sounded quite pleased with himself, and why not? The trout was hooked.

"I have in mind the perfect one," Ellene said. "What could be better than festival day, the anniversary of our meeting?"

"The very thing!" Famagost exclaimed.

"But—" Ricold began. It was still most of a year to the next festival.

Famagost understood him perfectly. "Patience, my lad, is a virtue, or do you doubt it?" And then, with real sympathy, he patted Ricold on the shoulder, adding, "The day will come round sooner than you think, I promise you. You are young yet; you can afford to wait."

Hilarion's flat forbidding of even the possibility of marriage surfaced for a moment in Ricold's mind, but he could do nothing save nod.

As the months went by, Ricold came to judge Famagost a better prophet than the High Haruspex. Only now and again, when he happened to spy Hilarion treading his unyielding path through the city, did he remember his doubts. But Hilarion never so much as glanced his way, and it was easy to dismiss the forebodings the sight of that gaunt, angular countenance raised.

The unstinting hospitality of house Caffilos also helped lay them to rest. For the family was delighted in the catch Ellene had made, and determined to make him welcome whenever he visited his betrothed, which he did as often as he could. He found himself compelled to let out first one pair of tights, then several, because of the way they heaped his trencher when he sat at meats with them.

At each visit, he came to esteem Ellene the more. Not only was she beautiful, but possessed of a hard common sense invaluable in the women of a merchant house. Lest it grow too severe, however, it was tempered by the playful wit she had displayed to his embarrassment when she consented to be his wife. In short, he found himself altogether captivated, and happily so.

Seeing that, Famagost and the other elders of house Caffilos smiled to one another in satisfaction over the young couple's heads. No danger here of the engagement failing. And so, little by little, as Ricold's visits became an accepted part of life, the strict chaperonage with which they had begun gradually ebbed, and he and Ellene even began to find themselves alone together.

As would have been true of any boy of nineteen, he soon sought out the taste of her lips, and reckoned the wines of house Caffilos as vinegar beside them. As would also have been true of any boy of nineteen, he soon sought out more than her lips alone. But there, to his disappointed surprise, he found himself balked.

It was not that Ellene was less drawn toward him than he to her. On the contrary; their kisses left both of them alike dizzy with longing. But she had been taught from girlhood to preserve her maidenhead. And so, when his hand moved to the rounded softness of her breast, she pulled away, saying "Gladly I will give myself to you on our wedding night, but not before."

"What difference can it make, when the marriage is certain?" Ricold asked a trifle sulkily.

"If nothing else, then this: I have no intention of entering the temple with my gown tight against a bulging belly, and hearing the dowagers of your house snigger at me." She touched his arm, concern on her face. "Dear Ricold, surely you cannot doubt my love for you?"

"No," he said. It was the truth, and it did not help.

Still and all, most times he was happy enough for three men. Whenever he saw Dayne (less often than he had, before he met Ellene), he teased his friend over the festival night gone by. Being an even-tempered young man, Dayne took it well. "I'm pleased for your good fortune," he would say.

He had the grippe, though, the day he was to meet Ellene.

But half Cathaly had the grippe that winter; the old men said it was the worst they could remember. Of course, they said that one winter in three. And spring, when it finally came, drove out all memory of cold and damp. Never had the jasmine bloomed so fragrant by night; never had the nightingale sung so sweetly. A lovers' spring, people called it.

As the snows melted in the streets under the cheery warmth of the sun, Ellene's resistance to Ricold's importuning also faded, albeit more slowly. Even if passion did betray her, she told herself, the fruit of it would hardly be so obvious by festival time as to embarrass her. Yet somehow, oddly, knowing she might slip with relative safety kept the slip from happening: looking forward to later pleasure became pleasure in itself.

So matters progressed, while spring grew into summer and festival time drew near. In the month before it, Ricold and Ellene saw less of each other than they liked; both were caught up in their families' plans for the wedding. There were silks to be chosen, and groomsmen, and rare wines, and a thousand other things. Had Ricold known the preparations were so elaborate, he told himself, he might have chosen a tavern-wench after all. He laughed at the lie; he wanted no one but Ellene.

Three days before the festival, he contrived to see her. Both of them, by then, were aglow with anticipation. Ellene sat in an overstuffed armchair, chattering on about the wedding. A cup of wine next to him, Ricold lounged on a couch nearby, listening, watching her. They were the only two people in the little anteroom. The door to the hallway was closed.

"Here I've been doing all the talking," Ellene said after some small time had gone by. She made a face at Ricold. "What have you to say for yourself?"

He did not answer, not in words. Instead he rose, and in two quick strides came to stand before her. She looked up at him, in her eyes part question, part certainty of what he would do. Her mouth was waiting when he bent to her.

The kiss went on and on, like none of those that had gone before. When at last he drew away, her lips stayed parted, awaiting his return. Her eyelids fluttered halfway closed; her breath came quick and short.

He went down to one knee beside her, kissed her again. His mouth wandered to her ear, to her white neck. She sighed once, and shivered, though the room was warm.

She sighed again when his lips found hers once more. One of his hands was beneath her skirts. The silken hose she wore were of finer weave than a man's. Under them, the flesh of her thigh was soft, smooth, firm.

Then her own hand pressed on his, kept it from advancing farther. With a little moan, she twisted away from him, stumbling toward the door. Clumsily, he got to his feet and started after her.

"No," she said, her back to him. The word was all breath and no voice.

He took one more step, then sat down, hard, on the edge of the carven walnut table in front of the couch where he had been reclining. He buried his head in his hands. "Why not now? What difference could it possibly make now?"

She turned toward him. "You know how much I want you." He could see that; she was shaking with it, as was he. But her arms were outstretched, pleading with him to understand. "We've come this far. Why make a mock of our wedding night, with it so close? Is three days so long to wait?"

It seemed an eternity. "No," however, was the only thing Ricold could say, and he said it.

He hated the way she flinched from him when he approached her, and cursed himself for a heartless brute. Setting his hands on her shoulders, he gave her a chaste kiss in the center of her forehead. Her skin felt warm to his lips.

"Are you well?" he asked, concern at once banishing lust.

"Of course I am." She laughed at him, her eyes bright. "You'd best go now, I think. Who knows how late it is?"

When he returned the next morning, he brought a ruby pin for her wedding gown. He did not see her, though; one of her maids told him she had a touch of the fever, "nothing to worry your head about, dear," and urged him to come back that night.

He did, just as a physician was leaving the grounds of house Caffilos. The man would not say much, but he looked worried.

The next day it was not one physician there, but four. They would not let Ricold near Ellene's chamber.

"The illness is catching, you know," one of them said sternly.

"Of course I know," he raged. "If she dies, do you think I want to live?" But they would not listen, and in the end held him away by main force.

Ellene died not long after sunset.

On what was to have been his wedding day, Ricold had to endure the torture of Cathaly at festival. He had spent the night mourning with Famagost and the rest of house Caffilos, while messengers raced through the city to let all the invited guests know there would be no marriage, and while the undertakers bore his beloved away to a cold marble tomb in the family necropolis outside the town.

Then he had to return to his own home, through streets already full of jolly celebrants. Their songs, their laughter flayed him at every step. The sympathy of his kinsfolk was more than he could bear; he sought the shelter of his own room, as a wounded animal will lay up alone in its den. There he stayed, neither eating nor drinking, while the sun crawled across the sky.

The shadows of evening were growing loud when the knock came upon his door. At first it did not penetrate his grief. When he finally heard it, he set his teeth and ignored it. But it went on and on, even after he roused himself to cry, "Leave me!" Whoever was knocking owned endless patience.

With a curse, Ricold got up from his bed and flung the door wide. "Thank you," Dayne said, as if he had not been standing there a quarter of an hour. He stepped past Ricold, shut the door behind him.

Ricold stared at his friend with something approaching hatred. "Are you come to gloat, then?" he snarled. "In the end, I would have done better with you festival night a year ago. You had the right of it after all—and damn you for it!"

"When have I ever wished you ill?" From most men, such a question shouts a warning to beware the knife. Dayne meant it as he asked it, and waited for an answer.

"You have not," Ricold admitted, unwilling. He did

not think to pray pardon, and Dayne did not expect it of him. It was enough that he said, "Why are you here?"

"First, to share your sorrow, as much as anyone can," Dayne said. Ricold bowed his head. His friend went on, "And second, to ask you to keep festival with me."

This time, Ricold's stare was of astonishment. "Keep festival? Are you mad?"

"No. Hear me: she is dead. Not all your lamenting, not all your tears will bring her back. Come with me into the city. I will drink with you until oblivion takes you, too, for a little while. Let the wine blunt the edges of your grief and help you begin to forget, as you must to go on living."

"Forget?" Ricold said. "Never, by the gods; I will spend my life remembering. Even now, I can see my Ellene as she was when first I set eyes on her, how she lay, how the lamp glowed on her face." He had to stop then, for fresh weeping choked him, but he finished in a whisper, "She will live within me so forever."

"Think twice," Dayne urged. Ricold shook his head. Sighing, Dayne said, "Perhaps later this evening you will change your mind. You will find me then at the tavern called Lion's Brew. The gods grant we meet there." He sketched a bow, made as if to clasp Ricold's hand. When his friend did not reach out to him, he sighed again and left.

Ricold sat, looking at the blank wall opposite him, until the night grew too black to let him see it any more. When he stood, his joints creaked in protest at being made to move after so long a stillness. The hateful sounds of festival dinned in his ears as he walked through the halls of house Botron's stronghold.

He met his father just as he was about to leave the building for the streets of Cathaly. "Where are you going?" Rigobert asked, more sharply than he had intended. Something in his son's eyes chilled him; even when they swung toward him, they seemed focused on a point two feet behind his head.

But Ricold answered readily enough: "To drink with Dayne, and take what forgetfulness I can find."

Rigobert nodded and let him by. Dayne was a good lad; he knew what was needed.

The tavern called Lion's Brew was not far from the marketplace. To reach it, from the stronghold of house Botron, one bore left on coming to Stonecutters' Street. Ricold paused for a moment, then turned with firm decision to the right.

His step quickened as the city wall drew near. On festival night, with Cathaly at peace with its neighbors, all the gates were wide. People came in, people went out. Many of those leaving were couples, seeking privacy and soft grass; their happiness only hurt Ricold the more. The guards, passing a wineskin back and forth, paid no attention as he walked out into the darkness.

The dead of Cathaly dwelt outside the city, by the edges of the roads. Some graves had no mark to show what they were. A stone topped others, or a board with a few scrawled lines, maybe now too weathered to read even by daylight, telling who the deceased had been.

The tombs of the merchant houses were grander. Bronze and marble commemorated their dead. Some rested beneath statues grander than half those in Cathaly's marketplace. Others slept their eternal sleep in vaults of stone modeled after the mansions where they had lived.

House Caffilos followed the latter custom. Half a mile outside Cathaly, a veritable village of tombs sprang up. The outlines of the older ones were softened by years of rain and snow and heat, but not so much that they did not show Ricold the different façade the stronghold had once worn. The more recent monuments faithfully depicted the building he had come to know as well as his own. A few were unfinished, empty; in the moonlight their doorways gaped like black mouths, waiting to swallow down a corpse and shut forever.

Ricold ignored the uncompleted tombs. He went from one closed monument to another. At last he found the one where a glow showed in the crack between door and crypt: the two-day memorial candle, left behind by the undertakers with Ellene's body. Vents in the tomb ceiling kept it from smothering. Such a candle would also burn in the parlor of families who buried their dead in simple graves, to light the path of the departed to the next world.

"Let me look on her, at least, one last time," Ricold said aloud, though there was no one to hear him. The lock holding the bar in place was strong, but it did not stand up under his assault. With a squeal of abused metal, it broke in pieces. He drew out the bar, set it down, opened the door. Silent on newly oiled hinges, it swung shut behind him as he stepped into the vault.

As far as such things are possible, death had been kind to Ellene. Clad in her white linen grave raiment, she lay on her back on the marble bier as if asleep. The orange, flickering light of the memorial candle lent her still face color and a sense of motion, however lying.

Remembering her first words to him, Ricold murmured through his tears, "What a sweet dream you were."

And that one memory, once released, brought all the rest in its wake. He gasped to realize how closely the inside of the tomb echoed the arrangement of her bedroom that magic night a year ago. The position of the bier, her placement on it, even the color and drape of the cloth around her and the angle of the light, all of them conspired to reproduce the most exciting single moment of his life. He realized that, and was undone.

Moving as if caught up in a dream himself, or in a nightmare, he stepped toward the bier. His second gasp, moments later, sounded altogether different from the one that had gone before.

For some time, Dayne stayed sober in the tavern called Lion's Brew, waiting for Ricold. Stolidly he endured Taurizo's jeers and the incredulity of the rest of the youths they ran with. After a while, though, he knew his friend would not come. And not to drink in a tavern on festival night proved in the long run impossible. Having started late, he perforce swilled harder to catch up with his comrades. The potent wine, drunk swiftly, went straight to his head. Before long, he was drunk asleep, slumped over a tabletop, his hand loose round the stem of his goblet.

It must have been close to midnight when he sat bolt upright, his eyes wide and blindly staring, a cry of incoherent terror on his lips.

Taurizo laughed. "Behold the evil of drink," he declared to those of his friends who still kept their senses. "Tell us, Dayne, what you fancied you saw— purple spiders, perhaps, or lizards with the face of Hilarion? There would be demons to fly from!"

But Dayne only looked about in confusion before his eyes rolled up in his head and he slid back into unconsciousness.

In another part of Cathaly, Hilarion also sprang from sleep. Ever abstemious, the High Haruspex took no part in the revels that swept over the rest of the city. And since his wits were not fuddled with the grape, he remembered all too well the vision he had seen.

Regret penetrated even the granite fastnesses of his will. His family had given Cathaly haruspices for generations uncounted. It was bitter to know he would be the last.

Tomorrow, he told himself, he would have to begin making ready to leave. Nodding to make sure he would not forget, he went back to bed.

Festival still clamored in Cathaly when Ricold passed through the gates again. Most folk, by then, were intent on their own pleasure, and had no time to spare for him. Those who did recognize him murmured in sympathy at his misfortune, and took no offense when he did not reply.

When he reached the stronghold of house Botron, he found his father waiting for him where they had parted earlier in the evening. Rigobert eyed him keenly. "You did not go drinking with Dayne."

"No, sir."

Pity pierced Rigobert as he pictured his son wandering aimless and sorrowing through the glad streets. He clasped Ricold in a strong embrace. "Oh, lad, lad, it will get better. Time will make it so."

"No, only worse," Ricold said, shuddering, with such certainty in his voice that Rigobert almost recoiled from him.

Then the master of house Botron recalled his son's circumstances. "When did you last sleep?" he asked.

"Sleep?" Ricold echoed vaguely. It had not been this night, or the one before, and hardly the one before that.

"Come, son." Guiding Ricold by the elbow, Rigobert led him to his chamber, laid him in his bed as if he were a child of three. Ricold plunged headlong into welcome nothingness before his father had left the room.

He had to be roused almost forcibly the next afternoon to attend the memorial service at Ellene's tomb. No one remarked on how readily he found the proper monument among the many in the necropolis of house Caffilos. Along with the rest of the mourners, he poured his libation in front of the tomb, cut off a lock of his hair and left it there.

In the days that followed, Rigobert sought to draw him from his grief by forcing him to take a greater part in the affairs of house Botron. At first, as was only natural, he performed dully and without much skill, for his heart and spirit were far from the work. But as days became weeks and weeks months, he did better.

As his father had planned, the demanding tasks kept him too busy to drown himself in sorrow. More and more often, he found himself speaking with animation over a complicated piece of business, smiling, once laughing. Rigobert, who heard, went off with a smile on his own face.

Then the dreams began.

At first he did not remember them on waking. That was in a way merciful, for he would rouse shaking, sweating cold. He did not, he would not, think on why dread came visiting.

After the memorial service, he never visited Ellene's grave, as a moody young lover might have been expected to do. Rigobert noticed—he was not a man to miss much—but said nothing, reckoning it a good sign.

Wine held the evil dreams at bay for a time. One snowy winter afternoon, Ricold remarked on its sovereign property. Suiting action to word, he took a long pull at his mug. It held steaming spiced wine, mulled with a red-hot poker, the very thing for such a day. His friends, seated like him close to the taproom fire, nodded in agreement with him.

"Oh, indeed, I too drink to forget," Taurizo said, "but I never forget to drink." He drained his own mug and shouted to a barmaid for more.

"On festival night—" Dayne began. Ricold's head whipped round sharply, but the rest of their comrades jeered Dayne down: "On festival night, you were lucky to remember to breathe!" "You were nothing but a great sponge with eyes!" "You drank enough to make an amethyst tipsy!"

Laughing, a bit shamefaced, Dayne threw up his hands in surrender. The talk drifted elsewhere. Ricold tried to steer it back, but his friend said, "Truly, I do not recall. Some nightmare from too much wine, no doubt."

"No doubt," Ricold said, lacking the temerity to press further.

As winter wore on, his own tippling no longer served to shield him from his dreams. He would wake at midnight with a scream, eyes full of horror in the dark. And yet the dreams, what he remembered of them, were innocuous enough, even amusing, in a way, in their irrelevance. Most had to do with sowing a crop; regardless of whether or not snow lay on the ground, as a merchant's son he hardly knew one end of the plow from the other.

He bore the nightmares as long as he could. But after a dose of poppy-juice failed to give him rest, he took himself to Hilarion, in search of whatever relief the High Haruspex might offer.

As had happened before, he spoke first with the lesser haruspices in the temple forecourt. When he asked for Hilarion, they looked at him oddly. "Did you not know?" said one. "Just last week he sold all he owned and set out for Gosra, far to the southeast, there to live out his days. Already we are working toward the election of the next High Haruspex."

At that news, Ricold sagged like a man taking a mortal wound. "May we not be of assistance?" asked the haruspex who had told him of Hilarion.

"It's of no consequence," Ricold said, and left. He might have fled Cathaly himself, but he did not think running would save him.

Rain began falling from the sky more often than snow; the sun sometimes peeked from behind its veil of clouds. Ricold's dreams shifted their pattern. Though they retained their agricultural theme, they came to deal now with harvest.

There was one other change. He no longer woke screaming in the night. His fright was too great for that.

As spring took hold, he began to hear a voice in his dreams, a voice that gave him orders as an overseer commands field-slaves. On the one hand, he dared not disobey. On the other, he could not understand what it said. He thought that was worst of all, until it occurred to him that one day he might.

He went back to the poppy then, a triple dose that brought him unconsciousness, aye, but for two days and two nights. When at last he woke, he found his father bending over him. "No more of that, son," Rigobert said, concern on his face. "What makes you seek to fly so from life?"

"Bad dreams," was all Ricold could say. He knew it was no fit answer, but he had none better to give.

After that, he drank no more poppy-juice, or wine either, but enjoyed a respite from his nightmares nonetheless. A week went by, a week when he plunged as never before into the work his father set him. Still, he was not too busy to see how fine a spring it had become: almost one to match the previous year's, when he had been courting Ellene. In the midst of flourishing greenery, a tiny sprig of hope blossomed in his heart.

But then the dreams returned, and the voice, and at

last he heard it clear. "Go," it said: "Go to Ellene's grave and open it."

Of everything it might have said, that he dreaded most. He lay shivering in his bed, waiting for the dawn; not the voice, not anything, could have forced him to stir by night. At first light he rose, hurrying from the stronghold of house Botron before anyone else was up and about to ask him where he was bound.

He had nearly reached the gate when he heard his name called. His blood froze, but it was not the nightmare voice; it was Dayne, several blocks behind him. "Because you were right, my friend," Ricold said, sobbing, "for your sake I go now to prove it without you." He trotted on, not looking back or waiting for Dayne to catch up. Dayne also broke into a lope.

Though he had not visited the necropolis for nine months, Ricold would have known which crypt he sought had he been away nine years, or ninety. He stood a moment before it, as he had once before Ellene's lighted window.

The voice spoke again, from within the tomb: "Open, and behold the child you have begotten."

The bar, that accursed bar, came away easily when Ricold wished with all his heart for it to stick fast. He opened the door, peered inward. In the bright, prosy sunshine of early morning, he could make out nothing inside the vault.

Out flew a head, grinning and hideous. Black batwings flapped where ears should have grown. It hovered in front of Ricold, smiling at him with terrible glee. "Well, father, are you not proud of your newborn?" it cackled.

But Ricold made no answer. He would never make answer again. Eyes wide and staring, mind behind them burst from horror, he stumbled backward until he fetched up against another monument. Then his legs gave way as well, and he slid slowly to the ground. A line of spittle ran from his slack lips down his chin.

With a ghastly chuckle, the head soared on high. The first to see it was Dayne, still in dogged pursuit of his friend. It spied him, too, and stooped like a screaming hawk.

Dayne proved himself made of stern stuff. His lips were white, but he drew his sword and cut at the monster descending on him. Yet his courage availed him nothing, for with a flick of its wings it evaded his stroke. It struck him square in the center of his forehead. The sword flew from his fingers as he toppled. The head, quite unharmed, rose into the sky again and streaked toward Cathaly.

It coursed over the city the whole day long, shrieking the tale of how it came to be. Along with the rest of Cathaly, Famagost heard, and Rigobert. The lord of house Caffilos, driven near mad with grief and rage, gathered his minions and those houses that responded to his call and hurled them against house Botron. Rigobert was shamed and sickened, but fought back, along with the houses that held to Botron despite abomination. The streets of the city ran with blood.

Above all flew the head, laughing, laughing.

Civil war still raged when a great earthquake smote the city and all the land around. Buildings and wall alike crashed in ruin, crushing combatants beneath them. When the trembling stopped, not a stone of Cathaly was left atop another, nor a soul alive. Well-pleased, the hideous head took wing, whither no man knows, nor wishes ever to learn.

Hilarion? He died old.

KAYLI'S QUEST
by Paula Helm Murray

Paula Helm Murray is a good example of what I mean when I saw I'll break any or all of my rules—if the story is good enough. As a rule, I only have to see the word *dragon* anywhere in a story to reach for a handy rejection slip; but Paula Helm Murray made her first bow in SWORD AND SORCERESS IV with the very well received "Kayli's Fire" which starred a young sorceress—well, fire-wizard—and her dragon. And this was of the same kind; which I felt would go very well in this anthology.

Ms. Murray has also written a story which appeared in the first issue of Marion Zimmer Bradley's Fantasy Magazine; which is an unabashed plug. You won't find the magazine on the stands, but only in fantasy bookstores (or you can get subscription information from MZB Enterprises, Box 72, Berkeley, CA 94701). If you like this story, everybody, rush right out and buy the magazine. It contains work by many of the young writers who are appearing in SWORD AND SORCERESS—which is what an editor always wants.

Paula Helm Murray lives in Prairie Village, Kansas, and is currently working on a book series (as she says, "Isn't everybody?") has been a member of fandom for ten years, and was perennial ConSuite Mommy at conventions. She also has the three "mewses" which I presume are cats, but could, for all I really know, be ferrets—or alligators. One man's nightmare is another's cherished pet—some people even keep rats and mice—which would have given my mother instant cardiac arrest. To each his own taste, as the old lady said when she kissed her cow.

———

Kayli drowsed in the lazy summer sun, soaking up the warmth as she watched her sheep on the hilly meadows above her castle.

Something dark passed overhead briefly, blocking the sun. *Too dark for a cloud,* she thought, opening her eyes slightly, *looks like smoke.* How odd! She sat up and looked around, wondering where it came from.

The sheep grazed close by, white-gray clouds on the emerald grass. Fyl, her dragonet, had given up on hunting field mice. He lay, sprawled with a total absence of dignity, dozing on one of the large boulders that dotted the meadows; his silvery scales glittered in the sun as he breathed.

The sound of horses' hooves roused Kayli completely in time for her to see someone gallop through her flock, scattering the sheep in a panic.

"Hey, stop that!" she yelled, standing, then realized she didn't recognize the rider. She winced as he jerked hard at the horse's mouth to wheel it around.

That he rode a horse, not one of the shaggy local ponies, told Kayli he couldn't be from her village. A bandit? she wondered. Many men wandered the hills, scattered after a war waged and won by a Western king two months before. For the most part, they posed no threat to folk willing to defend themselves.

Kayli grew angry as the sheep scattered, some out of sight. Then she saw a lamb lying limp where he had passed.

"Don't try that again!" she shouted. Even from where she stood, the lamb looked dead.

He pulled his horse up sharply, making it rear a little. He grinned evilly as he looked her over. "Told me a woman tended the sheep alone up here. You're white-haired, but you'll do."

That does that, Kayli thought, losing her temper. She began to gesture as he goaded his horse to come back toward her. She made certain no sheep, save the hurt lamb, were near, and completed her spell.

A flashy, noisy fireball exploded in front of the horse; Kayli had chosen a spell to scare, not to hurt. The horse squealed, reared, threw its rider and galloped off in the opposite direction.

Fyl slid off his rock in a heap, off-balance and surprised awake by the commotion.

The rider stood and drew his sword. "Blasted peasants!" he growled. "Didn't tell me you were a wizard!" He advanced on Kayli, sword raised.

Kayli glared at him. "Begone," she said sternly, "or I SHALL hurt you." He didn't stop.

He kicked the obviously dead lamb aside as he approached. The gesture infuriated Kayli. As she prepared another fireball, Fyl slipped around behind the man to help in the fray.

Kayli cast a small, hot fireball that exploded in front of the man's face. His shirt burst into flames. He shrieked, dropped his sword, and wheeled just in time to trip and fall face down on the grass over Fyl. As he looked up, stunned, the dragonet bit him several times, then worked himself up to blasting the man right in the face with a small fireball.

The man, face blackened with soot, hair smoking, scrambled up and fled, screaming, back down the hill. Kayli's anger evaporated into laughter as he disappeared.

Fyl trotted up to Kayli. "Scared him off, we did," he said proudly, in his small, squeaky voice. He slithered gracefully up to sit on her shoulder, bracing himself by winding his long, lithe tail around her arm several times. Wisps of smoke still trailed from his nostrils. He turned to look at her, nose to nose, with amber eyes that matched her own. "Good job, ma!"

A sudden fear came to Kayli. "The village!" she said.

"What's wrong, ma?" Fyl asked, "You look worried. Shouldn't be, sounds as if THEY told him you were alone up here."

"Down, Fyl," Kayli said, stooping to let him jump off. "No matter what, I'm their . . . protector." She shouldered her carry bag and picked up her staff. "That peddler who came through last week, he said a gang of bandits had leveled and looted a village near here not too long ago. Oh, Fyl, I hope nothing has happened to them!"

"What can I do, Kay?" he asked, sitting up properly.

"You watch the sheep," she said. "The wolves have been so bad, I dare not leave them alone. If it gets to dusk and I'm not back, head them back to their pen. I know you cannot manage the gate, but I do not think the wolves will come inside the walls. You be careful, little one." She leaned over and lightly kissed his upraised muzzle.

She looked around. The sheep had clumped together again, grazing as if nothing had happened. The horse, a bay mare, walked up to her timidly. *Probably trained to return if the rider falls off,* she thought. She lay her staff aside. *May as well ride, much faster.*

Before she mounted, she unfastened the stirrup leathers, let the steel stirrups drop, careful not to touch them, and refastened the leathers so she could use the loop as a stirrup. Due to her nature, iron and steel burned her flesh, and she wore no shoes in the summertime.

Kayli mounted up carefully, unused to riding, though she knew how.

"You be careful, too, ma." Fyl went back to his rock. Kayli gently turned the mare down the path that led to her castle, over the bridge and into the village.

She paused at her castle, noted her smashed-open front door, then turned the mare and urged her into a trot across the stones of the bridge.

Disaster confronted her. All the cottages had been damaged in some way. Two still smoldered, mostly burned down, and smoke came from the granary. The villagers huddled together in the small square. The still body of the man she'd driven away lay on the ground behind them.

"What happened?" she asked.

The village headman came forward, clutching his cap nervously. "My lady . . ." he started, "he attacked us. Attacked us all, like a madman.

Most of the men still held staffs and hoes. The dead man looked as if he had taken quite a beating. The headman had one eye swollen and blackened, as well.

Kayli dismounted. "Bedaru, are you all right?" He looked quite unsteady. She looked around. "Is anyone hurt?"

Zoe, the headman's wife, came up to Kayli. "My lady, we are all right . . ." she paused, looking around nervously.

"What is this 'my lady'?" Kayli asked, with mock seriousness, "I have never been 'my lady' to any of you before. I asked if anyone was hurt." She looked Bedaru over, lightly touching the blackened eye. "This just wants a cold compress."

"We were afraid for you," Zoe said quietly, timidly. "Dal told that man you were up there alone. I think he did it out of spite."

Dal, Zoe and Bedaru's oldest son, had tried often to court Kayli, despite her lack of interest. "I have come to no harm," Kayli replied, "and I have promised I would never use my talent against any of you. You know that. What else is wrong?"

"They took Sylva," Zoe said, "and . . . oh, Kayli, it is just too horrible!" Tears started down her cheeks.

Kayli went to her and hugged her. Sylva was Zoe's oldest daughter, only a little younger than herself, and their pride and joy. She sensed Zoe's grief.

"Then she is dead?" Kayli asked quietly, looking down at the silver-haired, plump older woman.

"Worse than that," Bedaru said grimly, "they took her East, into the Borderlands. Goddess knows what will become of her there."

Kayli stood silent. This side of the river was safe to these people. The far side, closer to the magical East, started the Borderlands. Magic, for the most part, scared them almost witless.

Dal emerged from behind one of the ruined cottages. "I . . . I apologize, lady," he said, looking down. "Could have gotten you raped, or hurt."

"Well, you didn't," Kayli replied sharply, "but I do not think better of you for what you did."

Kayli turned and started to get back on the mare, to go and see what damage had been wreaked on her own household.

"Wait, Kayli . . ." Bedaru asked hesitantly.

"Yes?" She turned and looked them over again."

"So what are you going to do about Sylva?" he asked, more firmly.

"If I go after them, will someone look after my sheep?" Kayli asked. *Wonder what disaster will come to me,* she thought. *Last time I tried to save someone . . .*

*saved someone, Ylgs, my old bridge dragon, was killed.
And if Ylgs still lived, we might not have bandit trouble.*
She sighed quietly.

"I will," Dal volunteered, "only promise to take
your dragonet with you. Please?" His pleading tone
caused the other men to snicker.

"All right. But, begging your pardon, why?" His
request puzzled her a little.

Dal looked around, blushing deeply. "He doesn't
like me. He's always hot-footing me or hot . . ." The
men started laughing.

"I am certain he will go with me. I shall leave as
soon as I get my things, so you will have to drive the
sheep in for the night." She didn't laugh, though she
knew Fyl's reaction to Dal related to how she felt
about him. Anything to discourage the boy.

Dal walked into her kitchen as she finished filling
the mare's saddlebags. "Your castle intact, my lady?"
he asked, looking around uneasily for Fyl.

"They turned out my kitchen," Kayli replied, "took
most everything they could recognize as food, as well
as a few of my hens. That, and my front door is
ruined."

"What'll you be paying me for tending your sheep?"
he asked, more confident after he decided the dragonet was out of the kitchen. He approached her and
reached up as if to touch her shoulder.

Kayli drew back. "Seems I am the one owed," she
replied sharply, "even if I cannot return your sister to
your family."

"You never did know how to be grateful," he said
nastily, "I want you, woman. And that big, red-haired
man from the West won't be coming back, no matter
what he said. What would a Dragon Lord want with a
plain, foul-tempered woman, especially one with fire
at her fingertips?"

"Dal," Kayli struggled to control her temper, "you
just take care of my sheep. I shall not discuss my
needs or wants, or absence of such, with the likes of
you. Try and touch me and I will break my oath."

He pulled back. "Kay, I think I'm the only one who even likes you . . . think of your future."

"Dal, you shall take no familiarity with me," Kayli said sternly. "We have been over this before, several times. No. End of discussion."

Dal opened his mouth as if to continue. "Don't press your luck," Kayli said firmly. She turned and left.

After getting Fyl, Kayli rode up into the hills in silence. The trail was easy to follow. *At least a half-dozen horses,* she thought, *maybe more.*

She tried to let go of Dal's words. *Foul-tempered you are,* she thought to herself, *but grandmother always said that went with being a fire mage.*

Dal's words about Hugh not returning stung the most. That she cared had surprised her, at first. The man had promised most solemnly to return. He probably died, she thought, his wound seemed quite grave. It had surprised her that he had been strong enough to ride away with his brother, the Dragon King, after only four days. *Best not to worry about it,* she thought, looking around her. *No point to it. I manage alone, perhaps that is best. But should I feel so lonely at it?*

"Couldn't have picked a better day for a ride," she said, trying to change her thoughts, "warm and sweet."

"Even if we go deeper into the Borderlands?" Fyl asked quietly. "What if we have to cross into the East to follow them?"

"Shouldn't worry you," Kayli replied, "after all, you are a little dragon."

"But that is where BIG dragons come from," he said, voice squeaking, "Ylgs was familiar, but what if he wasn't senile, what if they are all just plain bad-tempered?"

"Don't be silly, fire won't hurt us," Kayli said, smiling a little and reaching back to pat the little beast. She had made a pillion out of a worn scrap of blanket, so he could ride and hold on without pricking the mare with his claws.

"But teeth can," he said, climbing up to perch on

her shoulder, holding on with his tail. "Is this such a good idea?"

"Hush, little one." Kayli stroked the warm little being some more. "There is nothing to fear, especially since you travel with me." Kayli wondered if she really should be so confident. They rode on in silence.

Better to be confident than afraid of shadows, Kayli told herself. *After all, grandmother said your mother had come from the East, and your father, her only son, was born in the Borderlands. That you have magic of a sort proves you won't come to harm.*

Rumor had it that a mortal who traveled too far into the Borderlands risked his life, or at least his sanity. As West passed to East, magic became more and more the law, and reason became myth. Or so she had been told.

The men left clear tracks. After a day and a half of hard riding, Kayli realized she could see them, riding across a ridge a few hills ahead. Kayli wondered if they were mages. They traveled with confidence, unafraid of traveling in the Borderlands.

"Ma, isn't that who we are chasing?" Fyl asked the obvious, stretching up precariously, perched on her shoulder.

"Crouch more, or if you slip, you will claw me," Kayli ordered. "You are too heavy to jiggle about so." She sat up straighter. "Yes, you are right. Seven horses, looks like Sylva on that last horse. She doesn't seem bound or anything . . ." Kayli stopped, pulling up on the mare as a large, dark shadow passed overhead.

She looked up to see a red-gold dragon, flying so low she could feel the strong backwash of its wings, and see that it had a white hind foot. She reined in the mare, though she realized, as she did, she was too late to stop a panic runaway. But the mare merely looked up with curiosity.

The dragon flew lower over the bandits, wheeling once as if to examine them more closely, then banked and soared upward toward the craggy, steep cliffs that made the northeastern edge of the hilly landscape.

That one seems larger than Ylgs, Kayli thought; she

had always believed Ylgs to be too big and heavy to fly. Perhaps his wings had simply withered from disuse and age.

The men ahead seemed unconcerned about the dragon, as well, though Sylva nearly fell off the horse in a screaming panic. Kayli hoped the men wouldn't look back and notice her. She froze, then slid off the mare quickly, putting the horse between her and the riders.

The bandits paused to calm Sylva, then rode on toward the cliffs where the dragon had gone. No one seemed to notice Kayli.

It crossed Kayli's mind that they acted almost as if under some sort of spell. *Nonsense,* she thought, *no one could possibly have that much power, certainly no natural mage like myself. And wizards . . . grandmother said they were unable to use their learned spell magic in the East. In fact, she said it grew weaker as one went farther into the Borderlands.*

She waited, allowing the mare to browse a little, wondering where the dragon stood in the matter of Sylva's kidnapping. *Or does it even care at all,* Kayli wondered. *Perhaps it is just curious.* Ylgs ignored people, though he had gotten downright cranky right before his death, but he had been very old and even the slightest disturbance would make him come roaring feebly out of his bankside cave.

She heard Fyl sigh a little as the great dragon sailed out of sight.

"Still worried?" she asked.

"A little . . ." he looked around at her, eyes round and almost glowing with excitement, "but . . . mmm . . . she was so beautiful. And she can fly!" He arched his neck up proudly.

Kayli laughed a little, looking over her little dragon disdainfully. "And what would SHE make of you, little one?" She immediately regretted her unkind tone. If the little beast could have blushed, he looked as if he would have.

"Yup, I'm not much of a dragon," he said regretfully, "not a very worthy creature at all." He slithered off her shoulder and curled up on his riding pad, looking dejected.

Kayli shut her mouth. *Anything I say now will be wrong,* she thought; *Goddess, but I wish I could learn to watch my mouth! Fyl is your only friend, you stupid clod, your nasty temper keeps everyone else away. Perhaps that's why Hugh hasn't come back . . . stop it, Kay,* she told herself.

Kayli patted the mare's neck firmly, then mounted up and gently urged her on with her heels. The horse moved willingly on down the trail.

The riders' tracks ended abruptly at the base of a high, sheer cliff face, about an hour's ride from where Kayli had seen the great dragon.

Fyl stirred as she stopped the mare. "What's wrong, ma?" he asked.

"They cannot have ridden through solid rock," she said, "any ideas?"

He stared at her, round-eyed, for a moment. "Am not worthy of suggesting anything," he said finally, curling back down on the pad, holding on with his tail and covering his muzzle with his forepaws.

"Oh, Fyl." Kayli reached back and lightly touched his little, wispy, totally useless wings. Only dragonettes could fly. "I am truly sorry for what I said. Come here." She helped him slither around to the front of the saddle, then took him in her arms, belly up like a baby. The mare stood quietly.

"Fyl, you are a fine dragonet," she said gently, patting his round little belly, "you know I sometimes work my mouth when I do not mean what I say. Apology accepted?"

"Mmm . . . yes . . . this time." He reached up and pressed his head up against the bottom of her chin for a moment, then wriggled out of her arms and back up to her right shoulder, again bracing himself with his tail on her arm. Then he looked the wall over carefully.

"Perhaps . . . mmm . . . spells?" he asked finally.

"Then we are quite locked out," Kayli replied, "all I have is my fire magic. If there is a door, I cannot imagine how I might open it."

"Well . . . hmm . . ." he slithered off and hopped

down to the ground. The mare fidgeted. Kayli gave the reins a little jerk to distract before the mare could kick Fyl.

Fyl coughed a little, then worked himself up for a little fireworks as he trundled along the edge of the cliff, peering carefully at the wall. Then he stopped and cut loose with a small fireball, aiming for a point just above his head.

"Something glowed," Kayli said, "looked almost like runes . . ." she dismounted and led the mare back a few yards, tying her securely to a small tree. Then she gestured and cast a large, hot fireball directly at the wall above Fyl. Glowing white runes appeared briefly, then faded as they cooled.

Kayli stood for a moment in silence. "What's wrong?" Fyl asked, shaking off ashes of the weeds her spell had crisped and jogging back to her. She picked him up and held him a moment, then let him climb back up to her shoulder.

"Well, I expected some sort of grand spell-poem or something . . ."

"That was just writing," he interrupted, "I had hoped we could make the edges of the gate show up." He sounded irritated.

"Well, you shouldn't expect things to come too easily. But this is ridiculous!"

"So what did it say, ma?"

"It said, 'State your business and I shall get to you.' Waste of a spell, if you ask me." Kayli walked back and untied the mare. "Perhaps, little one," she said, gently stroking the mare's muzzle, "you know what lies behind the wall. I wish you could talk." She led the mare back so they stood in front of the now invisible runes.

Kayli cleared her throat. "I am seeking the maiden, Sylva, taken from the village of Riverwer by raiders," she said loudly. "I feel stupid talking to a wall," she said, more quietly, to Fyl.

A black tunnel, only faintly illuminated by a crystalline glow that seemed to come from its walls, opened before them silently, as if a curtain lifted before them. A feeling of foreboding fell over Kayli. "Wish I had grandmother's talent of divination," she said softly, "I am afraid we are going into danger."

"Don't worry, ma," Fyl's voice sounded terribly small, lost in the hole ahead of them. "Look, the horse wants to go in. If she's not afraid, I'm not."

The mare tugged at the reins, pulling Kayli and Fyl along. Kayli sighted. "Well, this must be the way they went," she said, "let's go."

She climbed back on the mare and let the reins go. The mare willingly walked in through the gate, calmly, as if into her own stable. *Probably IS her own stable*, Kayli thought. *Goddess, I do not like this. But it looks as if this is the only way to find Sylva.* The gate shut behind them as silently as it had opened, leaving them in darkness.

As her eyes adjusted, Kayli realized the blue glow gave barely enough light to see her hand in front of her face. The mare walked on confidently in the darkness, hooves making a thunderous clatter that seemed to echo forever. Kayli wished she could see better.

"Ma," Fyl whispered in her ear, "can you see?" His eyes shone golden, reflecting the faint light.

Kayli started at the sound of his voice, then reached up to keep him from slipping. "No," she whispered, "I'll make a light." The sound of her voice seemed lost in the clatter of the horse's hooves.

She gestured and made a cool, bright blue fireball in the palm of her hand. It illuminated the tunnel much better. The mare shied a little at the strange light on her back. "Calm, lass," Kayli said, gently patting the mare's neck with her free hand. The mare relaxed and moved on steadily.

Soon, Kayli heard the sound of rushing water ahead, quickly growing loud enough to drown the clatter of the mare's hooves. At the sound's loudest, the tunnel opened out into a huge cavern. The mare halted at the edge of the tunnel, nose down, as if carefully looking at the path ahead. A faint reflection of Kayli's light glinted off a wall far to the back of the cavern.

"Ma, look," Fyl said quietly, nose pointing in the same direction as the mare's muzzle.

A narrow stone bridge crossed a deep gorge ahead

of them, a crack in the cavern floor that echoed with the sound of rushing water beneath. Kayli felt a small thread of fear as the mare started carefully out across the railless bridge.

"Sit still, Fyl," she quietly ordered, "I think she has us barely balanced. You are enough of a weight to throw her off. That looks like a long fall."

"Yes, ma'am!" he said, voice tiny in the din of the water.

Kayli held her breath, daring to exhale only after the mare stood again on solid ground. Her blue lightball faded as the mare stopped, the spell dissipated by time and Kayli's lack of concentration.

Kayli dismounted and started another lightball spell.

"Don't do that," a huge, quavery voice ordered, echoing around the cavern.

"But I need to see," Kayli replied impatiently, and completed her spell. A thought she might be wrong crossed her mind. She quashed it. *Makes no sense to stand here in the dark, helpless,* she thought. Another lightball bloomed in her hand.

A pained roar filled the cavern, echoing off the brilliant crystal walls. Kayli looked around, blinking from the sudden brightness. She stood at one end of a vast, open cavern.

At the far end lay an enormous, pulsing white creature, soft-looking, almost sluglike. The men she had followed, and Sylva, stood near what seemed to be the head end of the creature. It made a gesture with a ridiculously small forelimb. The faint blue glow of the cavern walls increased to a soft, muted light.

Kayli doused her light spell. *As long as I can see,* she thought, *may as well not displease the creature.*

"Come forward, brave human." The strange, wavering voice seemed to come from the white monster.

Kayli paused. "You had probably best obey," Fyl whispered.

"Ahem . . . I said, come here!" the creature whined impatiently.

Kayli approached the great beast cautiously, then more confidently as she realized the men didn't seem to notice her. Sylva also seemed possessed by the same force.

Kayli felt the creature's almost overwhelming presence, but felt no compulsion to obey it, as the others seemed to do. *I am doing this because I want to,* Kayli thought, *not because I am being forced to.* Fyl sat silently on her shoulder, staring at the monster.

She stopped near the head of the creature, silently realizing that it seemed to be a dragon, despite its grossness. *Some sort of brood dragon?* she wondered, *or just a huge, unique monstrosity?*

"That was what I wanted you to bring back," the whiny voice now roared, "not that pathetic, magicless creature." Kayli thought she could detect a certain amount of petulent whine in the roar, of a spoiled child that didn't get exactly what it wanted. The men staggered a little. "But you succeeded, nonetheless. I will let you live. You are released."

The bandits stood for a moment, gathering the wits that had been returned to them, then fled in total disarray up what seemed to be another, wider tunnel going west. Sylva turned to stare at Kayli, released from the monster's spell.

"Why did you wish my presence?" Kayli asked, curious. Her voice seemed very small, muted in the vast cave.

The creature looked down its long, warty muzzle at Kayli, eyeing her with curiosity gleaming in its pale, piggy eyes. "I wondered what manner of wizard lived at the edge of my domain. I can feel your spells, you know." The creature modulated its voice to a relatively quiet, quavery whine.

That irked Kayli. "You mean . . ." *Control your temper, woman,* she thought. "Begging your pardon, but you wanted me kidnapped simply to satisfy your curiosity?"

The creature shuffled its soft mass closer to Kayli and leaned its head toward her. Sylva screamed and ran behind Kayli. Kayli realized she could reach out and touch the beast's great, rough muzzle.

"Why not?" it asked, sniffing her over. "Cute pet. Looks tasty!" It grabbed for Fyl.

He squealed and leaped off Kayli's shoulder, landing with an "oof" on the rock floor. "Stop that!" Kayli slapped the huge muzzle hard, to give Fyl time to escape. "Sylva, get back to the mare, NOW! Don't argue." Fyl followed the young woman, nipping at her heels to hurry her along.

The beast pulled back at the slap, surprised. "That hurt!" It cut loose with a small fireball that engulfed Kayli.

Rather a feeble attempt, Kayli thought. *Old Ylgs could do better on a bad day.* The dragon looked startled to see Kayli still standing as the fireball dissipated.

"Some hospitality," Kayli said angrily, "you drag me across the countryside to settle your blasted curiosity; would have had me kidnapped; worried me to death over Sylva, not to mention her parents; then you try to eat my dragonet and cook me. You're lucky you don't get your fireball back, and more!"

The creature drew back, looking worried. Kayli heard Fyl snicker.

"You're no wizard," the creature said, after a long pause, "you're a fire mage! How silly of me!"

"Of course I'm a mage, you sotting great . . . thing! Do I look like a Westerner?" *Are all dragons daft?* she wondered. She paused, interrupted by a clatter of wings and clawed feet from the end of the cave where the men had disappeared.

A pair of huge, golden dragons, eyes glowing bright gold in the dim light, came to the side of the white monstrosity, tucking back their immense, delicate wings as they approached. They seemed identical to Kayli.

"Mother, what mischief have you been up to?" one of them asked. "We just saw men run out of the cavern mouth."

The other looked Kayli over closely, sniffing her carefully. Its jaws seemed big enough to bite a grown ewe in half, but she sensed somehow that she need not fear it at all. It was somewhat larger than Ylgs had been.

"Many pardons," it nodded a little, as if to bow, "I

hope Mother hasn't troubled you too much. Sometimes our watch on her lapses."

Kayli stood silent, awed. She realized they weren't
identical. The one talking quietly, soothing the Mother,
was smaller, and a clear red-gold, with no markings.
The one looking her over had faint, darker markings
amid the clear gold of its scales, as if tabby-striped,
and a small dot of white between its eyes.

"I'm Thyr," it said, "and this is Swrm."

Its politeness surprised Kayli, and deflated her anger. "I'm Kayli," she said, bowing politely, "and that
is Sylva," she pointed, "and the dragonet is Fyl. We
are from the village of Riverwer." Fyl had wandered
back when the dragons had appeared. Kayli helped
him climb back up to her shoulder.

"Pretty, ma," he sighed in her ear, staring in awe at
the golden dragons.

Thyr's eyes narrowed, curious. "The little ones talk?"

"Yes," Kayli replied, "didn't you know that?"

"Oh, no, we have little to do with them. Excuse
me." Thyr turned to help Swrm with the Mother.

Kayli watched as they silently prodded and shoved
the Mother back to a worn, straw-padded groove in
the stones. Once settled, it lay its huge head down and
seemed to fall asleep. The dragons then both turned
their attention to Kayli.

"Our greatest apologies, Kayli-Mage," Swrm said,
"Mother is . . . well, is very old. And, after when she
said she felt her brother die, two months ago, she has
not been quite the same."

"She must be the sister of my old bridge dragon,
Ylgs." Kayli said quietly. She silently wondered how
such a gross, sluglike monstrosity could possibly be
related to slender old Ylgs. No telling, she thought.

"You knew an Elder Dragon?" Thyr asked, eyes
rounding in excitement. "How did he die?"

"Defending our home," Kayli replied hesitantly, "a
Western king's war with a wizard spilled over a little
into my lands."

"Hope he wasn't as senile as Mother," Swrm said.

"Well, he was, in some ways," Kayli replied, "he
had forgotten how to talk. When I was very small, I

would visit and he would tell me stories. But he did remember his duty when we needed him, despite his age. He had no magic either, as far as I knew. That Mother can spell-summon people to do her bidding from so far away . . ."

"She usually cannot organize her thoughts well enough for such things," Thyr said "and usually one of us stays around to control her. I think someone has to live here on a more permanent basis, eh, Swrm?"

"Mmm . . . think I shall," the other dragon said.

"I think, perhaps . . . mmm . . ." Thyr looked Kayli over curiously, "that I think I shall travel west for a time, if Kayli-Mage approves."

"Me?" Kayli asked, startled at such a grand being asking her permission for anything.

"You DID say bridge, mmm?" Thyr asked, eyes glowing even brighter.

"Yes," Kayli replied, "the river Farand runs between my castle and the village. It is too deep and swift to cross easily, so someone long ago built a great bridge across it."

"Big river . . . big fish?" Thyr asked, peering at her closely.

Kayli realized it had the same expression as Fyl when the dragonet spoke of fresh eggs.

"You have said the magic word," Swrm said. "Thyr, best not frighten Kayli-Mage."

"Mmm . . . mayhap Kayli-Mage needs . . . wants a new dragon . . . mmm?"

"Well, now that you mention it," Kayli said, smiling a little, "we have had a great deal of trouble with bandits lately. I cannot imagine what shape the den is in, though. Ylgs was not tidy to start with, and I have not been down there for a long time."

"Oh, boy . . . please, Kay?" Fyl chimed in. "She's so beautiful!"

Kayli patted the warm little being. "She seems to want to come." She didn't want to know how he could tell Thyr was a she, but she trusted his judgment.

Thyr looked at Sylva. "And your villagers, Kayli-Mage? What will they think? She looks scared to death."

"I think . . . once they get used to the idea, they won't be scared . . . hmm . . . you don't eat dragonets, do you?"

"Oh, no!" Thyr looked shocked. "They ARE cousins, you know!"

"Mother tried to munch up Fyl," Kayli said, "and many dragonets live in the hills around my castle and the village. For myself, anyway, I would rather not have anyone hunting them."

"Mother probably thought he was a rock lizard . . . she doesn't see very well," Swrm said, "the lizards are her favorite treat. Eating IS the bright point in her life. We do not hunt from your people's herds, either, unless such food is offered. Neighborly relations are too important."

"I am certain that if fishing did not provide enough food," Kayli said, "a sheep or two a month could be provided, even more if needed."

Thyr looked her over, still curious. "Prefer fish, but mutton will do. We do not eat as much as you might think, either."

Kayli lightly touched her outstretched muzzle. She felt a surprising quiver. Then Thyr raised her head and looked Kayli over critically. Thyr reached to nuzzle Kayli again. Kayli stretched a little and scratched Thyr behind one of her ear scales, a place that Fyl always seemed to need a good rubbing. A soft rumble came from deep in Thyr's chest. She pulled her head back to look at Kayli again.

"I think I shall like living near you," Thyr said, almost so softly that Kayli couldn't hear her. "You will be a good partner. That an old dragon favored you . . . you must be very special."

"Well, I wouldn't quite say that . . . Ylgs came at the bidding of some forgotten ancestor."

"But you said he told you stories when you were a child, a rare treat even for dragon younglings . . . enough, we can visit all we want later. I would wager your friend." Thyr pointed with her muzzle, "would like to be out of here."

"I wouldn't mind it, either!" Fyl chimed in.

Thyr made a noise that Kayli realized was a chuckle.

"Yes . . . we are all creatures of air and light. The cave is beautiful, but it is still a dark cage. Follow me!"

"Come along, Sylva," Kayli said, "lead the mare so she will come." They left Swrm soothing the Mother, crooning softly to her.

Thyr led them upward through the much larger westward tunnel. Kayli didn't want to follow too close; Thyr's long, slender tail trailed her vulnerably in the tunnel. It wouldn't do to step on it. The same dim glow that lit the cavern filled the tunnel as they passed.

After a short time, Thyr paused and said a word in a tongue unknown to Kayli. Sunlight and fresh air suddenly bathed them as a huge stone door groaned open. It shut itself after they were all well outside, with a huge creaking and a scattering of small stones.

Thyr looked even more splendid in the bright sunlight. The striped markings showed up quite strongly. Kayli realized she had one white hind foot. Fyl sighed deeply and stretched upward on her shoulder to ogle Thyr.

"Fyl, control yourself," Kayli said, after stumbling, "you are too heavy. You will pull me over if you keep leaning so!"

Thyr turned and looked the little dragon over, almost touching noses with him. "Come along," Thyr said quietly, then lifted Fyl up by the scruff of loose skin behind his tiny wings.

The dragonet squeaked and struggled a little, then calmed down as soon as she sat him down on her shoulders, in between the broad bases of her great, delicate wings.

"Kayli-Mage, another horse still stands . . . one Sylva rode . . . I can smell that. Men didn't want to take a loose horse . . . perhaps they left it to appease . . ."

Kayli realized Thyr wrinkled her nose a little at that. "What is wrong?" she asked.

"Horses . . . upset the stomachs of most dragons," Thyr replied matter-of-factly, "and they are too tough, as well. Ycch!"

Kayli walked to the front of the great dragon, where she could see around the boulders of the gateway. A dappled gray mare stood, nibbling on the bush she had been tied to. They hadn't unsaddled her.

"Why do we have to ride home?" Sylva asked petulantly. "I'm tired of riding. Can't one of you two just . . . well, just magic us home? Or we could fly."

"Sylva, you know I have only my fire," Kayli said, a little irritated.

Thyr made a chuckling sound in her chest, looking closely at Sylva. The young woman stepped back as the huge muzzle came too close. "I doubt I could take off with even one of you on my back," Thyr said, "and I ought not go near your village without Kayli-Mage. Seems simplest to carry Fyl and walk, while you two ride the horses."

"But I don't want to ride anymore," Sylva whined.

"Then walk," Kayli said, feeling her patience shred, "and we will be seeing you in a week or so." She took the bay mare's reins from Sylva and mounted.

As they walked away, Sylva ran to the other horse, quickly untied her and mounted up, urging her into a trot to catch up.

They rode back at a much more leisurely pace than before; it didn't hurt Kayli nearly as much as the ride to the dragon's cave.

At dusk the second day, as they slowed to look for a good campsite, Thyr suddenly froze, then raised her head high, as if listening for something.

"What is wrong?" Kayli asked.

"I hear people . . . your kind . . . talking," Thyr said softly, "not very far away."

"Oh, perhaps others came to save me," Sylva said loudly.

"Shut up," Fyl said sharply.

The young woman glared at him. Kayli felt a little sorry for her. The pretty girl, well-liked in the village, obviously felt quite out of place in the company of mage, dragon and dragonet, even though Sylva and Kayli grew up together.

"Kayli," Thyr whispered, "I think they are just over the next hillock. They speak of looting your village, Riverwer."

"I will go," Kayli replied. Anger rose in her at the thought of them burning and looting the village again.

She slipped quietly up to where she could just see over the ridge of the hill. Six men sat around a small campfire. Kayli's anger grew when she saw they had tied their horses without unsaddling or feeding them.

"Well, damn," one of the men said, "we could've gotten ourselves killed, and for what? Nothin'! Didn't even have time to rape the girl. That spell . . . whew! worse than that old wizard we used to work for."

"Aye," said another, "perhaps we should go back to that village . . . there HAS to be some kind of treasure in that old castle. Maybe that's why we were forced into this wild goose chase . . . some sort of protection spell. No one lives there anymore, that's plain. I'd bet that spell was a one-shot."

Kayli startled a little as Thyr stepped beside her. The huge animal held her head down low, chin nearly brushing the ground, to keep from being seen.

"I hear that, Kayli-Mage," she whispered, "shall we stop them?"

"Yes," Kayli replied, trying to control her anger.

Fyl scurried up between them. "Me, too!"

"Oh, yes!" Kayli said. "Come along." She helped him climb up to her shoulder.

She stood up, tidied herself, then strode over the hill. Thyr held back.

"Let's go back, then," the first man replied, "to-morrow, though."

"You shall do nothing of the sort!" Kayli said firmly.

The men stopped talking. All turned to stare at Kayli as she started gesturing.

"And what are you and your little toy dragon going to do about it?" the ugliest of them said, "Beat us up?" He leered at her, baring broken green teeth, and stood up.

"You didn't harm the girl, and you managed not to kill anyone in Riverwer," Kayli said, "so I shall let you live. But I bid you to go and spread the word that Riverwer is again protected by a dragon as well as its fire mage."

"Bluff some more, woman," the first man said.

"What is an old lady, or a toy dragon, going to do to stop us?"

"She don't look so old, Borl," the ugly man said, starting to walk toward Kayli, "looks fine enough for me."

Kayli held back until the ugly man came too close. Too close was three paces, when she could smell him. "I warned you," she said sternly. "Thyr!" She finished the spell, a bright, loud fireball that singed the ugly man. He turned to run.

"Yeah, toy lizard indeed!" Fyl got off a fairly respectable fireball that hit the man in the backside, igniting his breeches as he ran.

Thyr came over the crest of the hill, neck frill fanned out and wings outstretched to add to her size. She emitted a stream of fire directed at the center of the camp. The campfire exploded into a shower of sparks.

The would-be raiders showed remarkable speed in getting on their horses and fleeing. The ugly one, breeches still smoking, had a hard time mounting up. The horse didn't want him near. Kayli started laughing.

Sylva came over the hill just as the raiders rode away in terror. "What IS all this about?" she asked. "Those are the men who kidnapped me!" She looked indignant. "Can't you stop them?"

"Too late and no point. They talked of returning to finish sacking Riverwer," Kayli replied, still laughing. "Somehow I don't think they will stop there."

"We showed 'em, didn't we, ma!" Fyl said proudly.

"Aye, we did." Kayli patted him. Thyr leaned over, crest down now. Kayli gave her a good head scratching.

Her sheep scattered as they came over the hill behind Kayli's castle. Their bleats startled Dal awake as Kayli halted her mare in front of him."

"What the blazes, Kayli?" he asked, standing as he saw Thyr come over the hill behind her. "Have you brought a monster back. . . ?" He looked afraid.

"Oh, shut up," Kayli said impatiently. "Thyr will not harm you. She has come to live in Ylgs' old den. I am certain she will be more pleasant company for the village and castle, as well." She studiously ignored Fyl as the dragonet snuck up behind Dal. It surprised Kayli that Sylva, beside her on the gray mare, ignored the dragonet as well.

"Boo!" Fyl said, and nipped Dal's ankles. "Surprise, we're back!" He galumphed away, snickering as Dal turned and fruitlessly kicked the air behind him.

The sheep regrouped as soon as they realized the dragon wouldn't hurt them, staring, stunned, at this new beast in their world.

"Best go off to look at my new den," Thyr said, "no use in putting that off."

"Yes," Kayli replied, "though you are welcome to stay in my great hall . . . you will fit . . . not that it is any protection in the rain. Place leaks like a sieve." Fyl came back and perched on her shoulder.

"You cannot get the villagers to fix it?" Thyr asked, as they walked on down to the castle. Sylva stayed behind with her brother. "I thought being a liege, as you seem to be, entitled you to more than a bow and a nod as you passed." Thyr continued, "though Sylva does not seem at all respectful."

"Perhaps when the castle was new and a great lord lived there, respect was given," Kayli said, "I am just Kayli around here, raised up with the other children."

"They can ignore your fire magic?"

"Oh, Thyr! It would be cruel to use it on them, especially since I have a hard time controlling my temper. If I blasted them every time I got mad, they would have stoned me, or something, long ago."

"And you live alone." Thyr cocked her head a little to look Kayli over with one of her great golden eyes as they walked along. "I thought humans needed one another more."

"The only local opportunity is that man, Dal. I am not interested in him." Kayli found herself wanting to avoid Thyr's gaze.

"Is there another?"

"Well . . . yes and no . . . I think he died. Around the time Ylgs died, a Western lord, they call themselves Dragon Lords, was brought to me for healing. He had a spell wound and they thought it needed a wizard's cure."

"It did not?"

"Just a Yll-worm, anyone could have taken it out of his shoulder and killed it. In fact, it bit me and Fyl killed it, cooked it after I tossed it onto the floor."

"Yeah!" Fyl chimed in, preening proudly.

"Those . . . things are a cruel magic. You do not know if he died?"

Kayli sighed. "I would rather not talk of it."

Thyr looked away. "You do not have to keep your gates locked?" she asked, changing the subject tactfully as they approached the back gates of the castle, the gates that led into the sheep fold and stables.

"No . . . when did that happen?" She realized, as she turned her thoughts back to her surroundings, that a rough rope and post paddock had been built just outside the stable gates. A pair of rotundly pregnant Great Horse mares grazed lazily. They looked up when Kayli's mare nickered at them, then went placidly back to the grass. "Those are not my horses." Kayli said, "in fact, you would have to go a long way just to find such." She paused, pulling the mare to a halt and dismounting.

"What is wrong, Kayli-Mage?" The dragon asked, looking around, alert for danger.

"Oh, do not worry . . ." Kayli unsaddled the mare and put her into the makeshift paddock, trying to stay calm. She looked up at the castle, but couldn't see anyone on the roof. *Almost dinnertime,* she told herself. *Anyone with any sense would be fixing their meal.*

"Where is this den?" Thyr asked, looking Kayli over curiously.

"Around beneath this end of the bridge. The first bridge pier makes a front door and landing spot."

"Then I will go see my new home. If you need me, call out." She turned to look at Kayli face-to-face, great muzzle almost touching Kayli's nose, a hint of worry in her expression. Then she turned and went on her way.

"May I go, too?" Fyl asked, "Perhaps I can help."

"Aye, little one," Thyr said gently, "come along." She reached over and lifted him from Kayli's shoulder to her back, to save him the indignity of having to scramble. Then she strode away, following the path that led around the outside of the castle wall to the bridge.

Kayli gathered up saddle, bridle and saddlebags, and walked through her castle's back gate. *Restrain yourself, Kay,* she thought, *could be other raiders, taking advantage of your absence.* The castle grew dark as the sun set.

She left saddle and bridle in the stable, noting other, strange tack, of a size to fit the mares, hanging there. *Now who . . .* she wondered, *Hugh? No, cannot be,* Kayli thought. *I already decided he would not come back. He most likely died.* She had to walk around to the front gate; the stable door to the main building was locked. *Did that before I left,* Kayli remembered. The shattered front doors lay to one side of the doorway; taken off their hinges. She realized half the roof of the great hall was gone, too.

A light shone from her kitchen. A strange, tall, blond-haired man stood in the doorway, blocking it. He still had some of the slenderness of youth, not quite filled out into manhood yet.

"Those dragon scales," he said, gesturing with a piece of bread, "are going to make a fine roof. And if we run short, the slate in the river banks will serve just as well to hold out the rain, as well as be fireproof." His voice was firmly deep, not a lad's.

Kayli froze. He had the same Western accent as Hugh had. Someone unseen in the kitchen mumbled assent, as if around a mouthful of food. Kayli could smell stew.

She steeled herself to stay calm, setting the saddle-bags on the floor quietly and walking up behind the young man. "Ahem, what might you be doing in my kitchen?" She tried to sound angry.

The young man stepped aside, turning to look at her. "Excuse me, my lady," he bowed a little, looking not at all surprised. "It seems we are in the middle of our meal right now, but we are also mending your roof. You fit Hugh's description of the lady of this place. Come, join us."

Kayli stood just outside the door for a moment, stunned by the young man's resemblance to Hugh; square face, aquiline nose, blue-green eyes. His only differences lay in that he had no mustache, no freckles, and that Hugh had redder hair and a deep scar cutting across the bridge of his nose, between his eyes. She heard whoever was inside drop his silverware and scoot his chair noisily back on the stone floor. Kayli took a deep breath and walked into her kitchen.

Hugh stood, smiling at her. She stood still a moment, not wanting to believe her eyes. *He looks well,* she thought, *fiery red-gold hair bleached blond from the sun, and it seems his freckles have run together, as well.* His right arm, permanently withered from the injury the Yll-worm had done to his shoulder, was held to his body by a clever leather harness-sling.

He walked to her and hugged her one-armed, lifting her off the floor a little. "Kayli, lady, I have come back as I promised. The villagers told me you had gone off east, to save some lass. I brought Wilse with me," he nodded to the younger man, "as I am still learnin' what I can and canna do one-handed. He is my youngest brother, and a skilled carpenter, as well."

"Hugh . . . I don't know what to say!" Kayli realized she stared like a fool.

"Then come along and have some stew and bread," he said gently, smiling. "Rough fare, but I'd wager you've been ridin' all day. You dinna strike me as a picky eater, either."

Kayli filled a plate with stew and cut off a hunk of bread. "Hugh . . . I hoped you would come back . . . I'd decided. . . . I thought you were . . ." She could not make herself say it, it seemed too obscene with him here, looking fit and in good spirits.

"Dead, lass?" he asked, looking serious for a moment. "Aye, I got quite ill, would've been better off if Troy left me here. But you remember his mood . . . there was no stoppin' him. Mother wasn't very happy with him when he brought me back in that state."

"And Mother wouldn't let Hugh leave," Wilse said, "until last week."

"You said she was a healing mage," Kayli said. "If she thought you were not fit to travel, she was right." She sat next to where Hugh had been sitting. "At any rate, I am glad you came back. How long can you stay?"

"Well, lady," he sat and looked at her, bright blue-green eyes meeting her amber ones, "I told my people to come in a month . . . we'd either be havin' a wedding or they'd be escorting us back. I figured you'd either be wantin' me to stay . . . or happy to see the back of me."

Kayli looked down at her plate a moment, then back at him. "You jest," she said, looking away again, "there must be someone better for you than I . . ." She stopped, unable to go on.

"Lady, I spent most of two months dreamin' of a white-haired lass with big amber eyes, strong of mind and body and quite hot-tempered; a fire mage, in fact," he said softly. "Troy kept runnin' the girls past me, tryin' to change my mind. They all seemed so . . . well, not worth my attention when compared to you . . . not that a one-armed man's worth much."

"One-armed or not," Kayli replied, "you are quite more than I ever expected. However, we shall see if my temper makes you want to stay, after a month. I even succeeded in offending Fyl on my journey, running my mouth when it was not necessary."

"Fyl?" Wilse asked, after swallowing a mouthful of stew.

"Mention me?" Fyl asked, waddling through the kitchen doorway.

Kayli picked him up into her lap as he came to her, realizing he looked a little droopy. She smiled when she saw Wilse's amazed look. "What is the matter, little one?" she asked, rubbing his belly gently. "He is quite safe, Wilse. Didn't Hugh tell you about him?"

"N-no," Wilse stammered, "though he did tell me you were a fire mage, you could start fires and such with spells."

"What is the matter, little one?" Kayli asked, "Thyr throw you out?"

"Once we got down there," she said, 'How could YOU possibly help ME?' " he replied dejectedly.

"Thyr?" Hugh asked, eyebrows raised.

"A dragon came back from the East with me," Kayli replied, "she's quite lovely, can even fly. She wanted to come, and I felt she would help with the bandit situation."

"Dragons?" Wilse asked, eyes even wider, "Brother, what have you gotten me into?"

"Wants discussin' later," Hugh said calmly, "let's finish our meal. I want to show Kay what Mother sent for her. Peace, lad, you'll come to no harm here."

"All . . . all right." Wilse reluctantly turned back to his stew.

Kayli started eating, stroking Fyl and thinking of her future possibilities.

THE SEVEN YEARS' NIGHT
by M. H. Lewis

I am an absolute sucker for comedy; so much of fantasy—
and that's especially true of sword and sorcery—is not only
coldly humorless but positively grim. When anything involv-
ing a lighter touch comes along, it's almost an assured
sale—but my sense of humor is, to say the least, strange.

This is a short little story—I don't want to give it away, so
I'll only say that sometimes a night can be very long indeed.

This is no day to walk the Highslopes Trail. The warm
sunshine on Oaktree Tavern this morning deceived
me.

Now lightnings glare in the black clouds hanging
over me around ThunderPeak. Their thunders echo
back from the haunted DeathPass below Highslopes
Trail. Old ballads say a passage to the Otherworld lies
in DeathPass. Those ballads are popular elsewhere in
the four and one realms but not in the neighborhood.
Folk here no longer use DeathPass trail for fear and
Highslopes Trail above it offers no shelter from fre-
quent storms.

The chill winds off the snowfields of ThunderPeak
beat at my back. Gusts blown back from the walls of
DeathPass draw tears and blur my eyesight.

The uneven stones of Highslopes Trail are no sure
footing. I have to stop until my sight clears. I use the
time to rewrap the muffler Kareth, owner of the Oaktree, knitted for me. Then I flex my fingers in the
gloves Kareth's sister Inor, owner of the Brookside in
Farslopes, gave me. A harper and balladsinger has to
keep her voice and fingers supple or end up begging.

No need to care for my face. Andrith the harper has no fair cheeks needing creaming against wind and cold and shielding from the sun. A swordsman scarred my right cheek for me when we were both young and foolish over a juggler lad. My dagger through the swordswoman's knee ruined her for selling her sword-skills for silver instead of hiring out to drive supply-wagons for coppers.

The scar on my face ruined my chances of ever having a place on a high lady's dais, fine livery, rich foods, soft bed, horses to ride, a pension instead of beggary at the end when my fingers cramp and my voice cracks. High ladies choose their harpers by their looks. I've taken enough prizes at festivals from their choices to know.

After all, the juggler lad left both of us that were marred for his sake for a fire-eating sword-swallower from his own troupe. Now I tramp this trail for my youthful folly. Somewhere this cold weather reminds a wagon-driver of a knife-stroke through the knee for hers.

If I don't mind my step now on this trail, I'll not have to worry about begging in old age. It would be a pity to slip and miss Inor's hot meat-pie tonight. The new I'm bringing, that she will be name-mother to another great-niece or nephew at the Oaktree by next full moon, will surely be worth one.

I can tell her the child will have a ear for music. When I placed my harp next to Kareth's daughter's great belly and played a lively jig, the child's kicks could be seen dimpling the taut cloth of her smock. Poor girl, wan with work and her burden, it was good to see her laugh.

It will be good to see Inor's grandson, too. I wonder if he'll remember me from last year when I played him through the fever from his teething. I sat by his bed the whole night when only my music gave him rest from crying with the pain and let him sleep.

That lightning stroke hit this path just twenty paces ahead. My skin tingles. The hair is rising on my head. Those are the foresigns of lightning stroke. It's going to hit here, right where I stand. I must not run, glare-

blinded, nor stand here. I will fall down. On my belly, I
crawl downslope, feeling the drop with my boot toes,
clutching the rocks, handhold to handhold. So I work
my way just over the edge into Deathpass. I won't go
down onto the haunted trail, just hold on high up here
until the lightning stroke's over.

Warm, the rock against my cheek is warm. I am
breathing in thick, sweet, warm, wet-smelling air like
that of a town's most expensive perfumed bath. There
is no more wind pushing against me.

My ears clear from the thunder and I hear a rasping
sound—loud, soft, loud, soft—the scales of a snake as
wide as an ox, crawling over rocks. Dragon noise. A
dragon's breath, is that what I'm smelling? I never
heard that a dragon's breath smelled sweet. I never
heard that any woman close enough to a dragon to
smell its breath ever lived to say what it smelled like.

I might as well see what's coming, eyes open. This
rock's a tree root attached to a tree trunk. Through
the branches overhead a clear night-sky and stars show.
If I find a clear spot, I can take directions.

The Plough doesn't show in this sky nor the Fishnet
nor the Goodman's Spindle nor Heaven's Harp, none
of the constellations I've guided my feet by so many
nights. This is the Otherworld. Well, who knows the
ways of the Otherworld better? I've sung all the ballads and told all the tales of the Otherworld known in
the four and one realms. All I have to do is not eat of
their drink nor drink of their food— That's not right.
My wits are muddled.

The rasping sound has never stopped. I must get out
of here. I will have to find a witch or a warlock and
compel the creature to send me back to the real world.
My hatchet's cold steel, holy steel, it will have power
over them.

I take it from my belt and pull the leather cover off
the blade. The weight of it in my hand is some comfort.
The starlight shines back from the polished stones of a
path between the trees. A path must lead somewhere
to someone. Step by step takes a sovereign to her
throne, says the proverb.

This path leads to the hilltop's edge where wooden steps with railings that shine in the dark lead downward. On either side of the steps are vines of white flowers. Their scent is what I have been smelling.

From the steps a walk of square white stones leads to a gate into a garden. Over the garden and the houseroof behind it on a high pole is a white jewel as big as a great turnip the size of six ordinary turnips. This jewel shines a white and ghastly light with none of the warmth of sunlight in it, a light which never flickers like firelight or candlelight. But the flowers of the garden are not withered by it and the moths among the flowers are not blasted by it.

There beyond the garden in the ghastly light is the house of a great wizard or warlock. Unless its owner can be made to return me from the Otherworld, I will never eat Kareth's bread at the Oaktree or drink Inor's beer at the Brookside again.

At least the garden gate is not guarded by spells or spirits. It is passed and all is still quiet. There is a shelf built round the house two or three feet off the ground with poles holding the roof up off it and a wooden railing around it. It is a whirling house or a flying house out of the old tales but just now standing still.

There are four and one steps, the death number, up to the houseshelf. That shows its owner is a servant of the Evil Other. Whoever comes by the steps up to the dwelling comes by four and by one, the number by which persons are delivered into the power of the Evil Other.

Not me. I set the steel blade of my hatchet against the boards of the houseshelf so it cannot fly by magic or begin to whirl, then heave myself by my hands softly up onto the houseshelf.

Something stirs in the darkness by the housewall. Then it says "Mow" loudly. Into the light at the houseshelf edge comes a white and yellow spotted cat, its green eyes looking up as if pleading. If I strike this seeming-cat with the holy steel, it must turn into its right form of witch, warlock, or monster.

The cat rises up on its hind legs and clasps my leg about the knee with its forepaws like a person begging mercy or vowing service. Cautiously, I put my finger to its head and mark it between the ears with the sign of the Holy Triangle, the lines of the Power, the Love, the Righteousness of the Holy One. An evil creature could not endure that sign.

The cat does not flee squalling into the dark. It rubs its head against my hand as if in delight. Then it turns and walks away around the houseshelf, sunwise, not against the sun as evil things must go. It stops at the corner and looks back at me. I follow the cat.

Around the corner the shelf-edge and wall-edge of the floor are lined with magic plants. Some stand in pots, some hang overhead. Some stretch out serpent-shaped branches with thorns, probably poisoned, as long as a woman's thumb. Some are like roses whose petals had been turned to thick chunks of greenish-gray rot, most awful to look at. There are ferns enough to provide fernseed to make an army of wizards or warlocks invisible.

The cat trails in and out of the plants, showing the safe way through them. Around the corner there is a chair, its legs set into half wheel-rims. The cat jumps into it. It tilts back and forth as a ship does when storm-tossed. A magic chair for raising storms at sea. How many innocents have been drowned by means of it?

On the far side of the houseshelf is a long bench with a back suspended from chains as hanged folks' bodies are hung up at crossroads. Whoever lies there chanting spells must be able to speak with the ghosts of hanged robbers and learn where they hid undiscovered bloodstained loot. Before the bench lies a woven round straw mat, a circle within which the ghosts of the damned criminals must appear smoking out of hell.

The cat jumps from the tilting chair and walks across the light from the small gourd-sized jewel over the door in the midst of this side of the house. It jumps onto a windowsill and sits looking in. I follow the cat and look in.

The window drapes are tied back. The window is a wonder. There isn't a Sovereign Lady in the four and one realms has such a window, a whole sheet of glass as big as a table top and as clear as still water, not a crinkle nor a ripple in it. Perhaps the bones of babies went into the cauldron that melted such glass to work such magic.

Through the window I see the witch, a little old woman with long white hair tied back with a red scarf behind her, wearing a rich red robe with black magic signs all over it. No hope to catch her without her robe of power on. She sits before a table holding a magic board and a green glowing magic ball, not round properly, a square with rounded corners held in a wooden frame.

The magic board holds square stones popped up from square holes, each with a black rune on it. The witch's fingers play across the runestones and the green runes of her spells appear glowing in the magic ball, march across it, and disappear.

The cat nudges my shoulder with its head, then jumps down. Startled, I step on it. At the yowl, the witch whirls and sees me. I hold up the holy steel hatchet blade between us to ward off any spell. With one leap the witch reaches the far wall and strikes it with her hand. The lights go out. There are three small birdlike chirps. Is it thus she calls demons? Then the witch's voice, low and fierce, reciting some spell.

The cat meows to me from the shelf-edge, then jumps down and runs. It stops and looks back for me to follow. We crawl under a line of bushes next to the front fence which have huge white flowers as big as a blacksmith's fists. All flowers in this world are white and monstrous.

The two trees by the witch's front gate have leaves as big as half a loaf of bread sliced through lengthwise and flowers as big as butter firkins or wheels of cheese.

The great flowers on the bushes are so strongly scented I can scarcely breathe. Certainly no pack of hell hounds the witch can summon could scent us here. The cat and I snuggle together for comfort.

A sort of roaring, humming, grumbling noise comes from behind me. Light shines over the road outside the fence, a dirt-track with black-shadowed potholes showing in it like sores on a beggar's face.

A flying kettle, as big as the village bake-oven, white-glazed with a middle blue stripe, comes bouncing and bumping and lurching from one side to the other up the road, more lively than any boiling kettle that ever bounced on a hearth. A glowing red coal burns on top as when a househusband piles coals on a kettle lid to bake in the kettle. The two sides of the kettle pop open and out come two spirits which the witch must have summoned.

By their mustaches they are men-spirits, but they are dressed in women's clothes—shirts and breeches—and those clothes are blue-black with magic signs and symbols on them. Blue-black is the deadly color Sovereign Ladies dress their torturers and executioners in.

The spirits carry metal cups in their hands. When they tilt the cups, light pours out for them to see by. Both have silver shield-shaped talismans over their hearts so they cannot be killed and on their belts a pair of magic silver circlets with which to secure any enemy and on their other side a scabbard holding a short metal rod set into a wooden handle because its magic is so powerful they cannot hold it in their bare hands.

They swing the circles of light from their magic cups all around the yard saying spellwords. One hand on the cat, one hand on the cold steel of my hatchet, the spells have no power upon me.

They go up to the house. The witch comes out on the houseshelf, holding her own magic rod set into a wooden handle, four and one times greater in length than the length of their small metal rods, so much greater in her magic power. She lays further commands on them by spoken spells and goes back inside.

The witch's spirits go about the yard against the sun poking into every bush. I'm ready with my steel. The cat walks out of the bush as I loose it, preparing to leap out and fight. Laughing, the spirits pick up the cat and walk away from me, back to the house.

The poor cat twists in their arms, trying to escape and meowing piteously, but they deliver it to the witch and she takes the poor creature into her lair. The two evil ones return to their kettle, set it aboiling again, and go bouncing away.

Now the witch's house stays dark belowstairs, but a light appears in the loft upstairs. I grip my hatchet and creep out of the bush. Now, I must not only dare the witch to get back to the Oaktree again, I owe that cat a rescue. It swore itself my servant. It delivered itself up so I should not be captured. I must be true lady to it.

My knife in the left hand, my hatchet in the right, I come up to the house door and use my knifepoint in the lock.

The lock is guarded. Demon spirits howl around, but nothing touches my skin. The holy steel protects me. No more delay. Three chops of the hatchet blade and I am through the door.

A light above shows a stairway. Up. Light shows through an open doorway. It is the witch's bedroom. The bed is empty. Its covers are thrown back. I see two closed doors. The cat mews behind one. It opens easily. The cat leaps out. I look inside it for the witch.

There is a black-stone-topped altar with a gleaming red stone basin set in it. Over both is a great round mirror set in a gilded frame. I touch the mirror, thinking it might show me the witch. It swings open. Behind it on concealed shelves all manner of vials and potions have runes and spell signs fixed to them.

The other side of the altar is an oval-shaped stone stool with a single pedestal under it. In front of it is a great black stone trough for mixing magics in. There is a red glass curtain hanging in soft folds like cloth over the trough. The witch could draw it when even she could not bear to see what she had summoned up. So this is where the witch comes to work her most awful spells. I am fortunate the witch did not reach this magic chamber.

I see the cat mewing at the other closed door. I bend to put it aside out of harm's way before I open that door. A thundersound rings in my ear. I feel a blow on my shoulder. The door is shattered.

Through the door, I see the witch inside pointing

her long magic rod at me. I snatch the rod from her and fling it to the far side of the room. It falls to the floor making another thunder and plaster showers down from the ceiling.

I pull the witch out from among her magic robes and show the edge of my steel hatchet blade to her. She understands that and stands quiet. Just then the howling demon voices, which have not stopped shrieking since I entered, fall silent. The cat is waiting by the door for me.

I haul the witch along with me, in front of me, the hatchet blade against her throat. From the top of the stairs I see the witch's two spirits from the flying kettle standing in the doorway with their metal rods drawn. But they see I have my hatchet blade against their mistress' throat and slowly they back from the doorway before me, the witch, and the cat.

The witch tries to trip me as we back around the houseshelf, but by a trick of balance the juggler lad taught me, I turn our fall into a leap to the ground. I drag the witch backward step by step to the hillside. Once I reach the spot where I first found myself in the Otherworld, then she must send me back.

A cold wind is blowing against my back. Lightning makes the spirits following me blink. As I back through the garden gate, there is a great streak of lightning and the jewel of light on the pole goes out. The witch's power is fading. I am winning.

At the bottom of the steps up the hillside, the desperate witch drives her bony elbow into my stomach, forcing out my breath. She flings herself free and her spirits rush me.

The cat streaks between us and one falls over the cat and the other falls over the first one. I turn and strike my hatchet into the hilltop over my head and jerk myself up by the handle. I scrabble with my free hand and then with the hatchet hand, releasing the hatchet to grab for a hold.

I am soaked in cold water, blinded with lightning glare, ears ringing. When my eyes clear, I am clinging to cold stone in pouring rain and the hatchet handle before me is charred wood. If I lie still, soaked, in the cold, I must die.

I struggle upslope on hands and knees until I can stand again on the Highslopes Trail. I had not reached the midway cairn. Last-fields is nearer than Farslopes, so I turn back.

The sun's warmth is welcome when it rises as I stagger into Last-fields and down the rutted track to the Oaktree. Its door stands open even this early. There are some old women warming the benches there from dawn till midnight.

Kareth steps into the sunlit doorway, beermugs in hand, to see who's coming. The sunlight shows the hairs straggling in her eyes are gray. I don't remember seeing Kareth was gray before. Her mouth drops open and there are only five teeth left in it. I don't remember noticing that. She stares at me like a ghost.

"Andrith? Is it Andrith?"

"The storm on Highslopes last night was too bad," I answer. "I couldn't get over."

"It is Andrith. Set a stool for her. Fetch beer. Something hot. Sit down, Andrith."

I drop onto my stool by the door where the smoke won't affect my voice and my singing. Harper's place.

"Here's bread and cheese now and a mug of beer. Then you shall tell us where you've been these seven years."

"Seven years?" I stop the beer mug at my lips. "I left here yesterday to cross to Farslopes and the storm caught me. The night in the storm felt like seven years, but the water's still sloshing in my boots."

"See this young-un fetched your bread." Kareth points. "It was her danced to your music unborn when last you played for us, Andrith. Folk at Farslopes sent word they hadn't seen you, so we searched the trail and down into DeathPass for your body. We dared even that for you. You might have let us know, sometime this seven year, you were alive."

"Pull off my boots. You'll see the rainwater from the storm I walked into on Highslopes setting out this morning from this place." I answer.

The child does and water pours out and sinks into

the straw on the hardpacked dirt floor. I stretch my cold, wet feet in soaked socks in the warm patch of sunlight.

"We've had no rain for a ten-day. All the creeks between here and Highslopes Trail have gone dry," croaks an old woman.

"And was you in the Otherworld, then, where a night can last seven years?" asks Kareth.

"I must have been. I let myself down into DeathPass to escape the lightning and then . . ."

So I tell my tale and all in the village are there listening when I finish it.

"Well," says Kareth, "I'm sure that after that we could all use a cheerful tune, even to a seven-year-old song. Have out your harp, Andrith."

I draw out my harp from the harpcase. It parts in my hand, the wood frame splintered, the strings dangling, and among the ruin the piece of crumpled metal the witch's rod cast at it.

Without a harp to play, I can't earn my bread. The price of a new harp is more coin than I've ever seen or ever will see.

"Won't she sing, then?" a querulous old woman asks from the back.

"Hush, her harp's broken. The witch smashed it in the Otherworld."

"Can't it be mended?"

"No, now, she must have a new one."

"New one takes silver. Singing for the likes of us, Andrith never sees silver."

"Enough copper makes silver," says a young lad. "I'll give over my copper fairing."

"I've a silver piece," says old Lor. "Saved it for my burying. Guess I'd rather hear some tunes from Andrith while I'm living."

"I save a silver piece each year for fines to my lady's bailiff," says Kareth. "Let her take 'em out in chickens this year. The hens had good settings this spring."

Coins clink in a mug and the mug comes to me full.

"Count it out, Andrith. Is there a harp's price there?"

There is a harp's price there unless they've changed a deal in seven years. If I had a fair face and served a great lady, she might have tossed me a harp's price like a bone to a dog. Perhaps the scar that has kept me harping for the poor was not such bad luck as I thought.

"Mow" says the white and yellow spotted cat in the doorway, looking up in my face with its green eyes.

All around me I hear the whisper of knives sliding from sheaths for fear of this Otherworld creature.

At once I scoop the cat up to my knee and sign it with the triangle of the Holy One, enclosing it in the Love, the Power, the Righteousness. All see that the cat rubs its head contentedly against the hand that has blessed it with the sign no evil creature can abide.

"Fetch some scraps and the broken clay bowl," commands Kareth. "Andrith's cat will need feeding, too."

"It walked through all our dogs and none so much as barked at it," says the old woman. "It will have no trouble traveling about with her, that's certain."

The cat snuggles against me, purring.

THE DANCE OF KALI
by Richard Corwin

Richard Corwin is a nice-looking young man whom I have known since he was in high school; I knew him first as a costumer, now married to another of same, either of whom who could easily have become a professional in that over-crowded field. He chose instead to try his hand at architecture, advertising, commercial art, photography, book illustration, early childhood education, textbook publishing, and now, writing. He is working on a novel—where have I heard that before? He is a former Berkeley resident, currently living in Los Angeles, and his wife Leslie is now a museum curator. He has sold before this to SWORD AND SORCERESS, Volumes II and IV, and the present story is a direct sequel to "The Eyes of Kali" in Volume IV. Success at writing short stories is not an absolute concomitant of success at novel writing, but for most writers it comes first; and we'd suppose Corwin would write novels as well as he seems to do everything else.

Stealing along the back of the night, Kali the Black, Kali the Destroyer, flew up, servant clutched in her arms, through the darkness until she reached the Bridge of the World's End. She had come to contemplate how to destroy the world now that the Wheel of Law had been shattered.

Placing her servant, named only Kalidasa, on one of the rock promontories of the bridge, Kali settled herself down to contemplate what should be done. As she sat, her girdle of skulls rattled about bare hips that were the color of the midnight sky. With hands that were the color of the infinite voice, she smoothed the ornate chignon of raven-colored hair that framed her

193

beauteous face. Her Dasa's hair and hands were black
also, but only tattooed. The Dasa's skin was a dark
tan, and her hair of equal color.

Hugging one knee close to her body, leaving her
other leg to dangle freely over the bridge, Kali allowed her foot to whisk about the smoke from the
burning of the Golden Temple of the Law, from which
she had just been released of a millenium's imprisonment with the help of the Dasa. Her blue-black lips
curled into a smile as she drew in the scent of the
universe. Freedom felt wonderful.

The Dasa sat beside her mistress and turned over the
day's events in her mind. She had stolen the eyes of the
gods from their statues in the Temple, effectively keeping
them from seeing the events that would next transpire on
the Earth. She had also defeated Yama the Destroyer in
battle, broken the Columns of the Ages of the Law, and
freed the Staff of Kali from the Column of the Kali-Yuga
before finally turning the Wheel that had imprisoned
Kali for three full Ages.

Clutching the powerful Staff of Kali, the Dasa looked
up at her lady. The Kali-Yuga, the Golden Age of the
reign of Kali, would be a short one. The tales had
spoken of this, too. It would, and could only last one
day. It was all the time that Kali was fated to have.
Soon she would see mighty Kali spread her arms across
the fields of Earth and crush it in the folds of her
night-body. Earthquake, flood, hurricane and volcano,
the tales told, would be called to complete the story of
the Earth. It was a story that Kali alone would write.
None knew the dance but the one called Kali, who was
truly neither goddess nor human. Not a goddess, because
the gods now slept with the turning of the Wheel. Not
a human, for no human could do what she was to do.
Reflexively, Kali called herself "The Fated Warrior."

Kali turned to her Dasa and spoke with words that
were the winter wind blowing across the Delhi plain.
"You have freed me as you were always meant to.
You have done well. For your struggle you will be
permitted to be free of the Wheel of Existence. You
will live no more on Earth, but rather you will sit
forever by my side in the Western Paradise."

The Dasa smiled at her mistress. "Thank you, Great One," she said humbly.

"Now," Kali said, "the time has come for me to destroy the Earth and make way for the new world that Vishnu will create when the rending of Earth's core wakes him from his dreaming."

"What does he dream, Mistress?" the Dasa asked.

"None know. Perhaps not even the Great Boar himself. But his dreams are the essence of what the new world will be: the very fabric of the next eternal Age of the Law. And as he sleeps, so must the rest of the gods. None must hear the cries of the faithful as they are plunged into the abyss as I extinguish the stars with my dance. With my waking, no more may be saved. The Day of Judgment has passed this way. It will not come again until the Wheel of Law turns again, and the gods are awakened."

"A sleep that we would prefer them to remain in," said a voice as velvety as the cracking of bones. A new form had lit upon the Bridge of the Earth, and squatted there, regarding Kali with eyes of volcanic fire. Its skin was a clotted red splashed with tongues of gold. Its body was shaped somewhere between that of a man, a lion, and a toad, bulbously formed and squat. The head was like that of a huge red bat, ringed with a mane of fingerlong black and gold scales. Its wide mouth was brimming with shining silver fangs. But its wings were by far its most remarkable feature, for they rose along its back like the feathery, spiny fins of a lionfish that swayed like leaves in a gentle breeze. Each of the three oily red wings was tipped at the end of each individual spine with a small black poisonous quill. "They must sleep through their own ages for a time," the splintery voice continued, "so that we may preside over the earth as its true rulers. And to accomplish this, we must ask you, great Kali-Ma, Author of the Destruction, to stand aside while we rule. For if you do not do this, we will make you stand aside."

"You call me by the name that is the name of my aspect of destruction. I know your kind, but I do not know your name. Tell me what it is, O little rakshasa," she said to the thing.

"I am Radmairas, King of the Rakshasa, and Lord of the New Earth of the Age of Kali. So, will you stand aside for us, Great One? We only ask that you stand aside for one day," it said, stretching out a claw at the end of a long webbed finger.

"Why should I stand aside for you, or any other lesser king of the Heavens?" she asked. "It is my way to destroy the world. To fail to do so would be against my nature. Like all those who are only like the gods, I would be forced to spend an existence on the new Earth in penitence if I did not succeed in crushing it."

"But Great One, if you destroy the Earth, will you not also be destroying all those who worship you? In eliminating your worshipers, you eliminate your own existence, do you not?"

"But I am not a god. Their worship does me little good, except this once to set me free," she smiled down at the Dasa.

The Dasa lowered her eyes in embarrassment, then spoke up to the beast, "And if she is meant to be a god in the next Turn, we will be reborn as our reward for our faith!"

"And if they are not?" Radmairas asked Kali in a sinister snarl that resembled a cat's.

"Then I will cease to be. Or cease to be godlike. But if that is my fate, what am I able to care?"

Radmairas addressed the Dasa. "She says she does not care. What do you think of that? She is so cavalier with your fate."

The Dasa turned her nose up at him, and did not reply.

"You, not care?" he mused quietly to Kali. "You are a coward, then, if you do not care about your own fate!"

Kali's mouth frowned, then said, "A coward does things that are against his better judgment because of his fear. I fear neither the destruction of my followers, nor the possible cessation of my own existence. How, then, am I a coward?"

"Because you are afraid of rebellion. Because you are afraid to take control of the universe for our own. We are not afraid of rebellion, therefore we will be the new rulers. And as the new rulers of the Earth, we forbid you to any negative acts of ultimate destruction," he hissed.

"The creation of the new world from the ashes of the old is far from a negative act. It is an act of affirmation. An act of cleansing the whole of the universe. But few, even among the old gods, could understand this. It is also an act that I will no longer let you stand in the way of," she said stroking her fingers across her necklace of skulls. "Kalidasa, attend me." The black-clad servant rose and bowed.

"It is time we left this place," she said to the rakshasa. "I will not have my servant see such quibbling, even if you claim kingship. You are no king on the upper planes, and thus, beneath such time as I have given you. It was foolish of me to have lingered here so long to listen to the jabbering of an idiot who calls himself the new ruler of the Earth. I have a spell to weave."

"Twice a fool, Kali-Ma." the rakshasa snarled like warm honey. "For I have diverted you long enough for my legions to silently mass beneath the bridge. As I had said, 'If you will not stand aside, we will make you stand aside.' " He chuckled a hideously malevolent chuckle, and said in his loudest bark, "Beasts of the old world, make her obedient to our will!"

And suddenly, the stars dimmed away as the sky filled with the silent fluttering of spined wings as thousands of rakshasa fanned to attack.

The only sound was the clicking of their long, curved nails. They were legion. Ancient horrors, each, smelling of bile and sweat. Some were red as dried blood, some a leprous greenish hue, some the sickly blue-purple of badly bruised skin, others the black of brackish water. They each carried vicious weapons: long steel swords that opened and closed like obscene flowers, lances thrice their height that bristled with poison-tipped spines, and axes that were twined with serpentine quills. They spread their wings until they formed a curtain that obscured even the darkness of the night sky. "Kali," they whispered softly.

One rakshasa, larger and more toadlike in form, who dripped with folds of sagging flesh, broke from the ranks of the demons with a heronlike roar and darted straight at Kali, brandishing its fanged sword. Quietly, she sat. Waiting. The Toad whipped its sword about its body, preparing to behead her. As he swung the blade toward her, she spoke a fragment of the spell of destruction, then whipped her hand up into the path of the swing. When the sword touched her hand, it shattered like thundering glass into a thousand shards, sending splinters to shower into the smoldering volcano beneath them.

The Toad sputtered obscene mouthings, drooling as it did. Kali paid him no heed, and moved not an inch. The wings rustled quietly above, curiously waiting for an end to the odd tableaux that was unfolding.

The Dasa, feeling the specter of fear coil about her in the air, reached into her garments to retrieve a long tulwar. Whispering deadly spells, she arched herself into fighting posture, prepared to defend her mistress to the death. But Kali turned to her and said, "You need not take arms against a sea of demons on my account. By opposing, you alone cannot end them. There are other things that you must do."

The Toad, waxing angrier, hissed and spat until his claws dripped nightshade. Extending his wings to their full height, he snapped them back, diving at the seated Kali with his nails and hindclaws aimed at her face.

For a few moments, the beating of his wings covered her body, and she could not be seen. Kalidasa began to glance about warily, winding her stance tighter, waiting for the first of the demons to come at her. But they did not. They waited, watching with their horrid nails clicking away, until the sound of breaking bones stilled all other noise. Kali had ripped her hands through the flesh of the Toad's wings and had begun to shred his body into long, lifeless strips of oozing flesh. Then she tied the refuse into the remnants of the wings and threw the ball toward Radmairas, who skittered out of its way.

"That is enough," she said coldly. With that, she stood up, along the Bridge of the World's End, and stretched her black form against the un-darkness. Like morning fog, the night crept back through the wings of the demons and clothed itself with her, shimmering like velvet. "It is time that I returned your graciousness, Radmairas. Dasa, attend me."

"I am here," the Dasa replied, easing her readiness.

"It is time for us to do what we must do," Kali said.

The rakshasa all moved forward with a clattering of swords. But Kali waved them back with a single finger. "You must wait your turn," she said to them with a hiss as cold as their own. The rakshasa moved back quietly, and waited. They knew that the time to begin the true battle was at hand.

Kali removed the necklaces from her neck and placed them around the neck of the Dasa. Then she tugged the bracelets from her wrists and handed them over. Finally, she unbelted the girdle of skulls from her waist and wrapped the clattering heads around the Dasa. "These," she said loudly, "will protect you from harm as I fight. If it becomes too thick for you to see me, then you must run to the far end of this bridge, and wait until the battle is done. Is that understood?"

"No," the Dasa said, "I am a warrior and a priestess. It is my sacred duty to defend you to my dying breath. I would rather die here in your service and forgo my chance to watch the universe end. It is my life to serve; that is the meaning of 'Dasa.' "

"And you will serve. I have a higher purpose for you," Kali said in a whisper so soft that no other could hear. "You must do the killing of Radmairas while I fight these demons. For him, the purpose of this battle is to divert my attention from him and my destiny. For me, the battle will be a diversion to allow you to kill him. His opposition was known to the gods long ago. It has always been a part of the great plan. But the plan may come undone. As I am neither mortal nor godlike, I alone may speak the spell. As he is also neither mortal nor godlike, his blood will make the potency to weave the spell."

"Do you think that they can truly defeat your destiny?" Kalidasa asked. "Can we stop them all before the day is out?"

Kali's eyebrows knotted together. "We must not think of that now. You must go to the end of the bridge when the fighting is hard, and slip away unnoticed. These bracelets will help your own strong sorcery to change your human form into one that will go unheeded by their kind. In this form, you must seek out Radmairas and kill him. Take the blood of his body and smear it on your hands; it will enable you to destroy with a touch any rakshasa that would oppose you. Then bring me Radmairas' head. There will be enough blood in it to cover my body. That is all that will be needed to work the whole of the spell of destruction.''

The Dasa nodded.

"Radmairas!" Kali shouted across the bridge, "I have given my Dasa leave to go should the fray become too thick. I demand your word that she will not be harmed if she does so.''

Radmairas, slouching on a promontory, curled back his hideous face into a toothy smile and sneered, "And if I do not?''

"Then I will jump across this bridge and do to you what I have just done to the one foolish enough to touch me.''

His smirk faded. "Of course, Great One. I am always happy to be honorable in combat.''

"Give me my staff, and go sit upon yonder rock and wait," Kali said.

The Dasa handed her the black iron staff, bowed deeply, then fell to the ground and kissed the black feet of Kali. Scrabbling up with a hidden, knowing smile, she ran and sat, legs crossed, upon the rock.

Kali ran her fingers along the length of the staff, sizing up its qualities. Then she raised it over her head and struck it upon the bridge beneath her. A shower of sparks flew upward to the sound of a distant anvil being hammered. With a single blow she had forged a long black sword from the staff. It was as black as the night, black as her skin, slender as she, with a long, slow curve that ended in a point so sharp that the eye could not see it.

Testing its weight with a quick stroke that slit the sky, Kali smiled long enough to admire her handiwork, then shouted a shout that could be heard across the heavens. "I am ready! This day my Dasa has broken me free of the Temple, free of the prison that has held me for centuries. This day I have flown to the Bridge at the End of the World. This day, too, I will take the world in my hands and crush it. And then I will destroy the very fabric of the universe with my fingers. It is my way, it is my destiny. The path to destruction has been laid. I will not be stopped by man, gods, or demons who think that they are better than both!"

She widened her legs into a broad stance and lowered the sword to her eye-level. "I am ready," she whispered.

At once the fabric of the sky came down upon her in the form of ragged wings. With long arcs, she slashed at the demons, scattering dozens of them with each stroke. Jagged swords swiped at her, but fell far from their mark, as she parried and riposted with blinding skill. Now and again a pithy squeal or howling shriek would be heard as she disemboweled another rakshasa. Unseen in the fray they would tumble Earthward, their bilious bodies becoming the heads of meteors as they crashed into the blueness of the day sky.

Her fight turned from the minutes into the hours as time wore on. There seemed no end to the rakshasa who came to fight her. No sooner would she kill a dozen when another dozen would appear to take their place. Down on the Earth below eyes gazed upward to see stars fall from the heavens as they never had before. Children giggled with glee and wiser minds pondered what the blaze of bright light might mean, until the sky began to blacken. The Reign of the Dark Ones began. Having slipped away from the diverted Kali, Radmairas led his second army downward to begin the conquest of Earth. The capitals of the world became blood-drenched thronerooms to the rakshasa as they rapidly raped and ravished and ravaged without concern or qualm.

Above the Earth the hours stretched long into the night of her day, and Kali began to fear that the day of her duty would slip away. Should the day pass, her destiny would be undone, and the world would slip into the Age of the Rakshasa.

Finishing a long slash at her attackers, she began to swing her sword in such a fashion that the long curving strokes began to form patterns, patterns that created larger patterns that mesmerized, for a moment, the whole of the rakshasa horde. And in that moment, she spoke two silent words that told Kalidasa it was time to follow Radmairas.

Down the Bridge of the World's End slipped Kalidasa, until she reached the edge where it became part of the Earth. There she smelled the air for the scent of Radmairas. His sickly smell was not hard to locate. She looked at the sun. It told her that she had about an hour left in the day to do her deed and return to Kali. She contemplated a prayer for a moment, but then decided that it would waste valuable time. Picturing wings to fly in her mind's eye, she caused wings of filigreed silver to form on her back. The bracelets did their work well. With an unexpected grace she lifted herself away from the bridge and sped on toward the ruins of the Golden Temple at the top of the world. While flying, she began to picture herself in the form of a rakshasa so that she would go unnoticed in the volcanic ruins. Slowly, the beautiful tanned skin became black leather, her tattooed hands became talons, and the wings that had formed on her back scaled over.

Touching down on the ruins of the Temple of the Law, Kalidasa looked to all the world like one of the foul demons. Covered, as they were, in jewelry, she was differentiated only by the belt of skulls that girdled her waist. But none took special note of that, for it seemed but a baroque fashion. All about her feet was strewn the wreckage of the temple mixed with the carnage of the rakshasa. The ground, slippery with blood, was strewn with piles of violated bodies, torn apart by evil whim. Her people, the worshipers of Kali, lay prominently among them. She did not shed a tear, for it would have given her away. Instead, she vowed to kill all the rakshasa on the mountain before returning to Kali, if she had the time.

Kalidasa the rakshasa trudged up the hill to where a pavilion of human skin and bones had been erected. It could only be the new palace of Radmairas. Only he could have so little taste. Around the pavilion milled fawning demons. The demons were scraping before two large black rakshasa in hopes of getting past the entrance that they guarded and into the pavilion itself. Once in the pavilion, they could oblige other demons in order to gain a final audience where they could be obsequious before Radmairas himself. Kalidasa approached one of the two guards who was being fondled by a corpulent female rakshasa with irridescent wings. "All I wish," said the female, "is to give all-mighty Radmairas the bounty which he is due by a subject as loyal as I. Perhaps if I shared my bounty with you, I might gain audience . . ."

The black guard grunted with a sneering leer as her hand inched down his belly.

Kalidasa strode up to the guard and regarded the female with an undemonic smile. "Let me help you show your bounty to this beautiful black one, sister-mine," Kalidasa said.

The guard smiled a demonic smile. Kalidasa bent low to her knees, drew back her rakshasa hand, and drove it full into the bloated belly of the black giant. With a groan, he folded over and onto the irridescent female who obligingly straddled herself atop the fallen giant and covered him with toothy kisses.

The whole scene, going largely unnoticed by the pleasure-prone rakshasa, enabled Kalidasa to step into the first room of the pavilion. From there, she stole through the various rooms of murdering, copulating, or gorging demons until she found herself standing outside of the open throneroom in the pavilion. It had taken her half of the hour to make this much progress. There was so little time left. Her only hope lay in striking Radmairas down quickly. An icy chill crept across her heart as she thought for a moment that even if she killed him quickly, there still might not be enough time. But she knew that she had to try. She bit her lip and moved forward.

She stepped into the throneroom and was amazed at

how much squalor had been accomplished in so little time. The room was filled with scores of groveling demons, scraping for the small favor of the king. Braziers burned with obscene perfumes, sending up a sickening smoke to coalesce among the hungry vultures in the rafters. The walls were spattered with red pearls of blood. Great works of art hung torn and defaced on the walls. Like the mountainside, there were corpses everywhere. Only here, they were partially consumed. The sight of the heaps of steaming flesh sickened Kalidasa, but they also made her angrier.

Radmairas sat on a throne of bodies. The bodies were the worshipers of Kali. His fat body was draped with the regalia of a dozen royal treasuries and the great temples of the world. His skin was dripping in slopped wine and human fat. He alternated between hearing appeals, gulping bowls of wine, and toying with the naked body of a half-dead woman.

Kalidasa rolled in the muck of the floor to further camouflage herself. It reeked. She rapidly crawled over broken bodies, under tables and through entwined legs to gain half the distance to the throne. Then she groveled, like the rest, over the last few feet. Bored with the human at last, Radmairas threw her from his throne to the floor. With a soft thud, she landed before Kalidasa. It was, as she had expected, one of her fellow worshipers. The woman gurgled out an unheard plea as she died. This was too much for Kalidasa. She stood up, separating herself from the grovelers.

"I have a gift for the Great King of the Rakshasa," she cried out to Radmairas. "I have for you the belt of mighty Kali. The belt of skulls that she fashioned from the skulls of the elder gods before they perished in the last turn. It fell from the waist of her Dasa on the Bridge at the Edge of the Earth. Seeing it fall, I have brought it to you, new king of kings."

Spilling his winebowl onto the floor with a hasty gesture, Radmairas lept up from his chair and peered at Kalidasa the rakshasa with excited eyes. She unfastened the belt and held it up for the demon king to see. He lurched down the steps and stood before the belt of skulls. The court was silent for a curious moment. Even the scented smoke seemed to still itself to peer at the talisman she held in her hands.

Radmairas extended his taloned finger toward the skulls and touched one of them. A tiny spark snapped between his claw and the bone's dry eye socket. A maniacal grin crossed his face. "Yes!" he shrieked. "It is true. This is the one. The true belt of Kali, the belt of the heads of the elder ones who imprisoned us so long ago. We have a talisman of the Elder Time." He gazed around the room, making certain that he had the eye of all present. "You are all witness to a historic moment. With this talisman, we become the inheritors of the earth! We will add to this string the heads of some of the young gods when we kill them. We are the inheritors! We are the ones!" He began to roar with vicious glee.

She was afraid that he might never stop bellowing and that her time would be stolen away forever when he suddenly said, "Give me the belt, my pretty. Your gift shall bring you the boon of your naming. Anything is yours. Name your price for this token that you have given me."

Knowing that she had him, and that she had won, she spoke her request in words so soft that he had to bend to hear them. "All that this humble servant requests of the mighty Radmairas . . ." as he bent closer, she roped the belt about his neck, "is the rightful destruction of the universe . . . which will commence with your death!"

She tightened the belt and twisted her body under his, forming a lever with her hip. She bent her body from the waist and threw Radmairas over her back with deft speed, cracking his neck with a sound like dry splintering ice. His body splattered onto the floor with a second, wet, cracking noise. Stooping down, she tore his head from his body with her demon claws and bathed her hands in his blood. There was so little time left in the day, and she had yet to make her way to the bridge.

"Only one skull will be added to the belt of Kali,"

she said, refastening the belt to her waist with her prize, "and it will belong to no young god."

The rakshasa in the room were stunned for a moment. Radmairas' death had happened so quickly that most thought it to be some trick or illusion. But the passage of a few seconds proved enough to dispel the disbelief of most in attendance. A hissing whisper began to spread through the room. Elegant claws began to reach for silver-chased knives.

"Draw what weapons you would," Kalidasa said, feeling an odd sensation come over her. "They will do you no good. It is time for you to pay for the foul indignities that you have heaped upon the bodies of mankind."

And with that, her flesh began to shimmer before those assembled in the pavillion. The charm of the blood was beginning to take effect. She could feel her body move faster than she could keep track. Her rakshasa form began to slough away, melting into an ectoplasmic puddle that mingled with the wine and blood on the slick floor. Her human form passed into view for a moment, and then was obscured by the radiant blue of the two tattooed and bloodstained hands flying about her body, crackling the air like angry ravens.

The room, which had been moving toward her, began to suddenly fall away from her. At her feet demonic bodies began to wiggle backward in a wormlike fashion. If a black blur could be said to smile, it smiled. "None will escape here . . ." she said.

She clenched her fists and spun them at the nearest rakshasa. Upon contact, the demon's body shook with a resounding thud, then ignited into a giant black flame that flickered up and out of the roof of the pavilion. She struck at a dozen more demons with such speed that she appeared to be only obsidian lightning, and they, too, became incandescent blackness that floated skyway. Within a space of a few moments, the inhabitants of the pavilion had all died screaming deaths. Then the obsidian lightning sped down the mountainside, striking all within its path and leaving behind a jet-colored fire to fly to heaven.

Then, taking two quick steps, Kalidasa crossed the world and stood upon the Bridge at the End of the World. There was time. Only minutes, but there was time!

Standing still, she looked across the bridge to where Kali the mighty was slaying the rakshasa with her long black sword. Kalidasa called to her mistress, and Kali replied with a jubilant laugh, "You have the power, my precious one. Help rid me of these masterless demons."

The Dasa smiled. Taking the belt from her waist, she plucked off the head of Radmairas and tossed it to Kali, following that with her belt and other jewelry. The Fated Warrior caught them with one hand while piercing her sword through the throat of an algae-green beast. Redressing herself, Kali rubbed her body in the blood that oozed from the head and spoke again the first lines of the spell of destruction. With the speaking, her body suddenly grew to thrice its size and its flesh melted away until only her glittering black bones remained. She had become the form of Kali-Ma, Kali the destroyer.

Kali-Ma squared her shoulder blades and turned toward the fray of demons that remained. Her Dasa joined her and together they began to strike at the rakshasa with a whirling legion of arms. The sky rained with black stars as the opponents of the destruction died. Killing the last of the rakshasa, Kali-Ma expanded herself across half of the Earth's sky and let out a victorious cry that cracked the edges of the universe. Her day was not undone.

Reaching out with a giant bony hand, Kali-Ma took Kalidasa upward into a protected corner of the heavens and spoke to her. "You have served your mistress well, little one," she said. "You have gained a place next to me when the next turning comes. For now, you will be the sole human witness to the end of all things."

The Dasa smiled softly, "To have been your servant, to have worn your belt, your bracelets, to have changed into another being, to have done your bidding for a moment of time has been enough for this one."

"You are deserving of much, much more," Kali said.

Taking four steps that circled the earth, Kali then stretched her fleshless arms across Earth's sky and brought her skeletal hands down to touch the ground. And as she touched the ground, the Earth quivered for a moment, then shook itself into a huge black flame that exploded into the huge black body of Kali. The body doubled in size and began to shine like a black diamond.

Kali took five steps and stood before the sun. Her hand reached out and plucked the light from the sun. In six steps she strode to the corners of the universe. And standing on the corners, with the whole of that which is and that which is not beneath her, she began to dance. She danced the dance that was herself, the dance that was Kali-Ma. She stepped lightly, nimbly across the fabric of the firmament, extinguishing suns as her feet touched them. And one by one, the Dasa of Kali watched the lamps in the skies darken. Eternal night fell, and the heavens were torn asunder by the gentle dancing feet of Kali.

And out of that darkness a voice that was softer than the blackness from which it spoke whispered, "Vishnu, it is your time."

Deep within the protected womb of the darkness, the Kalidasa curled into a warm corner of desolate nothingness to sleep. She would sleep until she awakened in the new Western Paradise, beside her beloved Kali. Remembering the Earth, on which she had grown, the Kalidasa shed a single tear. And as she slept, that single tear became the form of Kali the Unfated One, for she had dispatched her single duty. Now, she would wait for the new universe to begin to see what wonders it might hold for her. But this time she would not see them alone. With a gentle caress for her Dasa, Kali wrapped her arms around her, and slept.

ANCIENT HEARTBREAK
by Diann Partridge

Diann Partridge has been writing for me since the days when I was producing fanzines; she was well known to all readers for her winning stories in my first couple of fanzine contests. She appeared in one of the Darkover anthologies—maybe more than one—and in my last volume of SWORD AND SORCERESS.

She lived in Wyoming, and all over everywhere as a member of the U.S. Army—I think if I'd had to live in the army I'd want to live in Wyoming, too. She is married to another ex-army man and though I don't remember what she does for a living (this is why I ask people for an update of their bio every year—I don't keep the letter from year to year and I am notoriously short on memory), I do know that she is one of the people whose stories always surprise me by being extraordinarily good. And after all, what else do we need to know about a writer?

———————————

Nicolenna had been awakened in the middle of the night by a mysterious piping. The sound was compelling and a little frightening, but at the same time it called to her in a way she could not resist. In the warm peaceful hours after midnight she had dressed quietly so as not to disturb her sleeping sisters and slipped out of the house.

She was used to roaming around at night, but of late it had become harder to escape unnoticed. She had never been one to remain safe behind walls simply because everyone said it was the appropriate behavior for a girl. Now with rumors of armed brigands in the area and strange beings skulking around the forest's edge, her father had increased the nightly guard. Her brothers had taken to strutting around in new importance with their tinkling mail shirts and shiny swords. Of course the women kept to their regular jobs (only more so now) in the cook house and still room and with the washing tubs.

Not that for Nicolenna di Stadda. She hated being confined to the house and escaped as often as possible to the barns where the horses were or just into the woods. Away from prying eyes. Her older sisters huffed and 'tsked, but her mother merely shook her head and let her youngest daughter run. Lady di Stadda knew and understood her children. Let Nicolenna enjoy her stolen time for now. Lessons for gentling could come later.

Though now, there was only the piping.

Hiding in the shadows at the edge of the main gate she waited until the guard had stomped past, then she ran across the clearing and into the forest. None of the dogs so recently pressed into guard duty barked when they scented her. She had handled them all as pups.

The piping greeted her, begged her to wander deeper into the silvered trees. Hurry, hurry. The farther she went, the more insistent the music became and she began to feel as though she were dream walking.

In a tiny moonlit glade she found the music and the piper. He sat gracefully on a log, a small wooden pipe to his lips. Light from the moon cast a halo around his thick golden curls. His eyes gleamed as green as the tender spring leaves entwined in his hair. She stopped several feet from him, taking in his magnificence from the tips of his velvety spike horns to his dainty hooves. When he lowered the pipe and smiled at her, she thought her heart would burst with happiness.

Time held no meaning for Nicolenna after that. Moonlight or daylight, there was only the piper in the glade and their lovemaking.

She stirred in the pine-bough bed and sat up. Knuckling the haze of sleep from her eyes, she scrambled up and looked around.

"Where am I?" she wondered out loud.

The day moon Neva hung full above the tree tops. When she had seen it last, Neva had been four days to full. And there was no mistaking that rosy glow of Neva when she was full. Looking down at her clothes she saw they were torn and grass-stained, full of stick-tights and leaves. There were scratches on her arms and legs as though she had run full tilt through the bushes.

Her feet were bare and filthy and her hands the same way and even her face felt dirty when she yawned. Her worst problem was the uncomfortable empty feeling in her stomach—as though she hadn't eaten in days.

Blinking like an owl in the strong sunlight, she stumbled out of the glade to look for a path. She found a bush covered with new spring dew berries. Ignoring her dirty fingernails she stripped the branches, stuffing the berries into her mouth. Their taste was tart and tangy, just what she needed to clear the last of the cobwebs from her head. When the pains from her stomach had been taken care of, she looked around for a stream. The gurgling of a brook could be heard not far off and she headed for it.

After satisfying her thirst, she walked about gathering wood.

"I wonder if the spell will work for me now?" she said to herself. She closed her eyes and wiggled her toes in the bare earth. Raising her hands over the kindling she called up the energy from within herself as she had been taught. She felt a gathering inside, then a tingling that spread from her mind to her arms and then to her hands, then heard a *snap!* When she opened her eyes and looked down, the branches were smoking. Quickly she dropped to her knees and blew softly to encourage the flame. When the fire was properly established, she jumped up and did a little victory dance around it.

"It worked, it worked! Oh, it worked! I knew that what the piper and I did couldn't have been a dream. How wonderful!"

She stripped off the filthy clothes and anchored

them with a rock to soak in the brook. Then she jumped in herself and splashed around as quickly as she could in the cold water, trying to remove as much of the dirt as possible. There was dried blood on the inside of her thighs, which should not have come as much of a surprise but it did. She knew she was weeks from her moontime, so this was just further proof that her piper had been real.

She scrubbed out her tunic and breeches as best she could, then wrung them out and hung them over some branches she had rigged up over the fire. She danced around and around the fire to dry herself off and stay warm, then went to find something else to eat. The forest was generous and she picked up last year's blacknuts, cracking them open between two rocks and eating the sweet meats inside. There were even early spring mushrooms to pick and eat.

Her clothes were still damp along the seams when she put them back on, but she could spend no more time waiting. Her newly acquired power seemed to bubble and jump inside her, causing her to jump and twirl on the outside. She couldn't wait to get home and *tell!* Dousing the fire she set out to find her way out.

She had always been at ease with the forest, but she had never been in this deep before. Even keeping Neva over her right shoulder, it took her the greater part of the day to walk out. Close to the edge she caught the scent of something burning. She stopped and closing her eyes, thinking how the long tedious hours in the classroom when her mother had instructed them in how to do this were paying off, she turned her sight inward. Something big was burning. No, something big *had* burned, now what was left was smoldering. There was no fear here among the trees, so it could not have been them that had burned.

Fear began to uncoil inside her as she walked closer to the smell. When she stumbled free of the trees and stood in the clearing that had circled her home, for the first few minutes she could not believe what she was seeing.

Even the very foundation stones of her home had

been blasted up and lay smoking. The house and all the barns and sheds, everything was in ruins. The sense of outrage that replaced the fear told her this destruction had nothing to do with magic; this was vilest sorcery. What she had used to start the fire was inner magic, called for from within and paid for by herself. But this—this desecration was only evil.

Nicolenna forced herself to walk through the ruins when all she wanted to do was crawl away and hide. There wasn't a piece of furniture left unbroken. Cooking utensils lay in twisted lumps of metal. The huge copper stew pot was identifiable only by its color; otherwise, it was a melted blob. She wandered slowly from room to room, seeing nothing and praying she could wake up from this nightmare.

She found what was left of her father and brothers and the other male servants in the main hall. Their bodies were laid out side by side, but not peacefully. With her new-found magic she could sense their dying agony. It hung in the very air around her. They had been held in place by sorcery, then cut open from throat to groin. Their insides had been methodically pulled out while they were still alive.

She dropped to her knees by her father's head. With one hand she closed his sightless eyes, then stroked his cold lifeless cheek. One by one she did the same for her brothers.

When she came to her brother Timen, she cradled his head in her lap and wept, finally allowing the tears to fall. He was just older than she and her worst tormentor. The scratch was still there on his cheek from their last fight and they had parted angry. Now she would never have a chance to set things right with him. Nicolenna had been the youngest in a large family, the most teased but also the most loved and spoiled. Even while the tears ran, the anger grew in her. To Timen's lifeless body she made a vow to find the one who had done this and kill him!

Then her stomach spasmed in rebellion. Gently she laid Timen's head down and crawled off into the corner to retch. All that she had eaten in the forest came back up. When the heaving was finally over, she crawled farther away and collapsed.

There were voices arguing softly around her when she awoke. Someone had wrapped her in a blanket and placed a folded one under her head. There was a fire burning. For a few seconds she allowed herself to believe she was back in her room with the rest of her sisters and what she had seen before was only a nightmare. Then the blanket was pulled down and someone lifted her head and held a cup of warm broth to her lips. She began to cry again.

"Sh, don't cry. You are safe now," comforted a soft voice. The woman sat the cup down and held Nicolenna close, rocking gently.

"Stop cosseting the brat, Heda," growled another voice that was deeper and rougher than the first, but still female. "Let her bawl an get it out a'her system. Ain't we got enough problems without you tryin' to mother every stray we come across?"

"Shut up, Til. For Mother's sake, the child has had a bad shock. That had to be her family we buried back there. She has a right to cry. Now leave off fussing at her and warm this broth up again."

Nicolenna could hear the one called Til moving around, but she didn't want to leave the comfort of the arms of the one called Heda. When the cup touched her mouth again, she drank. And when her crying ceased, Heda let her sit up.

Horses were tethered to a tree just at the edge of the firelight. The camp was some distance from what had been her home, far enough away that the smell didn't frighten the horses. There was a stew pot set up over the fire. The woman called Heda sat beside her and across the fire sat the one called Til, polishing a sword blade with a rag.

"You buried my family back there?" Nicolenna asked in a shaky voice, wiping her face on her sleeve.

"Yeah, girl, we buried 'em. Like we been a'buryin' 'em all along the river clear back to where the Aster joins the Victory. How come you weren't gathered up along with the rest a the women?" Til's voice matched her haggard face and rough cropped hair.

"I—I was out in the forest when it happened. When I came back all I found was the bodies. My father and all my brothers. It was—it was horrible."

"It was sorcery, girl. Magic wielded by a man, the most unnatural thing in our world. We don't know who he is or where he got his power, but he has been attacking farms and steadings clear up the Victory. He blasts the houses and kills the men. Then carries off the women. Your mother and sisters are with him right now."

"Tillie and I were up in the hills above our home to a healing when he attacked us. By the time we could get back, all that was left was what you saw at your place."

Tillie sheathed the sword and growled. "We vowed to find this sorcerer and kill 'im. I just pray he ain't et up with his own evil before I find 'im. I want the enjoyment of killin 'im. No man destroys what's mine and lives!"

Nicolenna shrank back from the raw hatred in the woman's voice.

"Now, Tillie, you are scaring the child. There's no need to burden her with all this tonight."

"Hell's balls, Heda!" Tillie swore, "She ain't no child, you said that yerself. She's got her magic. If she's any proper woman, she'll want revenge for her family. I say she goes with us."

"I will go with you," stated Nicolenna, letting the anger return. It blotted out the fear and helplessness she felt; with it she knew she could be strong. She sat up straighter and cleared her throat. "I want revenge for my father and brothers. And if my mother and sisters are still alive, I want to get them back. I can ride and like you said, I have my magic now. Just tell me what to do."

"Good girl," said Tillie, but Heda reached out and pulled Nicolenna to her.

"You are just a child, dear, for all that you have your magic. You don't know what this evil sorcerer is capable of. None of us do. But Tillie and me, we don't have anything to lose. You are so young, you could go anyplace. We will take you to the Green Sisters of

Middle Lake and leave you with them. You are just too young for this."

"I am not too young—she's not too young!" spoke both Nicolenna and Tillie at the same time. Heda found herself confronting two angry faces.

"We can't take her all the way back to Middle Lake. It would take days. By then that damned sorcerer will have blasted who knows how many more farms. If the girl wants to go with us, then more power t'her. She can ride the mule. When we find him, Heda, we will need all the power we have t'kill 'im."

"I still think she's—" Heda started to say.

"I think I should have the final say whether I want to risk my life in this," Nicolenna tried to make her voice sound as determined as she felt. "I am Nicolenna di Stadda and that was part of my family that was butchered back there. I am the only one left to avenge them and save the rest and I have already vowed to my brother's spirit to do it. Here and now, again, I swear before the two of you to kill this sorcerer for what he has taken from me. And no one will stand in my way."

Tillie threw down the rag and jumped to her feet. She pulled Nicolenna up and wrapped her big hand around the smaller one on the sword hilt.

"I will take your oath, brat. It's close enough t'my own t'make us sisters, even if you are young. You'd a made a good match for my third 'un, Sethan. He had your brass. Don't mind Heda none, she'll get used to the idea. She and me been friends since we were ten year old. But she never were as mean as me."

Heda just shook her head and didn't answer. With her new-found magic Nicolenna could see the bond that tied these two women together. A tightly woven bond of love and friendship now welded with an unquenchable, burning need for revenge. Turning her sight within, she found a similar need inside her own mind.

"Why do you think I am too young," she asked Heda.

"I studied under the Green Sisters in my youth, child. We are vowed to protect life wherever possible. Since we started after this evil man you are the first person we have found alive. I feel responsible for you.

Your magic is so new and bright, Nicolenna. I don't want to see you killed.''

"When'd you get yer magic, kid?" asked Tillie, changing the subject. As far as she was concerned, Nicolenna was going with them.

"About four or five days ago, from the piper in the woods.''

"Piper?" asked both Heda and Tillie in the same voice.

And Nicolenna went on to explain to them what had happened to her. "He had horns and gold curls and hooves instead of feet. He was so beautiful.''

"It must be one of the forest folk," stated Tillie without much surprise. "You don't see 'em much anymore, but I don't think this one is sly enough to lie about it.''

This time Heda made a rude noise and settled herself back on the blanket. "No woman lies about her first time and getting her magic, Til. Not even you.''

Tillie smiled sadly at her friend and sat down too. "No, Heda, not even me. A'course, me 'n Emory, now, we spent too much time rollin' round in the hay for me to even know the magic was mine till days after. He were a prime man, my Emory.''

Her voice caught on his name and Nicolenna looked up to see the glint of tears in her eyes. Looking with the inward sight, Nicolenna could see the raw heartbreak inside Tillie and knew instinctively that only vengeance could soothe it. Turning to look at Heda, she saw that it was the same with her.

The two women allowed the girl to look and share, remembering how it had been with them when first receiving their magic. Nicolenna's wonder and joy in this new talent gave them comfort.

"It's time we were asleep. There be a long ride tomorrow. If that damned sorcerer keeps followin' the Victory, he'll end up in the ocean. We want t'catch him before he gets away. You two sleep, I'll keep watch for a while.''

So Nicolenna curled up under the blanket with Heda. She had only known these women for a few hours, but her life was already threaded in with theirs. Magic could do that to women, she had heard, binding them close in seconds with feelings that each had known the other forever. She didn't feel the little sleep spell that Heda said over her. She merely fell asleep and didn't dream.

They rode together for three days after that, pushing the horses as hard as possible. Tillie refused to talk any more about their tragedy, but Nicolenna learned of it from Heda. Whenever they passed a blasted farm, Heda insisted they stop long enough to bury the dead. She always performed the ritual for the slain over the graves and fussed that just burying the bodies wasn't enough. They should be burned. Tillie argued back that they didn't have the time to gather that much wood and besides, dead was dead. Burying was just as good a way to go back to the great Mother as the flames were. The Mother'd understand.

Nicolenna quickly realized that these two argued about everything, quite amicably and from sheer habit. If Tillie had had her way, they would have ridden straight through the blasted farms, not stopping for anything. But Heda was the more stubborn of the two, even if she didn't look it, and she had taken a vow with the Green Sisters to protect and respect life. Tillie gave in, but made no bones about how she resented the time it took away from exacting her revenge on the sorcerer.

They rode on, the two women arguing and Nicolenna dozing on the padded pack saddle. When the arguing stopped, it was a few seconds before she looked up. Their horses were motionless and so were they. She tried to pull the mule up, but he blundered right along and into the holding spell.

She couldn't move, could hardly breathe. She could only see Tillie, who was a little ahead of her, straining against the hold. Then from a stand of trees to her left, three men walked out.

"Well, well, well. Look what we have here. *He* said there was someone following us. These two old hags don't look too dangerous. Won't be worth much either. But this young one is a prime catch."

The men walked around the women inspecting them. Each man wore a braided metal loop around his neck. The leader came close to Tillie and reached for her sword. Green fire sparked from the hilt to his hand and he fell back cursing, shaking his burned hand wildly. Tillie struggled against the spell, but it was useless. All she got for her pains was a hard punch in the thigh when the leader stopped shaking his hand.

"Tie them down," he said viciously, taking the ropes from their saddles. "We will see that they ride to *him* like proper women."

The other two thought this was extremely funny and laughed all the while they were tying slip nooses around the women's necks. The ends of the rope were knotted around the saddle horns and then their hands were tied in front of them. It meant they had to ride bent over or strangle.

"Can't we take the little one now, boss?" whined one of the men, running his hands over Nicolenna's legs. "She looks like she ain't never been used before."

"Sure, take her if you want, boy. But remember when *he* finds out you been messing with her, *he*'ll make you wear your balls for ear muffs. *He* likes the young stuff for himself."

That made them serious. It didn't take any explanations for the women to figure out who this "he" was.

The leader said the words to cancel the hold and Tillie immediately began cussing. She gave very accurate descriptions of the men's ancestors and future progeny and physical prowess. They just laughed jeeringly and jerked her horse forward. The noose tightened and she began to choke which made them laugh even harder.

Riding bent over as they were, it didn't take them long to wish they had been killed outright.

Following the Victory led them down over a hill and into a valley where the river widened out and then merged with the ocean. By turning her head to the side and leaning over the mule's shoulder, Nicolenna saw that there were two large ships at anchor in the bay. Off to the left were a number of pens. There were people milling around in them and when she sent her magic out and touched the people she found they were all women.

She craned her head around to look at Tillie and Heda. Their expressions were grim. Heda shook her head in warning to Nicolenna.

Their captors led them down into the valley to where the pens were. Tillie was still quivering with anger and now frustration, her eyes blazing and her short cropped hair all but standing on end. They had found out the hard way that their magic didn't work on these men. The braided chains they wore were some kind of guard. Whatever magic the women tried just slapped back at them.

"We will have to take this one," and the leader nodded his head toward Tillie, "to *him* to get the sword off her. I ain't about to touch it again."

"Do you reckon *he* will let us take this one when he gets through with her?" asked the same one as before. The ropes were cut and the women pulled from the saddles. He rubbed his hands over Nicolenna's breasts. She jerked away in fear and loathing, only to have him pull her back by the rope still tied around her neck.

"Around here, girl, women do what they're told to do and they like it." He grabbed her by the hair and shook hard. "When *he's* finished with you, I'll see to you personally. And believe me, by then you'll like it."

She had no doubt what he meant by "it." But she struggled away from him and spat, "The only thing I would like for you to do is die."

"You'll like it," he yelled, jerking the rope hard, "and you'll beg for more. Round here the women do the begging. *He* sees to that. And . . ."

"Come on, come on, stop jawing and let's get these three up to *him* so *he* can see them." The leader grabbed Tillie's rope and pulled her forward.

There were women hurrying around them, carrying water buckets and various bundles. None of them made any attempt to stop the men who passed from fondling them in a rude way or knocking them to the ground. They walked with heads bent and shoulders hunched. Since they didn't wear the metal chains like the men, Heda sent her sight out to touch them.

What she touched made her scream and she fell to her knees. As Tillie and Nicolenna turned to help her, they were pulled up short by the ropes and then a voice spoke.

"On her knees is an appropriate place for a woman."

The sorcerer stood in front of them, gloating. When Nicolenna looked at him, she didn't have to see with her eyes that this man was evil. It oozed out of him like sweat from a pore. It was all she could do to keep from throwing up. He carried the miasma of evil like the scent of an animal dead for a week.

"Cut them loose," he commanded and the men moved to obey. "Now women, you will hand over the sword to me. Women have no need of men's weapons."

Tillie ignored him as she rubbed circulation back into her numb hands. Then she helped Heda to her feet. The smaller woman was shaking from head to foot and at first Nicolenna thought it was from fear. But when she looked into Heda's eyes, she realized it was from insane rage.

"He has taken their magic, Til," said Heda in a deadly quiet voice. "With his sorcery he has taken the women's magic. They have no spirit left. Oh, Tillie, he has taken their *magic!*"

She screamed this last and threw herself at the sorcerer before any of the men could stop her. Tillie drew her sword and killed the leader as soon as Heda moved. The other two men turned and ran. The braided chains were no defense against simple steel.

Whatever shielding the sorcerer had sent Heda bouncing back into Nicolenna. He took a step forward and pointed his finger at her.

"Yes, women, I have taken their magic, just as I will take yours. Women have no right to magic. When I have finished with you, we will load the rest on those ships and sail away. I have captured enough women to last me for a long time and there are always more when those are gone."

Heda grabbed Nicolenna's hand and screamed at Tillie, "Join with me, Til! Give me your hand quick!"

Heda's eyes blazed and she threw her magic at the sorcerer with furious hatred. He stood confidently behind the shield made from the magic he had stolen.

A green shimmer went up around Heda and the

others. It flowed out and began to *push* against the
sorcerer. Slowly, ever so slowly, his shield began to
buckle inward. His eyes widened in surprise and then
fright. With his sorcery he began to suck up the energy
from the women in the pens, draining their life forces
to strengthen the power that wasn't rightfully his. The
women he touched simply stopped in their tracks and
folded silently to the ground.

Then the green shimmer turned to a blinding emerald
blaze as Heda used more and more of herself and of the
other two to pierce the shield. Nicolenna remembered
the cheery fire she had started in the forest so long ago
and she called up that fire now. She raised her free
arm and let the flames flow up her arm and then flung
the magic fire at the sorcerer. At the same time Tillie
changed her grip on the sword hilt and flung it like a
spear. The blade and fire touched the crumbling shield
and slid through as one into the sorcerer's throat.

When the cleansing fire blade touched the sorcerer,
he exploded outward in a shower of dull red chunks.
Bouncing and crackling along the ground the clinkers
were quickly extinguished in the dirt.

The silent force of the explosion was taken by Heda,
who was knocked to the ground. She lay there without
moving. Nicolenna stood swaying and panting as Tillie
staggered and dropped beside her friend. She lifted
Heda gently and cradled her in her arms.

Heda's eyes fluttered open. "Tillie," she whispered,
"he was going to take our magic, like he took it from
the others." She coughed and her whole body shuddered. Bloody froth appeared at the corners of her
mouth. Tillie wiped it away with a gentle finger.

"I couldn't let him do that, Til. He had to be stopped.
I had to break my vow and kill him. Do you think the
Mother will understand?"

Tillie choked back her sobs, unable to answer her
friend. Nicolenna came to kneel beside them and it
was she who spoke to ease Heda's dying fear.

"You didn't kill him, Heda. Tillie and I did. You
even shielded us when he died. You are not forsworn,
do you hear? The Mother will know. You still have
her blessing."

Heda coughed and this time the spasms racked her body.

"Til, promise me . . ." her voice was less than a whisper now.

"Anything, Heda, anything." promised Tillie, for once without arguing. She bent closer to hear her sister's dying words.

"The pyre. Not in the ground."

Tillie nodded. Then it was over. She hugged Heda's body to her and gave way to her grief in choking sobs. Nicolenna moved closer and put her arms around them, sharing the pain.

The ships were gone and with them most of the men. The ones that were left had gone mad after the sorcerer died. Tillie had killed each one quickly. For the women, there were only a few left that still had their magic. A great many of them had died in the sorcerer's last bid for dominance. The dead were consigned to the flames.

Tillie and Nicolenna built the pyre for Heda. Tillie laid the body of her friend and sister on the wood, then she and Nicolenna used their magic to start the fire. They kept vigil with it until there weren't even ashes for the wind to blow away.

"Where will you go now?" Nicolenna asked Tillie when the fire was gone. Tillie gathered up the horses and packed what supplies she could find.

"Don't know," Tillie answered in a tired sad voice. "There's some a our daughters still alive. Guess I'll gather 'em up and go back home. Don't know what else to do." She shrugged.

"Could I—do you think I could go with you? I found two of my sisters in the pens and they are willing to go with me, if it's okay with you."

"I s'pose you could. What all us women are gonna do without men is what I'm wondering about." She looked around at all the fires burning the dead. "But it wouldn't s'prise me none if there ain't any a these women that'll want men after this."

So they finished packing and rode out, following the Victory back to where the Aster joined in. To home, wherever that would be.

HERO WORSHIP
by L.D. Woeltjen

I had two good stories by Linda Woeltjen this year—and
was quite put out at having to reject them. Fortunately,
before I had to return them both, news came along that this
year I was doing two anthologies, which left me room for
one of them, so fewer agonizing choices were necessary.

And, as I've said before, that's what it's all about.

———————

Bracer grumbled to herself as she oiled the leather
sheath that lay in her lap. "Might as well keep it
supple, though if things don't pick up, I'll be trading
my sword for provisions."

Sunlight glinted off the silver-plated bracers on her
wrists. Wisdom said these should be the first of her
possessions to sell, but the warrior-woman cast off the
thought. They were her source of identity now. She
could get another sword, but they were irreplaceable.

Anyway, Roag won't let me starve. The idea rankled
her, for she was the better fighter.

But the blond, brawny soldier had found work that
morning. The caravan master took one look at the
broad, sun-bronzed shoulders and signed him on.
Though Roag vouched for Bracer, the beady-eyed master refused to hire a woman, when so many men
needed work.

So Roag had left her their tent and remaining provisions. She'd told him that she might not be there
when he returned. If a likely prospect presented itself,
she'd be off. Roag had shrugged. Such was their relationship, though they'd been partners, and bedmates,
for more than two years.

But, sad to say, the whole world seemed to be at peace. Bracer doubted anything would be offered her in the three days it would take for Roag to return.

"I win!" one of the men who sat nearby shouted. If she'd any coins left, Bracer would have joined in the gambling that occupied some of the other idle mercenaries. She looked at the men huddled over throwstones wistfully. Maybe if she hocked just the sheath . . .

A movement in the shadows distracted Bracer. Someone crouched there, watching her. More than once her wrist armor had given thieves false hopes about her wealth. She wiped the excess oil off her hands, sliding them over her tunic toward the knife hidden in her belt.

A shock of straw-brown hair rose up from behind a barrel, then ducked as Bracer casually stood. The fighter sauntered toward the gamblers, as though she intended to join them. When she reached the barrel which crowned the area for cast off rubbish, she turned quickly. Darting out with the speed that made her excel with the sword, her fingers closed about a handful of short, unkempt hair.

"What do you think you're doing?" she bellowed as she yanked the watcher to her feet. That the thief was a girl came as no great surprise to Bracer. Her own youth had taken her briefly down a similar path. Still, her own slender form had never been so obviously female. For a time, Bracer had passed as a boy. This buxom young woman could never have done that.

The girl's mouth hung open, eyes wide with terror.

"Speak up," Bracer demanded. "What're you doing skulking about?"

"I was just watching," the girl stammered. Her eyes lifted longingly to the sparkle beneath the hand that held her captive.

"Were these what you were after?" the swordswoman hissed, holding her other wrist up to the girl's nose. "Rotten little thief."

"Oh, no," the girl tried to shake her head. "I was only admiring them."

Bracer snorted.

"Sure, I like them," the girl said defiantly, "but I

have every intention of earning some for myself. Only perhaps mine will be gold."

"Earn them?" Bracer laughed as she released the girl. "And how do you propose to do that?"

"I want to be a soldier," the girl said with an earnestness that reminded Bracer of an earlier self. "I been watching you, 'cause I thought you might teach me. You don't seem to have much else to do." Bracer scowled at the obviously intentional barb. The girl had a quick wit, and was feisty.

"Well, you might make a warrior, but this is hardly the time for it." She waved her hand at the camp full of idle, transient fighters. "You're better off going back to your family and letting them find you a husband."

A sullen look clouded the girl's face. "If I'd wanted a man, I could a had one . . ." She swallowed hard and Bracer wondered if her captive meant what her words implied.

"Do what I did, then," Bracer said, feeling kindly toward the troubled girl. "Go to Zavorax. They train women to fight there, and allow the kind of life I think you're looking for."

"So I've heard," the girl's eyes misted as she spoke. "But Zavorax is halfway round the world."

Bracer was momentarily stunned at the realization of how far her travels had taken her. Zavorax had no special place in her heart. She'd not felt comfortable in a world where one's gender held no importance. Certainly, she'd liked being able to learn soldiering. But when a girl in her sword class had become enamored with her, Bracer had not known what to do.

Once she'd learned how to fight, Bracer left Zavorax. She'd said she wanted to get as far as she could from the place she'd been born. There was truth in that. The proximity of Zavorax to her homeland made too great the chance of meeting someone she knew on the battlefield. Now she'd put twenty-some years of travel between that world and herself.

Bracer's silence seemed to embolden the girl. She cleared her throat and spoke officiously.

"My name is Kinsa. I am seventeen, and old enough

to be on my own. My family wants nothing to do with me, and besides, they live in a village miles away from here. I want to hire you to teach me to use a sword. You're looking for hire, ain't you?"

"You have money?" Bracer asked, amused at the proposition.

Kinsa nodded. "I work at the inn, mucking the stables and emptying chamber pots. Been saving, hoping to earn passage to Zavorax." The girl's expression turned to disgust, "But at this rate it'll take me till I'm an old woman."

"All right," Bracer said. "I'm stuck here a few days, so I might as well pass the time with you. But answer me one question first."

Kinsa waited expectantly.

"Why does your hair look like that?"

The girl giggled and ran her fingers through the coarse, bushy stubble that resembled an ill-constructed wheat sheaf.

"Well, this was the only way I could think of to keep the men at the inn off me."

Bracer studied the girl a moment. Her face was as lovely as her figure. Even with the grubby clothes and bad haircut, she probably had to fight off unwanted advances.

"My swordmate's gone for a few days," Bracer told Kinsa. "Why don't you stay here with me?"

Her answer was a beautiful smile. Kinsa bent behind the barrel and came up with a sack. "This is all I have."

Bracer helped Kinsa stow her meager belongings in the tent.

"If I'm to teach you," Bracer told her, "you'll need a sword."

"Can't I just borrow yours?"

Bracer crooked a finger at Kinsa, beckoning her back outside. Kinsa tucked a coin purse into her shirt as she followed.

Once they stood in front of the tent, Bracer offered her blade to the eager girl. Kinsa waved it about with obvious inexperience, yet she held herself as though she'd been studying the fighters for some time. She let her arm drop suddenly after several mock thrusts.

"I see what you mean. Need a lighter one, don't I?" Bracer nodded.

"There's an armorer in town," Kinsa said, pulling the purse back out of her shirt. Its meager jingle told Bracer there wouldn't be enough, even before she looked inside.

Nearby, the men were still gambling. Bracer held a palm out to the girl.

"Give me my wages in advance."

Kinsa looked over toward the huddled men, then back at Bracer. After several moments of consideration, the girl emptied half the contents of her purse into the swordswoman's hand.

With her pupil at her heels, Bracer joined the game. She lost a few coins while she appraised the other gamblers. They were as poor as she; desperate. The greedy eyes that took in her wrists, made her decide to sleep light while Roag was gone.

As she took stock of her opponents, Bracer noticed one decrepit old man among them. He seemed too frail to bear a sword, which led her to look at the weapon he wore. It was a thin, light blade. Exactly what Kinsa needed.

Betting her few coins cagily, Bracer was able to increase her money, but if she emptied the pockets of every man there, she'd not have enough to buy a sword in town. The old soldier was her only hope, and his luck was bad. That worked in her favor.

Betting modestly, she conserved most of her coins, waiting for him to go broke. When he did, the old man began begging.

"Loan me a few coppers," he asked a companion. One by one, the other gamblers refused to help him.

"I don't have money to throw away," one man answered gruffly.

"Sorry," another said, shaking his head with sincere regret that Bracer took for an act. The old man had little hope when he turned to her.

"Perhaps a woman like yourself has more compassion . . ."

Bracer ignored the snorts of laughter from the other gamblers.

"You don't succeed in this line of work by having a kind heart," she answered. "But I'd hate to see you starve."

The man waited expectantly, his eagerness all too apparent.

"Still, I have to eat, too. What assurance do I have that you'll repay me?"

"My word?" he offered optimistically. His companions guffawed and he reddened.

"I'd prefer something more substantial," Bracer answered. She looked him up and down, as if she hadn't already taken appraisal of him. "What about your sword?" she asked casually.

"That's my livelihood," he said, his hand resting protectively on its sheath.

"Not in these times," muttered one of the others. He began pulling in his stake, as though the scene was making him realize the true value of his few coins. Bracer sensed that the game would end soon if the mood didn't change. The old man must have also seen that he was close to losing his last chance at winning anything.

"It's yours," he agreed, unstrapping the belt. "For all you've got there in front of you. And only till I can pay you back."

"Agreed," Bracer said. She counted the coins as she pushed them toward him, pretending he had hope of redeeming the blade.

"Well, that leaves me nothing to wager," she said, rising. "You know where to find me when you get the money."

Grabbing for the throw-stones, the old man nodded. As they walked away, Bracer passed their prize to Kinsa.

The girl took the blade reluctantly.

"That poor old man. How could you rob him of his livelihood?"

"Time has done that. He'd never earn his keep with a sword, even if the whole world was at each other's throat. We did him a favor, forcing him to retire."

Bracer did not feel as callous as she sounded. She knew that she, too, was aging. If being an old male soldier was a pathetic plight, how much worse would it be for an aged swordswoman.

I don't intend to find out, Bracer decided. She'd die in battle, not begging in some alleyway. But that time was still a ways off. She had a student to teach.

The girl was hardy and determined. She was more apt than Bracer remembered being.

But I was a bit younger, Bracer thought. *And she doesn't have my natural speed.*

The next few days went by quickly, and Bracer was almost sorry to see Roag return. The big warrior eyed Kinsa appreciatively as she gathered up her belongings.

"Who's this?"

Bracer explained, and he laughed a deep, friendly laugh. "Just what we need, another warrior-woman." But he did not seem to truly mind.

"Lessons tomorrow, as usual," Bracer told Kinsa before the girl disappeared through the tent flap. "Unless I find some real work."

Roag was already sliding his fingers under her tunic.

"You missed me," Bracer chuckled, and planted a kiss on his tanned cheek.

If anything, Roag seemed to welcome Kinsa's presence in the camp during the day. By an hour after dawn she had finished her work at the inn and was ready to practice. Since Bracer and Roag customarily spent the morning seeking employment, the girl kept busy by cleaning their tent or fixing them something to eat. Bracer never took any more money for teaching Kinsa, allowing her instead to keep food on the table. Not that they had an actual table.

The girl's helpfulness endeared her to Roag. Neither he nor Bracer had any domestic bent. For once, their bed rolls and spare clothes were clean, their meals tasty instead of merely edible.

Bracer found herself both resentful of Roag allowing the girl to be basically a servant, and relieved that he had no other interest in her. Bracer had grown fond of the fighter, even though he was a good num-

ber of years younger than she, and she was not eager
to share him. But when Kinsa finally caused discord
among them, it was in no way that Bracer could have
anticipated.

"Wake up," Kinsa was whispering. Bracer opened
her eyes, but the tent was still dark.

"Why are you here so early?" Confused by the dark
and her half-sleepy state, Bracer grasped little of Kinsa's
explanation.

"There's been a robbery in town. A big one. The
merchant's guild has a standing reward offer. If we
leave now, we can be first to catch these thieves."

Beside her, Roag sat up quickly. She could hear and
feel him pulling on his clothes. "Do you have any idea
which way they've headed?"

"Yes. I was just starting to work in the stables when
I heard someone coming in. Wouldn't have been the
first time some brute tried to sneak up on me, so I hid.
Was horses they were after. But I heard them talking
'bout all the loot they'd got. Soon as they left, I came
here."

"Get up," Roag ordered, jabbing Bracer with an
elbow.

She complied as Roag continued to question Kinsa.
"How many?"

"Only two or three. It was hard to tell in the dark,
but there weren't more than we can handle."

"Listen, kid, I appreciate all your help, but Bracer
and I are doing this alone. If we catch them, we'll give
you part of the reward, but I'm not taking a half-
trained girl out to do battle."

"If I don't go, you won't either. I'm not telling you
where they went."

"Now listen here, you little wench," he lunged
toward her, but collided with Bracer. She heard the
girl escape into the darkness. Over the rustle of Roag
getting to his feet came the sound of hooves.

"If we hurry, we can catch her. You know she'll try
going after them alone."

"Well, good riddance to her. I'm not following a
harebrained kid into disaster. She's riding north, that's
all we need to know."

"They'll kill her." Bracer was upset at her companion's lack of concern. He only laughed in response.

"Who'd take that girl seriously? They'll just have some fun with her. And while they're distracted, we'll sneak up on 'em that much easier. Hmm, maybe the girl will be useful after all."

Bracer kicked at him, but missed, then strode furiously out the door. Before she finished saddling her horse, Roag was beside her.

"Do you think it means nothing for a girl to be raped?"

"Come on, Brace. We're not talking about some innocent maiden. The girl works at an inn, empties chamber pots. She's seen real life. Anyway, maybe it would set her straight, show her the way things should be."

"What do you mean?"

"Girl pants after you like a puppy. That's why I've left her alone. Never could understand . . ."

"You're crazy," Bracer spat out. She mounted quickly, refusing to think about what he was saying.

Roag followed, and she was glad he was coming along, even though she knew their relationship was over. However weak his character, he was a good man in a fight.

As they rode along, Bracer found herself regretting the lack of instruction she'd given Kinsa. Had she foreseen the girl's eagerness to get into action, she would have taught her more about strategy and stealth and tracking. Now, the girl was probably riding headlong into danger, for surely the thieves were expecting pursuit.

Once the sun came up, they were able to make out tracks on the well-traveled road. Although they could not distinguish the trail of Kinsa or the thieves, it was clear when several sets of hoofprints veered off the road. They followed the tracks into the forest.

"Be on the lookout," Roag cautioned needlessly. Bracer was as aware as he that the robbers might be waiting to ambush their pursuers. Most of the day passed, but they did not lose sight of the tracks they were following.

Both were so alert that they turned instantly when a branch crackled behind them. Most likely another mercenary was following them and they'd have to share the reward. Bracer would welcome the help. But in case the thieves had circled around behind them, she readied her sword.

Bracer relaxed when she recognized the shock of straw-colored hair. Kinsa waved as she rode toward them.

"I didn't know how to track the robbers, so I hid and followed you." She grinned triumphantly.

Bracer was too relieved that Kinsa was safe to be angry. Roag, however, scowled at the girl.

"Go back to town," he demanded.

"No." Kinsa's green eyes flashed with defiance.

Roag broke a branch from a tree and hurled it at her. Perhaps he intended to spook Kinsa's horse into galloping home with her. He did succeed in frightening the beast. With a startled whinny it reared up. The noise echoed through the woods. It was answered by the thunder of nearby hooves.

"We'd almost reached them." Roag cursed and wheeled his horse off in pursuit. After seeing that Kinsa had her mount in check, Bracer followed him. In moments, Kinsa's horse was pacing Bracer's.

Why didn't Kinsa tell me she had such a fine mount? Bracer wondered.

A few minutes later they caught up with the robbers. Finding the dense forest blocking escape, the three men had dismounted. They stood, armed, facing Roag, but their fearful expressions hinted that his size alone might cause their surrender. Bracer and Kinsa swung down from their horses, drawing their swords. When the thieves saw the two women, hope replaced the defeat on their faces. Swords before them, all three robbers charged at Roag.

It was then that Bracer recognized one of the thieves. The scrawny old gambler. The weapon he bore must have been stolen, for he was obviously burdened by it. But this was a matter of survival, and nothing is more dangerous than a beast facing death.

Kinsa was already moving in to intercept the little

man. Bracer stepped in to battle another, as Roag dispatched the third man with a swift blow. As her companion turned to assist her, Bracer gave one jab that caught the thief's shoulder. She stepped aside, leaving Roag to finish him. She wanted to see how Kinsa fared. The girl's sentiment might get in the way of the little Bracer had taught her.

Kinsa did hesitate; neither she nor the old man seemed eager for battle, but then he rushed at her. The girl quickly assumed the stance Bracer had taught her. Bracer was impressed by the cool manner in which Kinsa parried the old man's blows, then struck back. She did not even wince as her blade sank into his flesh over his heart.

Bracer stepped up to congratulate her pupil, but Kinsa's face bore no triumph. She bit her lower lip and watched with misted eyes as the old soldier stopped breathing.

"Seems to me, that a quick death would be preferable to execution at the hands of the city authorities." Bracer put her arm around the girl's shoulder and led her away, leaving Roag to prepare the bodies for return to the city.

"You did well," she told Kinsa, while Roag tied the corpses onto the horses. "Let's check the saddlebags," Bracer suggested as a distraction. The sight of the jewelry crammed into the first bag made her whistle.

"We should get a fine reward for this!"

"Then we'd better be moving on," Roag said as he mounted. "Once the townfolk realize that mercenary soldiers gone bad were responsible for the thefts, they won't take kindly to so many of us camping on their doorsteps."

The grim mood did not last long. Soldiers accept death as a companion. Bracer and Roag were soon mimicking the reactions of the merchants when they found they had to actually fork over one of their promised rewards.

"When you deliver all this to the authorities," said Kinsa, "take him along, too." She patted her horse's neck. "They'll think he was stolen from the stable," she grinned sheepishly, "instead of just borrowed."

Roag laughed, but Bracer could not forget how willing he had been to let Kinsa fall victim to these same thieves.

By the time Bracer and Roag returned to camp, Kinsa had packed their belongings and taken down the tent. She quickly put away her third of the reward, then returned to folding up the tent.

"Just because you did all right today, don't think you're coming along with us," Roag told the girl.

"Please take me with you," she pleaded. "I'll cook and clean and do whatever you want."

Roag seemed to be reconsidering, but Bracer called him over to where the horses waited.

"Actually, Roag, I think it's time to end our partnership. How much for your share of the tent?"

Too amazed to argue, Roag named a fair price. Bracer counted the coins into his palm.

"All this time," he said, shaking his head, "and I never took you for being that way."

"What are you talking about?" she asked as he mounted.

"You . . ." he paused as if seeking the right words, "preferring her."

"Why . . . I . . ." but he rode off before she could stammer out a denial.

How could he think that, after all they'd been to each other? Even now, watching him ride away, she knew there would be times when she'd miss him.

Upset, she pushed his accusation aside and turned to tie her packs onto her own horse. Kinsa brought her the tent, now securely bundled.

Bracer glanced at the girl, noting the trail a tear had left on one grimy cheek.

"You know," she said softly, "your share of the money would buy you a decent horse."

"What good would that do me?" Kinsa asked with a sniffle. But there was hope in her eyes. Bracer swung into the saddle.

"Oh, I suppose I could put up with your company till I find some real work." She held her hand out to Kinsa, pulling the girl up to sit behind her. After

Kinsa had settled herself on the awkward bundles behind the saddle, she wrapped her arms around Bracer's waist.

The way her breasts rested on Kinsa's forearms made Bracer oddly uncomfortable. She was glad they could afford another horse. As they started toward the city, she called over her shoulder.

"Maybe we could work our way toward Zavorax." Without having to look, she knew Kinsa was smiling.

A MATTER OF LIFE
by Cathy J. Deubl

Cathy Deaubl says about herself that she is married "and the mother of two wonderful little monsters" and says that like me (MZB) she is more of a novelist than a short story writer—though she hasn't managed a book sale yet. That sounds like almost everybody else in this anthology.

She says she doesn't work outside her home—an ideal situation for a would-be novelist—and the one job she has held was the one place no reader would object to—the public library. She says she writes everything—from science fiction to horror—but her real love is fantasy, especially sword and sorcery.

In the last couple of years the dam has broken; she has made three sales in the last *two months*.

———————————

That chilly autumn day, Raessa knew there had been a battle nearby. Early that morning, she had seen plumes of smoke curling into the sky from far away. It was surely another of the endless conflicts between Sharda and Talvaria. For so many years the battles had raged, she wondered if either side knew why it had ever started. She certainly didn't. All she knew was that soldiers would attack each other and fight, then burn whatever they couldn't hack to pieces. It had been that way for much too long, patches of peace stitched into a quilt of war.

She had hoped the sporadic battles would stay on their side of the mountain and leave her and the others alone on theirs, but it wasn't meant to be.

It was just beginning to frost in the little valley she called home. Thick forest and tall, snow-covered mountains surrounded the green meadowland, making her feel more safe than she probably should have. Sometimes she felt as if there were no other world than what was near her.

To some it might have been lonely, living in the old stone house with only a boy and the animals for companions, but Raessa loved the peace. Occasional travelers would pass by. She enjoyed their brief company, but was always content to see them go. Her life would quickly return to the comfort of daily routines.

Brek disliked those rare disturbances. He became moody and took to the barn when other people were near, choosing to sleep with the animals. She never chided him about it. He had his reasons.

Late in the day, Raessa was just coming from the barn. Her mare, Empress, was getting fat as a barrel as her time came near, and Raessa was trying to keep a close eye on her. A yip from Zar caught her attention. He was near the house. The urgency in his tone quickened Raessa's pace, causing her dark auburn braid to bounce against her back.

"What have you treed now, Zar?" she asked as she saw the wolf's dun-gray form sniffing at the doorway. When she saw what he had found, she stopped in her tracks. "My word."

Holding himself upright against the door was a stocky, dark-haired man. His right shoulder had bled profusely, mangled by some weapon of war. The blood had dried and crusted on his tunic, but dribs of bright crimson still seeped through. His face was pasty white, his eyes beginning to glaze. Still he clung to a sword with his left hand, a useless gesture Raessa was sure, left-handers being as rare as they were.

She reached out and took the sword easily from his grip. "You won't need that here, my friend. Let's get you out of this chill and see what I can do about that wound."

Raessa's mother, rest her, hadn't shirked her duty as a dovati with a dovati daughter. Even with the hardship in her life, she had made sure Raessa knew the healing arts and some of the magics. They had served the young woman well on several occasions. It seemed they would do so again.

She supposed the man, helping him inside as she pushed the door open. He faltered halfway to the table, and she almost let him crumple to the floor.

"Bed," she said. "It's longer to go, but if I can only get you one place, let's get you to the bed."

Taking his uninjured arm around her shoulders, she helped him to one of the rooms in the back. They scarcely made it to the cot before he fainted. Raessa let him down as gently as she could and knelt to examine the wound. As far as she could tell, no bones were broken. If it didn't sour, he might yet have use of the arm. Only time would tell.

Stripping him out of his soiled and tattered clothing, she looked for other wounds. He had been lucky. The shoulder seemed to be the worst.

Raessa sensed being watched and glanced up to see Brek standing in the doorway. He was a gangly lad with shaggy blond hair that never seemed to stay out of his face. His eyes were gray as storm clouds ready to spill as he stared down at the stranger.

"I could have used some help," she said lightly, never sure of his reaction. "I still could."

Brek seemed not to have heard. "He's a Talvarian captain."

"So he is. Are you going to help me or not?"

His eyes seemed to clear as he glanced at her. "What do you need?"

"My herbs in the pouch near the hearth and a pan of warm water."

He nodded and went off to fetch them, his right foot scraping the floor slightly as he did. His was one injury she had been too late to heal. That leg would never be strong enough to carry him straight. She listened to his sliding gait as he gathered the things she had asked for and brought them to her. He stood there fidgeting, awaiting her next order, clearly uncomfortable with the man's presence.

"Best keep a watch for anyone who might come looking for this one," Raessa said. "Take Zar with you up on the hill."

He nodded and quickly disappeared. She heard him whistle for the wolf and an answering yip as they found each other. Satisfied the boy was in good keeping, she turned back to her work.

She cleaned and bandaged the man's wound, packing it with a salve she hoped would keep it free of poison. The murmured singsong chant of a healing spell enhanced her fingers' delicate work. The man roused once, just enough to let Raessa coax a bit of dosed wine into him. It soothed him quickly back to sleep.

As she sat with the man, she began to repack the herbs in her healing pouch. A bright glint of light on metal caught her eye, and she withdrew a pendant from the leather bag. Its delicate chain dangled from her fingers in a glittering cascade. It had been her mother's. She had worn it for as long as Raessa could remember. The young woman avoided wearing it, using it seldom. It reminded her too much of her own loss.

A mounting of twisted gold held a white cabochon alasha stone of unremarkable quality. As she worried it in her hand, the stone came to life. It always gave off a faint pulse of warmth. Now glowing light and pastel colors shimmered beneath its surface. The colors deepened with her mood until they were twining ribbons of sky blue and deep purple, hinting at her concern for what might soon become a difficult situation.

This was one of its powers, the sensing of emotions. Occasionally, Raessa had used it with Brek, to plumb his moods of melancholy. She could usually manage to get it into his hands. He liked the way it came alive. Most of the time, it would swirl sour green with threads of black, ugly and unsettling colors. That was her sign to get him involved in some trifle like berry picking or herb gathering before the mood could swing to black. She had never seen the stone black except at her mother's death. She didn't care to see it that way again.

The pendant had more powerful uses, but she never had need of them. Its nearness now made her remember her mother. Strangely, this time the memories weren't so painful. Slipping the chain around her neck, she tucked the pendant into her bodice. The warm pulsing against her skin took up the rhythm of her heart. Its presence comforted her.

Late that day, as Raessa was tending to a pot of soup cooking on the hearth, she heard the door open. A chill breeze ruffled her skirt as she turned to see Brek come in. Zar slipped in past him and came to sit at her side, watching both of them expectantly, sensing their mixed feelings. When Brek was upset, Zar shadowed his every step, sensitive to his moods. Lately, the two had become inseparable.

"How is he?" Brek asked.

"I think he'll survive, with care. How are you?"

He gave a careless shrug, but she recognized the trouble brewing in his eyes. Inwardly, Raessa sighed. When he decided to be stubborn, he was so difficult to deal with. She had learned to back away and leave him to sort things out on his own. Interfering with the current of his feelings made him even more dogged. She would have to give him time.

Time was also what her other charge needed. He woke, coherent, the second day, demanding to know where he was. His name was Koren, and he was indeed a captain in the army of Talvaria. Raessa answered his questions while she checked his wound.

"Lucky I came to the house of an ally," he said smugly.

Raessa couldn't let that bit of arrogance pass. "Did I say I was an ally?"

A flicker of uncertainty shadowed his face. "Then— you aren't?"

She chided herself for taunting him. "I didn't say that, either. Actually, I care as much for one side as the other—or as little." She finished with the new bandage and wiped her hands on a clean rag.

"I've seen the boy around here. Is that why he hasn't gone to the army?" Koren asked.

"He isn't fit for the army," Raessa said shortly. "Watch him a bit closer. His right leg is barely useful for walking. Do they take cripples now? Or did you think he was too spineless?"

He looked a bit flustered. "Of course not. I never meant to hint that he was a coward."

Raessa smiled as sweetly as she could. "You didn't have to hint. It was plain as day in your eyes. Well, he's a cripple. Leave him alone."

She didn't give him any chance to apologize, if that was his intention. She gathered up her healing pouch and left him to stew.

Koren didn't cross her again for several days. She supposed it took him that long to pluck up his courage. Her father had always accused her of having the temper of a she-demon when she was provoked. Apparently, he had been right.

After Koren had rested another day, Raessa invited him to sit by the fire while she replaced the herbs in her pouch. It was time he was building his strength. Brek had been conspicuously absent, so she didn't see the likelihood of a confrontation.

She helped Koren settle into an armchair by the hearth. The tension in his body told her about the pain he thought he was hiding. After seeing him comfortable with a cup of mulled wine, she took up her mixing bowl and the bunches of dried herbs she had gathered. She began breaking leaves and seed pods into the bowl as Koren alternately watched her and stared into the fire. Silence passed. Finally it seemed to weigh too heavily.

"What is it you're doing there?" he asked.

"Replacing herbs in my healing pouch. It wouldn't do to run out just at a time of need."

"No, I suppose not." He toyed with his cup. "I imagine my wound depleted your supply quite a bit."

His tone was searching. Raessa glanced up at him. "What is it you want to know, Captain?"

"Is it only herbs you use, or . . ." His voice trailed off.

"Or what?"

"I've heard stories about women called dovaris— davalis—" He continued to stumble with the fragment of memory.

"Dovatis," she supplied. "Women skilled in the healing arts."

"You know of them?"

So, that was his curiosity. "Intimately. I am a dovati."

"A magic healer." Koren looked thoughtful. "I suspected as much. I should have lost this arm."

"If the wound had soured, you would have lost more than the arm. Magic doesn't heal everything."

He sobered. For some time the only sounds in the room were the crackling of the fire and the dry rasp of the herbs as she crushed the pods and stems into powder.

"Is it true," he said finally, "that you favor neither side in the war?"

"True. Or I wouldn't have said it."

"Then why—"

"Take you in and care for you?" she finished. She had been expecting this. "Because I would do the same for any poor wounded creature. Sharda or Talvaria or woods or mountain. It makes no difference to me. I found Zar as a half-grown pup with a hunter's arrow through him."

Raessa glanced up to see his reaction. The slight flush of color in his cheeks satisfied her, whether from anger or embarrassment. She wanted this man of war to know she was not someone to be mastered or trifled with.

"Why must it always be one way or the other?" she went on. "Right or wrong, this side or that side, dark or light. Can you never give a person freedom to simply be neutral?"

"We don't see much neutrality in this war."

Raessa slammed the bowl down on the table, scattering the herbs. "Then you don't ask the right people. Go into one of your towns and find a woman whose husband is gone, or one who has a son nearly old enough to fight. Ask them if they care who wins as long as the fighting stops."

She hadn't meant to become so angry and looked away to gain control of her feelings.

"I didn't mean to upset you," Koren said.

"This started long before you came here," she replied softly. Her anger was spent, but an explanation might serve a purpose. "My father left to fight when I was a girl. He never came back. When my brother was old enough, he went off to another of the skirmishes.

It was all the same. My mother grieved herself to death over them."

"What side did they stand on?"

Her temper sparked at his question. "Does it matter? Would it make them any less dead? I wonder sometimes how men can be so ignorant that they leave family and home without so much as a backward glance to fight in a war that doesn't matter a damn."

"Perhaps it does matter to us," he flared back.

"And why is that? Do you have any idea why the fighting started this time, or has anyone bothered to tell you?"

"It began when Sharda's army attacked the capital on a day when only women and children were left. They are killers of children, Lady."

"All the men were gone?" she asked. "How unusual. I wonder what they were attacking?"

Koren's face purpled with fury. He lunged up from the chair, preparing to stalk from the room. He faltered with the first step. Raessa had to leap and grab him before he crumpled to the floor. He clutched at her for support.

"You should be in bed," she said. "We'll save the rest of our arguments for a time when you are better suited to the battle."

She put him to bed and dosed him with herbs until he slept. When he woke later, their conversation was never mentioned. Raessa had the feeling he was deep in thought, however. His eyes would meet hers, burrow deeply, then move on. The intensity in that stare made her wonder.

He never spoke about her lack of allegiance from then on, but he became adamant about getting back to his people. At Raessa's insistence, he agreed to give himself a few more days to heal.

During that time, Raessa became better acquainted with him. Despite his profession, Koren was a difficult man to dislike. When he felt more at home, she found he could talk about a great many things. He even made an effort to get inside the barrier that Brek had built around himself. Now that the weather was turning too cold for the boy to retreat to the barn, he was forced to accept the man's attempts at friendship. Raessa saw the slow unbending of the boy's manner and Koren's crooked smile at his success. Once or twice he even made Brek laugh, something she had never seen before.

Raessa was not so impressed with Koren's stories, but she was fascinated by his telling. He was a man who cared passionately about the things he did. It lent him an air of attraction she couldn't recall feeling in some time.

Finally, he was well enough to travel. By his standards, at least. Raessa knew he should put it off, but he wouldn't hear of it. Before winter could drop its first snow, he began gathering what was left of his belongings, prepared to leave on the morrow.

That morning, Raessa was cutting up vegetables for a stew. Koren was packing to go, and Brek was feeding the animals. Only the wolf had decided to stay at her side, coaxed, Raessa was sure, by the smell of what she was cooking. He watched her intently, expecting the tidbits she tossed his way.

Suddenly, Raessa saw Zar come to his feet, hackles rising, a low growl issuing from deep in his throat. She glanced over her shoulder and saw Koren standing in the doorway, a tattered piece of blue cloth in his hand. The muscles in his face twitched. She put her task aside and rose calmly to face him, one hand holding Zar at bay.

Koren shook the fabric at her. "What else have you lied about?"

"I have lied about nothing."

He turned the cloth until a faded outline of black could be seen. "I was looking for my things in that trunk you told me about. I found this. It is the crest of Sharda. Somewhere you're hiding a Shardan swine. Where is he?"

She had forgotten what was in that chest when she had put his things there. The die was cast. She could only hope to keep the impending explosion under control.

"You've met him."

Koren's eyes widened, then an expression of recognition came into them. "The boy?"

"Brek. He came to me just as you did, wounded. I nearly lost him. His crippled leg is a remembrance of it."

"Why didn't he return to his people?"

"Why should he? His family is gone. There was no home to return to." She wondered if Koren could understand the next reason. "And he was afraid."

The man snorted. "Then perhaps I was hasty to say he isn't a coward."

Her hand pulled back as if of its own accord to slap Koren. Brek chose that moment to walk in the door. He sensed the hostility in the room immediately. Only Raessa's call stopped him from backing out.

"Come here to me," she ordered.

Watching Koren as if he were a coiled snake, Brek crept closer to Raessa.

"A coward, is he?" she asked. "And how brave are you?"

The ice in her voice surprised her. With one hand she grasped Brek's hand. With the other, she hooked the chain that pulled the alasha stone free of her bodice.

Holding the pendant tightly, she recited the spell her mother had taught her, all the while concentrating on Brek.

The stone warmed to a heat that threatened to scorch her hand.

Its pulse stumbled then picked up again, becoming the true double beat of a throbbing heart.

The room began to fade around Raessa.

Suddenly, it was winter, the wind blowing like chilled spikes through her clothing. Her hands were numb from the cold. Pain throbbed through her like a living thing, driving every breath out of her in a gasp.

She had run from her pursuers until one of their crossbow quarrels had torn through her leg. After that, she could barely crawl. They drew near, and she hid until they passed by. When they were gone, she crawled and hid for a lifetime, dizzy and sick from the pain. She grabbed up snow and left it to melt in her mouth for water to slake her thirst, but she couldn't remember when she had last eaten.

It was so cold. Snow covered the ground in slushy patches, making soft pools of mud below. She dragged herself through several of them in her flight, shivering as the icy wet chill seeped into her body.

It had begun to snow, and she knew her struggle was over. She could drag myself no farther. The pain had taken over her mind. The light snow falling on her would make her grave.

She lay exhausted on the cold ground as she listened to someone approach, footfalls crunching in the snow. Was it the Talvarian soldiers who had wounded her? Their vile taunting and crude teasing returned to her, and her mind pushed the memories violently down into the darkness of oblivion. How much better it would have been had that quarrel killed her. Death was far more preferable to torment at their hands.

Fear made her belly into a writhing nest of snakes. She could feel the sobs rising in her as the moment grew closer. She kept them clenched behind her teeth. If the men heard her, it would only make their taunting worse.

Please kill me, she begged in her mind. A quick blade and a gush of warmth, and it would be over.

A gentle hand touched her shoulder. A woman's voice called to her. She couldn't answer.

When hands rolled her to her back, pain flashed up her spine. A cry escaped on a cloud of misty breath. The hazy image of a red-haired woman floated above her. Her vision cleared for a moment, letting her stare into her own concerned face; then the second wave of pain crashed over her.

Abruptly, the spell broke, and Raessa found herself reeling into her own body again. Dizzy from the strain, she looked up at Koren. He stared back, pale with shock. From behind, she could hear Brek sobbing softly. She put an arm around his shoulders and pulled him to her, as much to steady herself as to comfort him.

"What did you do?" Koren asked in a whisper.

"I invoked the alasha stone to let you see Brek's experience through his eyes. He had to relive it just now. We all did. Not very pleasant, was it?"

He reached out to steady himself on a chair back as he sank down into its seat. For many long moments, not a word was said. Brek became quiet, but he made no move to break away from Raessa. She was sorry to have put him through it again, but Koren's callousness had angered her. Perhaps now the boy could let go of the memories that were weighing him down. At least she had some idea of how to help him.

"Why don't you and Zar go hunting?" she said finally.

Brek pulled back from her. His eyes went to Koren and back to Raessa. Fear and loyalty warred with each other on his face.

"Go on." She smiled to reassure him. "It's all right now. All behind you."

Reluctantly, he limped to the door. When he held out his hand to Zar, the wolf came to him easily. They both looked back at Raessa as if hesitant to leave. She waved them out, and they slid silently out the door.

Raessa took a chair across the table from Koren. "Now you know."

Koren looked up at her as if she had pulled him from deep thought. "Brek went through—" He seemed to be searching for the right words. Failing, he simply finished, "—a great deal."

"He is a child terrorized and crippled by war. Don't saddle him with false courage. He would have died there in the snow if Zar hadn't found him. And he had nightmares for months. I'm not sure what was done to him, but the fear never stops."

Expressions chased one another over Koren's face too rapidly to identify. Raessa stroked the alasha stone briefly and murmured a spell. A glance at the yellowed stone told her about his misgivings.

"Men leading children," she whispered. "That is what it has come to. It has to end."

"You overestimate my power, Lady."

She smiled. "I don't think so. Great storms can start from gentle breezes."

She rose and left him with his own thoughts. Outside, her only stallion, Valas, stood tied to the porch railing, fidgeting nervously. She had insisted the night before that Koren take him. Brek and Zar were huddled on the hillside above the house. Hugging herself against the chill, she climbed to join them. Settling down on the other side of Zar, she put an arm around his furry neck.

"What is he going to do?" Brek asked.

"Leave as he planned, I suppose."

"And us?"

"Empress should be close to having that baby. We'll need to keep a close eye on her."

Raessa knew he wanted to ask more, but his eyes were suddenly pulled away from her by Koren coming from the house. Taking the stallion's reins in his hand, he looked until he saw her and the boy. Leading Valas, Koren approached them.

"Words can never repay you, Lady," he said.

"Deeds might," she replied.

A troubled looked passed over his face. "You don't know what you ask."

"Perhaps I know more than you realize."

A crooked smile quirked up one corner of his mouth. "Perhaps you do at that. Just remember, I'm only one man."

"You make that a difficult fact to forget."

Something else passed between them then. A feeling. A promise. Raessa suddenly knew she would see this one again. With a flush of surprise, she also realized she would look forward to that day.

The moment vanished. Koren swung awkwardly into the saddle. With a wave, he wheeled about and was on his way. They watched his figure dwindle to a tiny speck against the meadowland. Just before he was swallowed up by the forest, Raessa stood, pulling Brek up with her.

"We have a mother-to-be to see about," she said.

They started off for the barn, arm in arm, Zar trailing along behind.

THE MOON WHO LOVED THE MAN
by Robin W. Bailey

Robin Bailey is one of the few men I've found who writes sword and sorcery as well as a woman; he has appeared in SWORD AND SORCERESS, as well as in other magazines and anthologies. He has also sold five novels; the first *Frost*, from Pocket Books, three more from Tor, and another from Bantam. He is about to enter—as I write this—a five hundred mile bike race across the state of Iowa; (well, whatever turns you on; some people also like plowing, needlework and nursing lepers—any of which I would rather do than ride a bike.) He writes that if he doesn't survive, his "wife inherits the literary estate; the cat gets everything else."

Mee-yow!

The mournful songs of the Almees women still filled Hasan's ears as he drove his horse furiously across the Egyptian night sands. Tears blurred his vision and rilled down his cheeks, soaked the soft white cloth that masked his face. It didn't matter where he went. He rode and rode, forcing his poor beast to the brink of exhaustion. At last, it stumbled, nearly fell. Only then did Hasan consider his animal and stop his reckless flight.

Yasmin was dead. His beautiful betrothed would never be his wife, would never lie in his arms as he had dreamed so many nights. Even now, her family placed her in the ground before she was cold, and the Almees sang their sad songs over her. She belonged to the sand now, not to him. Never to him.

He cast a glance back over his shoulder toward Wadi Adan, cursing the city and its people, cursing his own tribe for setting their tents outside its walls. He cursed the fate that had brought them to this unfortunate valley. And he cursed Allah. Most of all, he cursed his god.

The sand stretched before him like a shroud that covered the world. It sparkled in the soft light of a half moon, rolling and dipping with a gentle dancelike grace that only a Ghawazee tribesman could truly appreciate. Yasmin was as beautiful as the night desert. She also rolled and dipped in the right places, and she danced—how she danced!—as all Ghawazee women did. As long as the desert endured, Hasan knew he would not forget Yasmin. Especially now that she was laid within its folds. The dunes would be her breasts, the valleys, the very valleys of her sweet body, its mystery her mystery, and its every wind her scented whisper.

Hasan wept, hiding his face with his scarf until his tears ran dry. His horse trembled nervously. Without direction from its rider, it stood still. In the evening breeze the sand eddied around its hooves and fetlocks. Finally, Hasan wiped his eyes and stared outward, empty of heart. There was nothing to see but the great white desert, a peppering of stars, and the moon.

The moon was as pale as the sand, as pale as Yasmin's milky flesh. It hovered just above the horizon, large and luminous even in its middle phase. He would not go back to Wadi Adan, to the town that had murdered his beloved, so Hasan nudged his horse and rode toward the moon.

The sky revolved above him as he rode. The constellations shifted, and the moon climbed the heavens. Yet the beauty of the night only sharpened his grief for he could not share it with Yasmin. He wept again, but this time not the violent tears of anger and pain, instead the slow soft tears of memory and of dreams that would never come true.

The horse plodded on, rocking him in the saddle with a gentle, consolate motion as Yasmin had sometimes rocked him under the date trees when they talked about their marriage plans. He smiled at that, a bittersweet smile that tore at his heart. To compare his love with a horse! She would have thrown back her dark hair and laughed at that, her laugh that sounded like the music of cymbals and zils. Everything reminded him of Yasmin.

Atop a crest he tugged back on the reins and stopped. Despite his grief, no desert dweller could ignore the smell of water in the air. He looked down, and moonlight glimmered on an oasis he had never seen before. He realized suddenly that he had fled Wadi Adan without provisions and, except for a small belt dagger, without weapons. At sight of his dead betrothed he had just leaped on his horse and ridden. He was somewhat thirsty, he admitted, staring at the oasis. He started down the rise, watchful for tents or travelers who might be camped within such a welcome place.

He was alone, though, in what might have been paradise. Orange trees and lemon trees poured their heady fragrances into the air. Clusters of date palms swayed in a gentle desert breeze, their broad leaves rustling like a beledi dancer's skirts. Coriander and anise, endive and cumin grew wild, and wherever Hasan's horse set down its hooves the aroma of herbs wafted fresh and sweet. He paused long enough to climb from the saddle, then continued, leading his mount by the reins. For the moment, he forgot his grief as he walked among juniper berries and cardamom shrubs and bitter almond. Over it all came the smell of clean water and a soothing, timorous trickling.

The pool was as beautiful and clear as the eye of Allah. Hasan caught his breath. Along its grassy banks poppies bloomed and large, white ladanum flowers. On one side grew a myrrh tree waving its purple blossoms, offering its fragrant resin to the winds. On the other grew frankincense. Everything in the grove was in perfect bloom. He had never seen such loveliness.

Except in the face of his Yasmin.

Hasan tied his horse to a pomegranate shrub, ignoring the plump red fruit, having no appetite. He sat down on the pool's bank, uncovered his face, and stared into the water. It was a mirror without blemish, and it reflected the stars and the crescent moon in all its pale glory. It floated, perfectly balanced upon the waveless surface, and if the real one traversed the heavens, this image seemed determined to remain forever. He dipped his fingers and moistened his lips. The moon trembled, and the stars wavered ever so slightly until the ripples ceased and the pool once more grew still.

A single tear rolled down Hasan's cheek and fell into the pool. *Yasmin,* he thought, gazing around sadly. *How you would have loved it here. How I wish you were here beside me now.* But the Compassionate, in His wisdom, had taken her and left nothing for Hasan in the world worth having.

He drew out his belt dagger and held it in his hand for a long time. Moonlight gleamed on the blade, on the intricately wrapped hilt of woven gold wire, on the small pommel with its inset emerald. Hasan thought of his father who had given it to him on the day of his betrothal, and he remembered how his mother had danced as all the Ghawazee women danced that night at the celebration. The memories made him smile, yet there was still the emptiness in his heart where Yasmin had been.

It was against the Blessed Teachings, but Hasan was past caring. He raised the dagger, and looked out upon the pool, drawing a deep breath as he unfastened the button of his assuit shirt and bared his chest. His gave fell upon the reflected moon, the beautiful moon, so mysterious and ivory pale.

Yet suddenly, it was not the moon, but a face on the water.

"Yasmin!" Hasan leaped to his feet, dropping the blade in the grass. His love regarded him with sad dark eyes, and he shriveled suddenly under her gaze. He clutched his knees and rocked back and fourth on the bank, weeping and calling her name under his breath, staring at her features in the pool.

A wind blew over the desert, then, shaking the leaves of the palms and oranges and lemons. It shook the bushes and stirred the grasses. A rustling rose throughout the grove, and in that dry music Hasan heard Yasmin's whisper.

My love, she said, and again, *my love.*

The wind died then, and the image on the water became once more the reflection of the moon. Hasan sat stunned, his jaw agape, fingers digging in the soft earth beside him. Here was his beautiful Yasmin, here in this garden. And she had come to him! He did not doubt his vision. He had seen her, heard her voice. Even the air had smelled of her perfume!

He remained on the bank late into the night, hoping she might come back, yet fearing in his heart he would not see her again. Still, she had not forgotten him. Death had not destroyed their bond.

At last, Hasan rose, took his horse's reins and rode from the oasis. His family would be worried. With luck, though, he would reach his father's tents before dawn touched the walls of Wadi Adan. As he achieved the crest of the rise where he had first glimpsed the grove, he remembered the dagger he had dropped and halted. A good blade was a precious thing, especially if it was a gift. But when he turned to go back for it he stopped again.

Nothing stretched before him but the sand made white and dazzling by the yawning light of the setting moon. There was no sign of the oasis. Confused, Hasan steered his mount toward home and toward the welcoming arms of his parents.

But next day as the sun declined, as the sand turned red as blood in its fading glow, as the world cooled and the wind began to blow, Hasan thought again of the grove. When his parents were asleep in their blankets and the fire before their tent had burned to coals, he saddled his horse and rode away once more.

When he reached the same rise he stopped and gazed downward. The oasis was there, shining in the moonlight.

Yasmin waited for him in the pool. *My love,* the breeze whispered, and kneeling on the bank he answered, *My love.* He strained his hand toward her, and she reached up to meet his palm. But he touched only the water, and the ripples fractured her image. When the surface smoothed she was gone. Only the moon shone there, thinner and paler than the night before.

Seven more nights Hasan journeyed to the oasis to catch a glimpse of his beloved. But on the eighth night he rode and rode and could not find it. He rested atop a rise, sure it was the right one. But below, there was no sign of the grove. He slumped forward in his saddle and rubbed a finger over his eyes.

"So this is how you spend your nights."

Hasan twisted around as his father rode up beside him. So intent had he been on his search, so full of thoughts of Yasmin, that he had not been aware someone had followed him. That was dangerous for a desert man, and foolish, and he chided himself for it. "I'm sorry, father," he said humbly, "for disturbing the peace of your sleep."

His father's hand closed on his thigh, a gesture of comfort and compassion. "What do you hope to find out here, my son?" The old man asked. He scratched at the thick white stubble that bearded his chin as he gazed over the glittering wastes.

"Yasmin," he answered simply.

The father stared at his son for a long time, neither of them moving or daring to say more. Then, the old man hung his head, slowly unfastened his scarf from his face and cast it back over his shoulder. When he looked up again he said, "Yasmin is dead."

Hasan interupted his father for the first time in his life. "No. Smell the air," he said. "It's her perfume. Listen, and the wind is her laughter. Be still, and you will feel her near." Quietly, he told his father about the oasis and the marvelous pool.

"Your grief has overwhelmed you," his father said sadly, shaking his head. "Come home with me, son. Your mother waits for us. Yasmin is in paradise with Allah."

Hasan turned away and peered over the white sands. "She is in paradise, yes, but not with Allah. She is here, somewhere, though tonight I can't seem to find her."

"Come home," his father repeated, touching his son's shoulder affectionately. "Tomorrow the Ghawazee must leave Wadi Adan and find another city where our dancing and entertainments will bring us fresh coins. Time and distance will mend your heart, and you will find another maiden to make your wife."

Hasan stared upward at the moon, only a slender crescent in the night sky. "Father, if we were any tribe but Ghawazee, you would need a son to tend your flocks and feed your camels, to defend your tents from wolves and raiders." He uncovered his face and met his father's gaze. "But we are Ghawazee. We move from city to city as performers, and no one molests us, nor have we much property to defend." He swallowed hard before continuing. "If the Ghawazee leave tomorrow, I will stay behind."

His father's eyes misted over, but the old man refused to shed a tear. "The Sacred Teachings," he reminded his son. "It is your duty to care for your parents. Who shall see to us in our old age? In the Name of the Compassionate. . . ."

"Don't!" Hasan snapped rudely. "Don't implore me in Allah's name. Yasmin is here, and here I will stay! It was Allah who tried to take her from me! Allah in a damned ox-cart on a muddy street. Don't speak to me of Allah!"

His father stared aghast. "My son! That is your grief talking. God knows that and will not hold it against you. But come home, come home to your mother and the tent where you were born. Come home to your people, and tomorrow we will seek a happier place."

Hasan shook his head. "I love you, father, and I honor both my parents." He took up the end of his scarf and covered his face once more. "But I cannot come."

"Then let me embrace you," his father said, holding out an arm. They reached out to one another clumsily from their saddles and pressed their cheeks together. After a moment, the old man withdrew and covered his face. Then he extracted a leather purse from his sash and pressed it into his son's hand. "Perhaps the desert wind will blow us together again someday. Until then, God keep you."

Hasan wearily watched his father ride away. When he could be seen no more in the darkness he loosened the purse strings and poured a handful of gold coins onto his palm. Almost, he repented and rode after his parent. The Ghawazee were not wealthy people. These coins represented most of his father's savings. But the wind blew suddenly, and in the rustle of the sand he heard a familiar whisper.

Hasan.

He turned. At the bottom of the rise there was the oasis.

Hasan, said the sand.

The lemon and orange trees smelled twice as sweet, their perfume a heady drug that made his senses reel. He rode past them, his heart thumping. The shrubs brushed his thighs, and the breeze made music in the leaves.

She waited for him in the water. Hasan dismounted and walked to the pool's edge. Her eyes regarded his every movement. Her lips parted ever so slightly. She bowed her head shyly, then looked up again. He reached out and plucked a purple flower from the myrrh tree, inhaled its fragrance, and placed it gently on the surface near her hand.

"If only you could speak," he said wistfully, folding his legs and sitting on the grassy bank. "My parents and my people are leaving tomorrow. I have only you, Yasmin."

The wind made a strange, soft sound. Hasan looked and saw a tear roll on the cheek of his beloved before the water rippled suddenly, and her image disappeared.

Hasan felt his throat tighten. He hadn't imagined it; he had seen the tear. What did it mean? He whispered her name, but the pool reflected only the crescent moon and a smattering of stars. Why wouldn't she come back? He remained there long after, tearing blades of grass, dropping them on the water. At last, he led his horse from the grove and started up the rise.

The first light of morning kissed the walls of Wadi Adan as Hasan approached. He stopped his mount. The tents of the Ghawazee were gone. Suddenly he knew how a leaf felt, torn loose from the tree. He drew a deep breath and sighed. Already the gates of the city were open. Up and down the streets he rode until he found an inn. He used his father's coins to rent a room.

Each night in the waning moonlight he rode to the oasis. Yasmin was always there in the water waiting for him. He sat on the bank and floated poppy petals and white ladanums to her, and she smiled up from the crystal depths. The wind and the leaves and the sand would whisper his name, and he would answer, *My love.* Then, the image in the pool would waver and fade, and he would be alone.

But on the first night of the new moon Hasan stared into a pool that reflected only the stars, and a terror gripped his heart. He waited, sitting on the bank, working his fingers into the earth, tearing blades of grass. The wind and the leaves remained silent, and the water showed him nothing but his own face. He closed his eyes, and the tears streamed slowly down his cheeks, dripped from his chin, and rippled the mirror-smooth surface.

The tinkle of bells and the soft clang of zils made him look up. Though her back was to him, he knew her, and his tears fell even more freely. On the pool's far side she moved, her zils beating a sensuous chifti-telli rhythm. Her dark hair made a cloud about her face as she whirled suddenly, and her silver-and-white skirts flashed like moonlight. She stopped with her back still to him.

Hasan rose to his feet. He wanted to shout, yet that would have shattered the strange stillness that filled the garden. Instead, he whispered her name. "Yasmin!"

The wind took it up and carried it through the trees. The flowers shivered at the sound and spilled their essences into the air. The leaves began to sway and rustle.

Slowly, she turned to face him. It was his own beloved! Unveiled, she smiled shyly, and her eyes danced with a heavenly light. The breeze stirred her hair, fluttered her garments. She made no other move, and even the bells on her ankles were still as she regarded him.

"Yasmin!" he cried, no longer able to restrain himself. He ran then, never taking his eyes from her, afraid that if he did not fling his arms around her and hold her tight she might leave him once more. It was a true fear. For an instant—just the barest moment—the myrrh tree blocked his vision. Yasmin was gone.

Hasan could weep no more. Numb, he stood by the bank and hung his head, sure that he had gone insane. His were the fantasies of madness. Allah was punishing him for his blasphemies. Praise Allah, praise the Compassionate, praise God. There was yet time to repent, if only he could find his parents and the Ghawazee.

But he held up his empty arms and knew he would not repent. A few glimpses of his beloved were worth the price of his soul and these nightly visitations worth far more than eternity in paradise.

The soft echo of finger zils rode the wind. Hasan looked up hopefully, but Yasmin had not returned. In the pool, though, shone the reflection of a perfect, full moon. He peered over his shoulder, turned in a slow circle, and wondered for the first time what magic he had given himself to. In the sky, there was no moon at all.

Hasan wandered the streets of Wadi Adan, waiting for night to fall. He couldn't sleep, couldn't remember when he last had eaten. People cut a wide path around him as they went about their business, but they watched him carefully from the corners of their eyes until they were a safe distance away. He could feel their sneers on his back. In truth, he felt shame, for he hadn't bathed and knew he smelled, and his clothes were filthy.

For two night he had avoided the oasis. For two nights he had shut himself in his dirty little room and cowered on the plain rope-weave mattress with his head between his knees. He knew she was waiting. Even through the odor of grime and burning lamp oil came the smell of lemons and oranges. Even here the wind sought him as it blew up and down the narrow streets whispering his name. *Hasan.*

But he didn't answer. He shivered and hugged himself and tried to stop his ears. And just when the wind died and he had regained a semblance of calm an ox-cart trundled by outside his door, its heavy wheels grinding the dust. An ox-cart, and so late at night! The clatter of its greaseless axles had made a rhythm too much like Yasmin's zils.

He knew, though, as he walked in the hot Egyptian sun through crowds of merchants and beggars and shoppers, as the noise of commerce filled his ears and the smells of tanners and blacksmiths and grocers filled his nose, that tonight he would return. He did not understand magic, and he was no philosopher. Yet, it was the last night of the new moon. He didn't know why, but he knew that mattered. And the lure of the oasis was stronger than his fear.

He rode from Wadi Adan as the sun set. In the fading rays the sand became a sea of dazzling flame. But in the desert, night fell quickly. He guided his horse across the dunes, leaving a trail of cratered prints on the windswept landscape.

From the top of the rise the oasis looked more beautiful than he had ever seen it. Strange, for without moonlight he wondered that he could see it at all. Yet, he saw. And as before he heard the gentle trickling of water, though the pool was perfectly still. Magic, he knew, and he did not even try to understand. He steered his mount down the slope.

She stood by the edge of the pool in the very place where he had often sat. When she turned around, she wore a look of infinite sadness. "I thought you would not come." It was Yasmin's voice, not the wind of the leaves that spoke to him.

But Hasan would not be fooled. He had thought long and hard in the lonely silence of the past two nights. "You are not Yasmin," he said. He walked to the pool. She held out her hands to him, and he took them in his own. Her flesh was the same ivory as his beloved's. But he repeated, "You are not Yasmin."

She slipped the zils from her fingers and let them fall on the grass. "I am not Yasmin," she answered meekly. "But I heard your tears as you rode across the desert the night she died, and I pitied you. I made this place for you to rest and spend your grief." Her hands touched his shoulders, and she pulled him down to sit.

"You saved my life." Hasan raised his arms as she slipped his assuit shirt over his head. The breeze was cool on his bare flesh. "I'd determined to take my life that night on this very bank, but Yasmin's face appeared in the pool and stopped me."

Her fingers burrowed deep in the grass, and she found the dagger he had dropped so many nights ago. She let it fall again. "I showed you what you most wanted to see," she said. "You didn't know what you were doing."

Then, they were both naked. She moved upon him, and he responded, unable to help himself, so great was his need. He ran his hands over Yasmin's form, exactly as he had dreamed so often of doing, twined his fingers in her hair, pressed his mouth on hers. She consumed him with a pale fire that went beyond passion, and again and again she raised him up and rode him like a great phoenix past the edge of the world.

"Who are you?" Hasan gasped helplessly as sweat ran down his brow and stung his eyes. He clutched her to him, though, trading that small discomfort for a greater pleasure.

"Night after night you came," she answered between clenched teeth. "And though I could never stay long, still I listened to your heart, Hasan." She threw back her head and drew breath. "A strange thing happened. As I saw how much you loved Yasmin, my pity began to turn to love for you."

They spoke no more until they lay quietly breathing in each other's arms. "Why didn't you come to me before?" Hasan whispered, gently stroking the silken strands of her hair. "Why didn't you tell me?"

"It was Yasmin you loved," she answered, tracing a pattern on his chest with one finger. "So I remained Yasmin. At first, it was to ease your grief. Later, it was to insure your return. I appeared to you in the pool those many nights because that was my only way."

Hasan untangled himself and sat up. "There was a moon in the sky those nights, and it reflected in the water." He gazed upward. "There is no moon tonight."

"Nor the last night you came when I danced for you." She threw her arms around him from behind and held him close. "On those nights when I do not sail the heavens, then I may take any form I please."

Despite himself, Hasan shivered. "I know you, now," he breathed softly. "Badr-al-Dujja!"

She released him, rose, and went to stand beside the pool. "Between man and Allah," she said, "there are many creatures and many things." She beckoned, and Hasan went to stand beside her. In the water he saw his own reflection, but also a bright shining orb. "I am Badr-al-Dujja," she whispered.

Hasan closed his eyes. "The Light of the Moon," he said.

She touched his cheek. "And though I did not mean for it to happen, I love you."

He hung his head. "I love Yasmin."

"No." She picked up his shirt and held it for him. He slipped an arm into one sleeve, then the other, and pulled it over his head. "You *loved* Yasmin. She is dead." Her fingers brushed over his heart.

He caught her hand with his own and held it trapped to his chest. For a long moment, he thought, feeling her flesh pressed to his. "I understand," he said meekly. "The hurt will heal after all.

She smiled mysteriously. "Of course. It's a kind of magic."

He embraced her and pulled her head against his chest. "Are you truly the Light of the Moon?"

Badr-al-Dujja returned his embrace and kissed his nipples. Then she backed away. "I am," she answered with unexpected sadness. "And because I am, we must part."

Hasan tried to embrace her again, but she stopped him. "No," he said. "I'll come every night to see you."

She shook her head. "That is no life for you, Hasan. You're an ephemeral, and I am the eternal Light of the Moon. We must be what we are." She brushed his cheek again, and he saw the tears that glistened in her eyes. "We've touched in a wonderful way. Let that be enough. And as you return to your people, ride knowing you have the love of Badr-al-Dujja."

"I would go with you if I could," he said quietly. "There is nothing for me here."

Again, she smiled, but she also wiped a tear with the back of her hand. "We must be what we are," she repeated, "and you will find much in the world to love before your days are done." She plucked a pomegranate and held it for him to take a bite. When he did, she ate from the same place. The remaining fruit she dropped into the water. "This garden will fade when I am gone," she said. "But from this pool and those seeds another will grow to quench the thirst of the Ghawazee when they pass this way again."

She bent and took water in her cupped hands, then held for him to drink. "This one sip will take you to your people. You will need no more as you cross the desert."

Hasan took her hands in his and kissed them. "Don't leave me yet," he said. "I shall have lost two loves." He touched his lips to the centers of her palms and closed his eyes. He inhaled her perfume. It was no longer Yasmin's, but it smelled just as sweet, just as rare. "I have gained so much," he whispered.

"And the loss is little beside the gain." She kissed him, and stepped away quickly. "Go now, Hasan. And I will give the world a sign of my love, a sign to make them marvel."

He did not try to stop her, but watched as she turned and waded into the pool. Deeper and deeper she went until she disappeared beneath the water. When the ripples stilled and the surface was mirror-smooth once more, Hasan smiled.

Badr-al-Dujja smiled back at him, and her reflection mirrored the great full glory that floated in the sky where no moon at all should have been.

The oasis lingered but a moment more, long enough for the wind to stir the leaves. *Hasan*, they said with magic voices. *Hasan*.

LAST QUARREL
by Dorothy J. Heydt

Dorothy Heydt said at her last bio update: "By now you probably know the facts as well as I do; I'm a Catholic, a soprano, a mother of two, and a crummy housekeeper." (Aren't we all—it comes with spending your time at a word processor—and processing words even when you're away from the keyboard.)

She has also written a couple of pretty good novels which are harder science fiction than I could ever manage.

The shadow had been passing over their heads since midday, back and forth like a blot over the ground, rising up like a solid body when it passed through the dust clouds the King's army left in its wake.

The high arid plains of Thesh stretched out for miles in every direction. A day's march behind them lay the inhabited lowlands, safe for the moment behind the shelter of the hills, but the plains were scoured bare with the wizard's malice; not even grass grew there now. Four days ahead of them, already visible among the mountains, the wizard's keep rose like a smooth-pointed fang in the jaw of a great cat.

It was not till two hours past the noon, when the sun had fallen from its highest point, that they caught a glimpse of the flying thing that cast the shadow. Captain Andraia held up a hand to block out the sun, and peered into the deep autumn sky. "What do you make of it?" he asked those who rode near him. "Bird, beast, or bat?"

"It's big, whatever it is," said the archer Valmai. She had taken her arbalest from its sling across her back and was giving it the dozen turns it took to wind it up. "See how it glides, hardly flapping its wings. It's riding the updrafts, like an eagle. But I wouldn't say it had the shape of a bird." She squinted up at the thing, deepening the lines that years of service had carven round her eyes. "Whatever it is, I doubt it means us well. Some spy of the wizard's, unless I miss my guess." She reined in her horse, and motioned those who rode behind her to pass by on either side.

Skill is one thing, and luck is another, and when they happen to coincide the damnedest things can happen. Valmai's bolt shot up as swift and vicious as gossip, and skewered the flying thing through the wing. It tumbled through the sky and fell.

They rode up to where the thing lay, downed but not dead, and stood at a cautious distance as it thrashed about with the quarrel through its wing. It was a long-necked serpent with bat's wings, like a dragon out of an old tale, but no larger than a man. The sheen over its scaly body was like glass, greenish and transparent. It wrapped its tail around itself, drew in its wings, and changed. A man lay on the ground before them, a thin, beardless gray-faced man in a shimmering green cloak, Valmai's arrow thrust through the palm of his hand.

He pushed himself to a sitting position with his good hand, and looked round the circle of watchers. When his eye fell on Valmai and her arbalest, the hood of his cloak spread like a cobra's and he began to speak in a hissing whisper. Andraia drew his sword and took a step toward him, but Valmai motioned him back and began to wind the arbalest again. The wizard smiled thinly and made a little gesture, as if throwing a handful of nothing toward her. Then he put his hand over his face and disappeared. The quarrel fell to the ground in a little puff of dust.

"Curse it," Valmai said without heat. "I should've shot first and asked questions later."

"No matter," said the captain. "We won't have him overhead now, not till that wound heals in his wing. Well done, Valmai." He looked about him, where the army had come almost to a stop with gazing and confusion. "Form up those lines, there! Where's the sergeant? Get them moving again; the circus is over." He turned back to Valmai. "Dine with me this evening? I've a piece of that venison left and we ought to eat it before it goes off."

But by evening, when the army stopped to make camp, Valmai was feverish and unable to eat. Her companions brought her water and sponged her body and her aching head, and eventually she slept. By morning she was able to ride again.

All day she could barely keep her eyes open, and her head kept nodding toward her saddlebow. She put it down to her lack of sleep the night before, and when they camped that night she swallowed some bread and tumbled into her bedroll before the sun was well down.

In the morning she was too weak to rise at first, and she lay long in her tangled blankets before she could muster the strength to rise and dress. She went straight to the physician's tent. He listened to her story and looked her over, and then he stood turned away from her, his hands clasped behind his back.

"Is it a sickness," she asked, "or the wizard's work?"

"Yes," he said. "It's both of those. And I fear there's no cure; I've seen it before, in the Koriath campaign. The man lasted three weeks, growing tireder and weaker all the time, till finally he stumbled and fell in the midst of battle and tripped up two of his fellows as he went. I don't know how long he would have lived if he'd stayed out of combat; a year or two, maybe."

"Well," said Valmai. "Will you send for Andraia, master physician? We've campaigned together a long time; I'd as lief he struck off my head as anyone."

"There's a better course," the physician said, "if you have the courage."

"Try me."

"Go back to the lowlands," he said, "and live there till you die. It's a cloud of his power that's on you, his chains on your limbs, his silk that entangles you. He can't draw it from you while you live. Live as long as you can, and you'll hamper him every day of it."

"So I will, then."

She drew her back pay and as much of her pension as the paymistress was willing to allow her, and she sold her sword and her armor; but she kept the arbalest. It was all her arms could do to wind it, but the trigger would loose at a feather's touch and she had no wish to cross the plains again alone and unarmed. She tied a bag of coppers to her saddlebow, and packed a few days' rations next her bedroll, and she said goodbye to her companions. When the army was ready to march, she turned her back on them resolutely and rode back the way they had come.

Since it was herself that was ill and not her horse, it took her only a day and a half to retrace the path that had taken the King's army two days. She rode slumped in the saddle, her eyes half-shut and her wits dulled, but no living thing came near her. She slept the first night under the unsympathetic stars, her horse towering over her like a forest.

The next morning she had to clamber into the saddle like a bear into a tree, and she was glad that her companions could not see her. That day the road began to descend, and a little rivulet sprang up beside it and lined its verge with green. As she descended, the stream widened into a brook a tired woman could bathe her face and her feet in, and keep awake a little longer. Bushes grew up beside it, and the air grew sweet and heavy with the scent of water, and when at last the stream fell in a little cataract of a dozen feet, she saw small fish flashing in it, and a pool beneath it where the shadows were deep and green. Beyond the pool was the village.

They had passed through it on the way up, but she had scarcely noticed it, her mind being set on her business and full of preparations for battle. Now the place seemed a paradise on earth, a shelter maybe for her weary bones as long as her flesh could hold them together. She had intended to ride farther from the plains before she stopped, but instead she turned her horse and went into the village.

The last of the crops were in and the men were plowing the upland fields for the winter wheat. The caller went before the plow, coaxing the oxen forward, and the plowman followed after with his whip laid at right angles to the plowshare, to space the furrows evenly. Three men followed him, breaking up the largest clods with heavy wooden mallets. They paused and stared at her, and one left the furrow and leaped over the hedge that rimmed the field.

"Good evening, mistress," he said. He was a youth of fifteen or so, grown tall and gangling but not filled out yet, a drift of yellow fuzz on his chin like the backside of a baby chick. "Is the battle over already?"

"Not begun yet; but I've fallen ill and had to come back. I need a place to live."

"We'd be happy to put you up for the night."

"Longer than that; I can't travel farther."

The youth raised one sandy eyebrow. "Well, my great-aunt Kinda died last month, and left my Dad her cottage. He doesn't need the cottage, and he needs a new cart-horse. Dad!" he shouted, his voice breaking in the middle, and the plowman rested the plow against the headland and joined them.

By nightfall the trade was agreed on, and in the morning Valmai moved into the cottage. The youth Kendrick carried water in for her, and helped her sweep out and build a fire.

The house was tiny, only a single room, a dozen feet from wall to wall and not quite square. There was a door in the front wall, a window in the back, and a hearth built in at one side. Kendrick set Valmai's bed against the fourth wall, and she collapsed into it gratefully while he set the place to rights.

Most of great-aunt Kinda's possessions had been shared out among her kin. A few other pieces Valmai sold, leaving the house almost bare. She had a shelf to hold a few dishes, a chest to hold a bit of clothing and the souvenirs of a dozen campaigns; she had a kettle and a broom and a water bucket, and (a touch of luxury) a change of bedlinen that Kendrick's mother would launder from time to time. There was a kitchen garden with a few turnips still left in it, bordered by a fence of rough split stakes, and a privy tucked discreetly around the corner of the house.

Thus she established the narrow limits of her life, in

the hope of keeping them within her grasp, and settled down to wait out the winter.

On her good days she could get up and cook her meals, draw the broom across the hard-packed earthen floor, even sit on the doorstep and watch the crows drifting across the sky. She found that she could portion out her time and her strength: half an hour to cut up a chicken and some vegetables and put them in the pot; an hour to rest while it simmered over the fire. Sometimes she could even walk a furlong's distance to a neighbor's house, sit for an hour swapping battle yarns with the stories of these strange quiet people who had lived in the same place all their lives, lives as rich and complex as her own.

On her bad days, she never heaved herself out of bed except to go to the privy. She slept all night and half the day. She quickly learned that the week before her courses fell due would be the worst week of the month, and made arrangements for Kendrick or his sister to come in and clear out the undergrowth, simmer the kettle and wash the crockery, and haul buckets of water from the well on the village green.

Her wits grew as weak as her body, and her soldier's life seemed a tale told of somebody else, long ago and in another country. Perhaps it was a mercy, since it kept her from longing to be out again and on the march; there were days when she could not even remember any more whether she had held her sword in her right hand or her left. Her ambitions were shrunken, and she dreamed not of marching into new lands but of walking in her garden and pulling up young carrots that her jaws had the strength to chew.

When the Frost Moon was new in the west, a cat invited himself into the cottage, a rangy young tomcat with gray stripes from his nose to his tail. Thin as a hop-pole when he came to her, he grew sleek on her broth and bread and spent hours lying heavily in her lap, purring soft and deep as distant thunder. It was a comfort. To eat, sleep, and watch the crows fly past was enough for him, and she tried to follow his example.

Kendrick also took to coming by, even on her good days, to stir the up her fire and listen to her battle stories when she could bring them to mind. He had decided to go for a soldier himself when he had his growth, and whenever the weather was dry he borrowed Valmai's arbalest and shot at a target he'd set in a dead tree.

Once or twice during the winter a messenger would go by, picking his way over the frozen road between the army and the King. Valmai learned that the wizard's keep was beseiged; the army had built its camp at the foot of the mountain and settled in for the winter. The wizard was said to be hard-pressed, his goblin troops faint for lack of fresh meat and his mercenary men deserting in droves. Some of them made their way to the camp and bought their freedom with what they knew.

Kendrick passed on these bits of news in a voice afire with eagerness. Valmai, barely listening, drew her blankets closer around her and tucked her hands under the cat's striped flank to keep them warm. The time now seemed incredibly long ago when she had marched in order of battle, wound up an arbalest and loosed a bolt at a gliding shape with a man's wicked heart wrapped in a green serpent's skin.

The spring came at last, with the distant honking overhead of the wild geese flying north and the steady drip of meltwater from the roof. Kendrick's sister came with an iron griddle and taught Valmai to bake oat-cake as thin as leather. On her good days she sat by the fire, her face splendidly scorched by the heat, casting the thin batter over the hissing griddle; on her bad days she need only stretch an arm to break it down from the rafters where it hung in folds, slowly growing stiff and brittle.

Spring, and she was still alive despite the wizard. She counted over her shrinking pile of coppers, and thought of hiring Kendrick to spade her garden.

Then the message went out that the King's army had broken camp and stormed the wizard's fortress. His tower was fallen, his armies dispersed; the wizard himself had taken to the air and barely escaped with his serpent's skin.

It was the warmest day they had had so far that

spring. Valmai sat in bed with her back to the wall and the cat in her lap, watching two flies dance in the doorway. From the yard outside came the occasional thump of a quarrel hitting dead wood, as Kendrick practiced his aim. He was losing her quarrels in the forest, one by one; soon she must collect herself and teach him to make some more.

A shadow drifted over the ground, too swiftly for a passing cloud. Valmai went cold, and the warm burden of the cat in her lap was suddenly a crushing weight, too heavy to shift aside. Kendrick shouted, and came inside at a stumbling run, the arbalest in one hand and a single quarrel in the other. "A flying thing," he said. "It came in low over the trees, I think it's landing on the green. I'll run and see."

"Set down the arbalest," Valmai snapped. "Never run with it wound. Besides, he might know it again. Ah! cat, you're made of lead."

Kendrick ran off. Far in the distance there was a murmur, a rumor of disturbance like a shaken beehive. The cat rose and stretched, sinking its claws into the blankets and opening its pink mouth wide in a yawn. The flies swirled in the doorway and made off for quieter places.

Kendrick came back at a dead run; scorning the gate, he leaped over the fence and burst through the doorway. "He's coming! Ai, ai, he asked them where you were, and they told him! He's coming this way."

"Get out of here," Valmai commanded. "Take the cat and go through the window. That's orders!" Already the shadow was at the gate.

Kendrick snatched up the cat with one arm and plunged headfirst through the open window. There was a thud outside, and a scrambling sound that died away in the forest.

The shadow in the doorway was not quite solid; the sun at its back seeped through in a green mist that swirled aimlessly on the floor. Deliberately the wizard advanced to stand at the foot of the bed where Valmai huddled silent under all her blankets, her knees drawn up as if with cramp.

"Archer, you have failed in what was expected of you," the thin voice said. "I meant you to be a weight on the arm of your comrades, a hobble on the feet of your army. Instead, you have inconvenienced *me*.

"I should have sought you out before this, but that my wing pained me. Now I shall pay you out, and returning to my own place wipe your army from the map." He raised a hand like a bundle of twigs, and smiled.

Valmai kicked off the blankets, and the arbalest that rested on her knee sang briefly as the bolt loosed from the spring. It buried itself in the wizard's breastbone, and he fell backward into the doorway flapping his arms like a half-fledged stork. The green shape writhed and darkened, by turns like a man on the rack or a snake with a broken back. It shriveled in the sunlight into a little dried-up thing, twisted round the shaft of Valmai's quarrel, looking like neither reptile nor man.

Pushing with her hands, Valmai got her backside under her and sat up. There was a clean smell to the air. Her lungs drew it in deeply, as if she had put on too tight a corselet in the autumn and only just now cast it off. A certain freshness was creeping into her body, slow and promising as the first drops from the frozen thatch under the sun. Maybe her strength would come back to her. Perhaps she would redeem her horse from the plowman's cart, leave the village and the forest and go back to the battlefield. She got to her feet, and her sight went dark; she must clutch at the doorpost till her blood rose to her brain again and the dizziness passed.

The earth, steaming under the hot sun, was furry and green with young weeds. She must borrow a hoe and clear a few rows; it was too cold for beans or turnips yet, but she could have a few lettuces ready to go with the venison, when Captain Andraia brought his troops back down the road.

CROOKED CORN
by Deborah Wheeler

Deborah Wheeler has been in almost every anthology I've edited. So naturally when I started a new anthology she was one of the first writers I solicited for a story. She has sold now to a magazine called *Pandora*, and has become a contributing editor to *Fighting Woman News*. She also has two daughters, and two novels "at the stage of waiting for a senior editor to make up his or her mind."

In other words, she's pretty typical of our writers.

A soft night breeze, barely more than a puff of air, ruffled the heavy-headed barley-corn, releasing its musky scent of ripeness, and whispered through the hedgerows of leatherleaf and dwarf-alder which ran between the fields like strips of forest trying to reclaim their own. Night birds erupted into song, quieted, and then burst forth again, while in the fields, crickets and flip-its kept up a constant chatter.

In the densest part of the hedge, hidden from the eyes of all but the keenest nocturnal hunter, a great black warhorse, still in saddle and bridle, dozed. At his feet, a warwoman in battered leather-plate armor also slept, her back against the trunk of an ancient leatherleaf. Her head had fallen forward on one arm, and the other hand rested lightly on the long, slightly curved sword at her side. On her left hand she wore a bloodstone ring set in silver, an odd ornament for a fighter, for it bore the unmistakable stamp of magic. Indeed, it was all Tyr of Arcady had left of the witch Elarra, who had fought at her side against her sworn enemy, the Djenne Warlord Chandros, and died defeating him.

Tyr had not intended to actually sleep, only catnap a little while Hellsteed rested, and it was a measure of how desperately she had driven herself that she failed to rouse instantly when first the field insects and then the hedge birds fell silent.

Not so the battle-trained stallion. His head shot up, nostrils flaring like red-scoured goblets. Tyr reacted to his movement, scrambling to her feet even before her mind emerged fully from sleep. Her sword left its sheath with no more noise than a hunting owl. The razor tip paused a hairsbreadth from a soft human throat.

It was the girl from Assire. Tyr had just ridden into the market town when she found two of the Duke's soldiers attempting to rape the child. Something deep within her, held under tight rein all those years she hunted Chandros, had snapped, and for a blood-crazed moment she was again a child herself, violated and battered by the Djenne Raiders. When she came to her senses, the two soldiers lay dead, and she was no longer the hunter but the hunted.

What was the girl doing here? Tyr wondered, her thoughts still sleep-muddled. *And how had she managed to follow so quickly?*

She lowered her blade. "Don't you know better than to go sneaking up on an armed warrior? I could have sent your head tumbling in one direction and your body in another before I realized you weren't one of the Duke's men."

"No," the childish voice was sweet, like dew on petals. "Not you. You would always look before you struck. You're a Swordsister."

Tyr slipped her sword back into its sheath, thinking she could do without that particular legend. "What're you here for, anyway?"

The girl dipped her head, eyes gleaming through the tangled mane of hair. "To warn you."

"It's not news the Duke's looking for me, I did kill two of his henchmen. That they deserved it won't make any difference."

"You won't reach the borders. Noon tomorrow the Duke'll name you outlaw. Then anyone can kill you for the reward, an' anyone caught helpin' you gets an eye branded out."

An eye . . . "A few days hiding in the fields, traveling after dark, and that won't matter."

The girl wavered, then blurted out, "No, they're countin' on that—and they're startin' the harvest early."

"I'll just have to be gone by then." Tyr slid her left hand along the reins and rested it on the saddle's high pommel.

Suddenly the girl was by her side, whispering, "Ye'r done for, lady—"

A heavy-laden grain stalk snapped, and then another, this time behind her. A man's voice rang from the nearly dark field. "You're surrounded! Surrender in the name of Lestro, Duke of Burien!"

Now she knew how the girl had followed her so quickly. "The Duke's men—you kept me talking until they had me surrounded!"

Tyr pushed the girl aside, sending her crashing into the hedge as armed men, jacketed in dark leather, appeared from their hiding places in the field. She did not know how many she faced, and the first thing was to pick off as many as she could before they rushed her.

Tyr brought her sword up and out in a smooth extension of her body. The foremost soldier parried, an awkward move that left the other side of his body unguarded. His sword was massive, his technique relying more on momentum than skill. Her lighter steel slipped along it, and with a flick she was past the stylized guard. The sword, its owner minus a thumb and bleeding profusely, tumbled to the ground.

Another man, featureless in the gloom, lunged at her. Tyr whirled to send him hurtling by and sever his hamstrings in passing. His screams multiplied those of his comrade, and the others drew back.

Tyr kept her sword tip level and ready as she swung up, one handed, to Hellsteed's back.

"Hold!" It was the first man's voice. "Archers, to position!"

Tyr's stomach turned gelid as the swordsmen moved back. Polished lengths of wood gleamed as they curved, wood and steel-tipped arrows. Her mouth filled with a bitter, unfamiliar taste. She reversed her sword and held it, hilt first, toward the leader. It took courage for him to approach her, to put himself within her reach. He took the sword.

"Not used to surrender, are you?"

"What makes you think this is surrender?" she said as she dismounted.

"What makes you think it's not?"

Tyr's lips twisted into a barely suppressed smile. There was something in this captain, with his curt words and his ruthless efficiency, that she understood and could respect.

It took a few minutes to remove Tyr's other weapons and get the party organized to move out. They'd left their horses well back on the road, which accounted for their quiet approach. Tyr was bound to the saddle of a bony-withered nag, hands tied behind her back. Once they were on the road, the captain reined his horse beside her and politely asked her name. For a moment she hesitated, but refusing seemed pointless, so she told him.

"What will this Duke Lestro do, now that you've captured me alive?" she asked in return. "Cut off my hands and ears, brand me, crucify me? I don't suppose I'll get a trial."

"If you were a man he'd castrate you before hanging, double penalty for the two deaths."

Tyr laughed, saying, "No doubt he'll manage to think of something appropriate. There was a peasant couple on the road who spoke of the Old Duke. I take it they didn't mean this Lestro."

"Once we had better things to do than raping children. The Old Duke kept us busy defending Burien against her real enemies. We fought against the Djenne Raiders and held them back until Chandros brought up his demons—"

"Chandros!"

"—slaughtered the Old Duke and half our forces. The Old Duke's son—Lestro, the present Duke—he was already a grown man with a son of his own. He stopped the bloodshed—how, no one's sure—the rumor is that he made a bargain with Chandros."

This Duke allied himself with Chandros, Tyr thought in horror. *Whatever happens now, he shall not have me, any more than Chandros did! I swear—* She remembered what she had sworn before, staggering from the smoking ruins of Arcady, and how Elarra fulfilled that vow in her place. But now there was no gray-eyed witch, prattling of earth spirits, at her side.

"Yet you still have a chance," the captain said suddenly. "The Duke holds Harvest Court in a few weeks. By the Old Law, that's when a prisoner can challenge to win his freedom."

"Why should I believe anything you tell me—you whose Duke made a devil's pact with Chandros!" She spat the name like a gobbet of distilled venom.

He rode in silence for a few moments, and then said, "I know that Chandros led the Djenne scourge across Arcady and Verithe, and only a handful of your sisters survived. Isn't it better to accept the honorable help of one who has suffered with you, than to die with your own stubborn pride intact?"

"The Duke would think you a traitor to speak this way to me," she replied cautiously.

"I have never broken my oath to serve."

"To serve Lestro, or Burien?"

"Ah, we understand each other, then. My name is Sirion Ancather."

"I ask you again, why help me?"

"You could have killed two of my men, and did not, and you have no love for the true enemy of this land. In a different time, I would be proud to count you as my friend. But whatever my feelings, I have no choice now but to deliver you to Burien's Duke, as I have been commanded to do."

Tyr spent a few uncomfortable days in the Assire stockade, a drafty structure suited more to housing goats than human prisoners. The jailer stripped her to her linen underthings and took her belt and boots, leaving her with nothing which could be used as a weapon, but only a flea-ridden blanket and a bucket in the corner.

Sirion Ancather led the contingent of guards on the ride to Kingsbridge. He was a tall, graying man, with one shoulder slightly hunched from an old injury. He commanded his men quietly, and Tyr did not miss the respect in their eyes, even when it was mixed with weaselly fear. He took no chances on her making a break for freedom, either on the trail or during their overnight camp, and she saw no point in a useless attempt.

Kingsbridge was one of the largest cities Tyr had ever seen, although not as beautiful as Rizenne by the Eastern Sea, or Malta-of-the-Golden-Towers. The Bridge was a stone-layer's triumph, a sweeping arch of silver-flecked granite spanning the muddy Shawan River. The company marched over it and up toward the fortress which now served as the Ducal palace. Tyr was given a meal of bread and badly cooked potatoes, and then thrown into a damp, smelly cell to await her sentencing.

So that's Duke Lestro, Tyr thought as she stood chained with the other prisoners in the far corner of the great hall. The central arena, thronged with courtiers, was spacious, the acoustics so clear that she could hear what was spoken on the dais. Tapestries on the walls glittered with reds and purples, and heavily applied metallic thread in geometric patterns.

Trumpet flourishes announced the entrance of Duke Lestro, followed by his entourage of lesser nobles and their ladies, dressed in autumnal russet silks and velvets. The Duke himself wore black satin, almost buried under a lord's ransom in gold-thread lace and moonstones. Tyr caught a glimpse of him as he took his seat on the immense, ornately carved bronzewood chair. In her years of training she'd learned to evaluate an opponent in the flicker of an eye. The hands upon the bejeweled armrests moved steadily as he gestured to his grown son at his side, but something in the movement suggested deceit.

The young man dressed in midnight velvet now bend-

ing to hear the Duke's private words was another
matter—a possibility, not yet wedded to his father's
path. His muscled shoulders and clipped waist suggested he had not yet abandoned daily arms practice.

I could take him, Tyr thought. *But it would be a
shame. Without his father's rank and with the right
teacher, he might yet make something of himself.*

The prisoners were brought forward one by one to
stand before the Duke. The ruby-robed vizier, a hawk-
eyed man with a wispy beard and ramrod straight
spine, read each name and charge before sentence was
pronounced. The other outlaws, men driven by des-
peration to petty thievery, cowered before the Ducal
throne, whimpering for mercy. Some, to her surprise,
were granted pardon and their ragged belongings re-
stored. Tyr was not surprised when the others were
sentenced and led away, leaving her standing alone.

"The ruffian Tyr, sometime styled Swordsister," the
vizier announced as he surveyed her with eyes of ice,
"charged with the willful and bloody murder . . ."

Tyr took a deep breath and stilled her thoughts, as
she did before a battle. Now she had no blade in her
hands, no war-trained stallion between her knees, only
a room full of uncaring strangers, interested only in
the spectacle of her death.

"Stop!" she shouted, and stepped forward. Her chains
clinked on the stone floor.

"Silence, prisoner!" the nearest guard said, and
yanked her back.

"I claim the Harvest Challenge!" There was a half-
breath of rippling shock, and then the hall exploded in
outrage.

"—to this nonsense! Proceed with the sentencing—"
Lestro's voice rose above the uproar, amplified by the
hall's specialized acoustics.

"The Harvest Challenge!" Tyr shouted, pitching her
voice the way she would a battle-cry.

The hubbub died quickly, with only a few chopped-
off exclamations of, "What is she talking about?"
"—what right has she—" "The vizier will know, shut
up so we can hear what he says!"

The Duke gestured the vizier to his side, and the

two conferred in muted whispers. Finally Lestro looked up and demanded, "By what right do you claim Harvest challenge?" His voice resonated through the hushed chamber. "By the warm day or the cool, by the straight corn or the crooked, by sweat or by blood?"

It's a ritual formula, and I don't know the correct response! For the first time in her adult life, Tyr felt utterly lost. Without certain knowledge, she had no idea how to answer, and no berserker rage, no trick from her years of training could come to her aid. *What would Elarra advise, if she were here?* she wondered, knowing she had only a few moments before the Duke took her hesitation for ignorance and she forfeited her only chance.

Elarra yammered away at me about earth spirits, about growth and life. I know nothing of such things, only vengeance and the shedding of blood. Then I will wager my answer on what I am not, rather than what I already am.

"I challenge by the cool day and the crooked corn," she began. *For any warrior would prefer a fair day and an easy enemy. Sweat or blood—neither is foreign to me . . .*

The Duke's eyes remained raised as he waited for her to make a fatal error.

"By the cool and the crooked," she repeated, "and by *my own* sweat and blood."

The vizier once again bent his head to the Duke's. The enormous room was so quiet Tyr could hear the blood rushing through her veins. The Duke shook his head but the red-robed advisor gestured emphatically, and finally Lestro nodded and waved the man away.

"The challenge is valid!"

This time Tyr was given a room in the palace, although there were bars on the slitted windows and she was kept under heavy guard. She gathered from the talk amongst the servants who brought her food that the entire city was preparing for the spectacle of the challenge.

On the appointed morning, servants brought Tyr her gear. Her sword had not been returned to her, nor

her cooking knife or the small dagger she carried in
the top of one boot. Instead of her armor, she pulled
on a loose-fitting flax-weave shirt and pants, tucked
into her laced boots. As she rummaged through her
saddlebags, looking for a good-luck token, she found
the bloodstone ring, still in its suede wrapping.

Tyr slipped it on her finger, surprised to feel how
warm the metal was. It seemed to welcome her like an
old friend. No, that was just because she was thinking
of Elarra, and missing their brief comradeship. Then
she changed her mind, for there came a whisper in her
mind, just beyond what she could understand as speech,
and it bore such a strong sense of the witch that Tyr
no longer had any doubt that some evanescent trace of
Elarra's personality remained in the ring.

I don't know if some part of your soul is tied here,
she thought, *or if this is only an emotional residue
because you owned the ring so long. But I swear by all
the gods, Elarra, that if I come through this alive, I will
bring this token of your courage to Ryley Witch-heart,
that you may be laid to rest in honor.* When the guards
came for her, Tyr was still stroking the bloodstone,
and feeling disturbed and reassured at the same time.

At the edge of an immense field of barley-corn just
beyond the western gates of the city, carpets had been
laid down around the Duke's throne and stands fes-
tooned with banners set up for the onlookers. Lestro's
son stood at his side, bare-headed in the late morning
sun. He had opened the neck of his embroidered linen
shirt and rolled up his sleeves. Several of the younger
court ladies cooed appreciatively, and the boldest went
so far as to toss rose petals in his direction, although
they fell far short and she was immediately hurried
away by a vigilant chaperone.

When everyone had assembled and the crowd grown
quieter, the vizier bowed formally to the Duke and
unrolled a vellum scroll. He read, "As in the days of
our ancestors, who measured the truth in their souls
by the yield of the earth, so we stand here today. In
this holy place, the field kept sacred to the memory of
the ancient High King, stand two contenders. For the

Duchy, Byrem, son of Lestro. Against him, Tyr the Outlander, sometime styled Swordsister.

"From now until the last rays of the day's sun, they will labor in the Field of the King, reaping the bounty of the Earth Mother. Whomever the harvest smiles upon shall prevail."

At the Duke's gesture, servants brought forth several sickles, a long-handled scythe and a rakelike thing with curved metal teeth which Tyr did not recognize. Fighting the despair which she knew would defeat her before she'd even begun, Tyr took the long-handled scythe and swung it experimentally, but it felt awkward. The last sickle ended in a long, open curve and Tyr knew as soon as she picked it up that she could manage it. She took her place beside Byrem at the edge of the field in front of the Duke.

"Begin, and may the harvest judge your hearts," the Duke proclaimed.

They began reaping side by side down a central strip. It was not necessary to tie the cut sheaves, for a cadre of well-dressed peasants, supposedly the same who had sown the field and would otherwise be doing the reaping themselves, followed them.

Tyr and Byrem both started out in a frenzy, slashing through the coarse stalks more by sheer muscle power and nervous energy than skill. Byrem, clearly fit, soon gained a substantial lead. Tyr had lost stamina during her imprisonment, and her first adrenaline-fueled rush quickly faded. The sun turned her neck and shoulders molten, and strength ran out of her in little runnels of sweat.

How long do you think you can keep this up? she wondered. She fought to relax without breaking the rhythm of her stroke, but it was no good. The tangled stalks resisted her at every turn. She had to shove and jerk the sickle to hack through their tough fibers.

I learned to flow with my fighting art. Why can't I work in harmony with this damned corn?

An enemy, that's what the corn was. The stalks stood in silent ranks, waiting for her to shatter her strength against them. There was no blood in those unfeeling bodies, no muscles to tire against her speed and skill.

Anger rose in her, a pale cousin to the battle lust she knew so well. She seized it, drawing it out as an energy source. For a while the blood rage masked her fatigue, but it was only a temporary respite. In a real battle, Tyr's cold-minded fury would carry her through a whole day's fighting. Now she felt her energy waver and wane.

The sickle felt heavy as a headman's axe. *I might as well slit my own throat here and now,* Tyr thought, *and save Lestro the pleasure.* She stumbled and the blade slipped, slicing open the back of her hand. Sweat and blood mingled as they fell on the earth.

She glanced up at the sky, once clear but now clouded over with gray. Cut off the sun's warmth, the day turned chill.

A cool day . . .

Tyr paused as her mind flew back to the ritual phrasing of the Harvest challenge. *I won a chance at life by choosing what I was not. I am a Swordsister and now must become something else—but what? Elarra would know . . .* She brushed her fingers across the bloodstone ring.

Feel the corn, Tyr, even as you feel the reaping blade . . .

Yes, the tool in her hands, like her sword, had an intrinsic rhythm . . . and not just the sickle, the corn itself. For crooked as it was, it had its own beauty, its own complex texture. The corn was not her enemy, or any man's. It had never stolen an undeserved crown, never raped or pillaged or made off with another's cattle. Instead it fed those cattle, and the children left hungry by the whims of kings.

Tyr bent over and cut another sheaf. The moment she began thinking of the corn as a thing of value and not a useless obstacle, the sickle glided through the tangled stalks.

Feel the earth, and the crooked corn. Feel the circle of the seasons . . .

Tyr dropped the sickle and yanked off her boots and socks. The dirt felt rocky at first and she wondered if she'd made a mistake, exposing her uncallused feet to a mixture of stone and knife-sharp stubble. Her toes dug beneath the surface, where the soil lay cool and moist.

Circles, circles, the whole world seemed alive with circles—the curve of the sickle, the sweep of her arm as she gathered sheaf after sheaf of cut grain. The rich earth curved up to meet her even as the azure sky stretched above her, a giant bowl spanning from the Forgotten Kingdom to the Eastern Sea.

Tyr's breath sizzled through her lungs and her skin tingled. She could feel worms pushing their delicate heads through the soil and crickets huddling in the fallen leaves. Fieldmice trembled in their burrows. To their dim minds she became the fullness of harvest, the completion of life's circle. They knew her tread, knew the whisper of her blade cutting away the ripe, fulfilled seed to make room for new growth after winter's rest.

On and on Tyr reaped, her body singing with delight, all physical pain forgotten. The whispering sigh at the back of her mind became a joyous song, the words now intelligible:

All this is passing, only change itself never changes, death gives way to life and then to death again, grief to gladness, autumn to winter to spring once more . . .

At last came the moment when the surging tension of the seasonal change grew still and Tyr's tears dried on her cheeks. The air softened, as if sinking closer to the earth in conciliation. Although the harvest frenzy had subsided, the powers behind it still filled her.

She straightened up, her sickle falling soundlessly to the earth, and looked around her. Her half of the field lay harvested, the peasants even now tying the last few sheaves. At the far end of the field, a great cry rang out as the onlookers realized she had finished. From his still unharvested corner, Byrem started toward her, his handsome face flushed with exertion.

Tyr ignored him and walked slowly toward the hushed crowd, unaware that as she did so, she seemed to tower above them. The ground reverberated to her footsteps, and her face was no longer that of a human woman, but the gleaming visage of a goddess. Currents of power rose from the earth to swirl around her in a turbulent aura.

Tyr halted before Lestro, who fell to his knees before her. In his face, she saw emblazoned the things she had only surmised before, both his cowardice and his cunning. She shifted her vision from the Duke to the crowd. They seemed to her a field of wildflowers and poisonous weeds, all mixed together. Here and there shone patches of brightness, a husband with work-roughened hands sheltering his pregnant wife, a towheaded boy with a toad in his pocket, an old woman grieving for the soldier Tyr had killed. Dark splotches marked those whose hearts had turned away from life, into greed, into hatred. Dotted through the crowd, like gleaming jewels, were souls who had also been touched by the earth spirit. The brightest of these stood a little to the left of the throne.

Sirion Ancather, his blue eyes full of light, moved to the Duke's side, took the coronet from his head, and held it out to Tyr. As she touched the warm silver, she understood the true meaning of the Harvest challenge. It was no gesture of clemency toward a prisoner whose freedom was little better than slavery, a prisoner who risked all while the Duke sat on his high seat and ventured nothing. Its origins lay in the deep past, when the King was chosen by the blessing—and the possession—of the very powers that now dominated her. Not the best fighter, but the one most in harmony with the land, the one on whom the Earth Mother smiled. And the proof had been in the harvesting.

Tyr had wagered her life and won a Kingdom. But could she keep it? Did she even *want* it? Did she have any choice now that the land itself claimed her as its own? Knowing it was an irrevocable commitment, she accepted the crown and put it on. The metal curved like a living thing against her brow.

"Burien is mine." Was that really her voice—ringing with the certainty of mountains, musical as a dancing stream?

The red-robed vizier picked up Tyr's sword in its sheath and handed it to her. He gestured her to Lestro's chair with the same courtesy as if she were born to it. She felt the earth spirit begin to leave her, and trembling weakness take its place. Human flesh was not made to play host to elemental forces for very long. Elarra had taken the Djenne land spirit into her own body during that last climactic battle with Chandros, and it destroyed her. *Elarra* . . .

Tyr wrenched her thoughts back to the present. She'd have to do something quickly, before Lestro recognized her vulnerability. He might be temporarily overawed, but once the power deserted her, he'd waste no time scheming his return to power. She needed an ally who could stand against him, before she ended up dead by poison, or worse.

Sirion knelt before her and touched his fingertips to her sword hilt. "I would be the first to pledge fealty to Burien's new Queen." *Queen*, he said, not *Duchess*.

I can't win this fight by myself, she thought. *Help me!*

From deep within her mind came a surge of renewed strength, a silken touch of reassurance. *I am here with you, as I was on the field . . .*

There was no mistaking the tone and inflection of the words, the unique stamp of the witch's personality. *Elarra! How—*

The bloodstone! The witch's anguished cry rang through her mind. Not dead, not alive, but goddess-touched all the same.

Tyr closed her eyes and felt new energy flood through her. *I owe Elarra more than my life,* she thought. *I cannot leave her imprisoned in the ring. There must be some way to free her!*

My masters—at Ryley Witch-heart— The words formed roughly in Tyr's mind, as if Elarra were reaching out with the last dregs of her strength.

Ryley! I knew all along I must go there, though not why. But I cannot abandon these people to Lestro's tyranny. Earth Mother, you chose me for this land— help me find a way!

She raised her arms above her head and the only sound was the whimper of a hungry baby. The power within her flared anew, bringing new insight. The easy life of a Queen was not for her, but now she was no longer alone. Elarra's presence whispered through her mind and Sirion stood beside her, as committed in his own way to Burien as she was. As the crowd waited, she began to see a way to make the Duchy safe and yet repay her debt to Elarra.

"Burien is mine," she cried, knowing that she would always feel a kinship with this land and the people who tilled it. "But I am not Burien's. I cannot begin to rule you honorably with a broken promise elsewhere. Therefore, hear me! I shall appoint a Regent to rule you in my stead, a man who has as little love for tyranny as I have. Sirion Ancather—"

She took the coronet from her head and held it out to him. "I charge you to keep this for me as token of your wardship of this realm. Neither rank, nor greed, nor custom shall stay your hand from justice."

Sirion cupped the outer edge of the crown with both hands so that his fingers met hers around a circle of silver. "I swear upon my honor," he said in a ringing voice.

The crowd burst into cheers, except for a few of the more wealthy courtiers, who scowled and slunk closer to Lestro. Within moments, though, Sirion arranged for an honor guard to escort the former Duke and his entourage to their new quarters. By that time, the earth powers had entirely deserted Tyr, and it was only by the discipline of her warrior's training that she was able to stay upright on the throne until Sirion got her back to the palace.

Sirion Ancather proved better than his word. By the time Tyr was able to travel, he had gathered trustworthy men from forgotten corners, and the city was afire with change—new governors for the provinces, an advisory council of guild elders, an upheaval in the officers' corps. Lestro departed for an obscure country estate with only a minimal household staff and few tears shed in Kingsbridge.

"I will hold Burien for your return, My Lady," Sirion said as she mounted a frisky, re-shod Hellsteed in the courtyard of the new Regent's palace.

Don't count on my coming back, she thought, and then decided that a monarch who might return at any time and demand an accounting was not a bad idea. No single man, no matter how honest to begin with, should be entrusted with the welfare of her land and its people. Years from now, the people of Kingsbridge would still speak of the goddess who watched over them, ready to return in times of trouble.

She said, "Rule wisely, for I will deal with you as you have dealt with Burien," and turned the stallion's nose east toward Ryley Witch-heart.